IF TRUTH BE TOLD

To Holly —

I love you like a daughter, and I treasure your friendship.

Lynda

7/14/07

IF TRUTH BE TOLD

LYNDA FITZGERALD

FIVE STAR

An imprint of Thomson Gale, a part of The Thomson Corporation

Detroit • New York • San Francisco • New Haven, Conn. • Waterville, Maine • London

LIBRARY OF CONGRESS CATALOGING-IN-PUBLICATION DATA

Fitzgerald, Lynda.
   If truth be told / Lynda Fitzgerald. — 1st ed.
    p. cm.
   ISBN-13: 978-1-59414-568-1 (alk. paper)
   ISBN-10: 1-59414-568-7 (alk. paper)
   I. Title.
PS3606.I8838I36 2007
813'.6—dc22   2007005117

First Edition. First Printing: June 2007.

Published in 2007 in conjunction with Tekno Books.

Printed in the United States of America on permanent paper
10 9 8 7 6 5 4 3 2 1

For Dee, who suffered through my moods and madness and believed in me through it all.

ACKNOWLEDGMENTS

I owe a real debt of gratitude to my daughter Nikki, and to Holly Bier and Sheila Reece who, besides being wonderful friends, were my first (and unofficial) editors. Your advice and support were and are invaluable. And to Alice Duncan, my official editor, who (thankfully) caught the rest of my inconsistencies—at least the written ones.

CHAPTER 1

August 1961

Todd stood a bit outside the wedding party, clearly unwilling to take part in the ceremony soon to commence. I had never before laid eyes on him, but I had met his mother at one of those duty meetings where everyone pretended to be natural and nobody was. She was all right, I decided, meaning she hadn't said or done anything that had offended me outright. According to my mother, she was low-classed and loose and would never be part of our family. Her criticism rolled off me, an insignificant gray fog, and I gave it no thought. A lot of people, including me, had found themselves at the cutting end of her tongue, either in person or in absentia, as she preferred.

It never occurred to me that my uncle and his new wife might make one another happy. I had seen a lot of married people in my fourteen years—my mother and late father popped immediately to mind—and none of them had seemed particularly happy unless you counted the people down the street I babysat for, and I was certain that their happiness was a fluke. I could not have spent the early part of my life surrounded by the cold war my parents called a marriage and thought otherwise.

My future—what? Stepcousin? Was there even such a relationship? Whatever. Todd was beautiful. Tall, straight, golden bronzed by the Florida sun, with his near-platinum hair buffeted by the ever-blowing breeze. My single thought was, "This gorgeous hunk is going to be part of my family?"

The thought seemed to carry with it some responsibility for conversation. I edged closer to him with a show of courage that belied the nervousness I felt and, as no one had thought to introduce us, said, "Hi. I'm Christie."

"I know," he muttered, with barely a glance in my direction. That was all. No, "Hi, I'm Todd," which, of course, I already knew, or "Good to meet you," which I could see he wasn't. Still, his words stung more than they should have, and I was about to edge back over to the group when he muttered, "Why in the hell do they have to get married?"

He wasn't talking to me, or even at me, really, but I was hurt and angry and embarrassed by his rebuff. As I moved away, I summoned up all the superiority I could muster and said, "Maybe she's pregnant."

His eyes widened, and he really looked at me then. Not with interest or admiration or any of the other things I might have wished for, but he looked at me.

I moved closer to my sisters and realized that, while they might have missed the words Todd and I had exchanged, they had not missed Todd.

Joanna, the eldest, was picture-book beautiful. Darlene was a year younger and was, as I delighted in reminding her, the "not-quite-as" sister—not quite as old, not quite as tall or as pretty or as popular. Fortunately, she was also not quite as intelligent and was content to paddle along in our big sister's wake. Appearance-wise, at least, I ran a bad third with my straight stick of a body and stringy hair.

Joanna, at seventeen, collected young men in very much the same way she had collected dolls when she was younger and discarded the worn-out ones with just as little feeling. I admired her tremendously and hated her guts. She was the tallest of the O'Kelly girls and, like Darlene and me, had the family dark hair and nearly black eyes, but somehow it looked better on her. It was as if God or that great universal intelligence had only so much beauty to dole out to our family. Joanna, first on the scene, got the lion's share. When he got to Darlene, he realized he might run a little short if Mother kept on spawning. Then I came along and got the scrapings from the bottom of the pot. It was with thoughts like this that I entertained myself daily as I gazed into my bathroom mirror.

Joanna's latest boyfriend, Larry, hadn't been invited to the wedding, and it was obvious that the slight rankled with Joanna. Her manner since our arrival at the church had exuded bored tolerance, but now, maybe because circumstances had forced her to go for hours without being the center of some male's attention, she looked at Todd with interest. He saw the look. His eyes met hers, and then slid away. "Big deal," his face said clearly.

I barely suppressed a giggle. Then, for an instant, I thought I felt Todd's eyes on me. I looked over, but he was staring at the sidewalk.

I felt Joanna shift impatiently beside me. "Will this thing ever get started?" she stage-whispered to Darlene. "I have to go home and do my hair." The wedding, of course, hadn't been important enough to warrant a special hairdo. She was our mother's daughter, all right.

If Joanna was a carbon copy of our mother—in all but appearance, that is—Darlene worked diligently to be a Joanna clone. Now she affected irritation she probably didn't feel. "Mother *said* Uncle Jack would probably do something to mess up his own wedding."

That seemed like too low a blow, even for them. I heard myself saying, "It's the minister's fault. He's the one who's late."

They both looked at me as if they'd just realized I was there. Joanna sighed a long, exaggerated sigh. Then they turned their backs on me and began to whisper. With a sigh of my own, I cursed myself for opening my mouth.

We were standing outside on a covered walkway between the church and a larger building where I guessed they held their Sunday school classes. I had never been to this particular church before. In fact, none of us regularly attended services. Mother worshiped money, Joanna worshiped herself, and Darlene worshiped whatever Joanna told her to worship. I worshiped my Uncle Jack, and now, having nothing else to do with my attention, I focused it on him.

It was hard to think of Jack O'Kelly as a groom, although he looked every inch of it, standing tall and straight in his navy suit and boutonniere, glowing with a pure happiness I'd never seen before. He had always seemed like a giant to me, but he had grown several inches since his bride had arrived. He also had the family dark hair—the spitting image of his deceased older brother—with eyes set deep under thick black brows. His face was as angular as the rest of his frame. In photos in the family albums I had seen him as a gawky boy, a wiry man. It was only in the past few years that flesh had begun to adequately cover bone. I thought him the handsomest man alive and stood very much in awe of his intelligence. He was the only member of our odd family who treated me as a person, who asked me questions and actually listened to the answers.

After my father died three years ago, I had lost Uncle Jack for the most part because, for some mysterious reason, my mother seemed mad at Uncle Jack about it. Maybe she was taking out the anger she felt at my dad for daring to die without first asking her permission, or maybe it was because Uncle Jack looked so much like him. Anyway, Uncle Jack gave her barbs and hateful looks the attention they deserved: none. But it couldn't have been pleasant for him to be around her.

My sisters, predictably, took Mother's view of things. I,

equally predictably, did not.

I looked from Uncle Jack and Carly to the two little groups of guests. It was because it was a second marriage, I suddenly realized. On one side of the walkway were clustered Carly's son and friends. On the other, a decidedly smaller group of those of my uncle's family and friends who felt it wouldn't be disloyal to Mother if they came, knowing Joanna would run back home and tell Mother who showed up. The two groups never glanced toward one another. They looked for all the world like two armed camps, and I felt a little sick at my stomach.

I was running out of places to look when a car pulled into the asphalt parking lot and a man jumped out, juggling his Bible and pulling on his coat as he hurried toward us. I heard bits and snatches. "So terribly sorry . . . accident across the highway . . . no one directing traffic . . ." as he began herding us into the smaller of the two buildings.

The groups merged a bit and darted furtive glances at each other as they reached the entrance. They split again once they were through the carved double doors. Inside the cool and quiet sanctuary, my uncle's friends made way for my sisters and me to precede them down the aisle. We had been instructed in proper wedding behavior by our mother, a staunch Emily Post fan, and the three of us marched purposefully toward the front, left-hand pew. It took only the two pews behind us to accommodate my uncle's following, but the bride's side was nearly full.

Todd, I saw, sat by himself on the long wooden bench across from us. It looked a very lonely place to be.

The ceremony itself was mercifully brief, with a few quiet words and no music at all. There was something about an exchange of rings, and my uncle kissed his new bride.

Before I knew what was happening, we were being ushered back outside amid handshakes and congratulations. We had been told that the reception was to be held at my new aunt Carly's house. There was a brief delay while she threw her bouquet to one of her friends. Then everyone began to move toward the parking lot. That presented another problem. Joanna, Darlene, and I had arrived by taxi, Mother unwilling to allow her car to be sullied by being part of any such proceedings. My uncle had a two-seater sports car—an attempt to regain his lost youth, according to guess who.

Aunt Carly solved the problem. "Todd, dear, why don't you drive the girls to the house?"

He nodded briefly, his face expressionless, and unlocked the passenger side of the two-door sedan. Joanna and Darlene lunged as a unit toward the open door, climbing in the back seat. I stood for a moment. It was either get in the back seat with them and make Todd look like the chauffeur he was, or take the front seat beside him. Feeling a bit presumptuous, I chose the latter.

His attitude screamed that it didn't matter one way or the other to him. He fastened his seat belt and started the engine without seeming to notice me, but then he stopped and looked over. "Put on your seat belt," he ordered.

"Why?" I asked before I could stop myself. "Is your driving that bad?"

I saw a flicker of something that might have been a smile, but it vanished before I could be sure. I reached over my shoulder and grabbed the seatbelt, pulling it across me and hooking it.

The ride to the reception wasn't a long one, but I could tell after one block that it was going to seem interminable. Joanna and Darlene were whispering between themselves in back, and Todd was staring ahead at the road with more concentration than was necessary for the late afternoon, lightly traveled roads of Cocoa Beach, where more than ten cars on the highway at any time outside of season spelled rush hour. The silence in the front seat was threatening to smother me. I struggled for something brilliantly witty to say. "Nice car," I finally managed.

It was a minute before Todd answered. I could see the muscle working in his jaw and didn't understand what the moment of decision was all about. "It's my mother's."

I decided to push my luck. "Don't you have one?"

His amazing blue eyes flicked over to me, then back to the road. "Freshmen aren't allowed to have cars on campus."

I was so thrilled to have someone talking to me that I plunged recklessly ahead. "You're in college?"

He shrugged. "Next month."

"What are you going to study?"

It took him a moment and a lot more jaw machinations before he answered, and I could see that he was sorry he'd gotten himself into this conversation. My uncle had always teased me about being the most curious person alive, and I did tend to ask a lot of questions, but how else were you going to find out things?

His voice, when he did answer, was sharp, his words precise. "I will be studying political science. My sign is Aquarius. I wear a size-nine shoe, and yes, my hair really is this color. Does that pretty much cover it?"

I swallowed hard. Yes, actually it did, and it didn't help a bit that my two superior sisters were sitting two feet behind me observing my disgrace. I turned in my seat so that I could no longer see Todd and hoped the icy atmosphere that filled the interior of the car would frost his most private parts.

CHAPTER 2

Aunt Carly lived in a house south of Melbourne Beach, about twenty miles from my own Cocoa Beach house. There were few motels and only a sprinkling of homes on the long stretch of shoreline that terminated abruptly at Sebastian Inlet. It was beautiful in its way, with palm trees and scrub palmettos lining the roads. Almost the only other trees, if they could be called trees, were the sea grapes, and they were so plentiful, they even had a motel named after them.

The white sand area in front of the house was crowded with cars when we arrived. Todd parked his mother's car in an empty corner and climbed out, walking away without a backward glance. I opened my own door and held the seat for my sisters.

"Isn't he the rudest thing you ever saw?" Joanna asked the world in general as we traipsed across the soft sand, and for once I had to agree with her.

By the time we made it up the steps and into the house, champagne corks had popped and glasses were being filled. A maid, hired for the occasion, I assumed, was passing around delicious smelling hors d'oeuvres, and I remembered I'd had no lunch.

My uncle and aunt were nowhere in sight, but I saw Todd moving among his mother's friends, being charming and gracious. "So that's what he was saving it for," I muttered loud enough for my sisters to hear. They looked at me without comprehension.

Carly's house—now my uncle's house, too, I realized with a jolt—was beautiful. I had been there once before but hadn't taken the slightest notice. Now I did. Not in a proprietary way, exactly, but at least with interest. It was right on the water, one of those newer beach houses with lots of redwood and glass and a deck that stretched far out over the sand dunes. Once the bride and groom arrived (had it taken that long to pay the minister?) and had gone through the congratulations once again, the party began to drift out through the sliding glass doors. My greatest wish at that time was to be invisible and, as there is no place to get lost quicker than in a crowd, I moved with them.

The reception signaled a truce between the visiting camps, and they laid down their weapons and mingled. Maybe the champagne helped. Evening was settling in. Soft music was somehow piped outside. The sun had almost completed its slow descent, bathing the scene in soft golden light. The lemony fragrance of citronella candles mingled with the beach smells of seaweed and fish and salt, while hanging Japanese lanterns glowed like a dozen small moons reflected in the stemmed glasses of bubbly liquid. A table in the center of the deck was covered with a white lace cloth, and in its center rested a towering wedding cake so elaborate as not to seem real.

From my vantage point off to one side of the throng and slightly behind the barbecue grill, I watched as my uncle and aunt cut the wedding cake and fed each other a bite, laughing as the crowd applauded. Flashbulbs popped, and I was certain I'd never seen my uncle look as happy as he did at that moment. When the amateur photographers moved, I caught sight of Todd's face distorted by a dark frown. *He really hates this,* I thought suddenly. Then his mother smiled over at him, and the moment passed. He returned her smile with a warmth that spoke unmistakably of love, stepping forward to hug her and shake my uncle's hand. He even smiled at my sisters. Joanna gave him the cold shoulder and walked away, but Darlene responded with a fluttery little smile before following her leader.

No one seemed to notice me, so I slipped off the bench and onto the floor of the deck, wrapping my arms around my knees and pretending I didn't know what redwood boards would do to a pale yellow dress. I could see perfectly well from there. My sisters sat off to one side wearing their best superior-to-all-present faces. Todd walked around with his mother and my uncle, smiling and nodding and shaking hands, and I realized that, while he hadn't chosen to demonstrate his manners to me, his mother had taught him some.

After a while, though, I realized that all was truly not well in his world. By that time, the cake had been chopped beyond recognition and I had filched two full glasses of champagne that careless celebrants had set down on the bench in front of me. Someone was taking pictures again, and I heard a man's voice yell, "Give her a big kiss, Jack." A moment later, I saw Todd slip down the stairs that led from the deck to the beach and walk purposefully away, shoulders hunched, his hands thrust deep into his pockets.

Curiosity and the unaccustomed alcohol gave me the courage to follow him. I slipped between the wooden slats of the deck rail and dropped down to the soft sand below, having no clear idea what I was going to say when I caught up to him.

It very nearly didn't matter as I almost lost him altogether. He had stopped a little way up the beach and climbed a sand dune. If the last traces of daylight and the first glow of moonlight hadn't been reflecting off the white sand, I would have walked right past him. As it was, I hesitated, undecided on how I was to approach this person who obviously didn't like me any more than he liked the rest of my family. He didn't make it any easier. He sat cross-legged on the top of the dune, playing with a piece of sea grass and watching me. Not speaking. Just watching. But I had come this far.

I scrambled up the steep rise with relative ease, compensating for the slipping sand by turning my feet sideways, as only native beach dwellers know how to do, and plopping myself down beside him, only a little out of breath.

I tried to smile, but it wobbled and died.

He regarded me through narrowed eyes. It seemed a long time before he spoke. "You're a pest."

His remark neither hurt nor offended. I had heard it all my life. "Tenacious," I amended, nodding. That earned me a sidelong glance. "At least that's what Uncle Jack calls me. Everyone else calls me a pest like you did," I added with a grin.

I saw a smile tease the corners of his mouth and win. He began chuckling deep in his chest. Suddenly it exploded into laughter. "And funny as shit," he said finally.

"The family wit," I agreed, nodding. "Somebody has to be it."

The laughter died away, but the smile remained. "Your sisters are assholes," he said without rancor.

"Tell me about it. I live with them."

"You seemed to turn out okay."

His praise left me lightheaded. "I take after my uncle."

His smile vanished, and before I could stop myself, I asked, "Why do you hate him so much?"

He looked surprised. "I don't hate him. Hate's too strong a word."

"Are you jealous?"

"No, I am *not* jealous!" he sputtered. Then, "You can't be any happier about this than I am."

"Why not, if it makes them happy?"

He ignored the question. "He was married before."

Was that his sin? "So was your mother."

"Why'd your uncle get a divorce?"

I couldn't resent the question since I had asked my mother the same thing. "My mother said because he's just like my father was."

"Meaning?"

I shrugged. "Beats me. I thought my father was great."

"Where is he?"

"He died."

The words hardly hurt at all anymore, but Todd must have seen something. "Sorry," he muttered.

"Why? You didn't do it."

That earned me another look. "Did he knock her around?"

My eyes widened. "My uncle?" I squeaked. "Knock my aunt around?"

He nodded, and it was my turn to burst into gales of laughter. He glared at me, but I couldn't help it. The mental image of my gentle, philosophical, book-reading, pipe-smoking uncle raising a hand to anyone was too much for me. I clutched my sides and rolled in the sand, tears of laughter making tracks down my cheeks. "I don't believe"—I stopped to spit sand out of my mouth—"you asked that question." Finally, I caught my breath. I sat up, trying to straighten my dress and shake some of the white grit out of my hair, most of it onto him.

He was regarding me coldly. "I'm glad you find it so amusing."

His words sobered me. All humor fled as I realized there was more to his question than idle speculation. I found myself suddenly wanting very much to answer his original question. "No," I said earnestly. "My uncle never hit my aunt." Then, tentatively, "Did your father hit your mother?"

Todd jumped to his feet and slid down the dune. When he reached the hard sand nearer the water, he started off in the direction opposite the house.

I stood up, brushing off the skirt of my dress. I knew it would probably be nicer to leave him alone with whatever demons possessed him, but I found myself wanting an answer to my question. I took off my shoes and, clutching them in one hand, slid down the dune. I ran to catch up with him.

He was walking along the water's edge when I reached him, ruining his loafers, I noted. I fell into step beside him, pretending that his three-foot strides were my norm.

The tide was out, and the sand near the water's edge was hard-packed and cool under my feet. The only sound was the constant slosh and hiss of the gently breaking waves.

He didn't look over at me, but after a minute, he said, "It's really none of your business."

"I know."

"You're too young to understand any of it anyway."

"Probably."

He sighed and slowed to a pace that more closely modeled a human's. "My father was a champ," he said in a low voice, "or at least, that's what they tell me. A cop. He died when I was five. I don't remember him. At all." His voice was flat, but I could feel the emotion vibrating just under it. "Mom has a picture of him in his uniform, and—" He glanced at me as if trying to decide if he could trust me. I must have passed some test of his, or maybe he just wanted to talk. "And she has his badge and gun. I found them one day. I wasn't looking for them or anything. I was just messing around. Anyway, I put it all back."

He walked on for a while before he spoke again, and for once I had the good sense to keep my mouth shut. His next words were hard, a curse. "My stepfather was a son of a bitch. My mother married him when I was ten. I don't know why she married him. He was a loser, you know?"

I didn't, but I nodded. It seemed enough. After a minute, he went on, "He really took her for a ride. Went through my father's insurance money like it was water. Stayed away for days at a time. She wouldn't dump him, though. I don't know why."

"Maybe she didn't want to admit she'd made a mistake."

He stopped and looked down at me. "You say some weird things."

"I'm strange," I agreed with a smile, "and a pest."

The corners of his lips twitched. "Tenacious," he corrected and began walking again.

The glowing compliment froze me in my tracks. I had to hurry to catch him. "So what happened?"

He shrugged, but his pace quickened. "When the money ran out, so did he, but not before he gave her a black eye and bloodied her face."

I thought about that as I raced to keep pace with him. I thought about the relationship I'd had with my father. I thought about what life had been like since he died, about the things my mother was constantly saying about him, and I blinked back the tears that suddenly filled my eyes. "My father wasn't like that, and neither is my uncle," I snapped. "He doesn't cuss or—or drink beer or—" I sputtered to stop before continuing. "He's good and kind and he works hard and—"

"So does my mother," Todd growled, "and she's had to work her butt off fifteen hours a day. Otherwise her precious son wouldn't be able to go off to college."

His bitterness was totally wasted on me. I was still wrapped up in my own feelings. "And he won't hit her either. He'll pet her hair and tell her she's beautiful and make her feel won-wonderful." As the last words spilled from my mouth, so, too, did the tears I had held in check for so long spill from my eyes. I wiped them away without even realizing what I did. I was talking about my uncle, but it was pictures of my father that I saw in the sand in front of me. I could feel Todd looking at me, and I raised my chin a half inch, unashamed of my emotional outburst. He said nothing, but his pace slowed and he wordlessly reached into his coat pocket and handed me his handkerchief. Then he walked on, with me trailing and mopping.

After a few minutes, with a "We'd better head back," he turned and started in the opposite direction, stopping after a few steps to let me catch up to him. I wasn't through crying yet. I hadn't talked to anyone about how great my loss had been when my father died and then when my mother decided to hate my uncle, too, and he quit coming around much. The feelings that surrounded it all had bubbled and sizzled and hissed inside of me for so long that any expression of them had been like a single trickle of lava down the side of an enormous volcanic mountain. Now that volcano had erupted—not in loud sobs. I had lived with my icky sisters so long that I knew how to cry silently. I stumbled along, awash, half-blind and heartbroken.

The tears dried to a sniffle about halfway to the house. I wiped my eyes and blew my nose loudly. Defiantly. I started to give the handkerchief back to him, but thought better of it, tucking it up under the belt of my dress.

We walked along in silence, kicking up bits of sand, watching the phosphorus buried in it sparkle like diamonds in the night. When we were nearly there, Todd stopped and looked down at me. The moon had risen and, bathed in its glow, he looked like some kind of god: tall and strong and beautiful. Better than the heroes I'd read about in books. More . . . touchable.

I could hear the music from the deck now, a soft love song with lots of saxophone and flute. The scent of citronella seemed to reach out and surround us.

A smile brushed his mouth. Then it crept up until it softened his eyes. It was the most romantic moment of my life, and I waited breathlessly for what was to come next.

After a long moment, he reached down and gently grazed my

chin with his loosely clenched fist. "You're all right. You know that?"

My heart swelled. From his lips, it was a compliment of monumental proportions. I felt dizzy, elated, before my obnoxious sense of humor rushed back to spoil it. "For a girl, you mean?"

He looked at me in surprise, as if the thought had never crossed his mind. "No," he said, grinning down at me. "For a kid."

The remark did nothing to diminish my newfound feelings. I had met the man of my dreams. Not that I'd had many dreams about men up to that point, but I was certain that if I had, he would have featured in them. The enormity of my emotions subdued me so that even my uncle remarked about it on the way home. I just smiled and snuggled deeper into the plush upholstery of his new wife's front seat. I loved him more than ever at that moment. I loved his new wife and I loved her car. I could even almost tolerate the two sisters sitting in the back seat.

Part of my euphoria stemmed from the invitation that had been extended to us just before we left. The guests had gone, and the six of us, Joanna and Darlene and the newlyweds and Todd and me, were sharing a private toast. Uncle Jack ignored Joanna's muttered remark about how scandalous it was to encourage a fourteen-year-old *child* (her emphasis) to drink alcoholic beverages. He offered a toast to the future, to the new extended family that had been created. Todd smiled over at me, and I grinned back deliriously, holding my glass higher than any of the others. Then my uncle informed us that we were invited the following weekend to a huge cookout they were planning as a send-off for Todd. It was the perfect ending of a perfect day.

I said, "All right!" spilling a bit of champagne down the front of my dress. Even Darlene looked interested, until Joanna said with a sniff that, of course, she would have to see what Mother had planned for us. I saw my new aunt flinch at Joanna's words, and I didn't envy her the task of winning over the eldest O'Kelly girl. I hope she had the good sense not to try.

Things were about as pleasant as I expected when we got home. The house was ablaze with lights and, through the open living room drapes, I saw Mother jump to her feet as we pulled into the drive. She was at the car before Uncle Jack got it into park and, hands on her slim hips, ordered us inside to wait for her while she had a "word with your uncle."

I tried not to listen, or at least I told myself I did, but still I heard something about the lateness of the hour and typical lack of consideration, just like his brother, before the front door closed behind us. Something within me rebelled. "You'd think she could leave him alone for one night!" I burst out.

"Why should she?" Joanna asked with a short, unpleasant laugh. "She doesn't owe him anything."

My cheeks flamed. "What does owing him anything have to do with it?"

Joanna shook her head, looking at me pityingly. "You're too young to know anything."

"What don't I know?" I demanded.

Joanna's eyes went to slits. "That he's just like daddy was, and that he's taking food out of our mouths and clothes off our backs and—"

"What are you *talking* about?" I almost shouted. "What food and—"

Darlene stood to one side, watching us with her mouth gaping open.

"Oh, shut up!" she spat out. "Mother said—"

"*Mother said,*" I mimicked, shaking with anger. "Well, I'll tell you something, Joanna. You're a liar and a pig. You're just like her—"

25

CHAPTER 3

Their widening eyes told me what I didn't want to know even before I heard the front door shut behind me. I turned slowly. My mother stood behind me, her face like darkening thunderheads.

"I didn't mean—" I began.

She held up her hand, her dignity perfectly intact. "I think I've heard all I want to hear out of your mouth, Christiana," she said in her best, brittle, you-are-lower-than-a-worm voice. "Go to your room immediately. I'll deal with you later."

I hung my head and tried to look unhappy as I trudged up the stairs but, truly, it was a fate devoutly to be wished. I closed the door softly behind me, leaned against it, and, looking around me, grinned.

I considered having a room of my own one of life's true pleasures, even, I thought as I looked around me, if the room looked outrageously childish for someone my age. My big, over-stuffed bear was propped against my pillows where I'd put him this morning when I made up the bed. In fact, stuffed animals and dolls littered the room. I was too old for this nonsense, I thought, rummaging in the bottom of my closet for an old pillowcase. I hadn't been too old this morning, but I was now.

As I began to gather up the clutter, I remembered hearing somewhere—maybe in one of my irregularly attended Sunday school classes—that when God dumps something yucky on you, he gives you something super to balance it out, or words to that

26

effect. Well, having two older sisters who delighted in calling attention to my bad points, whether to me or anyone else who would listen, was definitely yucky, but being able to close the door against the world (and them) was, in my book, really super. I had earned this great privilege through no efforts of my own, which was one of the reasons I was certain it was a gift from God. Age had dictated our sleeping arrangements. Joanna and Darlene were less than a year apart, at eighteen and seventeen plus one month. Being so close in age, the elder O'Kelly girls had always shared the same bedtime while I, being a full four years younger, required more sleep. Or so that rationale went. It suited me fine. I willingly crawled into bed at nine o'clock and read with a flashlight under the covers until eleven, which was when the others usually turned in.

When I got to my giant bear, which I had named Teddy at age four with a child's originality, my hand hesitated. I could easily part with Joanna's old dolls, the stuffed turtle, and my collection of Disney characters, but I shuddered at the thought of plunging Teddy into the darkness of no longer being wanted. In the end, I compromised, telling myself he was too big to fit into the pillowcase. I threw the pillowcase in the bottom of my closet and seated Teddy very comfortably on top of it, telling him goodnight before I closed the door.

I looked around the room again. It still looked childish. The prints on the walls were sad-eyed children and Holly Hobby–type girls; but it was better.

The actual redecoration of my room to reflect my advancing age had been in the works when my father was killed in a head-on collision on Highway 520. Dad had taken an active interest in my plans, carting me around to paint stores and linen dealers, matching paint chips to bedspreads. All that had come to a halt after his death. Mother had somewhat grudgingly offered to go on with the plans in one of her magnanimous moments, but I refused her offer. Keeping things the way they had always been seemed . . . safer, somehow back then. But now . . .

I heard footsteps coming down the hallway and jumped up on the bed, hugging a pillow to me since there was nothing else to hug, but they only hesitated at my door long enough for Mother to say, "Turn out your light, Christiana," and then continued down the hall. I could hear my sisters giggling in the next room. I had obviously been granted a reprieve, at least temporarily. I gave a silent yelp of joy and jumped out of bed. I took off my party dress, tossing it in the closet with the discarded signposts of my youth, and slipped into my nightgown.

As I crossed the room to turn off the light, I saw Todd's handkerchief on the floor where it had fallen out of the belt on my dress. I stooped down and retrieved it, holding it up to my face. It was still damp with my tears, this lasting reminder of the most wonderful night of my life. At least I hoped it was tears. Even I could see that I couldn't sleep with it until it had been laundered. I folded it neatly and placed it on my bedside table. Then I switched off the light.

I crossed to the window and knelt on the floor with my arms and chin resting on the windowsill, reasoning that if Mother looked in, I could tell her I was praying. My bedroom faced east and, although our house was a mile from the beach, I knew the ocean was there. The moon had risen high in the sky, and I could imagine it reflecting off the water as it had earlier this evening. I drifted for a long time, lulled by the breeze and the champagne and the lateness of the hour, thinking about divorce and marriage and young men about to go off to college. I tried to imagine what Todd was doing. Would he be talking to my uncle and Carly, or would he be asleep by now? I remembered how he had appeared standing on the sand near the house, silhouetted in the moonlight as he looked down at me, and a bit of poetry I'd read in one of my uncle's books came back to me with startling clarity. "God's in his heaven / All's right with the world." It brought a smile to my lips. I rose happily from the floor. All was definitely right with the world, I thought, climbing into bed and automatically reaching for Teddy and finding empty space. Well, almost all.

Morning brought none of the fireworks I'd expected. I came out of my stripped-down bedroom prepared for the worst. It wasn't every day you called your mother a liar and a pig, even if you didn't mean it that way.

They were all at the breakfast table when I came into the kitchen. Mother had taken a part-time job at a little boutique on the beach after my father died, "to make ends meet," she had told us with a sigh, and Sunday was one of her days to work. She was clearly ready to go, clad stylishly in a two-piece blue pantsuit and heels, with gold clip-on earrings. Her gleaming brown hair was swept back and up and sprayed ruthlessly into place. My two sisters, in contrast, were wrapped in bathrobes, yawning over cups of milky coffee. When I came into the room, their mouths snapped shut and their eyes focused on Mother.

"Good morning," I said, not looking at any of them. I got a bowl out of the cabinet and the cereal from the pantry. The milk was already on the table. The silence wrapped around me as I poured cereal into the bowl and spooned sugar liberally on the top.

"That's too much sugar," Mother said after the third spoonful.

It was a relief to hear a human voice. "Yes, ma'am."

No more was said until I finished eating. It was so quiet that I could hear the hum of the refrigerator, the occasional drip of the kitchen faucet. My cereal crunched loudly between my teeth. I knew what was coming, or at least I knew something was coming, so I ate as slowly as I could, but you can only make a bowl of Rice Krispies last so long. I should have had toast, I thought as I spooned the last bite into my mouth, but it was a tardy afterthought. Finally, I sat back and awaited the inevitable.

Mother's chastisement was brief and had all the sting of a direct hit from a half-filled water balloon. She pushed her coffee cup away from her and folded her hands on the table, a signal that she was getting down to business. She was an attractive woman, tall and slim, always well groomed, always under control. The perfect lady. Now, she began in her carefully modulated voice, "Your behavior last night was not what I would have expected of someone your age, Christiana, but—" She raised her hand as I started to speak. "But I understand your uncle had you drinking."

"Only a few sips," I lied.

"The rest of it went down her dress," Darlene said with a giggle. Joanna nudged her and frowned.

Mother looked at the two of them, then back at me. With exaggerated tolerance, she said, "Because of that and only because of that, I am going to overlook your behavior last night. I'm certain you didn't mean the terrible things you said."

I felt like jumping up from the table and executing a cartwheel, but I knew my future rested on my decorum at that moment. I lowered my eyes, trying to look suitably contrite.

"But something like that can't go completely unpunished," she continued as I had known she would. "I think you should spend the day in your room thinking about what you said. It's very easy for words spoken in anger to be misconstrued . . ."

Her voice droned on, but I no longer heard her. That was it? A day in my room left to my own devices? I had two new books from the library, for Pete's sake, and a bag of potato chips and two candy bars stashed in the top of my closet! I carefully avoided meeting my sisters' eyes. They would have known in a heartbeat what I was thinking.

My mother's voice slowly faded back into my consciousness. ". . . sale at the store, and Joanna and Darlene have a lot of shopping to do if Joanna is going to be ready to leave on time, so there will be no one here to watch you. I'm going to have to ask for your promise that you will not leave your room except to go to the bathroom and get a drink of water."

Potato chips and candy bars and water sounded fine to me, especially with two new novels waiting to be read. I looked her full in the face and solemnly said, "I promise."

She searched my face for any sign of deviousness or rebellion. Then, satisfied, she pushed her chair back from the table. "All right then."

I had never been one for timing. "What about the cookout next weekend?" I blurted out.

She hesitated. "What cookout?" she asked, looking first at me, then at my sisters.

Joanna rolled her eyes. "Uncle Jack wants us to come over next weekend. They're having some kind of stupid cookout for her son."

Mother's mouth became set, and my heartbeat stumbled. Then she relaxed. She tilted her head slightly to one side, looking at me. "And you want to go?"

I shrugged with what I hoped was supreme unconcern, but it was too late. She knew. I had given her a weapon, and I could have cut my tongue out. She drummed her elegant fingernails on the table for a minute, then said, "We'll see. We'll see what your behavior is like this week. That will determine whether you go or not."

She hadn't said no. There was still a chance. "All right," I said meekly. Then, "May I please be excused?"

I tried to keep the bounce out of my walk as I loaded my breakfast dishes in the dishwasher and carried my glass of water to my room. If they had known what I was feeling, they would have felt compelled to bring me down. This wasn't paranoia; the three of them took perverse pleasure in making me unhappy. "Keeping me in line," I'd heard them describe it, but it didn't bother me. Not as long as I got what I wanted.

Even in my room with the door closed, I couldn't rejoice as I wanted to. Our house wasn't built for privacy.

I retrieved Teddy from the closet and sat on my bed against propped-up pillows, hugging him to me as I listened to Joanna rummaging around in the next room. I knew she was getting dressed to take Mother to work so she could have the car for the day. Even when I heard the car start and drive away, I didn't move. Darlene was still somewhere in the house, waiting to pounce on the tiniest infraction of the rules.

Joanna came back twenty minutes later, and there was the sound of water splashing and conversation and laughter in the bathroom as they got ready to go shopping. It was what they lived for. I thought of the potato chips in the closet and the novels among my schoolbooks and willed myself to be patient. They had Mother's credit card. They'd be gone soon enough.

The water stopped, and I heard drawers opening and closing in their bedroom. I smiled a secret smile. The lack of privacy worked both ways. I knew exactly at what stage of dressing they were each moment, but as there were two of them and, for once, they weren't talking, I didn't move an inch.

My attention to detail paid off. The door to my room was flung open, and Joanna stood there, tall and stern-faced, dressed in her easy-off, easy-on shopping clothes. "We're leaving now." When I said nothing, she added, "We might have taken you with us if you hadn't been such a shit last night."

I looked down at the bedspread and said nothing.

After a minute, she said, "I don't know when we'll be back," which translated to "if you do anything wrong, we could show up at any minute and catch you in the act." They'd used that particular threat too often for it to have any impact. Besides, I knew better. They'd be back at six o'clock when the stores closed and not a minute before.

"Okay. Bye."

Joanna stood for a minute, considering me. She was trying to figure out why I was taking my restriction so well. I kept my face impassive. Let her wonder.

Finally, she shut the door.

I listened to their footsteps going down the stairs. To the front door closing. The car starting up in the driveway. I waited a full five minutes after the sound of the engine had died away. Then I got up and peeked out the window. No car. No sisters.

I let out a war cry, jumping up and down and making enough noise to bring the police. I flung Teddy up in the air and caught him. I jumped up on my bed and started dancing, holding Teddy in my arms and laughing aloud at the stupidity of mothers and sisters. What a present they had handed me! A day without having to listen to any of them.

I remembered Joanna's parting shot and threw Teddy ceiling-wards again. To have gone with them would have been torture; to stay home, bliss! They were idiots to force me to stay in my room. If going to the cookout rested on my behavior, I would gladly have scrubbed floors and walls and ceilings. I would have vacuumed and dusted and washed windows and cleaned the oven. I would even have made my sisters' beds.

The barest tip of my elation spent, I collapsed on the bed, breathing hard. As it was, I couldn't leave my room so I couldn't do any of those things. I had been forbidden. I had given my promise. I looked around me with glee. I was stuck in here all day.

I spotted Todd's handkerchief folded on my nightstand. On one of my bathroom trips, I would wash it. I could dry it with my hairdryer. It would make a lovely neckerchief for Teddy.

I sat the bear down on the bed. Then I crossed to my closet and retrieved the bag of potato chips from the top shelf, opening it and putting it on my bedside table at the ready. I opened the backpack I always wore when I went to the library and pulled out the two books I'd chosen, reading the flyleaf of each. I had my choice of Sacagawea's life story or a novel of ". . . deep passion and unrequited love." I chose the former for my entrée, saving the latter for a late-afternoon snack. I was a really fast reader. Then I curled up beside Teddy with a smile of contentment and opened the book to page one. Life, I thought before I lost myself in fantasy, wasn't so shabby after all.

Nor could I complain about the speed with which the next week passed. After all, Todd wasn't the only one going away to school. Joanna would be leaving next Sunday for the University of Florida, and the entire week was filled with shopping and sorting and packing. My eldest sister had an almost entirely new wardrobe, which meant that her old things would be passed down or thrown away.

The passing of the clothes was done in style. The four of us—Mother, of course, took part—were seated on the living room carpet, surrounded by carefully sorted piles of keeps and discards. As accepting and rejecting garments was hot work, the air conditioner was cranked down to frostbite and we all had glasses of sweet tea close at hand. My presence was demanded and then barely tolerated. I smiled blandly throughout the endless proceedings. The model daughter.

It was a teary state of affairs for poor Darlene, for whom acquisition of Joanna's much-coveted garments could scarcely make up for the loss of her most cherished companion. Still, she clutched the hand-me-downs to her as a drowning man clutches a passing log and only wiped her eyes on the wash and wear.

I, on the other hand, accepted the castoffs that even Darlene didn't want with good grace, thinking all the while of Joanna's precious dolls, still stuffed in a pillowcase in the bottom of my closet. I wanted nothing of my sister's, with one exception, and that exception almost proved to be my undoing.

It was a bathing suit, a gorgeous pale pink bathing suit with a burgundy sash that crossed under the bust and tied at the back of the neck. It shouldn't even have been an issue. It was one of the dozen that Joanna "hadn't decided on yet," one scrap in a living room piled high with skirts and blouses and such. She hadn't worn it in years, and Darlene rarely borrowed it anymore. No one would have wanted it if I hadn't opened my mouth but, true to form, I did.

"Can I have this one?" I asked, holding it up during an unexpected lull in the chatter.

Three pairs of eyes swiveled to look at me. They had heard no similar words out of my mouth all during the long passing-down ceremony and, in fact, had heard very few words from me during the entire week. Now they stared as if they'd been unaware of my presence until that point in time. Then, as a unit, six eyes turned upon what I was holding. I could have cut my stupid hand off.

Mother still looked noncommittal, but I saw the birth of new interest flicker across Darlene's face. "I might want that one," she said thoughtfully, pursing her lips.

Joanna made a growling noise and snatched it out of my hand. "I haven't decided yet whether I'm taking it," she announced more spitefully than even I would have expected. She tucked it protectively under her leg as though I might try to snatch it back, giving me a triumphant look.

I seethed inwardly. It wasn't fair! They didn't want that swimsuit. Not the way I did. I loved that suit as I had never loved any garment in my life. Now, because I had been dumb enough to express a desire for it, it was going to be denied me. "You don't want that bathing suit," I muttered under my breath, half hoping Joanna would hear me.

I needn't have worried. She turned to me and raised her eyebrows. "What are you whining about?"

I lifted my head and looked her full in the face. "You don't want it. It doesn't fit you. The last time you wore it, you said it was too tight."

I had her dead to rights. I had heard it with my own ears, and so had the others.

"I've lost a few pounds," was her offhand dismissal of my complaint.

"In your brain, maybe."

"Christiana!" My mother's voice warned.

"I might want it," Darlene interjected.

"You hate pink!" I cried, aware that I was being baited but unable to help myself. "You said pink makes you look putrid."

Darlene jumped to her feet. "I did not—"

"Christiana! Darlene!" My mother stood between us, or I would have bitten Darlene on the ankle, so great was my hatred at that moment. As it was, I looked up at my mother, making a rare appeal to her sense of fair play. "It isn't fair," I told her, trying not to whine. "Neither of them wanted it until I said something about it and—"

"It's my bathing suit," Joanna broke in. "I'll throw it away before I let you have it!"

There! I looked up at my mother. She had heard it. Even she would realize how cheap and petty Joanna was being. But she was scowling at me.

I looked back over at Joanna, narrowing my eyes. "You—

you—" Bitch was on the end of my tongue, but it never got any further.

"Act your age," Joanna said.

"She is." Darlene giggled.

Mother said, "That's enough, girls." She focused on me. "I really don't understand your behavior, Christiana," she said coolly. "First the other night and now today."

Warning bells went off in my brain. Red lights flashed. I bit my tongue as hard as I could. Then I bit it again. The cookout! I had worked hard all week, cleaning and vacuuming and doing all those things I couldn't do on Sunday. I had gone shopping with my sisters and had carried their bags without complaint. I had stood around for hours and watched them admire themselves in various department store mirrors. All without a word! I was so close to getting permission.

Mother had tentatively planned a big evening out for Joanna and Darlene and their respective boyfriends, with her heading the group as the grand matriarch, and I was going to be excused from going because I wasn't wanted anyway. It would have meant spending the whole night at my uncle's house, an arrangement he had enthusiastically agreed to. It was a night of joy beyond my wildest imaginings. Had I blown it? Had I ruined everything?

"I'm sorry," I choked out. "I didn't mean it. I just—have cramps," I finished, hanging my head. The lie nearly gagged me, but it was the one they always used.

Mother was busy considering my fate when the telephone rang. "I'll get it," Joanna said gaily, knowing it was for her. She jumped up and ran into the kitchen. In a minute, she called out, "It's Larry. He wants to know where we're going Saturday night."

Mother forgot me completely. She rose to her feet and started for the kitchen. Darlene followed her, unwilling to be left out of

37

anything this close to the end. But my tantrum wasn't the only thing forgotten. The beautiful pink bathing suit lay crumpled on the floor exactly where Joanna had left it.

I began inching over toward it as soon as they were out of the room. I considered grabbing it and running, but discarded that idea immediately. The sight of me running past the kitchen door hunched over like a linebacker protecting an intercepted pass might alert them. If I stuffed it under my t-shirt and vanished, they'd know the minute they got back that something was up. No one ever left the passing down before the fate of every last stitch of clothing was decided. It just wasn't done. Then I had a moment of brilliance that almost made up for my earlier stupidity. I used my fingertips to inch it under the couch until not a thread was showing. Afterward, I sat back and waited patiently for them to end the conference with Larry.

They came back discussing what they were going to wear for the celebration. The word "shopping" came up. It was late afternoon. "I'll start dinner while you're gone," I offered helpfully, and so it was decided.

They were gone in less than five minutes. After I made certain, I retrieved the bathing suit from under the couch, smoothing it out with loving hands. It was *mine!* They would come home with new clothes, and this old thing would never again cross their minds. I was ecstatic. I was thinking cookout. I'd seen Joanna in this suit, and I'd seen the way boys looked at her when she wore it.

I carried it upstairs to my room and looked around for a place to hide it. Finally, I took all the sweaters out of my "winter" drawer and spread the swimsuit out in the bottom. Then I carefully placed my sweaters back in the drawer, making sure no trace of pink could be seen.

I felt eyes boring into me and I spun around, but no one was there. Only Teddy. Looking accusing. "It was fair," I insisted, shoving him over so that he was face down on the bed. "It was fair and you know it."

CHAPTER 4

The day of the much-dreamed-about cookout dawned clear and warm, with a good September breeze. My uncle picked me up before noon, and in my excitement, I chattered nonsensically all the way back to his new home.

My first surprise was the dozen or so cars parked in front of the house. They weren't like the cars that had been there the night of the wedding reception. They were less sleek and shiny, more like the cars that belonged to Joanna's endless parade of boyfriends. Still, the reason for them being there didn't become clear to me until I entered the house and crossed the living room to the sliding glass doors that led to the deck and the beach below. A volleyball net had been strung on the beach, and there were people down there. Lots of people. Not grown-ups. Todd's-age people. I spotted him right away because of his hair, a bronzed god in cutoffs. He was right in the thick of it, laughing and waving his arms in the air for the ball. They weren't all guys down there. There were girls, girls that looked like Joanna and Darlene, or at least they had the same God-gave-it-all-to-me builds. I didn't have a build yet. I was "slow to develop," Mother said, with only the bare beginnings of something chestwise and no waist or hips. Nature had been kinder to my sisters, who had been fully developed at thirteen and were sure that what I had was all I was going to get. I had high hopes. What I didn't have was *time*.

I don't know what I'd expected; maybe a cozy family get-together with just us four. My uncle had said a "huge" cookout, but the word hadn't registered. I hadn't thought about Todd having friends, but they were down there, all his age and sunbrowned and gorgeous. And here I was, fourteen and pale and straight as a stick.

My aunt said something to me, and I tore my eyes away from the enemy below. "What?"

"Why don't you change into your swimsuit and join them?" she repeated with a smile. "Jack won't begin cooking for a while yet."

She stood at the door to the kitchen in a yellow two-piece bathing suit and an open fishnet cover-up that came to mid-thigh. She looked like the girls down on the beach, only more so. She'd had her hair cut since the last time I'd seen her, I realized, so that it curled softly around her face. She also looked years younger than I remembered, whether from happiness or the hairdo, I didn't know. None of it was as important to me as what I was feeling, and what I was feeling wasn't good.

"Okay," I said with a sigh.

"Let me show you where your room is," she offered, taking my overnight case from me and starting down the hall.

She gave me a grand tour of the house. The master bedroom was off to one side of the house near the kitchen. It was large, with sliding glass doors that led onto the deck and a bathroom of its own. We crossed the dining room and living room to enter a hallway that led to the other bedrooms. One, she explained, was Todd's and a mess, so she didn't open that door. The next one, she said, was mine. Mine. The words finally registered. Not the guest room or the "room you can use while you're here." For some reason, that seemed very important to me.

It was a beautiful room, even to my untrained eye, with deep blue carpet and a lighter blue everything else. White gauzy curtains moved slightly at the open windows, and there were a half-dozen white eyelet throw pillows on the pale blue bed-spread. It looked like a sky full of puffy clouds.

Her voice came from behind me. "Do you like it?"

I smiled up at her, and she nodded. "Good." She handed me my overnight case. "Why don't you put your things away and change. I'll be in the kitchen."

There was a dresser in the room for me to use, and I took my time putting my things away. There were sweet-smelling sachets—lilac or something flowery—in each drawer. I hadn't brought much with me. After all, it was only for overnight. So I ended up with one pair of panties and two socks in one drawer, a change of shorts and t-shirt in another, and a nightgown in the third, but the very act of putting my clothes in the empty drawers made the room seem more mine. The only thing left in my case was my toothbrush and the bathing suit.

The bathing suit! Just seeing it all shimmery and pink in the bottom of the overnight case made me feel better. I grabbed it out of the case with renewed enthusiasm, suddenly feeling like dancing. I yanked off my shorts and shirt with one hand while I held the suit in the other. I got it caught in my shirtsleeve and had to struggle to get it out, but it was worth any struggle, this bathing suit. It was my ticket, my key to competing with all those bosomy girls down on the beach. How stupid of me to have worried.

I pulled it on, and turned to look into the mirror on the closet door.

I cried out at my reflection. It was—*horrible!* Too horrible to be believed. It sagged and hung on me like an old sack. It mocked my skinny body. With no hips to fill out the bottom, the crotch fell down a full two inches below my own, and the bust with its metal stays that had looked so ripe and rounded and firm on Joanna was concave on me. I tried crossing the tie under the bust, thinking that might help, but the cups collapsed and the tie ended up around my neck.

I wished it was a hangman's noose. I sank down to the carpet, suddenly weak with misery. I didn't wonder what had happened; it was as clear as day. God was punishing me for stealing my sister's bathing suit, but I never would have thought even He could be so cruel as to make my beautiful bathing suit ugly. The room around me turned ugly. The day was ugly and I, with my stringy brown hair and shapeless body, was even uglier. The thought of going down to the beach with all those beautiful, almost grownup people, and me looking like this, was the ugliest of all.

I don't know how long I sat there. I had no intention of moving. Ever. But I was roused from the nightmare of reality by a knock on the door.

The sound startled me, soft as it was. No one at home knocked on my door. They just opened it and came in. I didn't stop to wonder who it was. If I had, if I had thought it might be Todd, I would have dived under the bed and stayed there for the rest of my life, but even in my non-thinking state, I knew it couldn't be him. He was down on the beach with his friends and all those girls with boobs. He didn't even know—or care—that I was there.

I must have mumbled "Come in," because the door opened. I looked up.

There was a flash of—something—on Carly's face, then she adjusted her smile and stepped inside, closing the door after her. "Well," she said brightly, "you're all changed."

"It doesn't fit," I said miserably.

"Is it new?"

"It's my sister's. She—gave it to me."

Again that trace of something, then, "Stand up and let's see."

I didn't have any choice. The only other option was stripping it off where I sat and standing up nude, and I was much too shy to do that. Reluctantly, I got to my feet, careful not to look in the mirror.

She put her hands on my shoulders and turned me slowly. Then she began folding and tucking pieces of limp fabric. "I think we can do something with this," she said finally. "Your sister won't mind?"

I could look her in the eye and answer, "It's too little for her. She was going to throw it away."

"Well then," she said, and there was a trace of relief in her voice, "let me get my pins and we'll see what we can do."

I had not one grain of hope that Joanna's bathing suit would ever look like anything on me other than what it was—my big sister's ill-fitting bathing suit—but I allowed her to adjust and shift and pin. When she got to the concave bust, she said, "We'll have to do something about this," and I couldn't think of what she had in mind unless it was to wait for years for me to finish developing.

Finally, she was done, and the mirror confirmed my worst fears. There were pouches of fabric sticking out everywhere and it looked, if anything, worse than it had.

Carly vanished with the suit and I sat on the bed in my panties and t-shirt, suddenly missing Teddy very much. It seemed like she was gone for years. I spent the time constructively, trying to think of ways I could pretend to like what she'd done to the hideous suit and still throw it in the trash without hurting her feelings.

Eventually she came back, again knocking on the door before entering. The sound still amazed me. I dreaded the humiliation of putting on the now-hated bathing suit, but I knew it was just another part of my punishment. The Almighty could be a fearsome disciplinarian.

She turned me from the mirror and stripped off my shirt and panties. Curiously, I felt no embarrassment with her, maybe because she'd already poked and prodded everything I had during the pinning process. The minute she pulled the suit up, I could tell there was a difference; I could feel it against my skin. Before I'd had to hold it up, and I don't think it had touched me anywhere.

I looked down with a trace of interest. I could see some of her handiwork. All the extra inches of fabric in the middle had been sewn into pleats that swept down and outward to where my hips would have been if I'd had any. The bust felt snug, which meant yards must have been taken out of it. The metal stays were gone and it felt soft and cushiony. The tie that had slipped up to my neck was sewn in place now, although I didn't need it. The swimsuit stayed right where it was supposed to without it. Still, Carly crisscrossed it once more between the new breasts and tied it around my neck.

She looked me up and down with obvious satisfaction. "There," she said, taking my shoulders and turning me around. "Look at yourself."

For an instant I didn't want to, but it felt so good that my curiosity overruled my fear. I raised my eyes. And smiled.

It was beautiful, as beautiful as I had imagined it would be, only more so. Of course, I was still in it, but I seemed transformed. The pleats gave me curvy hips where none had been before, making my straight waist just small enough. And I had a bust. Well, *I* didn't, but it looked like I did. Even my bare legs seemed more shapely, although I'm pretty sure that was just my overactive imagination.

"Do you like it?" she asked, but she already had her answer. I was turning slowly around, admiring myself in exactly the same way I'd seen my sisters do in store mirrors. When I got to the full back view, my confidence slipped a bit. I still had no butt. Then I shrugged mentally and turned back so that I could see the front. You couldn't have everything in one day.

My eyes traveled from the neatly fitting crotch to the pleats to the curvy bosom, ending up at my head. My smile faltered.

"What's the matter?" Carly asked.

"My hair's still stringy," I said before I could stop myself.

I don't know what I expected her reaction to be. Maybe, "What an ungrateful wretch you are!" or, at least, "Some thanks that is for all my work." But I didn't expect what I got. She burst out laughing. She had been kneeling beside me, and now she collapsed on the floor, wiping her eyes.

"But the bathing suit's beautiful," I said hurriedly, trying to get it in before she lost her sense of humor.

Her laughter died to a chuckle, and she wiped her eyes. "You are adorable, Christie."

I blinked. No one had ever told me I was adorable before. I didn't know if she was laughing at me or with me, and I was a little afraid it was the former. "I didn't mean to sound ungrateful."

Her smile faded. "You didn't sound a bit ungrateful," she said, pushing my hair back from my face. "You sounded serious."

She put her hand under my chin and turned my head this way and that. "We can't do anything major this afternoon or the party will be over before you get to it, but maybe this evening." She looked at me. "If your mother won't mind."

"She won't mind," I lied blatantly.

I didn't know if she'd mind or not, actually. I doubted it. She took about as much interest in my hair as I always had. I had to be dragged to the beauty parlor twice a year to get the ends trimmed. Mother's involvement in the hair issue consisted of doing the semi-annual dragging and saying "Run a brush through it" when I'd been out in the wind. I didn't know what Carly had in mind for my hair, but if she could do for it anything close to what she'd done for the bathing suit, I'd weather the storms of hell and even my mother's temper to give her the chance.

I thought that settled the issue, but I had underestimated my new aunt's talent for invention. She led me down the hall and into the master bedroom, sitting me down at her dressing table. "This is just for this afternoon, you understand," she explained apologetically, opening a drawer and pulling out a hairbrush and a box of hairpins. Then she proceeded to work magic before my unbelieving eyes.

She brushed my limp hair up and secured it with a rubber band. Then she stuck a pin here and a pin there until it was all on top of my head, adding a good two inches of brown height to my puny five feet. She brushed a few strands down in front of my ears and snipped at them with her scissors. Then she wound them around her finger and sprayed them with hairspray.

She was standing in front of me when she did that, blocking my view in the mirror. When she stepped back, I caught my breath.

I looked . . . different. Older. And very, very close to pretty. If this was just for this afternoon, I couldn't wait to see what tonight would bring.

"Wow!" I said, grinning.

"You like it." I was surprised to hear relief in her voice.

"Sure I like it. It looks great! For me, I mean," I added, suddenly embarrassed by my own immodesty.

She nodded. "It looks great on you, but if you go in the water, it will all disintegrate. It's not the most practical beach hairdo."

"I'll stay miles from the water," I assured her, still admiring the stranger in the mirror.

"Don't do that. Get out there with the kids and have fun. Tonight we'll do something more practical for you. This is just for show. For that important first impression. Those count, you know."

And thinking of Todd down there on the sand with all those girls shaped like Joanna, I sincerely hoped second impressions counted, too.

CHAPTER 5

The reconstructed bathing suit and sophisticated coiffure were a much-needed shot in the arm of undiluted confidence, but it was my legs that had to walk down those wooden steps to the beach, and they were decidedly wobbly. I wasn't normally shy about meeting new people, I guess because people rarely noticed me, especially if I was with my sisters; but I felt different today, pretty and noticeable and terribly self-conscious.

They did notice me. A couple of the guys stopped what they were doing and frankly stared at me as I came down the steps. Although their looks were complimentary, I had a bad moment or two until Todd saw me and came bounding up to meet me.

All activity stopped while Todd introduced me. "Guys—and gals," he said with a grin, "this is my new—" he stopped and grinned at me. "Uh . . . cousin, I guess. Christie." He put his arm around my shoulders and looked down at me, and suddenly it was all worth it, worth the cleaning and dishwashing and vacuuming and yes-ma'aming, all the boot-licking hypocrisy of the last six days.

"And Christie," he said, startling me out of my thoughts, "this is—oh, hell. Introduce yourselves. There's too many of you."

He released me, and his friends gathered around me, telling me names that didn't register. They treated me like an equal.

Then had taken their cue from Todd; I was accepted and welcome.

Sides were being chosen for the next volleyball game, and I ended up on Todd's team. I played volleyball well, as I did every sport that interested me, and I proceeded to play my heart out. I thought I felt Todd's eyes on me more than once as I reached up for the unreachable shot and made it, and my heart soared. Our team won, and I was unanimously declared player of the game. When sides were chosen again, the captains flipped a seashell (inside/outside) to see who got me. It was a heady afternoon, and all too short.

Midway through the second game, my uncle called, "Chow time," and the ball was discarded as people began to drift toward the stairs. I was furious. My team was ahead, and my moment of glory was being snatched away from me.

I picked up the volleyball and began bouncing it on the sand. No one missed me at first. Most of the group started for the house in twos and fours, arms linked and laughing, but a bunch of the sandier ones, male and female, sprinted into the water for a rinse-off. I stayed where I was, watching them frolic in the waist-deep water. I saw Todd pick up one particularly buxom blonde in a yellow two-piece suit and throw her out into the deeper water, and I prayed for a shark attack. Then, as if on cue, they all began to drag themselves toward the shore, shaking off when they reached the sand like a pack of soaked retrievers.

Todd caught sight of me and, grinning, ran over to where I was standing. "Steaks are on," he said, running his fingers through his dripping hair.

"I'm not hungry," I mumbled, dropping the volleyball to the ground and viciously kicking it up into the dunes.

He didn't read my mood. "Oh, you're not, are you?" he said playfully, lunging for me and capturing me in a wet headlock. "We'll see about that. Come on, dwarf. You're going to eat if I have to force-feed you."

"Stop it!" I barked out. I twisted out of his grip and started down the beach at a run. I was ashamed of myself before I'd gone five feet. What an idiot I was. But he had called me a dwarf, and for a whole afternoon, I had forgotten to feel like one. And tomorrow he was going away for four years. It was more than I could handle at one time.

I heard him cry out, "Hey, wait," behind me, but I didn't slow my steps. I had made a fool of myself, and I couldn't see any way out of it except to run away and keep running.

I heard footsteps pounding on the sand behind me; then a hand caught my arm in a vice grip. "Hold up!" he ordered, dragging me to a halt.

I turned and faced him.

He was frowning. "What's the matter? Did I hurt you?"

I looked down. "No."

"What then?"

"Nothing," I answered petulantly.

"Don't tell me it's nothing," he said, not releasing my arm. "Tell me what's wrong."

I had never able to edit my words as some people do during their journey from brain to mouth, and I still couldn't. So I said, "I'm not a dwarf."

His frown vanished, and he gave out a hoot of laughter. "Is that all?"

I didn't share his amusement. "It's enough."

He shook his head, still grinning. "But you are a dwarf."

"I'm fourteen years old," I began importantly, "and—"

"Jesus!" he exploded, cutting me off. "Dwarfs aren't young. They're short!"

It was a far cry from an apology, and I was in the mood for a fight. I drew myself up to my full height and, avoiding his eyes, said, "I'm not short."

"Yes, you are."

"I'm not either. I'm not short!"

His voice took on a teasing note. "Look at me and say that."

I didn't do as he instructed immediately. I continued to glare at the ground until he said, "I dare you."

Then I looked. And up. To where he stood a full foot taller than me. I squinted against the sun, and felt amusement bubble up from that bottomless well that was my sense of humor. It erupted into laughter. Mine.

"See?" he said, looking down at me. "You're a dwarf."

"Next to you, everyone's a dwarf," I countered when I could speak. "I'm only a . . . a comparative dwarf."

His grin turned into a chuckle. "You have a hell of a way with words. Did anybody ever tell you that?"

They had, but still, my slightly padded chest swelled with pride. I had a decent vocabulary. Everyone in my family did. It was something you picked up as you got older, like their views on politics; but coming from Todd's lips, the compliment fairly took my breath away.

"Thanks," I said shyly.

He released my arm, and I turned and started reluctantly back toward the house.

"What else is wrong," he asked, falling into step beside me.

"Nothing."

"Aw, come on, dwarf. Level with me."

"Nothing," I repeated, not rising to the bait. Then after a few steps, curiosity got me. "Is she your girlfriend?"

"Who?"

"The one in the yellow swimsuit."

It was a minute before he answered. He might have been trying to place the bathing suit, but I didn't dare look over. He might also have been laughing at me. Finally, he said, "Jennifer. No, she goes with Jack."

"Then which one?" I was determined to know my competition.

"None of them. They're all just friends."

"Everyone seems to be couples," I insisted.

"Then you'd better count again, dwarf, because there's twenty of them. Twenty-two counting me and you."

"Really?" My voice squeaked a bit.

"Really."

We walked a few steps further before my insatiable curiosity overcame what little tact I'd developed over the years. "Why don't you have a girlfriend?" I asked, then looked over quickly to see if he was offended.

But he was smiling. "Why did I know you'd ask that?" He reached over and ruffled my hair, sending hairpins cascading down to the sand.

"Because you think I'm nosey?"

He didn't answer. Instead, he asked, "Why do you ask so many questions?"

It wasn't asked with a great deal of seriousness, but I wanted to answer him. I had been teased all my life—and sometimes not very kindly—about the questions I asked, but asking them was as fundamental to my nature as primping in front of mirrors was to my sisters. I was accustomed to the teasing, but Todd wasn't teasing and suddenly it seemed terribly, terribly important to explain it to him. "Because questions come into my mind all the time," I began earnestly. "Sometimes it seems like life's just a big puzzle and like the answers to the questions are the puzzle pieces, and I keep trying to put the puzzle together. Like somewhere in one of the answers will be the truth, the real truth, and if I ask enough questions, I'll finally get to it." I felt ridiculous even before I finished speaking. I sighed. "I guess that sounds pretty stupid to you."

He made a noise deep in his throat that I couldn't interpret.

Then he said, "No, that doesn't sound stupid to me. It sounds pretty damned smart."

Our pace had slowed to a near stop, and he made no move to quicken it. "You asked me a question a minute ago, and it deserves an answer."

"You don't have to—"

"It deserves an answer," he repeated, "and you're going to get one whether you like it or not."

He stopped and looked down at me. "I don't have a girlfriend because I've never met a female who can hold a candle to that woman up there," he said, nodding toward the house.

It took me a minute. "You mean your mother?"

"Yes, and that doesn't make me a wimp or a mama's boy, either." He looked up toward the deck. "Most of those girls up there are so concerned with themselves and their looks that they don't give a damn about other people. Maybe they will when they get older. At least, that's what Mom tells me." He shrugged. "But in the meantime, I don't want a thing to do with them. Except as friends." He grinned, adding, "Mom's going to be a hard act to follow."

"I like her," I offered. It sounded trite. "A lot."

"Yeah," he said, starting forward again. "So do I."

"What about my uncle," I couldn't resist asking. "Do you like him?"

His pace slowed. A long way down the beach, I could see two little kids kicking a soccer ball between them. A pelican sailed overhead and then plunged into the sea. From here, I could smell charcoal and meat cooking on the grill.

"He's talked Mom into cutting down to part-time work. Did you know that?" He couldn't see me shake my head because he was staring straight ahead, but I guess he didn't expect an answer. "It used to scare me to death, her working all those hours. I was afraid she was killing herself. She wouldn't let me get a job to help out. She said my job was school and her job was to bring home the bacon." He shook his head. "Jack tried to get her to quit altogether, but she said she wanted to keep her hand in. And he's going to help with my tuition so I only have to work part-time."

"You're going to work?" I couldn't imagine working and going to school at the same time. Especially college. The only other person I knew who was going to college was Joanna, and it was impossible to envision her working. Ever.

"I want to," he answered. "I have a deal with a security service at the school where I can work twenty hours a week and they'll apply my earnings directly to my tuition."

"You're going to be a cop?"

"Sort of. A school cop."

"Will you like that?"

He grinned down at me. "I don't know. I haven't tried it yet."

"Where are you going to school?" I asked, having a sudden vision of him and Joanna sitting next to each other in class, passing notes back and forth.

"Florida State."

I was safe. Florida State and the University of Florida were at least a hundred miles from one another.

I knew I was bombarding him with questions, and I hesitated to ask the next one.

"Well?" he prompted.

"Well what?"

"Aren't you going to ask what I'm going to be studying?"

I laughed. "I already know that. Political science. What I wanted to ask was what you were planning to do when you graduate."

"Then do it," he asked seriously. "Don't ever be afraid to ask me questions. I won't make fun of you."

It was one of the nicest things anyone had ever said to me. I cleared my throat. "Uh—what then?"

"Law. I want to go on to law school," he answered with the same intonation a true believer might use to invoke the name of the Lord.

I was suitably impressed. "That takes a long time."

He nodded, scowling at the sand. "That scares me, too. You never know what's going to happen. That's another reason I want to work. Like Mom, I want to get my hand in and keep it in."

His insecurity was alien to me, but then, I had always had enough money, and my mother hadn't worked a day in her life unless you counted her occasional appearances at the boutique, which I certainly did not. I felt compelled to help him out, to give him some of what I'd always had in abundance. "My uncle said he's going to help," I reminded him.

"As much as he can," he agreed, nodding, "but he's got three nieces to put through college."

There was nothing I could say to that. I knew from not-so-subtle hints from Joanna that Mother had guilt-tripped Uncle Jack into paying for Joanna and Darlene's college. My own wasn't yet an issue.

By then we had reached the stairs that led up to the deck, and the smells coming from up there made my mouth water.

"So how about it?" Todd said suddenly. "Are you willing to be my girlfriend? Just for today?"

And forever and ever and always, I vowed silently. I nodded, afraid to trust my voice.

He laughed and took my hand. "Then you'd better help me get up there to that food, or your date for the evening is going to pass out dead on the sand."

Mother and Darlene were helping Joanna with her last-minute packing when I got home. The clothes that weren't already contained in Joanna's matching suitcases were confined to the two beds in her room, and the three of them barely looked up when I breezed by with a "Hi. I'm home."

No one said anything about my hair, although I could see that they noticed. Carly had styled it into what she called a "windswept," so that it waved softly back from my face, making me look at once older and softer. I had discovered almost by accident that hairdressing was what she had worked at so many hours a day, although I think I might have guessed that when I saw the final results of my haircut. She also confessed to me that her sewing skills came from making all her own clothes for years, at first out of necessity, I surmised. Although she hadn't said anything negative about her past, I got the impression she had seen some pretty tough years.

I wasn't upset about them not commenting on the improvements wrought by the new hairdo. The women in my family had a hard, fast rule that stipulated, "If you can't say something derogatory, don't say anything at all."

I floated into my room, closing the door behind me. Teddy grinned at me from the bed, so I picked him up, kissing him on the nose and straightening Todd's handkerchief around his neck. He—Todd—had offered to drive me home. He had called me dwarf and carried my overnight case and opened my car door for me. It would have taken an earthquake to shake me out of my euphoria. I should have known I could count on my sisters to try to give the Richter scale something to measure.

My bedroom door burst open, and Joanna and Darlene stood there, smirking at me.

"You could have knocked," I said amiably.

They ignored me, coming into the room and sitting down on my bed uninvited. "How was your weekend?" Joanna asked with feigned innocence.

"Fine."

"I'll bet it was fine," Darlene smirked.

Joanna silenced her with a look. "Did you enjoy wearing my bathing suit?" she asked with a sneer of pure malice. I said nothing. "How did it fit?" she demanded, and Darlene burst into a fit of giggles.

I held Teddy between them and me like a shield, refusing to drop my gaze.

Joanna grew impatient. "It didn't fit, did it?"

I thought about telling her that it did after Carly remade it, but if I had learned anything from living year after year with my sisters, it was to volunteer nothing. "No."

Darlene reached down and grabbed my overnight case off the floor, handing it to Joanna. The scene was well orchestrated. Joanna opened it and rummaged through my clothes. "Where is it? I want you to give us a fashion show."

"I left it there."

That reduced them both to fits of laughter. After a minute, Joanna croaked, "I'll bet you left it there—in the garbage can!"

Actually, I had left it in the dresser drawer in my room where people knocked on my door and didn't sit on my bed uninvited, but I held my tongue. It seemed like they were almost through with me.

They relished their moment just a little longer before they stood up. "I'll bet you looked like a complete idiot," Joanna said, starting for the door. "Mother was all for driving over there and demanding it back when I realized you'd stolen it, but I wouldn't let her. I knew how ridiculous it would look on you, and I wanted you to wear it. It serves you right for being such a little sneak thief."

She paused at the door, motioning Darlene out of the room before her. She glared at me for a long time. Then she said, "I hope it ruined your weekend. You only got what you deserved, and I hope it taught you a lesson."

Then she stepped out into the hall, closing the door behind her.

I sat back down on my bed, burying my face in Teddy's fur to hide my grin in case they came back. She was right. It had taught me a lesson. I would never again steal anything that belonged to my sisters without first trying it on.

CHAPTER 6

The house was quieter without Joanna, if not more pleasant. The telephone virtually ceased ringing, and the silence hung heavy for some.

Mother and Darlene were inconsolable. They wandered around the house for weeks like troops suddenly cut off from their battalion, seeming disoriented as to time or place, checking the mailbox three times a day in hopes of news from the front. But if Joanna was communicating, it wasn't with them. No letters came except for one brief request for more money. In time, the two shattered O'Kelly women picked themselves up, brushed themselves off, and valiantly tried to get on with their lives.

I kept very much to myself, hiding my traitorous contentment behind a mask into which I tried to put just the right touch of misery and making myself the smallest target possible. I threw myself into my freshman year in high school with enthusiasm that surprised everyone and delighted my English teacher; but Todd had said I had a way with words, and I intended to have even more of a way with them before he came home for the holidays.

Besides, I had a life plan now. I would become such an academic wizard that I would be buried under scholarship offers by the time it was my turn to go to college, thus freeing up my portion of money so that my uncle could use it to help Todd pay for law school. It was a brilliant plan. Of course, it depended on a couple of other things, like Joanna finding a suitable husband from among the many offered by the student body and marrying him before too much of Uncle Jack's cash had been thrown away on her education, but I had faith in my sister. Mother had always told her that college was the place to find a husband, and I had no doubt that she would do so forthwith.

Then there was the small matter of Darlene, but I was certain that as soon as Joanna had her "Mister Right" legally tied to her, Darlene would fall in line. Of course, the weddings would cost a fortune, but Uncle Jack wouldn't have to pay for all that. And then they would be their husbands' problems. I gave them each a year and was off by only two months and a few days, which I considered not bad for a fourteen-year-old fortune-teller.

In the meantime, though, there was work to be done, and work I did, spending every waking moment that I wasn't in school with my nose in a textbook, even taking study materials over to Uncle Jack and Carly's when I spent the weekends with them. Which I did a lot. At first my mother was concerned about me spending so much time "under their influence," but when she weighed the risk against the sheer pleasure of having me out of the house, the only question became how cheaply she could pick up a bigger overnight bag.

I enjoyed my weekends with Uncle Jack and Carly for a lot of reasons, not the least of which was the pleasure of being around a place where my uncle wasn't criticized in each breath. Carly talked about him a lot when he wasn't there, all good, and music to my bruised ears. When he was with us, she would sit and watch him, her face mirroring her feelings with a clarity I found almost embarrassing. It was no exaggeration to say that he was the sun in her solar system.

Then there were Todd's frequent letters. I would read them aloud to Carly as she trimmed my hair or whipped up something for dinner. I think even then she was beginning to realize what a crush I had on her son. College was great, he told me through one letter to Carly and Uncle Jack. He really enjoyed his job with the security service and "when Christie asks, tell her no, we don't carry guns. We carry walkie-talkies and billy clubs, which are weapons enough for me."

He came home for Thanksgiving, while the weather was still warm and the beach nearly deserted. Joanna was home, so my mother and Darlene were delighted to see the back of me. I tried to look suitably dejected and packed my already-worn overnight bag.

Todd and I spent hours walking on the sand and talking about his school and my school and how happy his mom and my uncle seemed, and he answered my usual two million questions with patience and good humor. Yes, he liked all his professors. Yes, every one, except for his history professor who was a bit of a stick. No, he hadn't met any girls he could get serious about. "How can I, with a dwarf like you waiting at home for me?" he joked.

Thanksgiving passed, and Christmas came and went with the speed of lightning. I spent every possible moment of it except Christmas morning at Jack and Carly's house. Mother was content to let me be influenced; Joanna was home again. Life was good for her, too. Todd told me I was looking very grown up. Most of that was due to Carly's ministrations, but I wasn't going to give away any trade secrets. We exchanged gifts. His to me was a giant ceramic question mark I could hang on my bedroom wall, and mine to him, a miniature genuine brass scales of justice, which he took with him when he went back to school.

He sent me a generic Valentine's Day card in February, but he signed it "Love, Todd." I nearly swooned.

The academic year then began in earnest, and I dug in my

heels with a vigor that made my earlier efforts seem half-hearted. My social life consisted almost entirely of study groups and random trips to the library. There were a few boys who acted as if they liked me, but I was a one-man woman. I was cited at the end of the year for academic excellence, and Todd decided to stay in Tallahassee and work through most of the summer.

"I think it's stupid," I told Carly, throwing his letter down on the kitchen table.

"What else does it say," she asked, sprinkling seasoning into the stew she was fixing for dinner. "Did he say why?"

When she had called to tell me there was a letter waiting, I had closed the book I was reading from the summer reading list and begged a ride over. She had sweetened the offer unnecessarily by hinting that she might be making Irish stew, my favorite, but no added enticement had been needed. Now the smells coming from the stove had turned sour. Grudgingly, I picked up the neatly printed page and read on. "He says, 'I was really honored when they asked me, although I think they were probably pretty desperate. The way they explained it to me, they offer a lot of summer classes and any time there are classes, the security service has to operate, but most everyone wants to get out of Dodge by then and they have a tough time keeping enough people for those three months.' Lousy sentence structure," I added, glancing up. "He says the pay's half again as much as during the regular year and, since he's going to be on campus anyway, he's decided to pick up a couple of summer classes. 'If it works out and I decide to do it every summer, I could graduate a year early. Tell Christie I'm sorry about all our plans for the summer, but I know she'll understand.' And I," I added, throwing the letter back on the table, "know she won't."

Carly wiped her hands on a dishtowel and came to sit at the table with me. "It sounds like it's important to him, honey."

"It sounds like he's becoming a workaholic," I argued.

She bit back a smile, but I saw it. "Think positive," she said. "Maybe he'll hate it and change his mind after two weeks."

But we both knew better than that. Todd really liked his job, and his supervisors had told him he was "uniquely suited for the work," whatever that meant. I didn't care at the moment. I was lost in visions of horses that wouldn't get ridden and skates that wouldn't be worn, and I wasn't ready to be teased out of my sulk.

I was just about to tell her so when she pushed back her chair and came around to stand behind me, lifting my hair this way and that in a manner that was now familiar to me. "I was just trying to imagine how you'd look with a body perm," she said. "There's a new one out that's not supposed to frizz even baby fine hair like yours. What do you say? Should we give it a try?"

"Sure," I answered without enthusiasm. "Why not?"

I didn't always take Carly's attentions so much for granted. I was usually quite grateful for everything she did for me, like teaching me to sew and showing me how to wear makeup. I tried to show my gratitude in as many ways as I knew how, including letting her use me as a guinea pig for any new beauty products that came on the market and trying to learn to touch. Because Carly was a toucher, and being touched was as alien to me as Todd's insecurity had been. No one in my family ever touched one another, except to poke or scratch or slap. We didn't even give the dutiful pecks on the cheek that some people did when parting or meeting again. Nothing. Keep your hands to yourself and you won't get into trouble. The first time Carly had reached out and touched my arm, I jumped a foot. In time, though, I had become accustomed to it, flinching only slightly when she surprised me and not at all when I saw it coming, and

I was beginning to find this touching and hugging people very pleasant.

Her touching had affected my uncle, too. He had blossomed under her loving hands the same way the herbs in her kitchen window spilled out of their pots in leafy glory. As long as I could remember, Jack O'Kelly had been a private kind of man, his words and his emotions measured. That was good because it meant he rarely lost his temper, even when my mother did all she could to provoke it. The down side was that his affection was as controlled as his anger; he gave words of praise instead of hugs. Not now. Now he would walk up behind me when I'd been studying too long and begin massaging my neck and shoulders the same way I'd seen Carly do with him. He hugged me when I began and ended my weekends with them, and we had even progressed to real kisses on the cheek. This touching had changed the whole character of our relationship.

We had always been close, especially after my father died, but it had been a sterile, intellectual kind of close, at least on his part. He talked to me and listened to me because he thought I had a good mind. We still talked about serious things, but now we also shared warmth and laughter. I could keep him in stitches for hours with stories about Joanna and Darlene. We ganged up together and teased Carly unmercifully, and she loved it. He taught me about football. I learned about quarterback sneaks and the wishbone formation, about cornerbacks and the two-point conversion. We always chose opposing teams for the fun of it and whooped and hollered and slapped each other on the back if our team-of-the-day scored over the other. I had thought I liked that earlier version of my uncle, but I had only hero-worshiped him. Now I loved him with all my heart.

I was growing to love Carly, too. It was impossible not to. She was no mental giant, and sometimes Uncle Jack and I would get deep into discussions and lose her; but our intellectual closeness was no threat to her. She would sit across the room watching us with a look on her face that told us louder than words that she thought we were both wonderful.

My uncle told me that Carly had taught him how to express his feelings and, in learning to express them, he had discovered how many he had. He thought Carly was the most amazing woman who had ever lived. The more time I spent with her, the more I agreed with him.

I survived that summer without her son, although I have to admit that my sisters helped me through it. They didn't know it, of course, or it would have ruined everything. It began when Joanna came home wearing a ring on the third finger of her left hand. Not Larry's ring. Larry hadn't gone away to college. His parents had insisted he remain at home and attend Brevard County Junior College, which, according to Joanna's thinking, instantly rendered him beyond the pale. In fact, I was certain she had forgotten Larry's last name before she was across the Brevard County line. Her diamond was small and the setting ordinary, but it fit in so nicely with my timetable that I was able to tell her sincerely that it was the most beautiful ring I'd ever seen.

Darlene must have seen the handwriting on the wall, because she started dating a young man with no chin named Fred. Chin or no, I was glad Fred had been in the right place at the right time.

Joanna's fiancée was named Doug. Doug had a chin. He also had a set of well-to-do parents, a good pair of shoulders, and about as much sense as I would have expected. He thought my oldest sister was the most beautiful, sweetest, most loving girl in the world. I don't know what Fred thought about Darlene. I don't think I heard him string three consecutive words together during the entire summer. Spending any time around the four of them gave me ample time to work on battling my intellectual snobbery.

By mid-summer, Darlene had a ring on her finger that was every bit as impressive as Joanna's, and Joanna and Doug were doing things in Mother's room when she wasn't at home. I turned the radio in my room louder and hoped that Doug had never heard of rubbers.

The high point of my summer, predictably, was Todd's visit home just before the beginning of the next school term. It had been over eight months since I'd seen him, and I was as shocked at the changes in him as he seemed to be in those the same time period had wrought in me. We stared at each other open-mouthed for a minute before I flung myself in his arms and hugged him. I was getting very good at this touching thing.

The changes in me, as confirmed by his expression, were all positive. I had filled out—I no longer had to pad my bathing suit tops—and had developed a rather shapely fanny. My hair (chestnut, according to my personal hairdresser) was glowing and healthy, cut in a style that was particularly flattering for my somewhat narrow face, and my height had increased to only five feet, three inches, so I still qualified for my beloved nickname, dwarf; but if I had nature to thank for some of the changes in me and Carly to thank for the others, Todd could give overwork and lack of sleep credit for his. In the harsh florescent glare of the overhead lights, I could see that his face was lined with strain, his Florida tan only a memory, and his clothes were looser on him than even the fashion of the day dictated. Carly, with her usual tact, said nothing about it, and my uncle took his cue from her; but I had never let good manners stand in the way of getting answers to my questions.

"What in the world have you done to yourself?" I blurted out as soon as I was out of his arms. "You look terrible."

He smiled at me affectionately. "That's my Christie," he said, turning to hug his mother and shake my uncle's hand.

"And that's not an answer," I insisted as he turned back toward me. I studied his face more closely. Even his eyes weren't their usual clear sky blue, and they had dark circles under them, I realized with alarm. "You're not doing drugs, are you?" My voice echoed off the walls.

We were standing in the busy Greyhound bus station. People were crowded around the ticket counter and sitting slouched on uncomfortable benches that stretched across the center of the cavernous room like vinyl and chrome church pews. Quite a few heads turned in our direction. I did have the decency to blush.

My bluntness didn't faze Todd. He was either too glad about being home to care or too tired to notice them. "No, you silly dwarf, I'm not doing drugs. Now can we get out of this miserable place and head for the house?"

In the car, he fell asleep with his head on my shoulder. I would have been in heaven if I hadn't been so worried. When we got home, he only roused himself enough to drag his suitcase into his room and fall into a different kind of bed. He slept the day away. Carly and I had planned a big welcome-home dinner consisting of all his favorite things, but we had to postpone it, settling instead for cheeseburgers that Uncle Jack went out and got. It was a strangely quiet night, even for the three of us. None of us seemed to feel like talking. I was trying to figure out what was wrong with Todd, and I imagine they felt the same. We kept the television on the whole evening, the volume low so it wouldn't disturb Todd, but I'll bet none of us could have recalled one program under penalty of death. At ten o'clock, Uncle Jack and Carly decided to go to bed. I left the television on for a few minutes, staring at the screen blindly as I had for hours, but then it began to irritate me. I got up and snapped it off. I went down the hall and peeked into Todd's room. He was still sleeping soundly.

I went into my own room. Sat down on the edge of the bed. Considered sleeping and knew it was impossible. Finally, unable to contain the restlessness that had been building in me during that long and disappointing day, I pulled on my sneakers and let myself quietly out of the dark house.

I started down the beach toward Sebastian Inlet, following the path that Todd and I usually took. It was a beautiful stretch of beach, although I could see little of it with only the moon to light my way. Unspoiled, my uncle called it, and it still was, pretty much. For as long as I could remember, Melbourne Beach had been nothing more than a narrow finger of land wedged between the Indian River and the Atlantic Ocean, where A1A remained two lanes for some fifteen miles or so before dead-ending into rocks and water, but recently some genius had built a bridge across the inlet, giving road access to Vero Beach and beyond, and more people had discovered this heaven on earth. Now houses were beginning to spring up among the scrub palmettos. There was even talk of putting a grocery store on the beach. The long-time residents hated it. The snake had arrived in Eden.

The currents at Sebastian Inlet were treacherous, which made for dramatic waves crashing on the huge boulders near the end of the bridge. It also made for great fishing if one were so inclined. At that hour I had it to myself. There was enough moonlight so that I could see pretty well, and when I got to the end of the sand, I stepped onto a boulder, picking my way carefully from rock to rock until I was out over the water. The jetty stretched out almost a quarter of a mile. It was low tide, so the climb wasn't as hazardous as it could be. Waves hit the rocks on their south side, sending salty spray into the air, but there was little wind to give it muscle.

Finally, I squatted down and looked out to sea, trying to understand the strange emotions churning in me. They all seemed—exaggerated, I decided finally, watching the frothy black water swirl around the rocks under my feet, and out of proportion with reality. Part of it could be that absurd moment when I thought Todd was doing drugs. I couldn't imagine where that had come from. Todd rarely drank a beer, and he wouldn't take so much as an aspirin except under duress. No, it wasn't drugs, but something was wrong with him.

And with me. I felt unsettled, antsy, like my skin suddenly didn't fit. I had been looking forward to spending the day with him, but it wasn't just disappointment I was feeling. It was as if I was already suffering the aftershocks of some event that hadn't yet happened, as if I could feel the tide of my life changing and I had no control over what direction it was going to take. I was frightened, and it had nothing to do with being alone on a deserted beach late at night. The fear was vague, unsettling.

I got to my feet, defeated by trying to understand something that was beyond my experience. Then a sound behind me stopped me cold. I listened and there was another. I spun around, poised for flight, and my foot slipped on the rock.

Strong arms reached out and caught me, steadying me. I looked up into Todd's face and thought that the dark circles under his eyes had almost vanished in the way you always think silly, inane things in the moment before something life altering happens. I opened my mouth to speak, and that seemed to be the spark that ignited him. As he brought his lips down on mine, I ceased thinking at all. Instead, I felt. I felt as if I were a part of the deep crosscurrents that swirled around the rocks beneath me. Behind closed eyelids, I saw the sky, not black as it was now, but a deep, almost indigo blue, unfathomable, as his eyes had been in the instant before his lips touched mine. I felt his hands like the sun, warm on my skin. Then the world went deep amber as he crushed me to him.

Then he released me.

I came back to reality in stages. The first thing I felt was cold, although the night was warm. Each place where flesh had touched flesh now felt chilled by the loss. Then followed the afterglow of knowing I was loved. I looked up at him, aware that the moment was measured and wanting out of it all that it could give. His face was a kaleidoscope of emotions ranging from sorrow to anger to hunger, and I lived each emotion as it crossed his face. Sorrow because we had lost something, some innocence that had existed between us, the naïveté of early discovery, the easy laughter of casual friendship. Anger, because he had exposed himself to me in the most fundamental sense. Never again could he pretend not to love me, because now I knew. I had felt it in the kiss and could see it in his eyes and, when I did, I realized that, in some way, I'd always known. In some spot buried within that child's brain, that child that had first met him a year ago, I'd known he would come to love me.

And in his kiss there had been hunger. I had felt it pass between us in that moment like a violent electrical current. I knew all that in an instant. It was all in his face. Then it was gone.

He stepped back a little, his arms dropping to his sides. When he spoke, his voice was harsh. "You scared the hell out of me. I just want you to know that."

"I scared the hell out of you?" I shot back, quick as always to counterattack. "I thought you were a mugger or something."

"And that's another thing. It isn't safe to come down here alone at night. Hasn't your mother taught you anything?" He spun on his heel and started toward the beach.

"So much for 'I love you,' " I muttered, hurrying to catch up with him.

"Hey, wait a minute, will you?" I said breathlessly as he jumped from the rocks to the sand with me a half step behind him. "Why is one of us always running from the other?"

"You're the one with all the questions. Answer that one for yourself."

"Because we're afraid what will happen if we ever stop running," I said, panting a little as I hurried alongside him.

That slowed him down. He turned to look at me through narrowed eyes. Turned away. Turned back again. "And I want you to forget what happened back there on those rocks," he said, wagging his finger under my nose.

"What happened?"

"It was a stupid moment of weakness and you're jailbait," he continued as if he hadn't heard me. "So forget all about it."

"Okay."

My easy agreement must have taken the wind out of his sails, because before we had gone many more steps, he slowed his pace a good deal more.

"Can I ask you a question?" I ventured when I thought it was safe.

"You're going to anyway," he said grudgingly. Then, "All right. What?"

"How did I scare you? I mean, I know how you scared me. You could have been a vicious sea turtle or a giant fiddler crab, but how did I scare you?"

The corners of his mouth twitched, but the smile died before it was fully born. "I thought you were gone."

"When?"

"When I woke up."

"I was gone," I reminded him reasonably.

"I don't mean gone here," he said, waving his arm. "I mean really gone."

I still didn't follow him. "Where would I go?"

"Oh, home. I don't know. I thought you were mad at me."

It was the second time I had come face to face with his insecurity, and I ached for him. "So you came looking for me,"

I said quietly.

"Yeah."

"And you found me, exactly where you knew I'd be."

His only reply was a grunt. He thrust his hands deep in his pockets and trudged on.

"I won't do that," I said with as much feeling as I could pack into the words. "I won't ever just walk away from you—no matter what."

We continued on in silence. When we reached the steps to the deck, he climbed them slowly like an old man, dropping into a chair at the top.

The quiet was tangible. No jets soared overhead, no traffic sounds intruded from the highway nearby. The house behind us was dark, sleeping. The stillness was broken only by the sound of quiet waves washing up onto the shore, so continuous, so natural, that they became just another part of the silence.

Todd sat, slumped over, rubbing his forehead and never once looking in my direction, but he couldn't fool me anymore. He had kissed me. He loved me. He might tell me to forget it, but I knew he hadn't. He knew I was there—and I knew he was hurting. There was no way I was going inside until I found out what was wrong. I curled up in the padded lounge chair across from him. "So, what's going on?" I asked. "You're skinny as a rail and you seem exhausted."

"I am exhausted," he admitted, rubbing his hand over his face.

I waited. After a minute, he sat back and stuck his feet up on the deck railing, sliding down in his chair until his head rested on the cushion. He closed his eyes. "I am exhausted," he repeated, "but nothing's wrong. Everything is great."

"Then why do you look like you just escaped from a POW camp?"

A smile flickered across his face. "Fitting description. No, it's not that bad. Just a lot of hours. We were really shorthanded this summer. I think I wrote you about that." I nodded, and he continued. "The gotcha is that the kids are rowdier in the summer months, always pulling some kind of prank."

I considered reminding him that he was supposed to be one of those kids, having fun and pulling pranks, but it didn't seem the right time.

"We lost two guys at the end of summer, so I doubled up on my hours. I knew the money would come in handy when school starts."

"If you're still alive when school starts," I countered.

"I'll be alive," he assured me with a weary smile. "Two weeks of Mom's cooking and your constant grilling, and I'll be as good as new."

I ignored the left-handed compliment. "I guess that accounts for the dark circles, but have you given up eating as well as sleeping?"

He grinned, looking almost like himself for the first time since he'd arrived home. "I'm on a diet."

"Bullshit."

His eyes widened. "Profanity from my little Christie's mouth? What has happened to you, girl?"

I wasn't going to be distracted. "I spent too much time around you. Now stop avoiding the issue."

"Yes, ma'am," he said with a mock salute. But then his face grew serious. "I've been cutting down a little."

"A little? Todd, cutting down a little means refusing the second piece of pie because you're stuffed. You've been starving yourself." He winced at the word. "Can't you afford to feed yourself on all the money you're making when you're not sleeping?"

"That money's not for food," he snapped. "It's for school." Then, with less heat, "I'm sorry, but that's the way it is."

"The way it is, is that you're an idiot," I said, my voice as angry as his had been. "You can certainly afford a sandwich or two a day with what you make and what Uncle Jack contributes."

"He won't be able to help anymore." He said it so softly I wasn't sure I heard him right.

"What?"

"He won't be able to help out anymore," he repeated, straightening up in his chair. "Not with Darlene starting school this year."

I smiled my "ah-ha!" into the darkness. I wanted to whoop and holler with laughter, but I was afraid of waking the family. I had shared my little secret about my sisters with no one, wanting to see everyone's faces when my fantasy became a fact, but now I realized that my continued secrecy would be counterproductive. "Is that all that's worrying you?" I asked, "because if it is, forget it. Darlene won't make it through the first quarter."

He turned to look at me. "What are you talking about?"

I was feeling very smug. "I predict that both my sisters will be married before Christmas and that the weddings will be rather hastily planned." I glanced over; his eyes were riveted on me. I began to enjoy myself. "Madame Christiana also predicts the strong possibility of little feet pattering on my eldest sister's floor less than nine months after the ceremony," I finished with a giggle that refused to be suppressed.

"What in God's name are you talking about?"

I laughed aloud. "Love in Cocoa Beach," I quipped. "Joanna came home wearing an engagement ring, and she and her boyfriend Doug have been screwing their brains out all summer."

"Christie!"

"Don't worry. I don't listen. I keep the radio very loud and pretend I don't know a thing about it. I've learned a lot of new songs, by the way."

He shook his head. "But what does that have to do with Darlene?"

"Everything. She's engaged, too. Just up and fell in love right after Joanna announced her engagement."

"I can't believe it," he said, shaking his head again. "Has she known the guy long?"

"I don't know and I don't care. What I know and care about is that when they get married, they'll quit college, thus freeing up all of Uncle Jack's money."

"You're a witch," he said, but he was grinning. Then his grin faded. "They're too young to get married."

"Who *cares* if they're too young?"

"I care."

"Oh great protector of the nation's youth," I mocked. "Do you really think you can stop them?"

After a minute, he said, "No."

"Then leave it alone. Let them have what they want and get what they deserve."

He looked at me strangely. "That's a very cold and unfeeling thing to say."

I knew he was right, but I also knew that I had a defense. "If it is, I learned it from masters." He was unconvinced. "I'm not wishing any evil on them, Todd," I explained patiently. "I wish they would both wake up tomorrow morning and not be the shallow, selfish pigs they are. I wish they could marry wonderful men and live happily after, but I don't think that's going to happen. All I'm doing is wishing them Godspeed in what they're determined to do anyway."

"It's still cold."

"It's reality."

"It's not reality. Yet. Not their marriages. It's just a—a—"

"Fantasy?" I offered.

"It's just a fantasy like those books you're always reading.

They could both break off their engagements and decide to go to school and graduate school and postgraduate school. You're not dealing in reality. You're dealing in dreams."

"Well, if I'm dealing in dreams, you're dealing in doom," I countered. "Why do you always have to live as if the end of the world is just two inches around the corner?"

He looked over at me in surprise. "Is that what I do?"

I hadn't expected him to take my offhand remark so seriously, but when he did, I realized I'd meant it. "Yes, you do," I said slowly. "A lot. I'm not putting you down for it, but you live so much in fear of what might happen tomorrow that you miss out on what's happening today." He didn't agree, but he didn't disagree, either. "What about those courses you took this summer while you were trying to amass your fortune for next year? How did you do?"

Silence. Then, "Crummy."

"Crummy," I echoed. "So you half-killed yourself to get money for college and pick up a few extra hours, and destroyed your grade point average while you were doing it."

"I didn't destroy it," he muttered.

I snorted. "I know all about grade point averages. I'm busting my butt to keep mine high enough to get a scholarship. Wait," I said when he started to speak. "I'm not trying to pick a fight. I'm just saying that today is important, too. If you have to be any kind of 'istic,' be optimistic."

He looked skeptical. "And the future will take care of itself."

I shrugged. "Sure. It always does."

Amazing how we can feel so smart and know so little.

CHAPTER 7

For a long time, though, it seemed that I might be as smart as I thought I was. Todd spent most of the next two weeks at home, eating his mother's cooking and sleeping and answering my never-ending questions.

I was an odd duck that summer. I seemed that way even to myself. One moment I'd feel mature and act as if I was a self-possessed thirty; the next, I'd be a brat in pigtails. The strangest part was that I seemed to have no control over it. Even my uncle and Carly seemed perplexed by my behavior.

Todd, as usual, seemed to take my mood swings in stride. We walked to the inlet and talked about the courses he would be taking and the classes I was scheduled for. I had been encouraged by my English teacher to take a course in journalism, and I was pretty excited about it. Todd said it sounded like a good way to channel my questions into something constructive. We talked about my grades and his grades and avoided any discussion of money.

The other thing we avoided mentioning was the kiss on the rocks. There was no reccurrence of that impulsive behavior. I wouldn't be completely honest if I said I was glad about that, but somewhere in that mature part of me, I knew I wasn't quite ready for the feelings that kiss had stirred in me. That didn't stop me from daydreaming about it and reliving it almost every moment I was away from Todd during those two weeks. I discussed it with Teddy, and he told me I was still too young for that kind of thing. That almost earned him another trip to the closet.

Todd and I never discussed my sisters' college careers. It was another of the things we had deemed off limits. Still, I would occasionally find myself smiling at nothing.

Todd left three days early in order to register and pay for his books and get his security service schedule. He didn't kiss me goodbye at the bus station, but his eyes did and, at that point in time, it was enough for me.

I noticed during the last week of summer that Joanna's smile wasn't quite as bright as it had been, and her laughter sounded a little forced on occasion. One night when she was out with Doug and Darlene and Fred, I checked the Tampax box she kept in her top drawer and saw that none were missing. I considered putting it back as I'd found it, especially when I remembered Todd's description of me as cold and unfeeling, but there truly was a cold and unfeeling side of me that made me leave it on top of the dresser where she would find it.

At eleven o'clock that night, she did. The door to my room opened with a crash, and Joanna stood on the threshold, white and shaking. I was curled up in my bed, happily re-reading *Pride and Prejudice* with Teddy at my side, but I lowered my book and looked up. "Yes?"

She took a step into my room, holding the blue box in trembling fingers. "What were you doing in my drawers?" she demanded, her voice nearly breaking on the last word.

"Snooping," I said evenly. "Why?"

Her eyes became saucers and her mouth dropped open. Then anger overrode surprise, and her eyes narrowed to slits, her lips thinning to a white line. I could almost see her as the Wicked Witch of the West, riding her broom and chanting, "I'm going to get that girl, I'm going to get that girl." The vision was almost comical, but I wasn't laughing. It was a moment that had been a long time coming.

When she was capable of speech, she said, "You may think you're going to get away with it, but I'm going to tell Mother—"

"Please do," I interrupted, "and while you're at it, tell her what I was looking for and what I found. In fact, as long as we're telling Mother things, I'll tell her what you and your little stud, Douglas, have been doing on her satin bedspread while she's at work."

"I—you—you wouldn't *dare*," she sputtered. "She wouldn't believe you."

"I would and she would and you know it," I told her, my voice bored. "She'd have to if anyone actually said the words. I'm not totally blind, and neither is she. That goon you're engaged to lets loose enough semen each time to cover the state of New Hampshire. She just pretends to ignore the puddle."

Joanna pulled a horrible face, clutching her throat. "You're disgusting!"

"I took a biology class just like you did, only I did all my lab work at school. Now get out of my room or I'll tell Mother you've been behaving like a common slut."

I watched the battle take place in her. I half expected her to dive on top of me, claws curled and ready, but I had underestimated the impact of my ultimatum. After a moment or two, her shoulders sagged and she started to turn, but I wasn't finished with her yet. "And Joanna," I said when she was halfway out the door. She stopped with her back to me. "Don't ever come into my room again without knocking."

She glared at me over her shoulder. Her face was chalk-white except for the two little circles of color on each cheek. "You're a rotten bitch!" she hissed.

"I know," I said as she pulled the door closed behind her.

I didn't hide my smile in Teddy's fur that night because there was no smile to hide. I closed the book I'd been reading and put it on the floor beside the bed. Then I switched off the lamp on my bedside table and lay staring into the darkness. The little mouse had roared, as I'd always known she would. She had truly roared, and she had made herself a little bit sick in the process.

But having roared, she was a mouse no longer. Everyone seemed to notice the change in me, but no one remarked on it. I wasn't sure if that was significant or not.

I didn't lord my new power over Joanna, but neither did I back away from it. My behavior might have made me sick, but I had meant every word I'd said.

During the remaining days that she was home, Joanna avoided me, and I wasted no effort seeking her out. Darlene followed Joanna's lead and stayed out of my way. Mother didn't ask what was going on, nor had I expected her to.

Our mother was something I'd given a lot of thought to over the summer months, coming up with more questions than answers. It was no secret that she'd hated my father, although I knew she would never have given him a divorce. She wanted her married status and his money. Not that he was rich, but he'd enabled her to stay at home with her children and play the married lady. I also wondered why she continued to hate Uncle Jack so much, and through association, my aunt Carly. She was always "that woman he married."

There was no understanding her. She was an unhappy woman, and I was afraid she was going to get a little unhappier, at least for a while. Inconsolable as she had been when Joanna had left for school, I questioned how she would handle sending her younger daughter away to college. Darlene, although a poor second, had been a great source of comfort to her during Joanna's absence. Technically, I was the third of her daughters, but I don't think Mother thought of me as that. I was a separate entity to her, or maybe a nonentity. Whatever I was, I knew my presence would be no real help to her. It was too late for us to develop a mother-daughter relationship. Strange. When someone said the word, "mother," I thought of my own mother, poised and cool and imperious. The word "motherly," however, brought a different image to mind, the image of Carly standing at the stove, laughing as I read Todd's letters to her, worrying that he wasn't taking care of himself or that I wasn't taking care of myself.

Over the last year, Carly had become as involved in my life as in her own son's. It was she who worried with me about my score on some big test. She and my uncle. They were the ones who attended the ceremony when I was inducted into the National Honor Society. They were the ones who planned a celebratory dinner when I became editor of the school paper. They were my family. But they were not who I lived with, and I worried about that woman I called Mother.

I discussed my concern with Carly, and she told me that everyone had to go through things their own way, and that the best thing I could do was "be there" for her. So I was there. I tried my best in those early September days to make things easier. I had dinner ready when she got home from work—she had volunteered for full-time—and offered to watch the programs she liked on television. Mother picked at her food and sighed all through her situation comedies right up until the night of the anticipated call from Joanna. After that, she wept more than she sighed.

Then she adjusted. While I had expected Mother to react pretty much as she did, as if Joanna's pregnancy was merely a *faux pas,* I had given no thought as to how the sudden turn of events would affect our uncle. Until that time, I think I'd forgotten he was *our* uncle. Joanna and Darlene hadn't acted much like nieces, accepting Christmas and birthday presents as their due and laughing behind his back at his still-awkward attempts at a hug. Joanna had only condescended to see him once since his wedding, and Darlene had agreed to spend a couple of hours a month with him because Mother insisted on it. It was some kind of value-for-money philosophy, the nuances of which I couldn't begin to grasp, and I'd always felt as if he came out on the short end.

Their shoddy treatment of him, however, hadn't altered his feelings for them, as I found out when I brought over the news that both of my sisters were home and both would be quitting college to get married.

At first he didn't believe it. "What are you talking about? They can't do that. They're both too young. Especially Darlene. I can't believe your mother has agreed to it."

"She has, though."

He studied my face as if expecting to see the beginnings of a smile. A joke. That's what he thought it was. When I didn't smile, he flushed alarmingly. "I intend to hear this with my own ears," he said, stomping over to the phone.

I watched him dial the number, feeling sick at heart. I suddenly felt as if I should have prepared him for this somehow. At least I could have told him they were engaged, but my mother had forbidden me to mention it. "They'll tell him when they are ready" had been her words, which sounded to me like it would be when they wanted his funding for something. Still, it was a direct order.

The telephone was answered at their end, and I listened as he said, "Who is this? Darlene, I'd like to speak with your mother."

It was a long time before she came to the phone, although I knew she'd been expecting his call. She had told me only an hour earlier that I could "tell him the good news." It was just her way to keep him waiting.

Carly and I were sitting on a sofa at one end of the long living room, he on a chair by the telephone at the other. He said,

"Evelyn, I'd like to know what is going on." There was a pause, and then, "I'm sorry you don't like my tone of voice, but I don't like hearing from Christie that my nieces are quitting school and—This has nothing to do with money. I—What in the hell can you be thinking?"

I always thought of my uncle as a gentle, loving man because that's what he was ninety-nine percent of the time. The other one percent sent you running for cover. He never became violent. He didn't have to. He had a tongue like a bullwhip and the vocabulary to give it sting, and when he resorted to profanity, it was time to check the homeowner's policy.

Mother must have remembered that, because he listened for a long time. I could gauge where she was in her explanation by the shade of gray on his face. His only comment during the lengthy monologue was the occasional "Jesus" muttered under his breath. Finally, he said, "I'll call you back and let you know," and slowly hung up the telephone receiver.

Neither Carly nor I was stupid enough to ask, knowing he would tell us in his own time. For what seemed like ages, he sat staring at the telephone as if it were still imparting information to him. His shoulders were bent under the weight of Mother's glad tidings, and I tried hard not to look at his face.

"Joanna is pregnant," he announced finally. Then he slammed his fist down on the table, sending the telephone clattering to the floor.

"Oh, no!" I heard Carly whisper.

"And because of her stupidity," he continued in a barely controlled voice, "Darlene has decided to quit college after less than a quarter and get married, too."

"Oh, Jack," Carly was saying at the same time I was muttering, "Predictable."

His eyes fixed on me, hard and glittering. I heard a bullwhip crack in the background. "I don't need your goddamn sarcasm,

Christiana."

I felt worse than if he'd slapped me in the face. "I just meant that Darlene always does what Joanna does," I explained, trying to redeem myself in his eyes. "She wouldn't have made it in college anyway, Uncle Jack. She doesn't have two brain cells to rub together, and Joanna was struggling to maintain a low C average. She went to college to find a man, not to get an education."

His face was scarlet as he got to his feet and came toward me.

Carly jumped up and planted herself between him and me. "Christie is upset, too, Jack," she said quickly, holding her ground against his advance. "It wasn't right that they made her come over and tell you. She didn't mean those things she said."

I had, but I wasn't about to contradict Carly right now; and if her words didn't have the desired effect of calming him down, at least they prevented an additional explosion.

He looked from Carly to me, and back at her. Then he spun around and slammed his way out of the house. Carly and I held our places like mannequins in Macy's window until we heard the roar of his car engine and the squealing of his tires as he peeled out of the driveway. Then Carly sagged slightly.

After a minute, she straightened her shoulders. "He'll be back as soon as he calms down," she said, more of a plea than a statement. "It was a shock to him."

I couldn't look at her. I couldn't think. I could only feel, and I felt miserable. I shook my head slowly as I walked down the hall to my room, wondering how an otherwise intelligent man could refuse to see the obvious truth.

I closed my bedroom door behind me and crossed over to the bed, for the first time sorry that Teddy resided at my other home. I used my pillow as a substitute and tried hard to pretend it had fur.

Hours later, as Carly and I were battering and frying a chicken we hoped my uncle would be home to eat, I realized she was really worried about him. I had been so busy nursing my bruised feelings that I hadn't given a thought to how she must have felt after virtually throwing herself between the two of us. Now I began to watch. She kept tilting her head, listening for the sound of a car engine. Every few minutes she would glance at the clock and bite her lip. Once we heard the squeal of tires on the two-lane highway, and she almost knocked the heating skillet off the stove.

"He'll be okay," I said, watching her as she mopped hot grease off the kitchen tiles.

She glanced up at me. "Of course he will." She looked at the clock again. "He has to be," she said, as if she'd forgotten I was there. "I don't know what I'd do if anything happened to him."

I was suddenly and unreasonably furious with Joanna and Darlene. "It's their fault," I muttered.

She looked at me without comprehension.

"Joanna and Darlene," I spat out. "It's their stupid behavior that caused all this."

Carly seemed to shake herself. She straightened up, nodding slowly. "In a way, I guess," she said, beginning to dredge chicken pieces through a bowl of flour and seasonings. "He loves all his nieces very much. He feels like he's their father now that your daddy is gone, like he's responsible. So when two of them decide to botch up their lives in one day, he can't help but feel like he's failed them somehow."

I was washing lettuce leaves for salad, one by one and without enthusiasm. Carly was teaching me to cook as well as to sew. "Why?" I demanded. "Why does he love them so much? They treat him like garbage. They don't deserve his love."

"It doesn't work that way, honey," she said with a sympathetic smile, understanding more than I had said. "Real love doesn't have to be earned. It just is."

"I think that's dumb. You're saying they can do anything they want and he'll still love them just as much."

Carly thought about it. "Not just as much, but yes, he'll still love them. It's not easy to love a child who treats you bad. That's why you're his favorite. You make it easy. He has to . . . work at loving Joanna and Darlene sometimes. They haven't learned to feel other people's feelings or to care about them very much."

What I perceived as her defense of them ruffled my feathers more than her praise could soothe. I threw the head of lettuce in the sink. "They're just like Mother and I hate them all," I blurted out, and was instantly ashamed of my words. In the year and a half that I had been practically living with my uncle Jack and Carly, I had never put my mother and sisters down except in an occasional joke. I stole a look a Carly, and the pity in her eyes brought me up short.

"I don't think you really hate them, Christie," she said slowly. "I think you're disappointed in them because they don't always measure up to what you want them to be, and they haven't always made life very easy for you. In a way, you ought to thank them for that." At my incredulous look she went on. "They've made you a lot tougher than you would be if everything had been handed to you," she said, wiping her hands on a kitchen towel. "In a lot of ways, you're mature beyond your years, honey, and you've got so much going for you. You're intelligent and you can talk a blue streak and you can make people laugh, and all those are important things. But if someone asked me if there was something you were short of, I'd have to say it was forgiveness. Sympathy and forgiveness. You mama and sisters don't have what you have. They don't have your bright mind and your sense of humor. They can't learn things as quick as you do, and they don't get awards for being smart. I imagine they're a little bit jealous of someone as smart and talented as you."

The idea startled me, but I didn't have time to dwell on it because Carly went on. "They're just trying to get through life like all the rest of us, and if the way they do it seems wrong sometimes, you have to know they're doing the best they can and forgive them if it sometimes hurts you. That's what your uncle is doing out there right now, trying to forgive your sisters for doing such a foolish thing and trying to forgive you for saying things about them. You have to learn forgiveness if you're ever going to be happy in this life."

I thought about what she said. I didn't believe it, necessarily, but I listened. "How do you—learn—forgiveness?"

"Practice," she said without hesitation. "You practice, and life will give you plenty of things to practice on. This is one of them. Your sisters haven't always treated you very well in the past, but Joanna at least deserves your sympathy now. I think it's time to forgive both of them for the past and wish them well in their new lives. It doesn't cost you a thing to forgive them, and it will make you a better person. And happier. You'll see."

I didn't take her words about forgiveness all that seriously at the time, although I guess from that moment on I did begin to practice it. I never ignored advice given to me by Carly. I had too often seen the wisdom underlying it.

It was a good thing I did because, as Carly predicted, the coming years would give me a lot to practice on.

The first was one day before the big double wedding. Mother and Darlene had run up to the mall to pick up a few last-minute things. Morning sickness had curtailed all but evening shopping for Joanna, so she and I were alone in the house.

I was in the middle of writing an article for my journalism class when I heard her cry out in the room next door. Without thinking, I hurried to her room and opened the door without knocking.

She was standing in front of her full-length mirror, a vision in her eight-hundred-dollar wedding dress. Then I noticed her hands at the back holding the dress together. There was a full two-inch gap between the left and right zipper teeth.

"Get out of here!" she snapped, spinning to face me.

Her words didn't register. I was thinking about how stupid my sisters had been to run out and buy their wedding gowns two months ago when Uncle Jack had agreed to pay for them. Joanna hadn't given a thought to the possibility of her waistline expanding, but expand it had. "It doesn't fit," I croaked out.

"I said get out," Joanna cried, her face nearly purple with rage. "I don't need you in here laughing at me."

I stepped back in surprise, but then I realized that her suspicion of my reaction wouldn't have been too far off until recently. "I'm not laughing," I said, starting toward her. "Here, let me see."

She backed away from me until the wall checked her progress. "Stay away from me," she half-threatened, half-pleaded. "I'm not letting you near this dress. You'll—you'll do something to it."

I had been murmuring the word "forgiveness" like a mantra for the last two months. Now it came to mind unbidden. "I'm not going to do anything to it. I just want to see if it has darts or something that can be let out."

"And who's going to do it?" she demanded miserably. "The bridal shop closed at noon today. There isn't time to get it altered. Oh, God," she moaned, collapsing on the bed on a cloud of tulle and white lace, "can anything else in my life go wrong?"

Tears began to stream down her cheeks and she buried her face in her hands. Her display of emotion surprised me. It was true that she was given to outbursts, but they were usually outbursts of anger. Tears weren't what one normally saw on her face, and that gave them an even greater impact value.

"Come on, Joanna," I coaxed. "Just let me look at it. Maybe I can fix it."

"You!" The word hung in the air. "What can you do about it?"

Forgiveness. Forgiveness. "Carly has been teaching me to sew. I might be able to let out a couple of darts." When she made no move to do as I asked, I added, "What are you going to do, get married in your slip?"

Her hands dropped from her face, and I could see the sharp retort fly to the end of her tongue, but it died there. She stood up and yanked the dress from her shoulders, letting it fall to the floor in a heap. "Oh, who cares?" she asked the walls. "Things can't get any worse than they are."

She stepped out of the circle of fabric and kicked it toward me.

I said "forgiveness" several more times before I reached down and picked up the gown. One glance gave me the answer I needed. There were two wide darts in the front and two in the back, not to mention big seams. If I took them out, the dress would fit easily.

"Stay here," I tossed back over my shoulder as I headed out of the room. "I'll be back in a few minutes."

I carried the dress back into my own room and rummaged around in my top drawer until I found a large safety pin. There were no fancy sewing tools like a ripper-outer in this house. The lack was based on the female O'Kellys' philosophy of "Why make it when you can buy it at the mall?" I would have to make do with what I had.

I sat down on my bed and began painstakingly picking at the tiny stitches that gave the dress its maidenly figure. It was grueling work. Each dart was triple stitched to hold up through many generations of brides. I sat back halfway through the first one, blinking and rubbing my already-stiff neck. Why was I doing this? Why was I doing this for the person who let me steal her castoff bathing suit only so people would laugh at me? Then I thought about Joanna in her slip, sitting on the bed in the next room, and I remembered the day I had sat on a bed in my panties and t-shirt after Carly had vanished with the hideous pink-and-burgundy swimsuit. I thought of my mother and Darlene, who would throw up their hands in surrender if they were faced with so much as lowering a hem. Suddenly it became very important to me to make Joanna's wedding dress fit her, and I tackled the chore with renewed enthusiasm.

I had just zipped it up on her when our mother and Darlene breezed into the room laden with bags and boxes. I don't know what surprised them more, seeing Joanna in her wedding dress or seeing me in the room with her.

Mother dropped her packages on the bed. "Why, Joanna! Don't you look lovely? I was—um—a little concerned about—oh—the fit." Mother didn't talk about the blessed event that would happen three months too soon, only about the wedding.

Joanna looked over at me with pleading eyes. She still didn't know me. I couldn't have said anything even if I'd wanted to. "It fits like a glove," I murmured, sidling out of the room.

"Yes," Joanna said, her face breaking into a wobbly smile. "It does, doesn't it?"

The double wedding came off without a hitch. Both grooms appeared a little stunned and confused, but happy, even if their parents seemed a little less so. My sisters were showstoppers in their nearly identical gowns, and our uncle looked a picture in his black tux and red carnation. He gave his two oldest nieces away bravely, and only I among the spectators knew how much the gesture cost him. Carly hadn't been invited to the festivities, of course. She was home baking pies for the upcoming holiday. It was a happy Thanksgiving for me. I was maid of honor for two beautiful brides and Todd was home for the holiday. Add to that my uncle had forgiven me my moment of insensitivity, and I was walking on air.

At the reception, I watched as my mother ignored Uncle Jack and turned her back on him when he was speaking or answered in sharp little monosyllables. He took it all with remarkable grace. There was nothing she could do to provoke him. It was his nieces' wedding day and, however much he might hate it, he wouldn't allow an ugly scene to spoil their happiness. I wasn't surprised, though, when about two hours into the festivities, he glanced first at his watch and then meaningfully at me.

I was more than ready to escape. I had smiled until my jaw ached. I had oooh'ed and aaah'ed with the rest of the crowd when Joanna and Darlene emerged in their traveling suits (even though they weren't leaving on their honeymoons until the next day), feeling that I had done my sisterly duty. Besides, Todd and Carly were waiting for us.

We said a brief goodbye to Mother, then went over to where the brides stood side by side, ready to receive the well wishes of everyone. Uncle Jack stood facing the two of them, looking into each of their faces for a long moment before he spoke.

Darlene, in a burst of newlywed enthusiasm, grabbed his hands and said, "Isn't this all fun?"

He smiled with effort. "Yes, honey. It's fun."

He looked back at Joanna, whose gaze met his briefly before dropping to the floor. He reached out and touched her cheek. "Be happy, sweetheart," he said softly. "That's all I ask. Just be happy."

A tiny sob escaped her before she bit her lip. "I'll try, Uncle Jack," she whispered through trembling lips. "I really will try."

He leaned down and kissed her forehead. Then he kissed Darlene's forehead and we left the house.

At the car, I said, "Want me to drive?" I often did when the two of us were together.

"No," he said briefly. "I'll drive."

I climbed in without another word. I already understood about needing to be in control.

We were almost home before he spoke again, and then what he said was disjointed, his thoughts not yet structured. "They're too young." He didn't look at me. "It was a mistake to go along with it."

"What choice did you have?" I asked only a little bit timidly. "They had Mother's consent. That's all they needed."

He let out a long breath. There was no answer to that. "They're so unrealistic," he said instead. "The whole lot of them."

"Does it matter so much if they're realistic as long as they're happy?" When he didn't answer, I added, "It's their job to make themselves happy now. They got what they wanted, and now it's their job to make it work. I don't want to make you angry," I said quickly as he opened his mouth to speak.

"That doesn't make me angry." He glanced over at me. "It makes me hopeful, hopeful that they inherited a little bit of the common sense their sister got so much of. You're a pretty smart kid, you know that?"

I felt a glow start somewhere in the center of me and spread outward. "I spend a lot of time around two really smart people. I'm learning all the time."

"What are you learning?"

The question caught me off guard. I had made the statement half-jokingly, but now that I thought about it, I realized it was no joke. I just wasn't certain I could put it into words. "I'm learning about—friendship. About love and friendship." I thought for a minute. "Carly is your best friend. You two have so much fun together. Dad and mom never had any fun together." I glanced over, to check his reaction, ready to retract and/or apologize if I needed to, but he was nodding.

Bolder now, I continued. "I don't know if they loved each other, but I don't think they liked each other." My words sounded silly to my own ears. "I don't know how to say exactly what I mean."

"I think you're doing a fine job," he said. "Your mom and dad—well, they . . . tried . . . to be happy. Your mom can be really hard to get along with." He ignored my snort. "And Howard wasn't perfect." He glanced over at me and smiled. "All right, he was pretty perfect. He was always my hero, but I wasn't married to him so I don't know what kind of husband he was." He was thoughtful. "Their marriage . . ." A glance at me. "My marriage to Carly—well, it's different. The more we know each other, the more we like each other. Kind of like you and Todd," he said, glancing at me again. "The two of you remind me of us. You seem to be better friends all the time. I wouldn't be at all surprised if something came out of it someday."

I blushed to my roots. I was a long way from ready to talk about what Todd and I shared. My mind flashed back to the night on the rocks, and I blushed even more. But I never wavered in my belief that Todd and I would one day be just like Uncle Jack and Aunt Carly, and it was another couple of years before that belief turned to dust.

CHAPTER 8

I was in the middle of my senior year in high school. Joanna had a nine-month-old bouncing baby boy that was the image of his daddy. Doug had quit school, and the three of them had moved to Alabama where Doug would work with his father. Joanna had thought at first that this would be a great adventure, but she soon discovered that south Alabama lacked the cosmopolitan glitz of even central Florida.

Mother took the separation better than I had anticipated, partly because she had never quite accepted Joanna's error in decorum and partly because Darlene, with chinless Fred, had settled within five miles of her. It didn't hurt one bit that Darlene was three months pregnant and fifteen months married. Personally, I found Fred an affable nonentity, and while I'd have trouble recognizing him if I ran into him on the street, surely that spoke more to my poor memory than anything to do with him.

Within months of the wedding, Joanna volubly hated her husband and despised her in-laws, but I guessed she was happy enough. Darlene, on the other hand, was the image of marital bliss. She found a reason for living in being Fred's wife. I was happy for her and hoped all their children would look like their mother.

I had two whole Thanksgivings and Christmases and one entire summer with Todd before my world turned upside down. I thought he and I were as close as two people could be and still remain in separate skins. I was growing up, quite the young lady by then. I no longer needed tissues to fill out my tops, nor did Carly need to take tucks in my clothes to give me hips. The lascivious reaction of my male classmates impressed me not at all. I looked for admiration in only one pair of sky blue, beloved eyes. Along with this sudden maturity in physique came a collateral explosion of hormones, and it became increasingly difficult for me to not let my feelings for Todd translate into action. In fact, that second Thanksgiving holiday I displayed none of the common sense my uncle had credited me with, and it was only Todd's tremendous self-control that kept us on the straight and sensible course we had charted.

My near-downfall occurred on a Saturday night after that second Thanksgiving. Mother had grudgingly agreed to accompany Darlene and Fred to Alabama for a weekend reunion with Joanna. They were all to stay with Doug's parents in their big house outside Montgomery. Although it was mentioned that the invitation included me, I murmured my regrets, packed a bag, and hightailed it straight to my uncle's after school on Wednesday. Todd was coming home; I had no thought in my mind other than that.

It was a beautiful weekend. The weather cooperated as it generally did, giving us sunny, warm days for frolicking on the beach and cool, breezy nights with the mercury dipping all the way down to fifty-five degrees, making it perfect for donning sweatshirts and walking along the waterline hand in hand, as Todd and I did every evening.

We were strolling along the stretch of beach between the house and the inlet that Saturday night, and I was regaling him with stories of Uncle Jack and Carly. Their ever-increasing enjoyment of one another was one of our favorite subjects. Todd had long since quit scrutinizing Carly on each of his visits for fading bruises and had accepted, as I had, the fact that sometimes love between two people did work.

As I was talking, my uncle's words to me popped into my head and, of course, straight out of my mouth. "Uncle Jack says we're just like them." I felt a slight hesitation in his step, but he said nothing. I looked up at him, but his face was turned away from me, and he was looking out at the water. "Well, what do you think? Do you think we are?"

He stopped abruptly, looking down at me. He had been laughing the moment before. Now his face wore a stern, almost angry expression. "I don't think we can even think about how we are. Not for a long time." I could see him almost physically withdraw into himself.

I was used to Todd's odd reactions. They were all part of the package that was him. Life to him was serious business, and it was only when I could get him to loosen up that he had any fun at all. I probably should have left it alone, but he was leaving to go back to school the next day. I couldn't let our beautiful weekend end on such a somber note.

I turned to face him, grabbing his other hand and wrapping it around my waist so that my body lightly brushed his. "Oh, come on," I said playfully. "Can't we be just the teensiest bit like them?"

His expression didn't change, but after a minute, I felt a trembling begin somewhere deep within him. I thought I had made him that angry. Then his face twisted with pain, and his arms crushed me against him until I was breathless. His mouth came down on mine with a force that yielded as much pain as pleasure, blending the two together until, for the first time in my life, I truly knew desire. Mindless, overwhelming desire. I laced my fingers in his hair, arching my body against his, willing the feeling to go on and on.

He tried to pull away, but I clung to him, burying my face in his neck. I heard him whisper my name, and I realized I was trembling as much as he. Then he kissed me again, a long, deep, searching kiss that seemed to last forever. I felt the breeze buffeting us softly, heard the tide gently whooshing up on the sand. I opened my eyes and saw the million brilliant stars in the night sky above us and knew that this was where I wanted to be for the rest of my life. In his arms. Loving him.

After what seemed like forever, he made a strange animal noise deep in his throat and tore his mouth from mine. "I want you, Christie," he moaned. "God, how I want you."

His words destroyed the last vestige of reserve I might have had if I'd had any at all. "Me, too," I whispered, my lips close to his ear. "I want you, too. I love you."

It must have been the word "love" that brought him back to his senses, although desire waged a mighty battle before it lost completely. He lowered me so that my feet were on the sand, but he didn't release me. He held me loosely, his hands stroking my back, reaching up to caress my hair. I felt the trembling in his body slowly lessen until it was just a memory, and he stepped back from me.

I was having none if it. I wouldn't let him release me. I wanted him to make love to me. I knew all about making love. What I hadn't learned from listening to Doug and Joanna that summer, I had made up for with my insatiable reading. It wasn't always the classics that rode along in my backpack.

I hadn't planned that it would happen or even given it much thought until his words about wanting me, but now it was what I wanted with all my heart. Now. "Todd," I said, reaching for him.

"Stop it!" he said harshly, grabbing my arms and pushing me away from him. "Jesus Christ! What do you think I'm made of?"

"Flesh and blood, just like me," I said recklessly. "And you want me as much as I want you. Don't try to deny it," I said quickly, even though he hadn't, "because you said it yourself, and don't try to tell me you don't love me, either, because I know you do and—"

His mouth came down on mine, silencing me. This kiss held none of the electric desire of the one before. It was warm and firm and controlled. When he pulled away, he put his hands on either side of my face and tilted it up so that I was forced to look at him.

The moon rode slightly higher, and in its reflection I could see deep creases of pain etched in his beloved face. "All right. So I love you. So what? That doesn't give us the right to start acting like Joanna and that chinless what's his name—"

"No, that's Fred. He's Darlene's. You mean—"

"Whatever. We're better than them. Don't you know that?"

"But—"

"Christie, you're seventeen years old. You don't even start college until next fall, and I'm facing law school. We can't do this to ourselves, and we can't do it to Mom and Jack, either. I'm all Mom has, and it would kill your uncle. We can't let them down like that. Okay, so I love you and you love me and someday we'll do something about it, but not now, Christie."

He lowered himself to the sand. He sat with his arms wrapped around his legs, his chin resting on his knees as he stared out at the black water.

I stood for several minutes trying to absorb all that had just happened. He loved me! The words sang out in my mind. He loved me. I had known it, of course, but he had said it. He loved me! I wanted to dance across the beach and frolic in the surf, but the tension in his shoulders stayed me. I also could have picked several obvious holes in his logic—I mean, we weren't exactly all Uncle Jack and Carly had; they had each other—but it didn't seem the time for that, either.

Finally, I sank down on the sand beside him. I sat cross-legged, picking up a handful of sand and watching the phosphorus sparkle like tiny diamonds as it trickled through my fingers. He would talk, I knew, when he was ready. What I didn't know was whether I would be ready for what he had to say. It was an anxious few minutes.

He reached over after a while and took my free hand, lacing his fingers through mine. "I can't do it, Christie. Not because I don't want to. Do you have any idea how often I think about you?" I shook my head, but I don't think he saw me. His fingers tightened around mine as he said, "Half of what we do in security at school is go around breaking up couples in parked cars. Every time I do it, I wish those people in the cars were us. God, Christie, I dream about you all the time. Not a day goes by when I don't think about you a hundred times, wanting to tell you things, wanting to just touch you. Sometimes I feel like I'm going to go out of my mind—" He broke off abruptly, rubbing his free hand down his face. "But I'll handle it. Somehow I'll handle it. I have to," he added, his voice vibrating with intensity, "but not by jumping in the rack with you and blowing everything that means anything to us. I want to keep what we have special. You're too important to me. I'm not going to let anything cheapen us. Can you understand that?"

Reluctantly, I nodded. I did understand. I didn't want to, but I did. I, too, felt that what we had was unique. Losing one's virginity had become epidemic in my school. I had watched the girls in the senior class dropping out en masse because of pregnancy and becoming the butt of the latest campus dirty jokes. I didn't want Todd and me to become a dirty joke. My rash behavior, I realized as my state of mind became more stable, was the result of those late-blooming hormones finally coming of age.

Seeing my nod, Todd turned and looked back out to sea. I wondered what he was seeing. Knights in shining armor, perhaps, and damsels in tight-waisted gowns with billowing skirts. The longer I knew him, the more I realized what an ideal-ist he was. Part of his pessimism came from real life not living up to those high ideals of his. I had fewer ideals and more optimism, but he was truly a man of honor and I had to respect him for it. "Great protector of the nation's morals," I said, remembering an earlier conversation.

He looked over at me, and a feeble smile curved up the corners or his mouth slightly. "Not the nation's morals, dwarf. Just yours. The rest of the nation will have to look out for itself."

Blindly, blissfully, I sailed through the fall school term, studying my little heart out and maintaining my 4.0. As editor of the school newspaper, I had to find a quick replacement when our star reporter left suddenly "to spend a few months with her aunt in Detroit."

I was drawn to journalism in the same way a cat's claws are drawn to the best furniture, and had long been known around campus for my in-depth interviews of faculty and students. The motto of our little school paper was "Truth Will Light the Way," which, to the amusement of my fellow students, I took seri-ously. I was just beginning to understand what the truth meant to me, to realize that, throughout my life, I had despised hypocrisy above all else. I had seen it personified in my mother and sisters, in their treatment of me and my uncle and Carly, to mention only three of their many victims. But it wasn't just their treatment of us. They dealt with the world at large that way. Equal-opportunity hypocrites. They would verbally pulver-ize someone behind her back and then kiss her cheek when they saw her. Then it would be, "Did you see how haggard she looked! I'll bet she's drinking again." Spite. Gossip. They thought it was a game, a contest, and funny. I thought it represented one of the true evils in life. They laughed at me because I took things so seriously; I despised their callous insensitivity. They hid the truth and hid from the truth. Not too surprisingly, exposure of the truth became my life's goal.

As editor, I could at least partially control the quality of what we put in the paper. Articles and interviews submitted by student reporters were returned with little red notes that said "Why?" and "According to whom? What proof do you have?" scrawled in the left-hand margin every couple of paragraphs. Finally, my insatiable curiosity and search for truth had a productive outlet.

I was too busy during the four weeks after Thanksgiving to spend any time with Uncle Jack and Carly. I scarcely noticed when the colored lights began to adorn the shops and houses in my neighborhood. My Christmas began when Todd arrived home and ended when he returned to school. He was the calendar in my life.

During his two weeks home at Christmas, Todd and I were models of decorum, chastely holding hands as we walked the beach, our windbreaker collars turned up against the chilly breeze. He seemed more rested and relaxed than I had seen him in a long time. If he had trouble meeting my eyes, I passed it off as his way of keeping his emotions in check. I was just that naïve.

Then he and I each went back to our respective schools and our respective lives and our respective glittering dreams of the future.

In March, the dreams turned into a nightmare.

CHAPTER 9

It was Friday evening in the middle of the month, and for two weeks the weather had seesawed between unseasonably hot and up-north cold. Finally the two had come together with a clash of hail and lightning and thunder and rain that filled the gutters until it spilled over into the streets and the winter-brown lawns. Mother had gone into the shop before the storm unleashed its full fury, and I hoped it would let up before she got off work. I was planning to surprise her with my new recipe for beef stroganoff and had just added noodles to the salted water when the telephone rang. I gave the noodles a quick stir before reaching to answer it. "O'Kelly residence," I said automatically, watching the white froth in the pot climb slowly up the side.

"Hi, honey," Carly's voice said in my ear. "What do you think of this storm?"

Her sentence was punctuated with a crash of thunder, and I waited for it to die down before I answered. "I think it's ear-shattering."

She laughed. "I agree. I was going to ask you to have dinner with Jack and me, but maybe we'd better wait until tomorrow. You don't need to be out in this mess."

"I agree one hundred percent. Anyway, I'm going to wow Mother with my cooking tonight. I have beef stroganoff simmering on the stove."

"Mmmmm. I wish it were simmering on this stove. It sounds

wonderful. Okay, then. We'll plan on tomorrow. Give us a call when you want Jack to pick you up. Oh, I got a letter from Todd. You can read it to us when you come."

The lightness of her tone didn't fool me. She hadn't heard a word from him for over a month, which was unusual since he usually wrote weekly. I had been worried, too. I was suddenly sorry I'd decided to show off my culinary talents that particular evening. I tried to keep the regret out of my voice. "Go ahead and read it tonight if you want. You don't have to wait for me."

"Of course I do," she said almost before I'd finished. "It wouldn't sound the same from anybody else's lips."

I glanced over at the pot, where my noodles were hovering dangerously close to the top. "Okay then. Gotta run. Call you tomorrow."

I was thinking about the letter from Todd and wondering why it had taken him so long to write when the phone rang ten minutes later. The noodles were draining in the colander by then. I answered it on the first ring. "O'Kelly residence."

I listened to the hum for a minute before I realized no one had spoken. "O'Kelly residence," I repeated, my voice louder. "Hello? I can't hear you."

After a minute, the hum was replaced by a click and a dial tone.

I hung the phone up slowly, shivering slightly as I heard the wind whistling around the corners of the house. I wasn't a scaredy-cat kind of person, but the call made me feel uneasy. Or maybe it was the storm. I shrugged off the feeling and turned on the cold-water tap, picking up the colander and swishing the noodles under it.

When the phone rang again, I jumped back from the sink. I crossed quickly to answer it, then stood looking at it for a minute before picking it up on the fourth ring. My voice wavered as I said, "Hello?"

"Christiana, is that you?"

I cursed my cowardly self. "Yes, Mother. Of course it's me."

"Well, I barely recognized your voice. Is anything wrong?"

There was a crash of thunder and she gave a little squeal. I could visualize her holding the phone away from her with two fingers, and I couldn't help but smile. After a minute, she said, "Are you still there?"

"I'm here. Isn't this storm awful?"

"Terrible! I think I'd better grab a bite here and stay until it lets up. Some friends have asked me to join them. Will you be all right there by yourself?"

I glanced over at my stroganoff, and visions of Todd's letter wafted up in the steam over the pot. "I'll be fine. In fact, I was thinking about going over to Uncle Jack's for dinner. Would that be all right? If it stays bad, I could spend the night there."

"How in the world would you get there?"

"I'll see if Uncle Jack can pick me up. If it's okay, that is."

There was a clicking on the line, then another crash of thunder. To Mother's credit, she didn't squeal again, but it was a minute before she answered. "What? Yes, that's all right. If you must. I'll see you tomorrow."

I dialed Carly's number immediately. Of course Uncle Jack would come pick me up, Carly told me. Bring dinner with me if I wanted, or save it for another night and we could whip up something over there. I insisted on bringing it with me. Unlike beef stew and meatloaf, stroganoff doesn't age well.

I can imagine now that my uncle's drive up that dark two-lane stretch of A1A with the wind blowing at gale force was hideous. I never considered it at the time. My mind was full of Todd's letter. I was waiting on the front porch when he arrived, carrying my two-quart pot with potholders. Uncle Jack ran up to the porch, grabbed my overnight case, and we raced each other back to the car.

It took us forty-five minutes to make the thirty-minute trip back to his house. Carly held the door for us when we arrived. I breezed past her, wet hair dripping in my eyes, and headed right for the kitchen. Once I'd put the stroganoff on the stove, I reached into my shoulder bag and pulled out a ziplock bag containing the noodles, holding it up in the air.

"Dinner," I announced, "will be served as soon as I warm it up."

Carly took the bag from me and pushed me out of the kitchen. "Dinner will be served as soon as you warm *you* up," she countered. "Go get dry. I'll make a fresh pot of coffee."

She had fixed it the way I liked it, with two teaspoons of sugar and topped with whipped cream. My sweet tooth was a family joke. Luckily I burned it off as fast as I spooned it in. She turned on the oven and left the door open. I sat down at the table and stuck my cold, bare feet up on a chair near it. "Wouldn't it be nice to have a fireplace on a night like this?" I asked dreamily, taking a sip from my steaming mug.

"Delightful," my uncle said, walking into the kitchen with a towel wrapped around his neck, "and we'd get to use it about once every two years." He sat down at the table and took the cup of coffee Carly handed him with a grateful smile. "Maybe."

"I know," I said on a sigh. "I guess I'm just a hopeless romantic."

Uncle Jack looked over at Carly and winked. "Speaking of romantic," he said, pushing Todd's letter across the table toward me.

I felt the heat rise to my cheeks and tried to attribute it to the warmth coming from the stove. "Okay," I said, picking it up. "I'll read it if Carly will sit down and have a cup of coffee with us. Dinner can wait a little longer."

"All right, bossy," she said with a smile in my direction. She poured herself some coffee in a blue and white china mug. The smell was even better than the beverage, and the beverage was wonderful. I grinned as she spooned sugar into it out of the canister, even though the sugar bowl was right beside it. She gave it a quick stir and put her spoon in the sink. A creature of habit, I thought, as she came to sit beside my uncle. They smiled that special little smile they reserved only for each other. Then they joined hands and looked expectantly over at me. I was struck suddenly by how much they resembled a Norman Rockwell painting. Parents of a World War II soldier waiting for news from the front.

I ripped open the envelope and pulled out the single sheet of notebook paper. I was disappointed that it wasn't longer, then instantly ashamed of my reaction. As busy as he was with school and work, it was a wonder he found time to write at all.

I unfolded the sheet and smoothed it out on the table. I took a sip of coffee and, propping my elbows on the table, began to read. " 'Dear Mom and Jack.' " Then stopped. That wasn't the way Todd usually began his letters. When he bothered to use any salutation at all, it was generally something like, "Hi, guys," or "Greetings from academia."

I felt a sudden sense of foreboding. The bright, cheery room seemed to lose some of its glow, as if the weather outside was creeping in through the walls. The warmth of the oven no longer quite reached me. I glanced over at Uncle Jack and Carly. They were both smiling, waiting for me to continue. I passed my uneasy feeling off as a reaction to the rain beating against the kitchen windows and, taking a deep, steadying breath, read on. " 'I know it's been a long time since you heard from me, and I'm really sorry about it. I wanted to write before, but I didn't know how. I didn't know what to say or how to explain what's been happening here. I'm afraid I have some news you're not going to like—' "

I broke off as my voice failed me. I looked up at the two

people sitting across the table from me. Their faces were no longer smiling, but were creased with almost identical frowns. In that split second, I remembered what they said about married people growing in time to look like one another and marveled at how true it was.

A gust of wind brought my attention back to the moment. I looked at the window and noticed that the storm had let up a bit. The lightning flashes were dim and distant, and the thunder now rumbled out at sea.

I blinked a couple of times before I looked back down at the letter. "uh—'some news you're not going to like, but I guess there's nothing to do but tell you. I tried to think of an easy way to say it, but there isn't any. I am—' "

The letter fell from my fingers as soon as my eyes focused on the next word. The room went from dim to black, then hazy gray. No! I heard the rain pounding directly on my eardrums, exploding inside my head like a thousand cannons firing at the same time. It couldn't be true. It was a mistake. Oh, God, no! Not Todd. I felt the ground tremble and the world tilt to one side. I tried to peer through the haze, but my eyes couldn't penetrate it. I felt a giant vice grip my shoulders.

My uncle's face came slowly into focus. He stood beside me, holding my limp and trembling body in the chair. "Are you all right? Christie, are you all right?"

The urgency in his voice demanded an answer, and I tried to nod, but my head shook from side to side. I felt the bile rise up in my throat and fought it back, gulping deep breaths.

I heard Carly's voice say, "Married! Oh, Jack! Oh, no!"

I pulled violently away from my uncle's grip and snatched the letter from her hand. "No!" I said, holding it before my eyes with trembling fingers. "No! It's some kind of joke. Let me see. Um—um—'it wasn't something I thought would happen, but we had no choice,' " I read aloud, not realizing that I did. "I don't expect any of you to understand or to forgive me, and I know I'll never forgive myself for the stupid things I've done or for all the pain I know you must be feeling. I don't have any right to ask you to do this, but if Christie isn't there when you read this, if you'll just try to explain to her that I meant everything I said to her—"

I heard a wild cry break out of my throat. I crushed the hated paper into a ball and flung it on the floor. "Liar! Goddamn liar!" I screamed. My feet carried me across the kitchen and dining room and out through the sliding glass doors to the deck before either of them could react. Four strides took me to the stairs down to the beach. On the next to the last step, my legs gave out, sending me sprawling on the sand. I picked myself up and looked up at the house. They were standing at the glass doors, looking down at me.

I turned and raced off down the beach, unable to bear seeing them. Suddenly I hated them both. I hated them for the love they shared and for their happiness. I hated them because they had each other and I would never have what they had, and because they knew me and knew what I was feeling.

Then conscious thought deserted me. I was caught up in something too powerful to comprehend. My mind was racing faster than my feet. I stumbled blindly along in the rain, not knowing or caring where I was going. *Why is one of us always running away from the other?* A sob tore the breath out of my body, and I had to stop, bending over at the waist, before going on. I blinked the rain from my eyes as I stumbled on. *Sometimes life seems like a big puzzle . . .* Where were the answers? God, where were the answers? *Are you willing to be my girlfriend? Just for today? Why are we always running from one another? Because we're afraid of what will happen if we ever stop.* I tried to shake the memories from my head, but they just came faster. *So I love you? So what? Someday we'll do something about it. Great protector of the nation's morals. Not the nation's, dwarf. Just yours.*

The rain hadn't lessened. It pounded down on me. The wind had picked up again, whipping the rain into my eyes and nearly blinding me. I blinked hard and saw the inlet ahead of me. I could see the waves crashing against its great boulders, fierce and black and ugly like my heart. *Someday . . . Someday.* His voice violated me.

"Liar!" I screamed into the wind. "You filthy liar!"

I fell to the sand on my knees.

Then suddenly Carly and my uncle were on either side of me, pulling me to my feet. "Come on, baby," my uncle said. "Let's go home."

He led me to the car, which was parked on the road at the top of the dunes. I didn't resist. There was no fight left in me. Carly ran ahead. As my uncle handed me into the back seat, she wrapped me in a blanket and put her arms around me. I didn't feel cold. I felt—nothing. But I began to notice little details. The car was hers. It had a back seat. I saw water on her face, but I didn't know if it was rain or tears. My own face was dripping, and I didn't care with what. I laid my head on her shoulder and garnered what comfort I could from the human contact.

At home, they led me inside, still wrapped in the blanket. Uncle Jack said something about more coffee and went off in the direction of the kitchen while Carly led me down the hall to my room. She stripped off my wet clothes, pulling a flannel nightgown over my head and a pair of socks onto my feet. I was ashamed that she was doing all this, but my hands and feet wouldn't work on their own. I let her sit me down at the dressing table, where she started drying my dripping hair. It was the warmth of the hair dryer that triggered chills in me. I was shaking violently, uncontrollably, and I didn't know how much of it was from the cold.

She stopped long enough to grab the quilt off the bed and

wrap it around me. Then she finished drying my hair and led me into the kitchen.

The oven was still on and the door open. It was an inferno in there, but it didn't touch the chill deep inside me. My uncle forced a cup into my hands and I took a gulp, choking and spilling some of the brown liquid down the front of my nightgown. It was harsh and burned my throat. "Drink it," I heard his voice order me. "Drink all of it."

Slowly things began to come back into focus. I finished the brandy-laced coffee, and my uncle refilled my cup—with plain coffee this time. After a long time, I looked up at my uncle. "How did you know—"

"Where to find you?"

I nodded.

Then Carly handed me Todd's letter, pointing to the bottom of the wrinkled sheet. My eyes followed her finger to the p.s. It said, "Please take care of Christie for me. This is going to hurt her too much. She's not as tough as she thinks she is. If she goes nuts and takes off, look down at the inlet. She'll probably be down there."

Tears filled my eyes, blurring the last words, and trickled down my cheeks. I sat sipping my coffee and crying soundlessly, trying, trying not to remember.

Later that night, Carly made me a bed on the living room sofa. I was afraid to go to my room, to turn out the light. Uncle Jack went on to bed hoping, I think, that I would talk to Carly, but I knew it would be a long time before I could do that.

She turned on the television to fill the silence, and we both sat staring at the screen without seeing it. I don't know what we were watching, but at one point, a thought struck me, causing me to groan.

"What is it, honey?" Carly asked.

I shook my head. "This isn't right. I should be taking care of you. He's your son."

Carly bit her lip. "He's still my son, Christie."

I didn't have to ask her what she meant.

Still later, another thought popped into my head, propelling me to a sitting position. "Promise me, Carly," I said urgently. "Promise me you'll never tell him how—how—I . . ."

She came over and knelt down beside me, taking her hands in my own. "I swear I'll never say a word. There are some things in this world that no one has a right to know."

I accepted her promise because, by then, I had come to trust her. I gave little thought to the wisdom in her words because, as yet, I didn't need that wisdom.

CHAPTER 10

I didn't die. I thought I wanted to, but his words, "She's not as tough as she thinks she is," made me angry enough to survive just to spite him. Not just survive. I was determined to thrive.

That year will always remain in my mind as a year of pain and of discovery. Until then, all my future dreams had rested on the fact that "someday we would do something about it." Now I had to accept the fact that we wouldn't. I guess I might have thrown up my hands and let go of all my non-Todd dreams for the future, but my anger wouldn't allow it. Instead, I let them coalesce to create my focus.

I made sure my uncle and Carly knew I was moving forward. I even managed frequent smiles for them. Especially Carly. After that night, I would see little lines of worry in her face when she looked at me, and I knew she felt partly responsible for her son hurting me. I had to make that all right for her. My feelings for her then were ambivalent. I didn't blame her for Todd's defection. Even in the complete self-absorption that seems a natural consequence to getting dumped in love, I knew better than to blame Carly. Still, I couldn't look at her without pain, and I couldn't begin to confide my feelings to her.

I owed something special to my uncle, too. Perhaps without even realizing it, he had instilled a lot of his own values in me. One of those was to keep trying, no matter what.

So I soared through the year instead of wallowing in the misery that threatened to engulf me. I aced every test. I shone as editor of the school paper, so much so that I made up my mind during those five months that journalism would be my life's work. Eventually, my uncle seemed convinced that I was back to being a happy, well-rounded high school student and even Carly could spend more than five minutes with me without seeming to take my emotional pulse.

Suddenly, it was graduation day. It should have been a day of great celebration for me. In my graduating class of sixty-three, I walked away with all the highest honors and three of the five available scholarships. As it was, I barely managed to get through it.

I had invited my whole family, figuring that, whoever couldn't handle it didn't have to come. Still, I worried myself half sick about it. They all came—at least those who were local—and while Mother was barely civil to Uncle Jack and Carly, I considered it real progress that no actual blows were exchanged. Joanna sent a congratulations card, but Darlene came in person, with a plumper but still chinless Fred in tow.

I stood at the back of the auditorium with my classmates, waiting to march up the aisle to our seats in front, resenting Todd for rendering my day of glory so much less bright than it should have been. Then the band began cranking out their slightly off-key version of "Pomp and Circumstance," and we started to move down the aisle two by two. As we did, I caught sight of a nearly white head of hair in my peripheral vision. I stumbled a bit, but it could have been attributed to the too-long gown I was wearing. I couldn't turn around and look without making a complete spectacle of myself. While that's exactly what I'd done most of my life, I felt that it wouldn't be appropriate this particular night.

Once we were seated, I tried to turn discretely in my chair so that I could see the back of the auditorium. It was dark. All the lights were concentrated in the front of the room. Still, I thought

I could just make out that head of white hair shining like a beacon in the darkness. It was on a body that, even sitting, appeared tall. More than that, I couldn't make out. I turned a couple of more times until my classmates on either side of me began to turn, too, trying to see what I was looking at. After that, I sat frozen, staring blindly ahead.

"Some people get white hair because of their age," logical thought chided. True, I had to admit. "If he was in town, Carly would know about it." Not if he was too ashamed to face her. And if she knew, would she tell me? "How would he get down here?" There are still two buses a day. "Why would he come down here?" That was tougher. As if sensing its advantage, my rational mind added another quick thought. "Why would he travel three hundred and fifty miles to spend a couple of hours sitting in the back of a shabby high school auditorium listening to speeches?" He cared about my graduation. He really cared. "Sure. So he told his wife, 'I think I'll just drop down to Cocoa Beach tonight and watch my old girlfriend graduate. Don't wait up for me.' "

The tortuous voices continued on the edge of my consciousness, one derisive, one pitifully hopeful, until I heard ". . . Christiana O'Kelly, recipient of the JEA Journalist of the Year award, the Frye Scholarship, and the Career Journalism Scholarship."

Mr. Pirckle was standing at the podium, beaming at me.

I got woodenly to my feet to the sound of applause, knowing that logic had the better arguments. Still, the applause coming from the middle of the room and the back corner sounded especially loud to my hypersensitive ears.

As class valedictorian, I was required to make a speech. The thought of getting up in front of hundreds of people had left me nauseous just hours before, but now, with bigger things on my mind, I sailed through the ten-minute, well-rehearsed monologue. I finished up by thanking my family—all my family, I added, looking straight at the place in the back of the room where I thought I had spotted the white head and eliciting a few titters from the audience—for their unending support and encouragement. Then I accepted my beribboned diploma from Mr. Pirckle and shook his limp hand, satisfied that, if Todd were in the audience, he would know I had spotted him and managed to function in spite of it. If not, I had probably given some sweet old geezer a thrill.

Because by then, the O'Kelly good looks had come together in their youngest beneficiary. True, I hadn't come close to Joanna and Darlene's lofty five feet, eight inches, but I carried my sixty-three inches as if it were six feet. Carly, despite the fact that she worked now only when she chose, still kept my dark hair well cut and shining, and I had adapted the makeup tricks she had taught me to my own unique O'Kelly features, emphasizing the large, dark eyes and minimizing the generous mouth. Heads turned now when I walked down the street, accompanied by the occasional wolf whistle. It was all wasted on me, though. I had tried to look beautiful for only one person and, if I still made an effort, it was only because old habits die hard.

I took my seat and Mr. Pirckle introduced the guest speaker, an alumnus who had made good in the real estate industry, like that was really hard to do in Florida. I gave the man a well-deserved five percent of my attention while the remainder of my mind tried not to think of how differently I had envisioned this night.

Eventually, the interminable ceremony ended. Mortarboards filled the air. I jumped to my feet, trying to get a look at the back of the room, but my excited classmates and their exaggerated heights interfered. Then my awkward little family group surrounded me. As we made our way out of the auditorium and into the warm night air, I again searched the crowd. No one noticed that I was distracted. They were too happy for me. Well, except for Mother, who was worried about having to drive the two and a half miles home in the dark. Fred saved the day, volunteering to drive her home while Darlene followed in their car. It was the first time I had ever heard Fred string more than five words together, and I was inordinately proud of him.

When they were gone, Uncle Jack and Carly and I stood on the sidewalk, almost as if we were waiting for something. I couldn't help but remember the night four years before when we had stood on the sidewalk outside the church, waiting for their tardy minister to arrive. And if that night had been the beginning of something truly wonderful, this one seemed for all the world like the end.

Chapter 11

June, 1973

"Freddie pinched me!"

"That's what brothers are supposed to do, honey," I told Lanie, unlocking the front door. "Sisters are supposed to pinch them back."

I suppressed a grin when I heard Freddie grunt. He was too much grown to cry and too smart to retaliate, especially since I had all but ordered Lanie to pinch him back.

The kids had been in a scrappy mood all day, snapping and pinching and whining that "Suzy's on my side of the car" and "Laurie touched me." Maybe it was end-of-summer blues, but after more than four hours of it, I was ready to drown them all in the ocean that was my back yard.

The small horde followed me into the house. Laurie and Lanie, seven-year-old identical twins, were too superior to walk with Suzy, who was a mere four. They reminded me painfully of Joanna and Darlene when we were growing up. I was beginning to realize it was human nature for the older kids to scorn the youngest. And here I had thought my sisters just hadn't liked me.

The girls walked straight through the house and, dropping shopping bags on various pieces of furniture on their way, out the glass sliding doors toward the beach. "Keep an eye on Suzy," I yelled to their disappearing backs, knowing they would as a matter of habit. Suzy belonged to my next-door neighbors,

Joyce and Leon Crenshaw, although she was at my house as often as her own. The twins might not want to be seen walking with her, but they loved giving her orders, which meant they'd keep her under close scrutiny.

Freddie made two more trips to the car for groceries before joining the other kids outside. I stopped for a minute to listen to the soothing sound of silence. Then I kicked off my sandals and made my way around the house, opening all the jalousie windows. My house wasn't big, really more a bungalow. It had two bedrooms and a bath, with a small living room–dining room combo, and an eat-in kitchen. It could heat up in a hurry in late summer, but the ocean breeze cooled it off just as quickly.

I was unloading the grocery bags—it was amazing how many groceries kids could go through in a week—when the phone rang.

"Hi, honey," my uncle's voice said in my ear. "How's my favorite gal?"

"Beat." I stuffed the two dozen eggs in the refrigerator and sank down into a chair. "I've been shopping with the kids all day. I wanted to get them some school clothes before the stores jacked the prices sky high."

"You spend entirely too much money on those kids."

I grinned. "Well, there's a news flash." It was a difference of opinion so familiar it had become a comfortable joke. "They grow an inch an hour, you know. Nothing I bought them at the beginning of the summer fits now."

"Still . . ." He let it go, unusual for him.

After a minute of silence, I asked, "How are you? How's Carly?"

"She's wonderful, as always. Actually, I'm calling to ask you if you're free Saturday night. Carly and I want you to have dinner with us."

I smiled. He made the suggestion as if there were a possibility

I would say no, which was absurd. I treasured every minute I spent with them, despite the fact that Carly and I never regained the easy camaraderie we had before her son's defection. Although I had tried with all my power to disguise my feelings, I think she, of all people, saw through me. My uncle didn't, perhaps because he didn't want to. I was grateful for that, and even though I couldn't see the two of them together without being reminded of those happy early years, I spent as much time with them as I could. They were getting older, both of them. I could see it in the fine lines around Carly's eyes and mouth, in the slight stoop in my uncle's posture and the slight tremor in his hands. If I'd had tickets to *Chorus Line,* I would have thrown them away to spend an evening with them.

Still, I played along with the joke. "Hmmm . . . I'll have to check my calendar. Yep, I'm free," I said, examining my finger-nails.

"Good. I've asked Darlene and Fred. I hope you don't mind."

I didn't. Much. "Of course I don't mind. I know I have to share you from time to time. Are we having some kind of do?"

"Something like that," he said. "Oh, and—uh—Todd's in town. Would it be a problem if he came?"

It took a moment for his words to register. When they did, I was glad I was sitting down. A problem? *Jesus!* Had he really asked that question? He could bet his ass it was a problem. I had spent years avoiding seeing Jack's stepson. He had visited occasionally, probably a dozen times in the last eight years that I was aware of. Uncle Jack and Carly had been kind enough to drop hints when he might be around, and I had managed each time to be unavailable for the little get-togethers they'd planned. Could they really be that blind? That insensitive?

"No," I said, as soon as I could trust myself to speak. "No problem at all." Since I had no intention of showing up.

"Is six too early?"

"Six it is. Gotta go. Give Carly my love."

I was planning my upcoming virus before I'd hung up the phone.

"Todd's in town," he'd said, as casually as he might have said, "It's going to be hot tomorrow." Maybe I really had fooled them both. Maybe I'd fooled everyone. Because that's what I'd set out to do eight years ago. My mother and sisters had been easy. If they had given a thought to my despondency during that last year of high school, which of course they hadn't, they would have passed it off to exam stress or just general bitchiness.

Carly and my uncle were tougher, but I thought I'd done a pretty good job there. I didn't run screaming from the room when Todd's name came up, nor did I actually cover my ears when he was discussed which, out of kindness to me, I suspect, was seldom. Because of that, I knew little about how his life had progressed and what little I'd learned was more than I wanted to know. Among the few tidbits I'd gleaned was the fact that his marriage had lasted all of six months. Regular sex for six months seemed a pretty paltry reason to toss away what we'd had for four years, but hey, they say everyone has his price.

I didn't know why Todd had married so suddenly or why it had ended, and I refused to speculate. I knew he had dropped out of college and joined the army shortly after his divorce, using that fancy, if unfinished, college education to raise him to the lofty position of military cop. I think I remembered Carly saying he had been overseas, although I didn't know or care where. I also knew he had returned to the States a couple of years ago and joined the Orlando police department. Beyond that, I was willingly and willfully ignorant, and I religiously obeyed the speed limit when I was within the Orlando city limits.

Would it be a problem if he came? I tried to imagine sitting across the table from him without wanting to dump the mashed potatoes on his head, listening to his casual conversation without accidentally spilling hot soup in his lap. It was impossible. Some things are just beyond the scope of even an imagination like mine.

I knew I shouldn't feel that way. Shouldn't. What a stupid word. You either felt one way or the other, and should or shouldn't had nothing to do with it. Still, it had been eight years, long enough by anyone's standards to come to terms with a teenage disappointment. Shit happened, and people got over it. That's how it worked. Or, more exactly, that's how it was supposed to work. But instead of lessening, the pain of Todd's betrayal had lodged itself somewhere in the center of my chest, a physical ache sometimes, a slight nagging feeling that something wasn't quite right at others, and it had festered. When it tried to get loose as sorrow, like when I saw one of those mushy anniversary commercials on TV, or anger, when I was around Uncle Jack and Carly, I shoved it ruthlessly back down.

Would it be a problem to sit across a dinner table from a man who had stomped my heart into the sand without word or explanation, who had never made any attempt to contact me in the years since? I rubbed my aching forehead with my fingertips and tried not to visualize how he'd look today. If my mind wasn't cooperating, at least it was kind to me. It added eight years' worth of wrinkles to his face, a belly, maybe, one he'd gotten swilling beer with his fellow MPs after their duty shifts. Jowls. Jowls were good, sagging, discolored pouches of dissipation. Bags under his eyes were almost a given. Maybe he had gained a lot of weight. No. That one wouldn't work. The police department would never stand for that. The others were possible, though, and made me feel marginally better, but not good enough to have dinner with him. No way. It wasn't going to happen.

"If you feel as mean as you're lookin', maybe I should come back another time."

I turned toward the open glass doors off the dining room and smiled. Stella, my next-door neighbor on the other side, stood leaning against the door, one hand on her hip and her usual sassy grin on her face. Stella had been a dancer—her word—at Bea Morley's Mousetrap, a somewhat upscale if tacky bar, years before when it was open on the beach. She was tall, fiftyish and outlandishly attractive, with mounds of improbable red hair piled on her head. She had a voice that dripped southern, and she was still built like the stripper I was pretty sure she'd been. Dressed in a halter and shorts as she was now, you could see that nature had been unnaturally kind to her. Stella didn't have a job, although she did go out a lot. What she did have was a paid-for house on the beach, a fairly new Mercedes in the driveway, and enough clothes to keep a girls' school going for a year. Some lucky investments, I reasoned.

"Come on in," I said, trying to shake off my nasty mood. "Want some iced tea?"

"Lord, yes. It's hotter than a bitch out there." She pushed the sliding glass doors closed.

"I like fresh air," I said mildly.

"Uh-huh. Me too, long as it's filtered through an air conditioner." She walked over to the wall control and turned the switch to cool. Then she flopped into a chair, fanning herself. "So what were you lookin' so steamed about?"

I raised my eyebrows. "Neighbors who drop in without calling?"

"Very funny. What'd you want me to do, holler out the window? Besides, I did call. Twice. The line was busy."

"I was talking to my uncle." I put a frosted glass of sweet iced tea and the sugar bowl in front of her. Stella had a sweet tooth that made mine ache. I fully expected her to collapse in a diabetic coma at my feet some day and, while that might very well happen, it wouldn't be me who stirred that final, decisive spoon of sugar into her beverage. I tried not to look as she added three heaping ones to her glass.

"Well, it wasn't your uncle who pissed you off. He's about the sweetest man alive." She glanced at me out of the corner of her eye. "Things still good between him and your aunt?"

I grinned. "You may as well give up on that one," I said, fixing myself a glass of tea and joining her at the table. "Those two are the proverbial happy couple."

"Sure. That's what the kids always believe." She yawned and stretched her arms over her head.

Could those boobs really be hers, I wondered, not for the first time.

"Speaking of hunks," she went on, "there was a pretty nice-looking one hanging around your front door earlier. You seein' someone new?"

Her words following so closely after my uncle's announcement set alarm bells off in my head. "Noooo . . . What did he look like?"

She smiled her catlike smile, deliberately crossing one long sun-bronzed leg over the other. "Big and tall and solid looking. Nice arms. Tight pants."

I couldn't help but laugh. "God, what a witness you'd make. Hair and eyes, Stella."

"Oh, he had 'em all right."

"Very funny."

"I couldn't make out his eyes. The eyelashes were too long."

I waited. Stella could be infuriating at times.

"Blond hair. Real blond."

I caught my breath. Had he actually had the audacity to come to my house?

"You got that look on you again."

Denial set in. "He was probably a door-to-door salesman or something."

"Uh-huh. Well, if he was, I'm in the market to buy anything that boy wants to sell."

I jumped on the word. "Boy?"

She flipped a hand in the air. "Boy. Young man. Stud. Honey, they're all boys to me." She reached into her halter-top and pulled out a cigarette and a pack of matches.

Maybe that was it, I thought idly. The cups were stuffed with cigarettes. "Don't even think about lighting that thing in here."

She made a face. "You are such a stick in the mud. You think one little cigarette's gonna matter, bad as air pollution is anyway?"

"It matters to me. And it stinks."

"Oh, all right." She stuffed the cigarette and matches back in her halter. "Kids outside?" she asked, looking around.

"On the beach, I suppose."

"Maybe I'll go see what they're up to."

"Good. Don't smoke around them."

"Honestly, sugar, you think a little smoke's gonna pollute their little lungs?"

I nodded. "And their little minds."

She rose languidly to her feet. Her height without the hair was close to six feet. She was an impressive woman. "You busy tonight?"

"Why?"

"Thought you might like to go out with me. Have a little fun for a change."

I grinned up at her. "I have plenty of fun. With the kids—and with Virgil."

She made a face. "Virgil's a dud."

"Go home, Stella," I said amiably.

When she was gone, I remained at the table, my forgotten iced-tea glass making a wide sweat ring on the table. I could hear the kids outside yelling to Stella. They thought she was great, probably because she treated them like miniature adults. I drew little spokes out from the water circle around my glass. Could it be? Had he really been here? At my house? I shuddered at the thought, and then dismissed it. He wouldn't dare.

When the phone rang again, I had finished putting away the groceries and was making tuna sandwiches for dinner. "Is that Stella out there on the beach with the kids?" Joyce Crenshaw asked, even though her kitchen window had much the same view as mine.

Joyce was nothing Stella was and everything she was not. Very married and even more conventional, Joyce was short and ordinary looking, a bit plump, with short, square-cut nails and a tidy cap of brown hair. She was an emergency room nurse at Cape Canaveral Hospital, and she looked and acted like it. No frills. No nonsense. She and Stella were dry tinder and the careless match, at least in part because Joyce's husband, Leon, who did something unremarkable with computers at the Space Center, spent a lot of time on yard work while Stella was outside sunbathing. While that might have washed if they'd had grass, you had to wonder how long it took to pick up bits of sea-strewn debris and toss them back into the ocean. Joyce thought Stella was a slut. Stella claimed that Joyce was even more of a stick in the mud than me. Actually, her phrase was "tight-assed," but I knew what she meant. Our houses were at the end of a mostly paved street. Nothing as formal as a cul de sac, just a kind of little cluster. We sort of shared a yard and a beach. My house was the official demilitarized zone.

I glanced out the window. "It sure is. Hi, Joyce."

"I can't believe she's wearing that skimpy outfit out in public, and she's smoking a cigarette! I have half a mind to march out there and tell her to put it out."

"It's her beach, too," I reminded her, hating her criticism of Stella enough to forget I felt the same way. "How was work?" I asked, more to distract her than because I was interested.

"What? Oh, fine. Busy. There was crash on 520. Nasty one. It was—what is she doing now? Is she taking off her top?" Joyce's voice had risen to a shriek. "Oh, thank God! She's just getting another cigarette. It is so bad for those kids to see her smoking. Adults are supposed to model behavior, not set that kind of negative example. I think—"

My not picking up on the accident was a clear sign of how irritated I was becoming with our conversation. My father had died in a crash on 520, and as a reporter, a crash on 520 meant news, but my antennae remained inactive. "Joyce?"

"What?"

"Go get Suzy and take her inside."

"Oh." Then, "I probably should. What about the others?"

"They'll come in when they're hungry."

"Are you sure? Don't you worry about them, I mean, about her influence?"

I realized suddenly that I didn't, particularly. "They'll be fine. Go get Suzy."

"If you're sure . . ."

"Bye."

I hung up the phone.

Once in a while, Joyce got to be too much, even for me. She was a lot like my sister Darlene. If marriage to Fred had given meaning to Darlene's otherwise second-string life, having children had given her a higher purpose. Life was simple for Darlene. If something related to her children, it was vital; if not, she didn't think about it. World affairs? Foreign policy? What were they compared to the tooth fairy and Freddie's science project? I had thought her boring when she was Joanna's clone. As her children's mother, she was close to insufferable. Even Joanna, when she came back for her rare visits, agreed with me. It was probably the only thing we had ever agreed on.

As I had predicted, the older kids came in about half an hour later, grabbed their sandwiches, and headed for the living room and the TV. I didn't mind. We'd had plenty of togetherness while we were shopping. Breathing space and the monotonous drone of the television in the other room seemed just fine right now.

I had just taken the first bite of my sandwich when the doorbell rang. I froze in mid-chew. Then I shook myself. It was undoubtedly Leon, here to retrieve Suzy's clothes. "Get that will you, Freddie?" I yelled into the living room as I grabbed the bag of clothes. "Here you go, Leon," I said, rounding the corner into the living room. Then I stopped. The planet skidded to a halt under me.

"Hi, Christie."

My legs were frozen. I couldn't speak. Or breathe. I just stared. No jowls. Not a wrinkle that I could see, and his belly was as flat as it had been eight years ago. Stella was right. His pants were tight.

I brought my eyes back up to his face. "Todd." The word was flat, emotionless. I was so stunned that I felt numb.

"I hope you don't mind me dropping in on you like this. I wanted to talk to you."

Thoughts were reeling through my mind faster than I could process them. What was he doing here? Where did he get the guts to just drop in after eight years? Did seeing me again mean so little to him? Of course it did. Why would he care? He was the one who'd walked away. How could he look so much the same? My feelings went from shock to panic and back to anger in a blink. My face, for once, didn't betray me. "Talk about what?" I asked evenly.

He was looking at the kids. They were looking back with undisguised interest. He gave an uncomfortable laugh. "Can I come in?"

The laugh did it. I felt like slugging him. "No," I said, starting toward him. As I brushed past him and out the front door, I said over my shoulder, "You guys finish eating."

I marched down the front walk toward the strange car in my driveway that must be his with Todd trailing along behind me. When I got there, I turned to face him, crossing my arms across my chest. By then, the numbness had passed entirely and my anger and a lot of other emotions were building with frightening speed. "Talk about what?" I demanded.

He was regarding me with that knowing little smile I remembered so well. "No 'how are you?' "

Insufferable lout. "Sure. How are you? How are the wife and kiddies?"

"There are no wife and kiddies."

"That's nice. Enough social chitchat. What are you doing here?"

He rubbed the back of his neck. Another tug of memory. "I'm sorry to barge in on you like this. I . . . uh . . . thought about calling."

"You should have. What do you want to talk to me about?"

He looked around him. "Is there somewhere we can sit down for a minute?"

I glanced around at the walk, the sandy yard. After a second's hesitation, I sat down cross-legged on the walkway. Then I looked up, shielding my eyes from the sun and gesturing toward the sidewalk with my free hand. "Please, have a seat."

He closed his eyes and shook his head. "I'm sorry. I guess it was a mistake to come. I just wanted to let you know that I'm in Orlando now."

Call out the bands. "And?"

"And—and I'm sorry about your uncle. I wanted to let you know I'll be around if you need me." He turned and started to walk away.

Alarms rang in my head, loud, clanging ones. "What about my uncle?"

He stopped, turning slowly. His eyes searched my face. "You don't know," he said finally.

I jumped to my feet. "I don't know what?"

He seemed to consider and discard a number of answers before he said, "I'm—sorry, Christie. I wouldn't have said anything if I'd realized you didn't know."

I could feel rage and fear filling me in equal parts. "Didn't know what?" I almost shouted.

Again, he hesitated. Then he seemed to come to a decision. "He's sick. I thought he had talked to you about it."

My eyes narrowed. "I talked to him an hour ago. He didn't say a word about being sick. He didn't sound sick." When Todd looked away, I asked, "Sick with what? What's the matter with him?"

"You need to talk to him," he said, his voice gentle enough to scare me to death.

"I'm talking to you, and I asked you a question."

"Which I won't answer," he said, sounding a lot more like the Todd I remembered. "Talk to your uncle. I had no right to come, but I thought—I thought if they had told me—well, I was sure you knew. I'm sorry."

He started down the driveway to his car. I was torn between chasing after him to beat the truth out of him and racing inside to call my uncle. Before I could make a decision, he had climbed in his car and was gone.

I walked back into the house in a kind of daze. It was too much. Todd showing up. His announcement about my uncle. I walked past the curious kids without seeing them and on into the kitchen, grabbing the wall phone. My hands were shaking slightly as I dialed his number. Carly answered.

"Is Uncle Jack there, Carly?" I asked without preamble.

If she noticed my abruptness, she didn't remark on it. "He ran up to Publix, honey. We were out of coffee. Want me to have him call you?"

"Then he's not sick," I breathed out in relief. "Thank God! I'll tell you what, your son scared the hell out of me—"

"Todd? Todd was there?"

"He showed up on my doorstep offering his help because he said Uncle Jack was sick."

I heard a sound, like a rapid expulsion of breath. Then, "This is my fault, Christie. I'm so sorry."

"You're not responsible for your son's delusions. Don't even worry—"

"I don't mean that, honey." Another sound. A long sigh this time. "Your uncle—is sick, honey. He was going to talk to you about it Saturday night. I only told Todd because he was here when we found out. I never thought—"

"Found out what?" I asked, my dread returning with a vengeance. "Carly!"

"Honey, you need to talk to your uncle. I'll have him call—"

"I'm coming over there right now."

"What about the children?"

"Joyce can keep an eye on them. She owes me."

"Christie, why don't you wait—"

"I'll be there in half an hour," I interrupted, hanging up the phone.

My mind sorted through the possibilities as my car ate up the miles between Cape Canaveral and Melbourne Beach. Traffic was light, and for once the stoplights cooperated. I passed through Cocoa Beach, Satellite Beach, Patrick, tiny beach communities that clung to their separateness even as they bumped up against one another. The ocean to my left was calm, the air fresh and breathable, although it was a struggle to get enough of it into my lungs to do any good.

It could be anything, I told myself, heart trouble, ulcers, diabetes, although I'd seen no signs of any of them. What I knew about medicine couldn't fill my first aid kit, as Joyce delighted in telling me, but I did know some basic symptoms.

There was no history of heart problems in my family, no high blood pressure that I knew of. While that might not rule it out completely, I also knew that Uncle Jack worked out regularly, walked on the beach, ate sensibly. Sensibly occasionally stretched to include tacos and pizza, with a salad, of course. That seemed to rule out ulcers, unless they were a very recent development. My mind was spinning. Diabetes didn't seem likely. Again, no history, not overweight, not a sweets freak like his niece.

Of course, the one I refused to consider was cancer. But then, I hadn't noticed any recent weight loss or signs of pain. Alzheimer's. Oh God! Don't let it be Alzheimer's. Had he been forgetful lately? No. In fact, he frequently reminded me of things.

At the back of my mind ran the constant refrain, my uncle couldn't be sick. My uncle was a rock. He'd never been ill in my memory except for the occasional cold. Even then he didn't complain. He just blew his nose and got over it. I tried to think back over the last few months. Had I noticed anything different, except that he was getting a little older? Nothing popped into my mind, nothing that gave me the slightest clue.

I passed a police car and automatically glanced down at the speedometer. Sixty, in a forty-five-mile-an-hour zone. I eased off on the gas, knowing that if he had radar, he had me. I waited a couple of minutes for him to pull out behind me. When he didn't, I floored it again which, in my elderly Mustang, meant my speed slowly began to creep up.

Suddenly I remembered Todd's words, that he'd be around. Did that mean he'd moved back to town? Todd, a cop in my neighborhood? God forbid! Maybe he was still in Orlando. It was only fifty miles east. That might qualify as "around." "If I needed him" was the rest of that phrase. What gall to think that I'd need him for anything. I had needed him eight years ago when I was eighteen and blindly infatuated with him. Did he think I'd be stupid enough to need him again?

I slowed down to execute the little left-right zag that put me on the two-lane portion of A1A. Once past the tiny town of Melbourne Beach, I floored it for real. There wasn't much out here in the way of traffic, no big condos or high rises. A few homes, fewer small motels. An inconvenient place to live, which made it perfect for my uncle and Carly, who valued their privacy.

I felt like I'd been driving for hours. My eyes felt gritty, probably from the pressure of the thoughts filling the head behind them. I zoomed down the road, glad that it was so little patrolled. Finally I saw their mailbox and, as I turned in, my uncle's and Carly's cars in the driveway. Suddenly I didn't want to go inside. I didn't want to know. Great champion of truth and the people's right to know it, I wanted a lie. I wanted my uncle to tell me he was fine, that nothing was wrong with him. I cursed my cowardice, but it didn't go away.

Uncle Jack was standing in the doorway when I got out of the car. As I walked toward him, I again searched for obvious signs, but I could see nothing that screamed "symptom." I accepted our traditional hug.

"Hi, sweetie," he said. Then, with his arm draped around my shoulders, we walked into the house. Carly was nowhere to be seen.

"Carly told me Todd had been by to see you," he began,

leading me into the living room. "Sounds like he may have scooped me," he added, using my own jargon.

He sat down in his favorite chair.

I sat on the ottoman at his feet. "He said you were sick. What's going on?"

He rested his elbows on his knees and leaned forward, his hands clasped tightly in front of him. "I went to the doctor recently. I had been concerned about some things, and Carly talked me into going to see Dr. Johnson—you remember him?— oh, about three weeks ago. He did some tests. The usual things, I guess, and didn't like what he found out. Anyway, he sent me over to see a specialist. A neurologist."

I could see the muscles in his jaw working. It was the only thing that gave away how agitated he was. His voice and demeanor were perfectly calm and even.

"It seems I have Parkinson's disease and a few other little complications."

My gasp was as loud as it was involuntary. Parkinson's disease. Oh, my God, no. I knew almost nothing about Parkinson's disease except that a college friend's father had it. When he came to visit her, it was actually painful to watch him try to control his movements, try to walk and then to communicate when speech became difficult. When my friend graduated, only her mother had been at the ceremony. One of my classmates had told me her father had died the month before.

I realized he was watching me and had undoubtedly seen the horror pass over my face. "It's not hereditary," he said quickly. "The doctor assured me of that."

"I wasn't—I didn't even think—" At that point, words failed me. Tears spurted from my eyes, and I had to bite my fist to keep from sobbing out loud. "Oh, Uncle Jack," I whispered as he pulled me into his arms.

He rocked me as I sat crying selfish tears. I was so ashamed of myself, and yet, I couldn't help it. Not my uncle. Not my tower of strength. He couldn't have that horrible disease. I couldn't bear the thought of watching him suffer the way my friend's father had, the way my friend had. Yes, I was that shallow, that self-centered. I was acting like one of my older sisters, and I hated myself for it.

"I know it's a shock, honey. I was pretty shocked myself when the doctor told me," he added with a chuckle that must have cost him dearly. "But it may not be as bad as it sounds. He told me that there are a lot of new medicines, and the disease itself isn't fatal."

I wiped my eyes on the back of my hand and eased away from him a bit, determined to pull myself together. "I'm sorry," I hiccuped. "I—I just didn't expect—that."

"Me neither," he said dryly. "I didn't really go because of that. I'd been feeling a little stiff for a while. I told Carly it was just age, but she insisted I get it checked out. Some of those tests Dr. Johnson ran told him I have rheumatoid arthritis. I guess I'd kind of expected something like that, so that wasn't too much of a surprise. Then he asked me how long I'd had the tremors in my left hand. Both of them, actually. I told him I couldn't really remember. Years, probably, but that it wasn't anything. Well—" he breathed out, "that's when he decided he wanted me to see the neurologist. He confirmed it. Said we'd get me started on some medication soon."

I had reached over and taken his left hand while he was talking. I could feel it shaking as I held it against my cheek. "What can I do?" I asked finally.

He wrapped his other hand around mine. "Not a thing, sweetheart. What you're doing right now. Care."

"Oh, I care," I said, rubbing my forehead against his hand.

"You probably think it's strange that Todd knew—"

"That's none of my business," I said, cutting him off.

"It certainly is. It happened because Carly had mentioned to him on the phone that I had a doctor's appointment that Wednesday. It seems that was his day off, so he drove over from Orlando. He was here when I got back from the doctor. I was glad. Carly took it pretty hard."

Carly. I hadn't given her a thought. My self-absorption shamed me.

"He spent the night. We sat around and talked some. I was trying to decide what to tell you kids. And when."

"Is that why you wanted me to come over Saturday night?"

He nodded. "I thought I'd fill you girls full of good food and wine and then—well, you know. It never occurred to me that Todd would come to see you."

"I'll bet."

"I wasn't trying to keep it from you, Christie," he said, misunderstanding my bitter remark. "Well, that's not entirely true. I did consider keeping it from you until I couldn't anymore."

I pulled back, looking into his face. "Why would you do that? Don't you think I have a right to know?"

"Don't you think I have a right to my privacy?" he asked gently. "A right to tell you in my own time?" It was another of our common arguments.

"But what good would it do to withhold the truth?"

"It might protect you from this." He wiped away a stray tear.

"Not protect. Postpone. This way I have a chance to—adjust—to get used to it so we can fight it together."

"There's really no fighting it, honey."

"There is!" I insisted.

"The disease is progressive."

"But there are medicines. You said so yourself."

He nodded. "To help control the symptoms," he said, stroking my hair. "Not to control the disease."

136

I was scandalized. "I can't believe you're just tossing up your hands and giving up."

He pulled me to him again. "Christie, you're trying to get mad because it hurts less than being sad, but I'm not going to let you pick a fight with me. I'm not giving up. I intend to work with the doctors on this, but I also intend to face the truth head on. I won't delude myself that if I ignore it, it'll go away. I did that with the arthritis. The doctor tells me he could have slowed it down if he'd known."

"Why didn't he find it sooner? What kind of doctor could overlook something like that?"

"One whose patient rarely came to see him. I'm sorry, honey, but you can't blame Dr. Johnson. If you're going to blame anyone, it's going to have to be me."

"Never," I said fiercely.

"That's my gal," he said, hugging me to him. "Loyal to the bitter end. Come on," he said after a minute. "Let's go for a walk."

I allowed him to pull me to my feet and followed him out to the deck. Carly was sitting there, her feet on the railing. She quickly put on her sunglasses when we came out, but not before I saw her red, swollen eyes.

Uncle Jack leaned down and kissed her. "We're going for a walk. Want to come with us?"

She reached up and touched his hair, giving him a weak smile. "I'll just wait for you here."

I leaned down and hugged her. "We'll make him fight this," I whispered to her.

She bit her lip and shook her head almost imperceptibly.

I followed Uncle Jack down the stairs and onto the beach, where I kicked off my shoes. The sand was scalding under my feet, and I dug my toes into the cooler sand underneath as we walked.

It was a beautiful late afternoon. Hot, but with a breeze off the water. The sky was cloudless except at the horizon, where I could see a storm marching across the water, a clean line of dark rain sweeping down from the sky. It didn't look like it was coming this way.

We walked without speaking for a long time. I couldn't think of a single thing to say. My usual endless stream of questions seemed to have fallen victim to some kind of internal drought. Finally, he began talking. "The doctor said the disease progresses differently in different people. He's pretty sure I've had it for a while, just like the arthritis. It's funny, you know. All my life people around me have been sick, but never me. Then bam! Two hits at once. I just can't get used to the idea of being sick."

I picked up a conch shell and heaved it back into the water. "Then don't. Don't think of yourself that way."

"I don't mean as an invalid. I mean that I don't know how to—oh, how can I put it?" He scowled down at the sand, his face tight with concentration. "I've never given any thought to my health. I've always just had it. Now I have to remember to take pills and things. It's not going to come naturally to me, I'm afraid."

"I thought he hadn't started your medication yet."

"The neurologist hasn't given me the Parkinson's medication, but Dr. Johnson's got me taking some kind of coated aspirin for the arthritis."

"That doesn't sound like much of a medicine."

"It's for the inflammation. He said it will help a lot. The Parkinson's medicine." He shook his head. "I don't know about that. I talked about it some with the neurologist. There's some kind of new drug. Levodopa, I think he called it. It hasn't been out of the experimental stage for very long. He said there are some side effects." He looked over at me out of the corner of his eye. "Mood swings and that kind of thing."

Again, I had nothing to say. I knew so little.

"I'm really worried about Carly," he added after a minute. "This has hit her really hard. It's not fair. She's had to be strong all her life. After Todd's father died, she raised him until she remarried. That wasn't a good relationship," he said carefully. He didn't know that Todd had told me about his abusive stepfather years ago. "Then she was on her own for years, taking care of Todd, working. When I married her, I thought I'd be able to take care of her for the rest of her life." His face looked angry suddenly. Bitter. "She damned sure didn't bargain for this."

"It was for better or worse," I reminded him.

He paused, then walked on. "Easy words to say, but hard to live with. Don't think I don't know what this is doing to her. Oh, she's doing all the stiff upper lip stuff you'd expect of her, but, damn it, it just isn't fair." The last words almost exploded out of him.

He suddenly looked like he was about to cry. He stooped down to pick up a few random shells and throw them back in the water. After we had walked a few more minutes, he cleared his throat. "I hope you'll be there for her, Christie. She's going to need a lot of moral support. Todd'll help. I know that. He's talking about moving back here to the coast."

Not if I could help it, he wouldn't. "There's no need for him to disrupt his life," I said, working to keep my voice mild. "I'm here anyway. There's nothing he can do that I can't."

"Except pee standing up."

It took me a minute to realize he had made a joke. I tried to laugh, but it was a pitiful effort. "Well, maybe that. Anyway, I already live here, just down the road, and he's not so far away." Not nearly far enough.

"That's what I told him. It could be years before the disease really gets bad."

Years. I wanted to weep.

We turned around at almost the same moment and headed back up the beach. "So there's nothing I can do right now?"

"Well, except be here when I tell your sister. I don't know how it will affect her. I'm going to call Joanna. I think I can tell her over the phone. I really don't think it will bother the two of them like it did you."

Not bother them. God. "Okay. You mean Saturday night?"

"If it's all right." He waited a minute before he said, "And I would like for Todd to be there. I think it'll help Carly."

I sighed inwardly, knowing even I couldn't be selfish enough to refuse to come now. My uncle needed me. Todd's mother needed him. Shit. "Okay. Six o'clock, right?"

We were almost to the house. Carly was no longer on the deck. She must have gone inside. Suddenly I didn't want to face her. I needed to be strong when I saw her, and I wasn't feeling very strong. I needed some time.

I stopped. "I'm not going to come in right now if that's okay. I think I'll head on back. I left the kids with Joyce. But I'll be here Saturday night," I added quickly when his face fell.

Before he could say a word, I hugged him and ran up the dunes and around the house to my car. I waved at the house in case Carly was watching, then climbed in the car and slammed the door. After I turned on the ignition, I sat for a minute, not wanting to go back and face the kids, not wanting to stay. As I turned the car around and headed down the drive, I knew there was only one place I could go.

I made a left on A1A, heading south. In less than five minutes, I was pulling into the unpaved parking lot of the bait and tackle shop at the inlet, a wooden shack painted a hideous shade of blue and sporting a tin roof. There was a Budweiser sign in the one dirty window, and the door hung open to let in what breeze it could. I grabbed a dollar out of my wallet and locked my purse in the car.

I peered into the gloom of the shack, but Jackson was nowhere around. Jackson—I didn't know if that was his first or last name—was a former history professor from Minneapolis who one day said "Screw it," and headed south. Well, his words were more like, "Taught history. College. In Minneapolis. Got fed up." But they conveyed his message. He had offered no more about himself in the years he had been around, and I liked him enough that I hadn't really pried. Highly unusual for me. From bits and pieces I'd picked up, I knew he lived by himself in a trailer park just up the road, and from personal observation decided he was one of the most contented individuals I'd ever met.

I was aware of the faint smell of beer and the stronger odor of old bait as I entered. Familiar. Comfortable. Pleasant. I grabbed a Coke out the cooler and put my dollar in the cash register, helping myself to my fifty cents change. Jackson was probably down watching the fishing.

I popped the top on my Coke and headed out toward the rocks, to a deserted spot on the eastern side. It was getting late. I glanced at my watch. Seven-thirty. It wouldn't be dark for an hour or more, but the light seemed to lose intensity after about six or so. I picked my way out over the huge boulders and finally settled on a big square one near the end.

The water was calm, amazingly so for the inlet. The waves slapped up against the rocks with more tenderness than force, as one would teasingly slap a lover's face. I watched the foam swirl away as the next wave drew closer. The sound was soothing, and I felt the tension begin to leach out of me, to be replaced by a fatalistic acceptance and bone-deep sorrow.

My uncle was ill, and he was right; denial wouldn't make it go away. I would find out all I could about it, but even the doctors didn't know how the disease would progress. I couldn't deal with things that hadn't happened yet. I couldn't control them, him, or the disease, and it was wrong to mourn what I hadn't yet lost. I would do as he asked. I would be there. I would start by being there Saturday night, even if it meant sitting across the dinner table from Todd.

As I thought the name, a shadow fell across me. I didn't have to look up to know who it was. Still, I did.

He was standing about three feet away, watching me. Dressed in a t-shirt and jeans, he looked like a golden giant with the setting sun behind him, like he should have been clad in a toga and sandals poised at the top of Mount Olympus. It was obscene.

"Are you all right?"

I nodded. I didn't want him there. I didn't want his concern. "Fine."

"I thought you might want to talk."

There was no anger in me at the moment. It might be back in an hour or tomorrow, but in the churning cauldron that housed my emotions of the moment, there was no room for it. I shook my head. "No."

He continued watching me for a minute. Then he said, "Your kids are really nice looking. I didn't know you had gotten married."

I barely registered his voice.

He waited again. Finally, he seemed to realize I wasn't going to say anything else. "I'll leave you alone. If you're sure you're all right."

"I'm fine," I repeated, staring back down into the water.

After a long time, I felt his shadow move off me. I felt the warmth, the rough texture of the rocks under me that merged somehow with the sense of loss that gripped me. I heard the ceaseless sounds around me, the regular, almost hypnotic movement of the water, the cry of sea birds above me, and as I listened, I watched clever fish that had eluded the determined fishermen across the way. They swam close to the surface, as if to say, "See? I beat the odds. I survived." I could only wish them well.

CHAPTER 12

It was well after nine when I arrived home. The cops didn't stand a chance of getting me on the way back. I drove the speed limit and under the whole way, which meant it took me almost forty-five minutes to traverse the eighteen miles, even though there were few cars on the road. The moon was losing its battle with the clouds and, before I was halfway home, the night had gone black.

I pulled into the driveway and sat for a minute, trying to make my brain function. Then I gave up and let myself out of the car. Joyce's front door opened before I knocked, and Laurie and Lanie's matching heads poked out. "We thought you were never coming home," Laurie scolded. "Suzy wanted to watch stupid baby shows, and Joyce wouldn't let us go to your house and watch TV."

I handed her the house keys. "Go on over now, honey. I'll be there in a minute."

They dashed out the door with Freddie close on their heels. God knew what gory drama they were missing on the tube.

Leon was in the living room on the sofa, his stocking-clad feet propped up on the coffee table. He was a nice-looking man in his late thirties, always a little disheveled, with brown hair that almost covered his ears and the earring hiding there. He grinned up at me. "Hi, gal. So what was it? Some big story? Cat stuck in a tree? Mayor had a fight with his wife?"

I shook my head and dropped down on the sofa beside him.

Leon loved to tease me about my job as a reporter. As far as he was concerned, New Yorker that he was, nothing newsworthy could possibly happen south of Washington, DC. "No. I got a call from my uncle. He's—" Why was it so hard to say the word? "Sick," I said, swallowing hard.

Leon pursed his lips. "Nothing serious, I hope."

My answer was postponed as Joyce entered the room. "I thought I heard your voice," she said, sitting on the arm of the sofa by Leon and leaning against him. "Did I hear you say your uncle is sick?"

I nodded at her. Swallowed again. "Parkinson's. He was just diagnosed."

She and Leon exchanged glances as she blew out a long breath. "Oh. Wow. That's bad news," she said as Leon hit the off switch on the remote control.

"And that's an understatement," I added. "The hell of it is, I don't know anything about it. I thought I'd pick your brain."

"It will be slim pickings, I'm afraid. I don't know much about it either. It's strictly a neurology thing. I know it's caused by some kind of deterioration of nerve cells in the part of the brain that controls muscle movement. They don't know why it happens. There are some new meds available for it. Oh, and it's not hereditary."

"That's what he told me. First thing. It's not hereditary, like that would be my first thought." I shook my head. "I'll have to get some information tomorrow. I don't like this feeling of total ignorance." I got to my feet and headed toward the door.

"There are support groups," Joyce offered.

I turned to look at her. "Do you think I'll need one?" I asked, only half-serious.

Joyce missed the joke entirely. "You might as time goes on. His wife, too. It can be pretty hard on the family."

"Carly's already having a bad time with it."

"I'm afraid it will get worse. You can help her a lot."

I looked at her doubtfully. "Right now I don't even think I can help myself."

I crossed the sandy lawn in the nearly merging light from our two front porches. There was a light on Stella's front porch, too. Good thing. The moon was only a memory now. No stars. Maybe that rain I'd seen earlier was moving in after all. Rain seemed appropriate. I opened my front door to the sound of screeching brakes and gunshots. And Joyce worried about cigarette smoking being a bad influence.

"Turn it down," I said automatically as I headed toward the kitchen.

I wasn't particularly surprised to see Stella sitting at my kitchen table with a bottle of wine and a half-empty glass in front of her. Her wine, my glass. "Finally!" she said when she saw me. "I thought you were spending the night over there."

I grabbed a glass of my own off the shelf and poured some wine for myself. A good Bordeaux, I noticed. Stella had taste. In wine. "I thought you were going out."

"I changed my mind." She tossed her hair; it bounced precariously. "So who is he?"

I was genuinely confused. "Who?"

"Who?" she sputtered. "The blond god. The dream man at whose feet you were sitting this afternoon. Boy, did that ever furnish me with a few new fantasies," she said, fanning herself with her hand. "So give."

I groaned. I wasn't at all sure I was up to this. Still, the quickest way to shut Stella up was to answer her questions. "My— cousin. Sort of."

"I should have known. He's just as good looking as your uncle."

"Stepcousin, Stella, as in my uncle's stepson."

She raised her eyebrows. "Oh. Better yet. No relation means

no incest. So where have you been hiding Mr. Wonderful all these years?"

I simply could not carry on this conversation. I'd had too much day, too much emotion. I drank half my glass of wine in one gulp, making a face.

"Is something the matter?" Stella asked as I finished the glass with one more swallow. She's nothing if not perceptive.

I closed my eyes, rubbing my forehead. "Yeah." I glanced toward the living room. They probably wouldn't hear it if a hand grenade exploded in here. Still . . . "Let's go outside and sit."

Stella frowned. "Okay, honey. I can smoke out there."

"I may smoke out there."

"Jesus," she said under her breath, grabbing the bottle of wine and both our glasses.

My backyard had no fancy deck like my uncle's, but it did have a little patio. Not much. Just a ten-by-ten slab of concrete with a grill built into one corner. A couple of lawn chairs, a table. I lived very simply.

The wind had picked up, but it still wasn't raining. Stella refilled my glass and handed it to me. Then she pulled her lawn chair up so she was facing me. "Okay, honey. Tell Auntie Stella what's going on."

The tears ambushed me again with no warning, spurting out of my eyes like the rain I'd been expecting. Maybe it was the wine that loosened them up. Maybe I was going off the deep end. I blubbered into my glass for a few minutes. "My—my uncle—he—he has Parkinson's disease," I finally managed.

She was beside me in an instant, removed the glass before I dropped it and wrapped me in her arms. "Oh, sweetie. Oh, you poor thing. That's terrible. Oh, God. When did you find out? I'll bet it was tonight. So that's where you were. And I thought—well, never mind what I thought. You must be dying inside. That poor man. That poor, lovely man."

Sincere as it was, her concern was almost comical in its extremity, and if I'd been in better condition, I would have laughed. As it was, I laid my slightly swimming head gratefully on her shoulder. "Thank God you're not clinical about it."

"Like her?" She tossed her mounds of hair in the direction of Joyce's house. "Nurses," she snorted. "Prissy little starched things in white uniforms who know everything."

Now I did laugh. A little. "I think that should be prissy little things in starched white uniforms. Or starched white caps. Or something," I said, wiping my nose on my sleeve. If Mother could only see me now.

"Whatever. Who needs them?"

Patients in the hospital, I thought, but I wasn't dumb enough to say it out loud.

Stella handed me back my glass of wine. "You stay right here," she said, jumping to her feet. "I'll be right back."

She was, in about four minutes, with another open bottle of wine and a roll of toilet paper. She topped off my glass and her own, sitting the toilet paper on the table beside me. "Continuous Kleenex," she said when I just stared blankly at it. She ripped off a few sheets to demonstrate and handed them to me. "Blow," she ordered.

I did. Sipped my wine. Knew I was going to feel like hell tomorrow and didn't care. I was on vacation. I could have a hangover if I wanted.

"Okay, now. Tell me everything."

Some time and a few of her continuous Kleenex—not to mention another glass of wine—later, I had told her about my conversation with my uncle, about Carly's red eyes, about my selfish insensitivity to anyone's feelings but my own. I think I had even told her a little about Jackson and his bait shack. I'm not sure. I got to the part about Todd showing up on the rocks and stopped. I noticed her hair was beginning to slip its pins.

She refilled my glass. "How did he know you'd be there?"

"It's where we used to go when we were kids."

"Ya'll were pretty close?"

I'm not much of a drinker, which is the only reason I can come up with for telling Stella the entire story of my relationship with Todd since I was fourteen.

I told her about Teddy and how he had understood being relegated to second best in my emotions. She equated it to Puff the Magic Dragon. Sometimes you had to love Stella.

I told her about the bathing suit fiasco. We both actually laughed over that one.

I told her about Todd going off to college, about his visits home, his sudden marriage.

"So you hadn't seen him again till today?" Her southern accent was slipping into her speech more and more.

"Not one time. I hid every time he came to town. Well, not hid, but you know what I mean. Made myself scared. Scarce," I corrected. I was surprised I could still form words at all. "I couldn't believe he had the balls—oops!" I covered my mouth, giggling. "The gall to come over here. Who needs him? The jerk made his decision eight years ago. Let him sleep in it."

Stella was grinning from ears to ears. Both of her. I remember her saying something condescending about beddie-bye time.

Then it was morning. The sun was shining into the window and I was dying. My mouth was so dry I almost gagged before I could get to the bathroom and scoop up enough water in my hand to fill my mouth. Then I really gagged. I had been poisoned. She had poisoned me with that damned wine. Had she put something in it? I discarded the thought even as it formed, but it was hard to believe someone could feel this bad from just a little fermented grape juice.

I fell back into bed face first. The room was spinning and I felt slightly nauseous. It hit me that I was still a little bit drunk. Then I realized I was naked.

Jesus! The kids! I forced myself back to my feet and moved as quickly as I could to the door of my room, slipping my arms into the sleeves of my robe. I opened the door slowly, expecting to see the three of them still glued to the TV set. Instead, Freddie was tucked into his sleeping bag on the floor. I crossed the room and opened the door to my guest room. The girls were sleeping like angels.

Had they witnessed their aunt's disgrace? Had I stumbled across the living room singing bawdy songs and backroom ballads? Did I owe any or all of them an apology?

Before I could worry much about it, Stella slipped into the sliding glass doors carrying a pitcher of something that looked like blood. She gave me a bright smile. "Good morning, sweetie. Come on in the kitchen and I'll fix you right up."

I growled. Then I obeyed. "What was in that damn wine?"

She grinned at me. "Alcohol. It's supposed to be there."

"What are you so damned cheerful about?"

She busied herself, getting two glasses and filling them with ice. Then she poured the blood into them. "Drink," she ordered, putting one glass in front of me.

"I don't think so," I said, pushing it away.

She pushed it back. "Just a few sips. It'll make you feel better."

I sincerely doubted it, but I knew it couldn't make me feel any worse. I took a sip. Nearly gagged. Took another. Better. It was some kind of tomato juice concoction. Not hot and spicy like a Bloody Mary. Kind of smooth. "What's in it?"

"Better you don't know, but it'll have you feeling a lot better soon."

She was right. I finished off my glass of whatever and reached for the pitcher. She pulled it away. "Not too much at once, or you'll be drunk again."

I almost knocked over my glass. "There's alcohol in that?"

"Just a teensy bit. Enough to take the edge off."

"Oh, my God." I laid my head on the table and covered it with my arms. "I'm going to have another hangover."

"No, you won't. This will just kind of numb you while you get over the first one."

I peered up at her. "How much did I drink last night?"

"Enough to loosen you up, and believe you me, you needed that more than you need a clear head this morning. I'm real sorry about your uncle, sweetie."

Her words brought it all back in a flash: Todd showing up at my house, the drive to Melbourne Beach, my conversation with my uncle, fleeing before I had to face Carly, Todd appearing like an apparition at the inlet, the interminable drive home. No wonder I'd gotten drunk.

I raised my head from the table. The wonder-drug-drink was beginning to work. "I can't believe how selfish my reaction was," I said, toying with my empty glass.

"There was nothing selfish about it," she argued. "You were upset for him. That's natural. If you were selfish, you would have cared when he told you it wasn't hereditary."

Had I told her about that? Lord.

"Your reaction was just what it should be."

"I didn't give Carly a thought," I argued. "That's pretty selfish."

"No it's not. If it was Carly who had it, you wouldn't have given your uncle a thought except maybe in passing. You would have saved all your thoughts for her and what she was going through."

Sometimes Stella's common sense surprised me. I nodded slowly as I thought about it. "You're probably right."

"Of course I'm right. You don't have a selfish bone in your

whole body. Look how you spend money on those kids. Look how you baby-sit them every time Fred wants Darlene to go somewhere with him."

Now I did groan. Darlene. I looked at the clock. She was due in half an hour to collect her brood, and they were still crashed all over the house. "Stella, will you wake them up for me? I need to get their clothes together before Darlene gets here. God, I don't even know where the stuff I got them yesterday is."

"It's in their suitcases, which are packed. We did that last night."

"We did?"

She dimpled. "Well, you didn't. I believe you were asleep by that time."

"Passed out, you mean."

"Whatever. I will go wake them up, though, while you grab a shower and put on some clothes."

I looked down at my robe, gaping open at the neck. "How did—never mind. Don't tell me. I don't want to know."

Gingerly, I got up from the chair, but my head was no longer pounding. My stomach was almost settled, and I was beginning to realize I was starving.

I started for the refrigerator, but Stella headed me off. "Shower. I'll get breakfast started for all of you. You're not really as hungry as you think you are. Maybe some nice hot cereal and toast."

This was an entirely new Stella, I thought as I stood under the pounding hot water. I had never seen her as a nurturer. I had never seen her as anything but a party animal who was funny and fun to be around. I would have to rethink my perception of Stella.

By the time I had dried my hair and slipped into shorts and a t-shirt, I felt very nearly human. Stella had all three kids seated at the table with bowls of oatmeal in front of them. They were sullen but quiet. It was usually like this when it was time for them to leave. I sat down at the table, pretending not to notice. I took a bite of cereal, a nibble of toast. Stella was right. I wasn't as hungry as I had thought.

Freddie was the first one to give voice to their discontent. "I don't see why we have to go home today," he muttered around a bite of toast. "School doesn't start for another two weeks."

"You have to go because your mother and father are back home. I'll bet they've missed you this week." Which they'd spent at some kind of convention in New Orleans. New Orleans in August. Masochists, the both of them.

"It's more fun here," Laurie piped up.

"You let us do good stuff," Lanie added, "and we get to play with Suzy." That earned her a look from Laurie. They were Joanna and Darlene all over again.

"Mom doesn't let us do anything," Freddie said. "She's afraid we'll get hurt." He sneered.

"She loves you and wants to take good care of you," I reasoned.

"You love us and take good care of us, but you let us do stuff," Freddie countered.

It was the first time he'd put into words what I'd been seeing for years. Darlene smothered the kids with her brand of love, which consisted mainly of anxiety. I'd had to bite my tongue more than once to avoid a head-on collision with my older sister. I couldn't imagine where she'd learned it. Our mother had modeled unconcern more than anything else.

"I'll see you tomorrow night," I said, remembering suddenly. "We're having dinner with Uncle Jack and Carly."

Freddie's face lit up. "Way cool!" he said. He worshiped Uncle Jack. How would it affect him to learn that he was ill? The girls were really too young to completely understand it, but

Freddie . . .

The doorbell rang as Stella and I were clearing the table. Domestic Stella? Cooking and cleaning Stella? It was almost too much to take in.

Darlene breezed into the kitchen without waiting for me to answer the door. "How are my babies?" she oozed.

"Growing up," I said under my breath. I looked around for Stella, but she had vanished. She and Darlene had met once. It seemed enough for both of them.

"I hope you were all perfect angels for your aunt Christie." She looked up at me. "Were they perfect angels?"

I nodded. "Perfect."

"I knew you would be," she told them, managing somehow to get her arms around all three. "Let's get your stuff together and go home. I bought presents for all of you."

"Aunt Christie bought us some school clothes," Laurie said, hanging onto her mother's neck.

"Wasn't that sweet of her?" Darlene practically pulled the girls out of their chairs. "Do you have all your things together? Freddie?"

Freddie, with obvious reluctance, pushed back his chair and stood, and I realized suddenly that my little nephew was growing up. His head came up to my chin. Why hadn't I noticed it before?

I walked over and ruffled his hair. "Come on, champ. I'll help you get it together."

He shuffled out of the room with me close behind. "I don't want to go," he said sullenly, as if we hadn't already had this conversation.

"I know you don't, hon, and that makes me feel like a million dollars. I must not be a half-bad aunt if you want to spend time with me."

"You're the greatest," he muttered and looked away, but not

before I caught the look in his eye. Hero worship? From my nephew? That really did make me feel like a million.

"So is your mom," I said, trying to sound convincing. "Don't worry about not liking her much right now. Every guy your age feels that way. Ask anyone at school. They'll tell you."

"Really?"

"Really. You want to grow up and she wants you to stay a baby, but trust me, one day soon she's going to tell you to grow up and you're going to want to go back to being a baby. It's the way of the world."

He shouldered his backpack and grinned at me. "No way I'm going to want to be a baby again."

"Well, to be babied, then. Cooked for. Shopped for. Have your laundry done. One of these days you'll wish she was there, doing all that stuff."

"Yeah. Well." He stood there awkwardly.

I walked over and hugged him. "Go home, bud. I'll see you tomorrow night."

As we walked back into the kitchen, Darlene said, "What's this about tomorrow night? Laurie said we're having dinner with Uncle Jack and Carly."

"He's asked us over," I answered, unwilling to say more than I had to in front of the kids. Besides, it wasn't my place to tell her about his illness.

"I hope you didn't accept for all of us. I don't know if we're free."

There were things I actively disliked about my sister. Her late-blooming need to be in control was one of them. "Please try, Darlene. It really means a lot to him."

She studied my face as if additional information were hiding there. "We'll see," she said finally. Then she beamed at her kids. "Come on, darlings. Your daddy's in the car waiting for us."

When she was gone, Stella slipped back in through the sliding glass doors. "What a twit," she said, leaning against the counter and crossing her arms.

"That twit's my sister," I said, although I didn't really mind her assessment since I agreed with it.

Stella snorted. "No way. You were given to the wrong parents at the hospital. There's no way you're any blood relation to— that."

"Of course, that would mean my uncle wasn't my uncle."

"Oh. Well, that's different. But your mother." Another singularly unsuccessful meeting. I could only be glad she'd never had the pleasure of Joanna's acquaintance.

"Go home, Stella. I think I want a few hours of alone time."

"Are you sure, honey? Wouldn't you rather talk?"

I gave her a wry smile. "I think I talked quite enough last night."

She grinned at me. "You did have a lot to say. I want to hear more about how you almost attacked your cousin on the beach."

"Cousin by marriage only. Oh God," I groaned. "I didn't tell you that!"

"Oh God, you sure did. Another new fantasy." When I said nothing, she pushed away from the counter. "Another time, then. Don't worry. I won't tell a soul about all your secrets. You call me if you need me. I'll be home all day."

She was almost to the door when I said, "Stella?"

"What honey?"

"You're a hell of a good friend. You know that?"

She smiled. "You'd better believe it," she said as she turned to leave.

CHAPTER 13

I spent the day at the Cocoa Beach Library pouring over medical texts. Although most of what they said was Greek—or, more accurately, Latin—to me, a few were in words I could almost make out. They seemed to say what Joyce had said: that the disease was a disorder of the brain, caused by a progressive deterioration of the nerve cells in the part of the brain that controlled movement. Reason for the deterioration unknown. Symptoms: shaking, stooped posture, difficulty with walking and coordination, among others. It usually developed in people past the age of fifty. It wasn't like diabetes that could be treated with insulin, or heart disease that could be helped by medication and diet and exercise and, in extreme cases, by surgery, or even cancer that might respond to chemotherapy and radiation.

I felt irrational anger at the medical profession in general. How the hell could they let this disease go on without finding out its cause and cure? What had the researchers been doing since 1817, when the disease was first identified, sitting on their lab stools while my uncle—contracted? developed?—a disease that couldn't be fixed? They had come up with one lousy medication, Levodopa, that sometimes helped with the symptoms—and that had only been available by prescription for three years—but according to my reading, the side effects of that were often as debilitating as the disease.

The helplessness that had flitted around the edges of my

consciousness the night before bloomed into near despair. Diet wouldn't help. Exercise might help some, they said, while the patient could still do it. It was painful. Mental faculties usually remained intact while the body deteriorated out of control. Usually. Sometimes, it said, the patients became severely depressed. Small wonder. In really severe cases, it went on to say, the patient might exhibit severe mental deterioration. Even hallucinations. And that same medicine that had terrible physical side effects sometimes caused or aggravated the mental symptoms. God, what a vicious circle. Did my uncle know all this?

The list continued. Decreased facial expression. Freezing in place when trying to move. Trouble swallowing. Difficulty brushing teeth, shaving, buttoning clothes. Balance problems. Difficulty digesting food. Eventually bladder and bowel dysfunction. And they all stressed that Parkinson's disease was not fatal in itself. There was a definite message in those last two words, but no one expounded on that. The closest they came was to say that the disease "weakened" the patient to make him more susceptible to other diseases.

I left the library feeling more depressed than enlightened. Essentially what they were saying was that my uncle had a painful, incurable, degenerative disease.

It pissed me off.

Lacking the will or energy to drive back to the house, I wandered around downtown Cocoa Beach for a while. Well, what there was of downtown, which was about four blocks of low-to-the-ground stores and restaurants. There was the Cocoa Beach Pharmacy, which had a real soda fountain and a pharmacist who remembered people's names. There was a laundromat, with its six washers and dryers. Alma's Pizza, which served beer. A German guy had moved to town about five years before and opened a restaurant called the Heidelberg Inn, which served better beer.

Cocoa Beach had two main streets one block apart, one going south and one north. A town that had been hopping with activity at the height of the space program, it suffered dearly now that the government had pulled the plug. But it survived. Like those little fish at the inlet, Cocoa Beach was a survivor. It had been there long before a man had gone to the moon, and it was still hanging on, albeit a little frayed at the edges. Real estate had plummeted and there wasn't a lot of new construction going on, but the town hadn't gone under as many had predicted. That was enough for most of the people who called it home, those who just wanted to live and work within walking distance of the ocean.

I ended up at Fischer's, a bar attached by family and proximity to Bernard's Surf restaurant, known for its incredible food and incredibly high prices. In contrast, Fischer's was unpretentious, friendly.

Paul Lansing was tending bar. Paul had been in my class all through high school. He was a relative by marriage to the Fischer family. I think his mother was married to a cousin or something obscure like that. Paul had been the butt of a lot of jokes when he decided to skip college and work in the family business. He'd started by working on their shrimp boats out of Port Canaveral during summers in high school. Then he'd progressed from dishwasher to bus boy and then, upon reaching the required age of twenty-one, waiter. Bartender was near the top of the heap, which was where he now stood, and now that he made more in a week during high season than most of us ever would in a month, the jokes about him had lost their punch.

He had sandy hair and a square, freckled face that lit up when I pushed open the door and stepped into the cool, dark bar. "Christie!" he called out as if it had been months since he'd seen me instead of a week. "Where have you been keeping yourself?"

Paul was my friend. He had long wanted to be more than that, but I could never think of him any other way. Good-natured and friendly to a fault, his parents and I knew he was too good for me, even if he couldn't see it. I refused to let that difference of opinion end our friendship, and Paul's forgiving nature helped there. He knew I dated Virgil Townsend, who had also been a classmate of ours. Virgil and I had even been in for dinner a time or two. Paul was always polite to him, but polite was as far as he would go.

"I had the kids this week." I slid onto a stool at the bar.

"You ought to have kids of your own," he said, pouring me a Coke without asking what I wanted. It was that kind of place.

"Darlene's are enough for me right now."

He put my Coke in front of me. "How are your sisters?"

"Snotty," I answered, and we both laughed. It had been my standard answer to that question all through school.

"How are you?" he said, leaning on the bar in front of me. My face must have given him his answer. "That bad, huh? What's the matter?"

I wasn't ready to talk about it with him, or anyone else, really. My confiding in Joyce and Stella had been a weakness of the moment. "Oh, family stuff," I answered evasively. "You know how it is."

He nodded. "Your mother on your case?"

"When has my mother ever been off my case?"

He chuckled. "True, but I thought she'd be too busy with that new boyfriend of hers to make much trouble for you."

I blinked. "Boyfriend?"

Paul looked surprised. "Sure. Didn't you know? She's been in for dinner with Lamar Gunter half a dozen times in the last few weeks. The two of them are considered an item."

No. I hadn't known. I had never even met Lamar Gunter. I had seen his name on the door at the Barnett Bank, where he was a vice president or something. He was a big man, with thinning hair and a kind face. I tried to imagine him and my mother as an item, but it was impossible. It was impossible to imagine my mother with any man, including my father.

I remembered the first time I'd realized my mother and father didn't love each other. It was Easter, and the whole family was dressed up for our annual visit to church. I got a camera for my tenth birthday, and I was making a nuisance of myself forcing everyone to pose for pictures. I had taken a picture of my sisters, and then I'd posed my mother and father together. They had looked stiff and unnatural. "Put your arm around her," I'd told my father.

"Just take the picture, Christiana," my mother had said through stiff lips without glancing at my father.

Somehow, in that moment, I knew, and the knowledge had stunned me. In the months that followed, I noticed that they never touched each other, never called each other "dear" or "honey" or any of those things that my friends' parents called each other. Not too long after the picture incident they had started sleeping in separate bedrooms. What a sad way to live your life. Then the accident—

"I'm sorry if I upset you, Christie." Paul's voice brought me back to the room.

"No. I'm just—surprised. I had no idea. No," I said again, "I'm really happy for her. It's just that she hasn't said a thing."

"She's probably embarrassed. You know how these older folks are about their love affairs."

Love affairs. Sexual? God forbid. If I had been unable to imagine them as a couple, coupling was ten paces farther into the unimaginable.

"They were here last night," Paul went on. "Had dinner next

door, then came in here for coffee and liqueurs."

She had been having dinner with her new boyfriend while I learned about my uncle's hideous disease. I added them to the list of targets for my newly found anger.

"Your uncle and Carly were in last week for dinner with that son of hers—what's his name?"

"Todd."

"Right. Todd. Didn't he move away or something?"

I nodded. We were drifting from unwelcome subject to intolerable subject. "Eight years ago."

"Does he live here now?"

"He lives in Orlando. I don't think he has any plans to move back here." Not if I could help it, I added to myself.

Paul was still watching me more closely than our light conversation warranted. Could he have been the only person outside my uncle and Carly who had seen what was developing between us? His next statement answered that question.

"I kind of thought you had a thing for him." He picked up a bar rag and made a few random wiping motions. His eyebrows were an inch closer to the center of his forehead than they'd been when I walked into the bar.

"Hero worship. You know how it is. Ancient history."

His brow cleared. "Yeah. I had a cousin like that. You probably remember her. Lucille. She was five years older than us, and I thought she was the greatest. She's married now. Four kids. Weighs about two hundred pounds."

I laughed dutifully, resisting the urge to wipe my forehead. I felt like I'd just tiptoed through a minefield and made it to the other side. I finished my Coke and pulled a dollar out of my wallet.

Paul looked at it in surprise. "You aren't going to have lunch?"

I slid off the stool. "Nope. Got to run. Thanks for the Coke."

"Sure. Take care," he was saying as I pushed my way out of

the bar and back into the hot, early afternoon sun. My hangover was gone, but I was suffering the residual exhaustion. I made my way back to my car. My time on the parking meter had expired, but I was lucky. There was no fluttering piece of white paper tucked under my windshield wiper.

I was dead on my feet when I got home ten minutes later. No more wine parties for me, I thought as I stripped down to only my t-shirt and panties and climbed into bed. I welcomed the oblivion of sleep, but I wasn't to have even that. Instead I fought my way from nightmare to nightmare, never quite waking from one before being plunged into the next. When I awoke to my doorbell ringing, I didn't remember the who, what, when, or where of any of them but was pretty sure I understood the why.

The doorbell rang again. I considered ignoring it, but if it was Stella or Joyce, they had seen my car in the driveway and wouldn't go away until they were satisfied I wasn't prostrate with grief. Sometimes being close to your neighbors sucked. The obnoxious bell rang twice again before I had slipped on my jeans and made my way to the door. I had a sharp comment on the tip of my tongue for whoever was so impatient they couldn't wait until I was properly garbed to come to the door, but it died when I saw Virgil standing on my front steps.

"Virgil! What are you doing here?" He was supposed to be deep-sea fishing with his father, who happened to own the newspaper where I worked. Virgils Junior and Senior had gone to Gainesville at the the beginning of the week to meet with the head of the Journalism Department at the University of Florida with an eye to developing an intern program at the *Brevard Sun*. The internship program was my idea. The university had agreements with papers all over the state to place interns during the summer to allow them to gain practical experience while they learned. I had done my internship at the *Miami Herald* because no such program existed in my hometown. I thought my paper should remedy that situation.

To his credit, Virgil bestowed full responsibility on me when he'd broached the subject with this father. Initially, Virgil Senior was only lukewarm about the idea. He didn't want to pay students to learn on his time, but he had finally agreed to meet with the department head since they were going "up north" anyway.

The fishing trip was an annual ritual. Each August, father and son packed up their assorted gear and headed up to the Florida panhandle. Two weeks later, they returned, with outrageous stories and peeling noses. Virgil wasn't due back for another week, and I noticed immediately that his nose was barely pink.

His gaze swept over me from rumpled hair to bare feet, lingering for a moment in an area that reminded me I was braless. It irritated me. Virgil and I weren't sleeping together. Not that he didn't want to, but I didn't feel that level of comfort with him yet. I wasn't a virgin at the ripe old age of twenty-seven, but I wasn't that far from it.

There were only two men who had carnal knowledge of me. The first had been an engineer at the Cape, temporarily in residence from Houston. I met him not long after my high school graduation. We had a two-week thing that ended painlessly for both of us when he was called back west. He probably had a wife and kids back there. I never asked. I was still angry and reeling from Todd's rejection, and I don't believe I would have cared if I'd known. I found sex with him difficult and embarrassing, in spite of his attempts to make it pleasant for me.

The second was a philosophy professor in my last year of college. He wasn't my professor—journalism students tended to steer away from courses as problematic as philosophy—just a guy I'd met at a dance. It was only later I learned of his exalted status at the university. The affair had lasted three months, although it was never particularly satisfying to either of us. Like me, he was always delving into the "whys" of life. Unlike me, he wasn't looking for facts. He was looking for the ultimate truth, while I just wanted the everyday truth. Still, he had been a step up from my engineer. Instead of beer and hot dogs, he served me red wine and Brie when I came to visit him at his garage apartment off campus. The sex was also a step up, although, I suspected, a baby one. He must have found me naïve and pedestrian, while I began to suspect that, deep down, he was a flake. We never exactly broke up. We just drifted away from each other. Neither of us made an effort to pull back. Love life, Christie style. It was pathetic.

"What are you doing here?" I repeated.

He pulled his eyes up to my face. It seemed to take a minute before my words registered. "Dad has poison ivy. Can't be in the sun," he added when he saw my confused look. He grinned. "He's itching like crazy and threatening to pave our entire yard."

I was still confused. "When did he get it?"

"I don't know, but he didn't break out until day before yesterday. You should see the blisters. He was cussing a blue streak the whole way back." He shifted. "Uh—can I come in?"

"Oh. Sure." I stepped back so he could enter. I considered Virgil a decent-looking guy. Half a head taller than me, which wasn't saying much, he had straight brown hair and hazel eyes. It wasn't his looks that had attracted me to him. He was a born newspaperman, sharp and analytical. He had risen quickly at the newspaper and was now editor in chief, and not only because his father owned it, as some people had hinted. He could spot news before it happened, and he had the knack of assigning just the right person to the right story. It didn't hurt that he'd been raised in the profession. I admired him. I even envied him a little.

I ran my fingers through my wild hair. "I'm sorry. I was asleep."

I motioned to the sofa, and he sat dutifully. "How was your vacation?"

"How *is*," I corrected. "I don't go back until Monday. It's fine. I had Darlene's kids until last night. They keep me hopping. She got just back."

"Good. That frees you up this weekend. I was hoping we might do something tomorrow night."

Tomorrow night. Saturday. "I'm sorry, Virgil. I have a family thing tomorrow night. Dinner with my uncle and Carly."

His mouth formed a little pout that I hated. "Can't you change it? I talked Dad out of his boat. I thought we might pick up some dinner and head out on the water."

Virgil Senior had a forty-two-foot cabin cruiser that he worshiped only slightly more than his newspaper. If Junior had talked him out of the keys for the night, he had done some fancy talking indeed. I wasn't particularly interested in going out on it, but I knew how much it meant to Virgil.

I shook my head. "I'm sorry. I promised Uncle Jack. It's really important to him that I be there."

"What's so important that it can't wait one night?"

I could have told him, but his insistence raised my hackles. Who was it who said, "Never apologize. Never explain?" "I can't."

"I told Dad you'd want to go," he all but whined. His father liked me, which I found convenient, as he was my ultimate boss. He liked the fact that his son and I were dating and made no secret of the fact to me.

"Then tell Dad I didn't expect you back for another week and have a family commitment I can't get out of. He'll understand. He knows about family."

"What about Sunday? Maybe we could take it out then."

What about Sunday? Would Darlene need me? Would Uncle Jack and Carly? Would I? I didn't have a clue. "I'll call you," I said after a minute. "It depends on how tomorrow night goes."

He looked at me sharply. "It must be something big if it'll keep you tied up two days." He waited a minute to see if I'd fill him in. Ever the reporter. When I didn't, he slapped his knees and stood.

I walked him to the door and opened it. When I turned to tell him goodbye, he pulled me into his arms. "I missed you, honey," he said, and kissed me.

We had progressed that far. I closed my eyes automatically. When I opened them, I was looking into Todd's, clear blue ice.

He was standing directly behind Virgil. "Christie," he said, nodding.

Virgil jumped back as if he'd been shot. He spun around and looked up at Todd. "Who are you?" he sputtered.

I stepped forward. "Virgil, this is my—um—cousin, Todd. Todd, Virgil Townsend."

Todd hesitated a minute, then he offered his hand. Virgil reluctantly took it. "Cousin," he repeated, looking from Todd to me.

"Did I know you had a cousin?"

"He's been away."

"Oh. Well."

He stole another look at Todd. I'm not sure what Virgil saw, but I thought Todd looked particularly dangerous. Big, a head taller than Virgil. Broad-shouldered and tough in his tight jeans and t-shirt. He had on what must have been his cop face, devoid of expression except for the chill in his eyes.

"Well," Virgil said, starting out the door, "uh—call me about Sunday."

"I will," I told his retreating back.

I looked up at Todd. He looked back. His eyes swept over me

much as Virgil's had, lingering in the same spot. I blushed from my unpainted toenails to the roots of my still sleep-disordered hair.

He took a step forward; I took an involuntary one backward. He pushed the door closed. His eyes seemed to take in every detail of my living room in a glance. "Kids not home?"

"No."

"Husband not home?"

The insinuation in his words was like a slap in the face. My color grew deeper, although not from embarrassment. "What are you doing here?"

"You didn't answer my question."

"Neither did you."

I half expected him to say, "I asked you first," but I guess we were too mature for that kind of conversation now. Instead, he said, "I wanted to see if you were all right—"

"What is this sudden concern with my welfare?" I demanded.

"But I can see that you were being well taken care of," he finished as if I hadn't spoken, but I could see that my words had hit their mark. He was the one who colored now.

My fury had me sputtering. "How dare you come into my home and accuse me of—of—"

He held up his hand in front of him. "Hey. How you handle your personal life is your business."

"It certainly is."

"I can see my concern was misplaced."

"Yes, it was."

The muscle in his jaw twitched. "It wouldn't hurt if you were a little more discreet, though. Anyone could have walked up to that door and you wouldn't have had a clue."

I was seething, but there was no way I would let Mr. Smug and Superior know it. "I'll take your advice in the vein in which it was offered," I said through clenched teeth.

He looked me up and down one more time. "I'm sure you will," he said and let himself out of the house.

I kicked the sofa. When I heard his car start and drive away, I kicked it again. Then I realized I was barefooted and my toes were probably broken.

"Shit." I sat down on the living room carpet and rubbed them. Why was this happening to me? Why had this man walked back into my life all jam full of concern and judgment? Insinuating that I was having an afternoon quickie while the hubby was away and possibly with the kids in the house. "God!" I didn't think I could take him showing up at my door unexpectedly all the time. But he wouldn't, I realized suddenly. He couldn't. He didn't live here. He was just visiting for the weekend, and the weekend meant he would be there for dinner tomorrow night. After his snide remarks this afternoon, I might be able to have a bit of fun with that. The thought soothed my pride, even if it did little for my throbbing toes.

The thought of rubbing Todd's nose in his suspicions helped me deal with the dread of being with my uncle when he told Darlene. I had absolutely no idea how she would react. Joanna was different. She had grown even more distant from all of us when she moved to Alabama, not that she was ever that close to our uncle. There her detachment was nearly complete. Mother still visited her occasionally, on rare occasions still accompanied by Darlene, but Joanna had only been back once in the last four years. Why come back to where you're the little fish when you can play upper muckety-muck in Wherever, Alabama?

Uncle Jack had said he would call and tell her. I could imagine their conversation. Uncle Jack would try to break the news to her as gently as possible to spare her what pain he could. Joanna would say something like, "Oh, Uncle Jack, I'm so sorry," and would forget about it by nightfall. Darlene, however, was an unknown.

I arrived fifteen minutes early. I had spent a little extra time on my hair and makeup, stage trappings. I wore pale yellow slacks and a matching silk shell. My monochrome outfit made my tanned skin glow and added inches to my height, which I desperately needed. I wore high-heeled sandals and had painted my toenails with a glaring polish that should have been named "Fuck-You Red."

Todd answered the door wearing cutoffs and a tank top. Flimsy armor. He stood blocking the door, looking behind me. His face still wore the insolent expression from the day before. "All alone?"

I looked behind me, then back at him with a bright smile. "As you see."

He made a sound of something like disgust. It was a moment before he stepped to the side. "They're in back," he said without giving me another glance.

I waited until he walked away, then stepped inside and closed the door behind me, fighting the urge to rub my hands together. Perfect. I couldn't wait until the next round.

In the kitchen, I fixed myself a glass of iced tea before joining the rest outside. Uncle Jack and Carly were sitting at the redwood table in the middle of the deck. Carly was again wearing dark glasses, although the sun umbrella was tipped to the west to keep the late afternoon glare off them. She looked slightly better. I couldn't see her eyes, of course, and her face was still puffy, but her smile was a little less tenuous.

She reached up and took my hand, pulling me down for a kiss. "Hi, sweetie."

Uncle Jack got up and enfolded me in a hug. "I'm so glad you came, honey. It means a lot to me."

I kissed him on the cheek. "I wouldn't have missed it," I said honestly.

Todd was sitting on the railing, looking at the water. He didn't acknowledge me in any way. Better and better.

Darlene arrived a predictable fifteen minutes late, her entire brood in tow. The kids preceded her out onto the deck and spied me. "Aunt Christie!" Laurie and Lanie squealed in unison, descending on me. Freddie smiled his shy smile.

Todd's mouth fell open. I wish I could have frozen the moment in time. Then I could have taken it out at my leisure, examined it, savored it as one does a really fine wine.

"Hi, Aunt Christie," Freddie said, allowing himself to be kissed and looking pleased despite his embarrassment.

"Hi, handsome."

Then Darlene unsuspectingly enhanced my precious moment. She swept out on the deck with Fred, as usual, a pace behind. "You spoil these children," she said, taking the chair my uncle offered her with barely a glance in his direction. "Designer clothes for school! Now what can I buy them that they'll like as much? You just wait. Someday you'll have a husband and kids and expenses and I'll spoil *your* children! Then we'll see how you like it."

I chanced a glance at Todd. He was regarding me through narrowed eyes. I gave him a sweet smile and turned back to Darlene. "You have to let an old maiden aunt have her simple pleasures, Darlene. Besides, they'll outgrow them in two months and it will no longer be an issue. Fred," I said, turning to her husband, "it's good to see you."

He looked shocked and pleased at being noticed. "Hi. Uh . . . good to see you. Too." Fred wasn't the world's most brilliant conversationalist, but his manners were nice.

Soon, Uncle Jack had steaks on the grill and Carly was in the kitchen doing something with a salad, having refused my help. I took the kids down to the beach and left Darlene and Fred and Todd with my uncle. Todd's eyes hadn't left me since Darlene arrived. I think he was trying to intimidate me. It wasn't working.

Freddie and I were sitting on the dry sand while the girls waded in the water, pretending they were jumping over nonexistent jellyfish. I could tell something was on Freddie's mind, but he hadn't seen fit to share it with me yet.

"So who's he?" Freddie asked finally, tilting his head toward the deck.

"That's your uncle Todd. Or cousin. Or something."

"Why didn't I ever meet him before?"

"He's been away." I was getting pretty good at this.

"So is he back now?"

"Not back to live, no. He lives in Orlando. He's just visiting." Thank God.

Freddie gazed up at Todd for a long minute. "He's looking at you real mean."

I shielded my eyes as I looked up at the deck. "That's his cop look," I said with a grin. "That's what they look like when they're off duty."

Freddie brightened perceptibly. "He's a cop?"

"Don't worry," I quipped. "We aren't doing anything illegal."

It wasn't until we were all eating dinner that I realized what I'd done. Freddie, sitting between Todd and me, had been awkwardly silent throughout the first half of the meal. Finally, he looked up at me, then at Todd. "Are you really a cop?" he asked in his little-boy voice.

Todd looked down at him, his face softening into an expression that tugged at my memory. "Yep."

"Wow," Freddie breathed out. When he looked up at Todd again, there was a gleam in his eyes that hadn't been there a moment before. "That's way cool. Do you shoot people and stuff?"

I tuned them out. I felt betrayed. I was fourteen again just for a moment and wanted Teddy. How could the little shit be so fickle just because the man wore a badge and carried a gun? Where was his loyalty? Where was his crush, which had been so flattering just an hour or so ago? After all I'd done for him! The thought sounded so much like something my mother would say that I almost laughed. Almost. Not quite.

Todd monopolized Freddie's attention through the rest of dinner, discussing such spellbinding subjects as the intricacies of handcuffs and how to make the siren and lights go on and off in the police car. I found that, after the first sting of rejection, I could accept the fickleness of his nine-year-old affection with good grace. I bided my time. After all, Todd would be gone tomorrow, and Aunt Christie would still be here.

When I finished pouting, I wondered when and how Uncle Jack would tell Darlene, but it seems he and Carly had choreographed the entire thing. When we finished eating, Carly had the kids clear the table and told them she needed them in the kitchen to help her whip up some homemade ice cream.

She brought the coffee pot and cups to the table. "Why don't you have coffee in here while the kids and I fix your dessert?" she suggested, looking from me to Todd before smiling at Darlene and Fred.

I noticed she squeezed my uncle's shoulder before she left the room. My emotions had been yo-yoing since my uncle first told me about his illness. Just seeing that tender gesture caused my eyes to prickle, a precursor of tears. I breathed deeply, trying to get myself under control for what lay ahead.

"I'm glad you and Fred could make it tonight," Uncle Jack said, looking over at Darlene. He took a deep breath. "I've had a little bit of bad news recently. Not too serious right now, but . . . but . . . still . . ."

He was floundering. I thought he'd have the words rehearsed in his mind. Maybe he did, and they just wouldn't come out right. "Well, the fact is, I went to the doctor recently and he's told me I have Parkinson's disease."

Darlene and Fred exchanged looks of horror. "Oh, my God," Darlene breathed out, "isn't that the thing that causes you to shake all over?"

I could have slapped her. Uncle Jack closed his eyes briefly, then opened them. "Yes, it is."

Darlene covered her mouth. Her eyes went involuntarily to the kitchen. "Is it hereditary?"

"No, honey," Uncle Jack said gently. "It's not hereditary. I asked that first thing."

"Thank God!"

"It's not fatal either," he went on. "Just very—difficult."

"I'm so glad," she said, then looked confused. "I mean—I'm not glad it's difficult, but . . ." She said nothing for another minute. No one stepped in to fill the gap. I could almost hear the wheels turning in her head. I could tell by the look on her face that she was trying to figure out just what his illness meant to her. Then she tried to think of what Joanna would say in the situation. You could see her brow clear when it clicked in place. "I'm so sorry, Uncle Jack. It must be really hard for you."

"And Carly," he agreed. "I'm afraid she's the one who'll bear the brunt of it down the road, but let's hope that's a long way off."

"I do." Darlene nodded. "I'm sure it is." After a minute, she said, "Did Fred tell you his big news?" She smiled affectionately at her husband. "He's just been promoted to sales manager. And we're thinking of getting a new boat."

My uncle looked relieved at the change of subject. "That's great, honey."

"We went to a boat show while we were in New Orleans. You should see some of those boats!"

She rambled on while I sat, stunned by the feelings of resentment that coursed through me. A new boat? Your uncle tells you he has an incurable degenerative disease and you tell him about your new boat?

Carly peeked into the room, and then stepped through the doorway with the kids right behind her. Freddie carried the ice cream freezer, while Laurie carried the bowls and Lanie, the spoons. The room was once again a flurry of activity. I chanced a glance at Todd and caught him looking at Darlene with the narrow-eyed glare he had earlier used on me. She was totally oblivious to his presence. Her eyes bounced from child to child and, occasionally, to her husband. I had a feeling she had already forgotten my uncle's illness, and I didn't know whether to be glad or sad.

Sad won. Not because I was surprised by Darlene's self-centeredness. I'd known her entirely too long and too thoroughly for that, and I had exhibited a bit of the same trait the day before. It was more a general depression that settled on me like fog over the river. I'd had my moment of revenge. I was tired of talking and responding and smiling. I wanted to go the hell home.

Through sheer effort of will, I managed to delay my departure until Darlene was gathering up her crew. Then I hugged and kissed Uncle Jack and Carly. "I'll call you tomorrow," I told them both. I hugged the kids. Darlene and I still didn't touch one another, and Fred would have fainted dead away if I'd tried to give him a brotherly kiss. For Todd, I didn't spare a glance, but I did see him offer his hand to Freddie when he said goodbye. Freddie puffed up like a blowfish. He shook Todd's hand like the man he was becoming. I was proud and exasperated at the same time. Male bonding. *God.*

I had to wait until Fred pulled his car out before I could turn around and head out. Just for a minute, I toyed with the idea heading south for the inlet. It wasn't late. Eight-thirty. There was a full moon. It would be beautiful down there. Then I remembered who was in town and pointed my car resolutely north.

There were no lights on at Stella's, which wasn't surprising since it was Saturday night. I could see the TV flickering through Joyce and Leon's front window. I could imagine them curled up on the couch with a big bowl of popcorn between them. I had no desire to go over.

I had even less desire to be cooped up in my house. I went in only long enough to change into jeans and my Miami Dolphins t-shirt. Then, slipping my feet into deck shoes, I headed off up the beach.

About a quarter of a mile from my house was another jetty, a sixty-foot pile of boulders that marked the Port Canaveral channel. They weren't as magnificent as those at the inlet, but they were great for walking on and fishing off.

Port Canaveral was a working man's port, where shrimp boats with names like "Molly's Boy" and "The Lindy Lou" set out at dusk to cast their nets, returning at dawn before most of us were out of bed. Fischer's Seafood (of Fischer's bar and Bernard's Surf) operated their own boats out of the port. To say their seafood was fresh was gross understatement.

The area wasn't scenic; it was comfortably run down and smelled of dead fish. Few of the roads leading to it and none of the parking lots were paved. Both were scarred with three-by-five-foot potholes that held scummy water for a week after it rained. The mosquitoes were man-eaters.

There was talk of running passenger liners out of Port Canaveral, but a massive clean-up would have to be affected before the average person setting out on a cruise would agree to get within a hundred yards of the docks. So far the talk had remained only that. I was selfishly glad. Although cruise ships would mean tourists with money to spend and time to do it before their ship left the docking area—all very good for the city and the whole county—it would also mean a crush of tourists. We got enough of those, in my opinion, with the curiosity seekers checking out the launch pads at the Cape. I considered where I lived, a mile from the Port, a paradise; I didn't welcome the serpent called commerce.

There weren't any other people there tonight. The moon lit my way up the beach to the jetty. I climbed on the rocks and picked my way toward the end. I wondered idly what a psychiatrist would make of my always wanting to be on rocks out over the water to think, but I didn't really care. I had spent my life jumping from rock to rock. It was my own personal form of yoga, my way to meditate.

The nearness of the jetty had played a large part in my decision to buy my house. The Atlantic Ocean as my backyard and the affordability because of the real estate slump hadn't hurt either. Now I couldn't imagine living anywhere else, unless it was at the inlet.

Rocks and water teaming with fish. Salt air. The sounds of waves. Hungry birds hovering overhead. It was all a part of what I was and had dictated where I had to live, just as my curiosity and command of the English language had dictated my profession. Virgil flitted through my mind. Should I call him tomorrow? I probably wouldn't. I probably wouldn't sleep with him either. I wasn't even sure I liked the way he kissed. As quickly as he had entered my mind, he was gone.

I sat for a long time, breathing in the incredible air, the beloved smells of wet rock and seaweed and salt. I remembered the times I'd come home from college. As my car turned east toward the coast, I could smell home. It always made my blood quicken and brought a smile to my face. People I'd met while I was in college, people from the north, had asked me how I could live in a place that was so hot, where there was always the threat of a hurricane destroying all you'd built. They were mostly too polite to mention the smell. I couldn't imagine living anywhere else. It was probably the same way people who lived in Los Angeles felt about living on top of the San Andreas Fault. You paid your money and took your chances.

I'm not sure how or why I became aware of the presence behind me, but this time I was truly annoyed. I glanced over my shoulder at Todd, who was looming over me. "You really have got to stop this following me around," I said tiredly.

"You intentionally misled me."

"I did no such thing."

"You let me make a fool of myself, making me believe you were screwing around—"

I went from weary to livid, from sitting calmly on my rock to on my feet in the space of a blink. "I made you think nothing! Your own dirty little mind did that."

"You could have at least told me."

Feet apart, hands on hips, I thrust my face into his. "I owe you no explanations about how I live my life. What I do is none of your damn business."

"I know that! That's why I didn't know whether or not you were married, for godssake, or whether you had kids. I never asked because it was none of my business, but when I saw you with them, I assumed—"

"Your assumptions are your problem, bud. Don't try to put them on me."

"I was worried—"

"Bullshit. You were butting in where you had no business!"

He seemed taken aback for a minute. Then, he said, "I was concerned—"

I waved a hand in the air, cutting him off. "I. Don't. Want. Your. Concern," I said, carefully enunciating each word. "Get that through your head. Look, it's very simple. I don't know why you showed up suddenly and started interfering in my life. Oh, I know," I said when he started to speak. "You keep talking about concern, but that just doesn't wash. If you're really concerned, then be concerned about the added burden your sudden presence in my life is creating. The bottom line here is that I don't want to see you. I don't want you around. I simply want you to go away and leave me alone. I'm a big girl now, and I can manage on my own. You and your—concern—are just one more unwelcome pressure on top of all the others. I don't want it and I don't need it. Can you understand that?"

It was dark, but there was enough light for me to see his rigid posture slump slightly. His hands, which had been fisted on his hips, hung limply at his sides now. I was unmoved.

"Yes," he said. "I understand that. I thought we should talk—"

"We are talking. This is it. Our big talk. I want you to know that I don't need your help to get through this situation with my uncle. I can handle it quite well without you. I've been on my own and coping with life's little challenges for a long time. I'll do everything I can for Uncle Jack and Carly because I love them, but my relationship with them has nothing to do with you. It hasn't for a long time."

I could hear him breathing, feel the heat of him. He started to turn, but I wasn't going to let him go until we had some ground rules established. "I know you'll be coming to see your mother."

"And your uncle."

"And my uncle," I conceded. "It's probably inevitable that we'll run into each other occasionally. I'd like your promise that you'll respect my wishes. I have a life of my own now. I have a job and friends and a boyfriend." More or less. "I don't want you in my life. I don't want to have to keep looking over my shoulder to see if you're behind me, watching me. I want your promise that you'll leave me alone."

He hooked his thumbs into the waistband of his jeans. I thought I saw the muscle in his jaw twitch, but I may have imagined it, dark as it was. "You've made your wishes clear. I'll leave you alone."

"Good," I said, honestly relieved. "Go back to your life in Orlando, and I'll go back to my life here. It's the life I've built for myself. The life I want."

"Fine."

I nodded.

He turned and made his way back toward the shoreline with remarkable grace. I couldn't help but admire his outline, and I felt free to admire it now that I had made myself and my wishes clear. He was an incredibly handsome man. Still. If the years had changed his appearance, they had only improved what was already good. I'd have been a liar if I'd said he didn't move me. Deeply. Too bad he was a man who didn't honor his commitments.

When I was once again truly alone, I sat back down on the rock, but the peace was gone. My head was beginning to hurt and my eyes burned, and I felt like I was coming down with a cold. After a few minutes, I pulled myself to my feet and headed back to the house.

CHAPTER 14

During the next three interminable years, Todd kept his promise. He didn't show up on my doorstep or on the jetty. I only saw him at the inlet one time, sitting at the edge of the rocks having a beer with Jackson, and he had arrived before me. They were absorbed in a conversation about something. He was deeply tanned, leading me to believe he might have been around more than I knew. At one point, Todd threw back his head and laughed. The sun made his hair glimmer like white gold. Jackson poked him on the shoulder good-naturedly. Feeling it was only right, I got back in my car and drove away, leaving them to it.

When we ran into each other at Uncle Jack's and Carly's, a rare occurrence, we were each polite and distant. Jack and Carly seemed to sense the wind direction and made sure only one of us was invited at a time. They also found subtle ways to hint to me that he might be around at certain times. I suspect they did the same for him.

Holidays were easy. Cops worked holidays unless they had seniority. Holidays were when the emotions and the booze ran high and freely, respectively. It was the time that domestic incidents peaked. Friends stabbed friends and family members shot each other, all in the name of love. If I hadn't known that from my job on the newspaper, I would have from Joyce, who also worked too many hours during the holidays for the same reason and always had stories that chilled the blood.

Those three years were pretty good for me. I decided Virgil was too far from Mr. Right to warrant any kind of compromise. He didn't take it well, and it was a tough few months at the paper while he adjusted, but eventually he became reconciled to it. His final acceptance occurred when he met and married a former Miss Orlando, Becky Everly. She was as beautiful as you'd expect, with curling auburn hair and skin that looked like it belonged on a Dresden doll. I saw her at the paper occasionally when she dropped in to see her husband, and she was as friendly as she was lovely. Virgil Junior was in the boughs. Virgil Senior almost equally so. It was truly a match made in heaven.

Paul didn't marry, although he did take heart from the fact that Virgil did. I could have told him that it made no difference, but he wouldn't have listened. He never put any kind of pressure on me. He just kept me aware that he was there.

I did meet a guy during the second year who had me going for a while. His name was Thomas Flaherty. He came to Cocoa Beach to write a book. I thought that as romantic as he was, with his flaming red hair and a brogue as thick as our summer humidity. He was there for a year before he returned to Ireland. He made me laugh. He also made me feel beautiful and unique and loved, and I hope I did the same for him. I shed a few tears when he left, but ours always had the feeling of a temporary liaison.

It was Thomas who first planted the idea in my head of writing a book of my own. "You've the gift of language, girl," he told me. "Don't waste it spouting daily drivel. You've got imagination and you've got staying power. You've enough stories from your own childhood to write a dozen books. I plan to use as many of them as I can in my own stories, and I thank you for them. You've so much to say, and you manage to say it with just a touch of humor. Tell the world!" he had finished with a flourish. I think he was a little foxed that night.

I hadn't done anything about it yet, but the seed was germinating. I began to look at what happened around me with different eyes, with an eye to fiction. How would I describe that person or that incident? How would I lead up to that story?

In the meantime, I liked the direction my career was taking. Once Virgil forgave me in earnest for my rejection, he began giving me decent stories and allowed and even encouraged me to follow up on them. He teased me about being a modern-day Diogenes with his lamp, always searching for the truth. I told him he had his stories confused, but I liked the concept. It was thrilling to dig beneath the surface of some seemingly commonplace event and find out why something had happened, then to put it on paper so that my readers could see the natural progression of the thing and, even more importantly, the truth. I was beginning to earn a name for myself, and my confidence was at an all-time high.

On the home front, Joyce produced a sibling for Suzy. Peter Phillip Crenshaw was born the day before my twenty-eighth birthday, and Leon and Stella and I celebrated both with two lovely bottles of wine. Joyce would have killed him if she had found out.

Stella was changing. I didn't know exactly what was happening, but she was becoming more and more mysterious about her comings and goings. Often, I would see her slip out of the house early in the evening and not return until late the next day. That wasn't unusual, but lately she'd been wearing jeans or shorts instead of her usual dress and heels. I noticed subtle changes. Her makeup was more understated, although just as flawless. She was wearing her hair an inch or so lower, and occasionally I caught sight of her in a previously unheard of ponytail. I thought she might have a serious boyfriend, but if she did, she wasn't talking about it.

My sisters remained the same, Joanna in her ivory Alabama

tower and Darlene as supermom. Big Fred hadn't changed a bit, except to grow a bit older and lose a little hair. Darlene thought it made him look distinguished. His namesake had changed quite a lot. Freddie was twelve now and quite the young man. He and I were closer than ever. So, according to Darlene, were he and his uncle Todd. Darlene told me Todd called him about once a week and always spent time with him when he was in town. Although the idea made me squirm, I was glad for Freddie. Nothing against his father, but it was obvious that Freddie needed a strong male influence in his life, and Todd was nothing if not that.

My mother surprised us all by marrying Lamar Gunter, the man Paul had mentioned to me. They had a small wedding, fifty people or so. Most were business colleagues of Mr. Gunter, bankers and financial wizards of one sort or another. Joanna condescended to come to Florida for the wedding, bringing with her enough luggage to clothe her for a month. She was fond of explaining she only shopped in Atlanta. She also brought Doug and her son, Edwin. He was a supercilious little twerp of thirteen who had nothing to do with his cousins. They didn't seem to feel the loss.

Joanna and Darlene were matrons of honor. I declined being part of the wedding party, although I did attend the ceremony with interest. Mother looked wonderful in her tailored suit of pink silk shantung. Mr. Gunter—Lamar—looked confused and wooden during the ceremony but seemed happy enough after it was all over. So did Doug, Joanna's husband, so happy that he was mixing bourbon with his champagne and made a pass at me before the night was over. I wasn't impressed enough with him to be offended. I pushed him into the pool at the country club where they held the reception. I never did find out how he explained his way out of that.

Lamar and Mother spent their honeymoon in Paris. As a

result, all of Mother's subsequent conversations were sprinkled with just enough French phrases to remind people she had actually been there.

The years that were so good to the rest of us were less kind to my uncle. His health declined with a rapidity that had his doctors scratching their heads. About a year and a half after the disease was diagnosed, the tremors began affecting him in earnest. He would be holding a glass and it would suddenly fall out of his hand. He had difficulty getting food to his mouth with a fork. There was a frantic round of tests, which only told them he had arteriosclerosis. The aspirin he took for his arthritis would help that, they said. Thin the blood. It did nothing for the tremors. They finally decided he must have had Parkinson's for much longer than they had previously thought and made the decision to throw caution to the wind and start him on Levodopa.

That was when I found out all the stories I'd read about the drug in my research on Parkinson's were understated. They damned near killed him with it. It requires a high dosage of Levodopa to wield any kind of control of the symptoms, and the high dosage sometimes caused violent nausea and vomiting. It certainly did in his case.

I learned later from Carly that the doctor had urged him to try to tough it out, promising that his system would adjust to the dosage in time. It didn't. He had lost twenty pounds and was severely dehydrated by the time I received the call from Carly. She was too upset to sugarcoat her words. "Your uncle— Christie—he's in the hospital."

I arrived there twenty minutes later. I thanked God a hundred times as I sped across the causeway that I had traded my ancient Mustang for a new Jeep. The trip in the old car would have taken an eternity.

Todd was already there when I arrived. Carly explained that

she had called him before they left for the hospital and was going to call me next, but then Uncle Jack had started vomiting
again. Still, Orlando was over fifty miles from Melbourne. He
must have broken a few laws to make it that fast. Good thing he
was a cop.

The three of us were in the waiting room on the second floor,
a big room with chairs placed around the perimeter and covered
in some kind of vinyl that stuck to the backs of my bare legs.
Rickety tables cluttered with old magazines dotted the room,
which smelled of old floor wax and disinfectant. In one corner
was a coffee machine that dispensed brown water in cardboard
cups. Beside it sat a Coke machine that had "Out of Order"
scrawled on a piece of paper and Scotch-taped to it. As we
always did, Todd and I avoided looking at each other.

I hadn't yet seen my uncle. Carly said they were cleaning him
up and getting him settled, and if she was any indication of
what this emergency had done to them, I wasn't sure I wanted
to see him. She looked terrible. Pale. Strained to the breaking
point. I knew his tremors had worsened significantly, and I
knew the doctors had been talking about starting the medication.

"How long has he been on Levodopa?"

She bit her lip and tried to concentrate. "About two weeks, I
think. He seemed all right at first. Then the nausea began." According to her, he began vomiting almost immediately after
that. The tremors had abated somewhat, but the nausea became
worse and worse until he couldn't keep anything down, including the medication. "He's lost so much weight," she said, wring-
ing her hands. "He was so weak, I almost couldn't get him in
the car. He refused to let me call an ambulance."

She bit her lip and blinked rapidly. At that point, Todd took
her hand and held it tightly. She looked up at him with
something that might have been gratitude. Or maybe a plea for

help. In either case, she seemed to gain strength from him. When she spoke again, her voice had backed away a bit from the edge. "They're giving him IVs now. They said they have to get his fluids up, and they're going to be feeding him intravenously. I don't know how long they're going to keep him here."

I took her other hand. My heart ached for what she was going through. It had been exactly two weeks since I'd been at their house. I had intended to stop by this past weekend, but Virgil had me following a story in Titusville and I hadn't found the time. I wanted to ask her why she hadn't called me, but I was afraid my words would sound accusatory. Instead, I sat there mute, holding her hand until Dr. Johnson came into the room.

He was a little man in an ill-fitting suit, and he had been my uncle's doctor for the last twenty years. Not that they had seen much of each other. My uncle had rarely required medical attention, and he was impatient with the idea of annual physicals—to his detriment, it now seemed.

"Here you are," he said with what seemed to me fake joviality. "I wondered where you'd gotten to." He walked up to Carly, who had risen to her feet, as had Todd and I. "He's going to be fine, Carly," he said, taking her hand and patting it. "Just a rough reaction to the medication. Takes a while sometimes to get the dosage just right. We'll get him fixed up in the next couple of days and you can take him home."

"Isn't twenty pounds a lot to lose from a drug reaction?" I asked.

He seemed to notice me for the first time. He beamed at me. "Is this Christie all grown up?"

I hadn't seen the man in fifteen years, but I had no intention of discussing my advanced age or size. I waited.

He seemed taken aback by my lack of reaction. "Well, yes," he said finally. "It is a lot of weight, but your uncle carries a good deal of weight. Not fat, you understand, but he's solid. He'll put it back on soon enough once we get the medicine regulated."

"Can I go to him?" Carly asked, wanting nothing to do with our medical discussion.

He turned back to her. "Of course you can. Room 210. Second door on the right. You can all go in if you want. He's doing fine."

Obviously he was not doing fine, I thought, as Carly hurried away, or he wouldn't be here. I managed to hold my tongue.

"How long do you think he'll be hospitalized?" Todd asked, speaking for the first time since my arrival.

Dr. Johnson looked at him without recognition.

Todd offered his hand. "Todd Harrington," he said. "Carly's son."

"Oh. Of course. Jack told me about you. A police officer, aren't you?"

Todd nodded.

"How long?" he mused. "Well, it depends. We have to get his fluids back up to an acceptable level, and we want to try to get his dosage regulated while he's here."

I was incredulous. "You're going to keep giving him the Levodopa?"

He turned to me. "We have to, Christie. If we can get the dosage correct, it will help significantly with the tremors."

"And if you don't, it'll kill him."

His professional manner slipped just for a second, giving way to irritation, but he recovered quickly. "That's a little extreme, Christie. You can trust me that we won't let the medication do him any more harm. In the long run, it could do him a great deal of good. Dr. Seegar and I will be monitoring him closely."

"Dr. Seegar?" Todd asked.

His head swiveled back to Todd. "The neurologist. He and I

will be working very closely on this. Hand in hand, if you will. After all, we have the whole patient's well-being to think of."

I thought they were a little tardy in thinking of the whole patient, but again I managed to keep my mouth shut. Maybe I was maturing after all.

"How long?" Todd repeated. "Ballpark."

Dr. Johnson tapped his chin, raising his eyes to the ceiling. "Oh, I'd say a week. Maybe ten days. A lot depends on how he responds to treatment."

I wanted to scream. A week or ten days. As badly as Carly was reacting to his hospitalization, I was certain she would be in a mental institution by then.

Todd seemed to be thinking along the same lines. He nodded. "I have some vacation coming," he said more to me than to the doctor. "It might help if she had me around."

"Fine idea," Dr. Johnson beamed. "Now, if you'll excuse me."

I watched Todd watch him scamper away. I almost could have hugged him. I had no vacation coming, and while my work schedule was probably more flexible than his, it wouldn't allow me time to give Carly the full-time moral support she needed right now.

Todd turned back to me. "You don't mind, do you?"

"Mind? No, I'm relieved. I was trying to figure out how to get some time off. I've used all my vacation. I could probably take some family leave, but I've been saving that as kind of an ace in the hole."

He nodded. "Good." Then, "Do you want me to wait out here until after you've seen your uncle?"

I suddenly felt like crying. Delayed reaction, no doubt. "No. We can both go in."

He was in the hospital for nine days. Dr. Johnson was better at guessing length of stay, it seemed, than correct dosage. In all fairness, my research indicated that the experts agreed on one fact: that finding the right dosage of Levodopa was as difficult as it was crucial. That knowledge did little to relieve my mind when I saw my uncle that night. His face was gaunt and as pale as the sheets that covered him. Flesh that had lost its underlying fatty tissue too rapidly hung loosely on him. His generous mouth was cracked and dry. Even the innocent IV needle taped to his arm seemed grotesque to me. I tried to keep my feelings out of my face, but I must have failed.

"I'm fine, Christie," he said almost as soon as I was in the door. "Don't worry, honey. It was just a reaction to some medicine I took." I pretended to believe he was fine, willed my face to mirror that belief. I don't think I was very successful, and I was quite ashamed of myself for being such a weakling.

Carly seemed improved by just being in his presence. She bustled about, pushing pillows behind him and straightening his bedside table. Instead of that reassuring me, it frightened me even more. I had seen her out there in the waiting room. What would happen to her when he wasn't able to rally as he seemed to be doing tonight? Todd must have been having similar thoughts. He watched her with worried concentration.

They finally made us leave at eleven o'clock. I was almost relieved. I was beat, emotionally and physically. Carly hadn't stopped tidying or straightening things for hours. Watching her was exhausting me.

She fidgeted all the way to the parking lot, brushing Todd's sleeve and pulling at her own clothes. Her face reflected the naked fear that must be gnawing at her. I was grateful when Todd insisted he take her home in his car. I had parked in the emergency room lot, as had both Carly and Todd. It was a ground-level asphalt lot open to the air and the sky, as opposed to the claustrophobic concrete monstrosity of a parking deck across the street. It was almost empty at this hour.

The air seemed cold to me that night. It was January, but we'd had an unusually mild winter. I'd been wearing a light sweatshirt and shorts when Carly called, and I hadn't even stopped to pull on a jacket.

I said nothing as we reached my car. I couldn't give Carly platitudes. I didn't know if everything would be all right. I didn't know anything. I hugged her in the parking lot, enjoying that moment of warmth. Then there was an awkward moment of silence until Todd said, "Would you like to ride with us? I could drive you home, too." He was looking at me, and I could see the battle in his face—his good manners at war with my own statement about being able to take care of myself. I felt a little sorry for him.

"Thanks. It's nice of you to ask, but I'm fine." It was a lie, but I was pretty sure I could drive home without running off the road.

"Okay, then." He looked sad. Beaten down. The night had been hard on him, too. "Goodnight."

He put his arm around Carly's shoulders and led her to his car. I watched the way she leaned on him and felt an unworthy pang of envy. I wouldn't mind doing a little leaning of my own.

I shook off my self-pity and climbed into the driver's seat. As I looked up at where I thought my uncle's window might be, I had the feeling I hadn't seen the last of this hospital.

I was right about that. Six months later, Uncle Jack was back in the hospital, only this time he was vomiting blood. An ulcer, they diagnosed. It would complicate things, Dr. Johnson explained, ever the master of understatement.

The aspirin he took for his rheumatoid arthritis and the arteriosclerosis was aggravating the ulcer, as was the Levodopa. Without the aspirin, his arthritis, already painful, was nearly excruciating when combined with the tremors from the Parkinson's disease. Besides, he had to have some type of blood-thinning medication, and it would be better if one medication, aspirin of some sort, could be used to treat both. His latest vomiting episodes had thrown his Levodopa dosage off kilter, and they were trying to balance him out again. It was a true conundrum.

He had never regained his full weight after the first hospital stay, and this glitch (Dr. Johnson's word) in his treatment had cost him ten more pounds. Carly was spending a lot of time altering his clothes so that the weight loss wouldn't be so obvious. It was hard on her, since she was putting in more hours at the beauty shop. She said it was to keep her spirits up, but I thought they might just need the money. His medication was hideously expensive, and the doctors weren't free. Neither was the hospital. He had insurance, of course, but it only paid a portion of the cost. His disability was only considered about thirty percent at that time, so that insurance hadn't kicked in.

When I hinted that I might help with the medical costs, Carly looked horrified. "Don't you ever let Jack hear you say something like that," she scolded me like a disobedient child. "It would humiliate him."

I thought knowing she was putting in sixty-hour weeks to help pay for his medicine might also humiliate him, but once again I held my tongue. I was in danger of developing real reserve.

Carly had lost weight, too. She looked haggard. The terror she must feel every time my uncle so much as flinched was taking a toll on her. She seemed more unsure than ever. She apologized constantly for no apparent reason. Todd stayed with her that time, too, during the six days Uncle Jack was hospitalized. Either the Orlando PD had a liberal vacation policy or he had been saving his up for a while. During this stay—as well as the ones that were soon to follow—he was all politeness. His manner never veered from the path I had set it on, always show-ing the proper amount of respect and courtesy without a trace of special interest or excessive concern. It was beginning to ir-ritate me.

My mother did more than irritate me. I had been scheduled to have dinner with Lamar and her the night Carly took Uncle Jack to the emergency room, but I totally forgot about it until I got home and found her message on my answering machine. The machine was a recent and extravagant purchase, motivated more by my fear that Carly wouldn't be able to get in touch with me than by any real need of my own.

"Christiana," the imperious voice said, "I believe we had made plans to have dinner this evening. You must have forgot-ten. I don't require an apology, of course, but I do think com-mon courtesy dictates that you call Lamar and apologize to him. He was *très* disappointed. He had special ordered your favorite wine."

Since it was after midnight when I got the message, I didn't return her call. Instead, I went by the boutique the next day. Mother still worked there three days a week. She said it got her out of the house, and I think she liked her employee discount. It was off-season and the place was quiet. The boutique was a smallish shop on Atlantic Avenue that catered to tourists and the few residents who could afford the prices. Fortunately, the owner raked in enough during the winter and summer months to carry the shop the rest of the year. It featured unique cloth-ing and jewelry fashioned by local artists who couldn't possibly have afforded their own creations. I couldn't walk in without wishing I were rich. That day was no exception. There was a sundress in the window, yellow chiffon over blue silk that shim-mered like the Atlantic on a clear day. Out of morbid curiosity, I glanced at the price tag and only barely contained my gasp.

Three hundred and twenty-five dollars—and it didn't even have sleeves.

Mother was behind the glass-fronted counter that held the more expensive jewelry. It amazed me each time I saw her that she had changed so little over the years. At fifty-five, she looked much as she had at forty. Her hair was still the same color, with a little help, of course, and her skin remained unlined and un-flawed except for the little commas of disapproval around her mouth. Her chin was firm, her figure trim. I hoped I looked half as good at her age.

When she saw me, she raised one eyebrow.

"I'm sorry about last night," I said, feeling once again fourteen and naughty as I always did in her presence. "There was an emergency."

"An emergency without telephones?"

"Uncle Jack had to be taken to the hospital."

She blinked. "Was there an accident?"

I realized suddenly that I'd never told her about his illness. Illnesses, by that time. I guess I'd assumed Darlene had told her or that she wouldn't care. "No. He has ulcers," I began.

"No wonder, the way he lives."

I bit back my frustration. "It's more than that. The doctors have also diagnosed him as having Parkinson's disease." I didn't tell her about the arthritis and arteriosclerosis. It seemed too much at once.

I wasn't sure she knew what Parkinson's disease was—I might not have if it hadn't been for my friend's father—but the word "disease" stopped her for a minute. I could see her gather herself together. The shoulders came back and down, the chin elevated slightly. "I'm certain it wasn't so serious that you couldn't call—"

"He was vomiting blood, Mother," I said in exasperation. "I wasn't thinking about dinner."

She looked stunned. I wasn't certain whether it was concern for him or revulsion at my grossness. I decided to assume the former. "He's really very ill," I said gently.

She seemed to shake herself. "Nonsense. The man will outlive me."

I stepped back physically, stunned by the curt dismissal in her voice. At the time, I thought her remark cold and spiteful, even for her. It never occurred to me that it was denial.

Her words propelled me out the door of the shop without another word. It was several months before we spoke to each other again, although I did call her husband and apologize.

When Uncle Jack got out of the hospital, he seemed remarkably better. He had gained back some of his much-needed weight. His color had improved. The tremors had lessened so that they were almost unnoticeable. I allowed myself to feel hope for the first time since his diagnosis. Maybe the doctors would get the dosage right. Maybe he would live out his natural life with a minimum of symptoms. Ever the optimist.

The next eighteen months held more peaks and valleys than the Blue Ridge Mountains. I didn't want to think what it was doing to Carly and Uncle Jack. He was in and out of the hospital five times for various reasons. His hemoglobin bottomed out, and he had to have gamma globulin shots. The ulcer continued to give him fits. They kept him off the aspirin, even the sugar-coated kind, for six months. They'd have to take their chances with the Levodopa because orally was the only way it proved effective—if you could call depression and those sudden jerky movements that publicly embarrassed him "effective." Apparently it was better than the alternative. During those six months, he gritted his teeth against the pain he felt and virtually became a prisoner of the disease and the house. He was hospitalized for chest pain and anxiety attacks.

If he had aged fifteen years in eighteen months, Carly had

aged twenty. She had the look of a panicked deer in a car's headlights, wondering how she had gotten herself into this fix. She never complained out loud to me about my uncle, his mood swings or his severe depressions, which were only partly, I thought, caused by the medication. Carly looked gaunt; her teeth seemed permanently ground together.

Then, magically, Uncle Jack seemed to stabilize for several months.

Suzy provided some much-needed comic relief about that time by falling head over sneakered feet in love with my nephew, Freddie. She was eight now, and quite grown up for her age. Having a baby brother had begun the process; her new love hastened it along.

I was there the day it happened. The kids were out on the jetty pulling their usual mountain goat routine, all except Peter Phillip, who was only two and a half and unable as yet to make it from rock to rock. I had brought them down with me and was sitting on the sand watching Peter Phillip gnaw on a gritty seashell when I heard Suzy cry out. I jumped to my feet, but before I could get two steps toward them, Freddie had swept her up in his arms and was heading toward shore. She had apparently fallen on one of the rocks and scraped her knee. Blood was trickling down her leg when Freddie put her down on the sand at my feet. She was biting her lip, trying not to cry. She looked up at him with her big, moist eyes, and I could see the exact instant when it happened. Her facial expression didn't alter a bit, but her eyes widened ever so slightly and suddenly her gaze had an intensity that hadn't been there before. As Freddie went to get some saltwater in a cup to pour over her leg, her eyes never left him.

From that moment, she followed him wherever he went, her eyes all aglow with worship. It must have made him crazy at times to have her glued to his heels, but he was always gentle with her. I only hoped he wouldn't one day break her heart.

I was becoming irritable in general, which made no sense at all. Uncle Jack was better, which meant, of course, that Carly was better. He was back at work on a reduced work schedule. His bosses had been more than understanding about his multiple illnesses, allowing him whatever time was necessary whenever he needed it. I doubted my boss, Virgil, would be as understanding under the same circumstances.

I had started a story. I was afraid to call it a novel, afraid that I'd get halfway through and run out of words. It was about ill-fated lovers, one from Ireland who was writing a book and one who couldn't commit her whole heart to the relationship. Hey, they said to write about what you know. I felt a little silly writing a love story, afraid I'd had too little experience with the subject matter. That made me irritable, too.

Stella attributed it to the same thing she attributed all my problems to. "You need to get laid."

We were stretched out on plastic webbed lounge chairs on my patio getting fried by the midday June sun. There was a breeze off the ocean; enough, at least, to keep us from collapsing from heat prostration. We each had a spray bottle filled with water, the kind for misting plants. When it got too unbearable, we would spray ourselves or each other.

I had been surprised and pleased when Stella showed up at my door that Saturday at noon. She wasn't around very much anymore, and she was still tight-lipped about what was occupying all her time these days. Her halter-top really should have been outlawed. I hoped Joyce didn't look out her window.

"That is not the answer to everything," I replied condescendingly.

She was unperturbed. "It's the answer to everything that's wrong with you."

"How would you know what's wrong with me?"

"Gosh, I don't know." She turned her head toward me, her eyes hidden behind ovals of black plastic. "Let's see. You spend an hour in your cousin's company and you come back home and snarl at all of us for a week. You don't see him and you're sort of okay. You see him again and you come back here and snarl at us." She lifted the glasses and squinted at me. "I thought maybe there could be some kind of pattern here."

"What does Todd have to do—" I broke off, remembering with appropriate humiliation my drunken confession of puppy love. I changed tracks. "Todd has nothing to do with anything. I told you. All that has been over for years."

She lowered her sunglasses and lay back on her lounge chair. "Uh-huh."

"I've just been worried about my uncle."

"Sure you have."

"And Carly."

"Right."

"Don't patronize me," I said hotly. "You know it's true."

"Then how come your uncle's better now and you're worse."

"It's just—" I was struggling. It didn't occur to me to wonder why it meant so much to me to convince Stella of what I was saying. "It's just that everything has built up these last couple of years. I'm afraid to hope, but I can't help it when he's like this. The last time I was over, he was almost like his old self. It makes me happy and scares me to death at the same time. I'm afraid it won't last."

Stella turned her head toward me. "I know you are, honey, and it won't, you know. Last. It can't."

"I know," I answered miserably.

We baked in companionable silence for a few minutes. I thought Stella had fallen asleep. I was fighting sleep myself. When she spoke, her words caught me off guard. "He's a real stud, that cousin of yours."

I had to laugh. "Stepcousin. You could tell that from one glance out your window?"

"I've seen him down at the inlet."

Now it was me who sat up and raised her glasses. "What were you doing down at the inlet? It doesn't seem like your kind of place."

"I get down there from time to time."

I thought about that. The inlet consisted of a long jetty, some wild beach on which Jackson had his bait shack, and a recently completed bridge. Then I remembered the handful of half-million-dollar homes sprinkled along the beach and on the river. Maybe she had a boyfriend down there. That would certainly explain her frequent absences. I was about to ask her when she went on.

"You could do worse."

"Than what?" I had lost the thread of the conversation.

"Worse than Todd Harrington."

"No, I couldn't." She knew his last name?

She yawned and stretched her arms over her head. I thought the halter was going to explode. "Suit yourself, but if I was a mite younger, I'd try to get my hands and the rest of me around what's filling out those jeans of his."

"You're vulgar."

"You're a prude."

I ignored her and tried to ignore her words, but the visual image they'd conjured up haunted me long after she'd gone home to shower and go wherever it was she went these days. It came to me later while I was soaking in the tub, starting tingles in places that hadn't shown signs of life for a long time. It attacked me while I lay in bed reading, and I pushed it ruthlessly out of my mind. It waited until I slept, and while my guard was lowered, it wafted in and out of my dreams like the refrain of some half-remembered song. When I awoke, I was smiling for as long as it took for me to remember what had made me smile. Then the smile vanished abruptly, and my mood for the day was set.

It was Sunday, and I'd promised Uncle Jack and Carly to come by for dinner about five. I spent the early part of the day ruthlessly cleaning my house, my own personal way of slaying demons. Stella dropped by early—early for her, which meant about noon. I was in no mood for her fiddling with my psyche and pretty much told her so. She smiled that knowing little smile of hers and left. Joyce came in as she was going out, with Suzy and Peter Phillip in tow. The two women gave each other a wide birth, although Suzy had a big smile for Stella and even Peter Phillip's perpetual smile brightened a few watts at the sight of her. Men, I thought in disgust.

I couldn't hold on to my nasty mood while Peter Phillip was there, though. He was the kind of kid who makes you want one. At nearly two years old, he was irresistible. He had only one mood—happy. He didn't fuss, he didn't throw tantrums. He just enjoyed the moment and everything and everybody in it. His enthusiasm for life was infectious. Even his big sister couldn't sustain a snit about all the attention he received wherever he went. He was that cute. Besides, she was a grown up woman in love now. She managed Peter Phillip as if she were practicing motherhood for when her and Freddie's first child arrived.

"Spring cleaning?" Joyce asked, looking around at the piled up furniture and the carpet shampooer I had rented that morning.

I had finished my bedroom and bathroom, and was working my way toward the kitchen. "Summer cleaning. I couldn't stand this place another day."

"So I see." Joyce looked around her again. "Fight with your mother?" Joyce and I had known each other a long time.

"Nope. Not this time."

"Your sister?"

"No," I said with a grim smile. "Just the age-old battle with dirt."

"Hmmm. Well, I just dropped by to see if you could watch the kids this evening. Leon just called me and asked me out on a real live date."

I gave her a sidewise look. "The last time the two of you had a real live date, Peter Phillip was the result."

Joyce laughed. "True, but I wised up and got back on the pill."

I put aside the bottle of spot cleaner I'd been using on the rug before shampooing and sat down on the corner of the sofa that wasn't piled high with debris. "I wish I could, Joyce," I told her sincerely. I loved taking care of Suzy and Peter Phillip. "But I'm having dinner with Uncle Jack and Carly tonight."

"Oh." A pause. "That's okay. Maybe I can get someone. It's just that it's the first night Leon's had off in two weeks that coincided with mine."

I knew she and Leon rarely got to see each other because their schedules rarely meshed. I also knew that she didn't have a single last-minute babysitter candidate she could count on. Except me, of course. At that exact moment, Peter Phillip climbed in my lap and pulled my arms around him, leaning back and grinning up at me. "My Christie," he cooed.

I looked at Joyce with suspicion. "Did you teach him to do that?"

She laughed. "No. I swear. He's a con man in his own right."

I ran my fingers through his silky baby hair. "I suppose I could take them with me. Uncle Jack and Carly would get a kick out of them."

"I couldn't ask you to do that," Joyce protested, although I thought a bit weakly. "They'd be too much trouble."

"They wouldn't be any trouble at all." I was thinking now. "You'll need to bring me Peter Phillip's car seat, and a change of clothes for both of them in case I take them wading. I'll need their pajamas. They can spend the night here." I looked up at her. "You're sure you're on the pill?"

"I swear," she laughed.

"Okay. But don't bring them over until about four. I have to get this house put back together."

"You are a lifesaver," Joyce said, grabbing up Peter Phillip and giving me a spontaneous hug. "This date seemed so important to Leon. I don't know why. It's not our anniversary or anything, but when he called, he said please try to make it. I'm meeting him for dinner over in Cocoa at that new steakhouse by the river, Land's End."

I nodded. "I've been there for lunch. It's really nice."

"I never get to go anywhere for lunch except the hospital cafeteria," she said as she took Suzy's hand. "We'll get out of your hair now. I'll see you at four—if you're really sure about this."

I leaned down to kiss Suzy on top of the head. "I'm positive."

The more I thought about it as I ran the shampooer over the carpet, the more I liked the idea. Uncle Jack and Carly both loved kids, and Darlene's were getting big now. They were all great kids and Freddie, in particular, worshiped Uncle Jack, but babies were more fun.

I was looking forward to spending some time with Uncle Jack and Carly that wasn't motivated by a crisis. I tried to get by often, but when things were going well, time just seemed to slip away.

The house fairly sparkled by the time Joyce delivered her children to me. She had packed two separate bags: one to take with us to dinner that included a change of clothes for each kid from the skin out and the other full of pajamas and stuffed animals and special blankets. It looked like they were coming to stay for a month, as I mentioned to her.

She shook her head ruefully. "I know, but Peter Phillip can't sleep unless he has his teddy bear and his Pooh blanket and Suzy likes to read for a while at night. I swear, it's only for overnight."

She departed after a lot of hugging and kissing and last-minute instructions for them and me. I was glad to see the back of her.

I had called to warn Carly that I'd be bringing the neighbor's kids with me, and she had said that was fine. She told me that Uncle Jack was still doing great. So it was with a light heart that I set out for their house with the two kids securely belted into my back seat.

I arrived a few minutes early. Uncle Jack and Carly made an appropriate fuss over the kids, who were on their absolute best and cutest behavior. I whispered to Carly that Suzy had a crush on Freddie. She gave me what I thought was a strange look, but a few minutes later, she invited Suzy to sit on the sofa with her. She pulled out the photo albums and began showing Suzy all our old family pictures, pointing out Freddie at all ages.

Carly looked better than I'd seen her in months. Thin still, but her skin looked healthier, as if she'd been out in the sun. Uncle Jack, too, had some color in his face. Maybe he and Carly were back to taking their daily walks on the beach. She was dressed in shorts and a shirt that was tied at her waist. The combination made her look more like twenty-five than—I realized suddenly that I had no idea how old Carly was.

She seemed calmer than I was used to seeing. Only her eyes gave her away, eyes that never strayed for long from my uncle. She would point out something to Suzy in a picture, and then her gaze would dart back to him as if she were afraid that if she didn't watch him constantly, something terrible would happen. Although he seemed unaware of her scrutiny, I doubt he really was. He had been sensitive to what was going on with his wife for far too long to miss something I could spot in ten minutes.

He and Peter Phillip were on the floor making car noises while pushing prime specimens from Uncle Jack's antique car collection across the carpet. I was standing near the front door enjoying watching all of them, but my heart was in my throat every time Peter Phillip reached for one of the fragile and outrageously expensive "toys." I should have known better. My uncle managed to keep him entertained and the cars safe with skill that left me breathless. In fact, they were making so much noise that I didn't hear the front door open and close behind me. I was unaware that anyone was standing behind me until a voice said in my ear, "So whose kids have you borrowed this time?"

CHAPTER 15

I spun around so fast that I nearly lost my balance. Todd's hand lightly touched my arm, steadying me. Stella's mocking words, all my unwelcome thoughts and my dreams of the night before flooded back in the space of that casual touch, and I felt an unwelcome heat suffuse my face. I spun back to Carly, who had looked up from the album. Her face was wearing that smile that only Todd could bring to it.

"Honey!" She closed the album and handed it to Suzy, getting to her feet. "I thought you couldn't make it this weekend."

He crossed the room, brushing by me. The heat in my face spread to other parts of my body. I cursed Stella and my imagination.

He put his arm around Carly's shoulders and kissed her on the cheek. "I didn't think I could until this morning. Last-minute schedule change."

He reached down and shook my uncle's hand. "Jack." His eyes came to rest on Peter Phillip. "Who have we got here?"

"Well, the young lady over there memorizing our family history is Suzy. This big boy is her brother. And this," he swept his hand out to indicate the floor littered with cars, "is the Indy 500. Peter Phillip here is a future racecar driver. Grab a car and join us."

Which, of course, he did. He chose the cherry red 1955 Thunderbird and stretched out comfortably on his side on the carpet, resting on his elbow.

I stood like a statue until Suzy came over and nudged me. "Who's that?"

"That's Carly's little boy," I informed her softly.

The little boy under discussion looked up at me, a half-smile on his face. I looked away, silently cursing Stella once again. I took Suzy's hand and led her into the kitchen where, I presumed, Carly had vanished.

"Oh, good," she said brightly when we came in. "You can both help me." She handed Suzy a stack of plastic plates. "Do you think you can set the table on the deck?"

Suzy nodded solemnly. "Mama taught me how."

"Good. You go put the plates around the table, and then come back for the silverware. Okay?"

When she was gone, the silence was as pregnant as I expected Joyce to get some time during the night. I didn't ask Carly when she had extended the invitation to her Todd. We didn't talk about things like that. I felt pretty certain she hadn't done this to trap me into an evening with him; she and Uncle Jack had been wonderful about keeping our visits separate. I had only received my invitation on Monday, probably after Todd had said he couldn't make it.

Just as I had decided all that, Carly said, "Isn't it wonderful that Todd could make it? It's so seldom we get a chance to be a normal family anymore."

I was trying to digest her words when Suzy reappeared, looking for the silverware. Then Carly had me traipsing back and forth carrying dishes of food to the table. Before long, we were all seated at the round wooden table on the deck. I sat beside Carly, with Peter Phillip propped up on four soon-to-be-food-spattered Encyclopedia Britannicas on my other side. Then came Todd, then Suzy and Uncle Jack. They had smoked a turkey on the grill, so there was no danger of a food shortage with all the unexpected mouths.

Jack made a big ceremony of carving the enormous bird, I think because he was glad he could still do it. He passed the part of one wing that was normal drumstick size to Peter Phillip and the other to Suzy. There was a lot of other food on the table: some kind of potato dish with cheese, green beans, corn on the cob. By the time I thought to cut the corn off the cob for little, nearly toothless Peter Phillip, Todd had already done it. In fact, he managed to handle the kids on either side of him with a smoothness I found astonishing. Where had he learned these skills? Not in a six-month, failed marriage. I had never asked Carly what had happened, but I had seen no pictures of grandchildren spring up around the house, which had led me to believe he hadn't produced one. Maybe he had a girlfriend with kids.

I tried not to watch him throughout dinner. Uncle Jack served some kind of lovely white wine with our meal, of which I probably drank more than my share. I feared I was turning into an alcoholic. He and Carly kept the conversation flowing, mainly about neutral stuff, like the work they were having done on the house. A house on the beach required constant maintenance. Sun and salt and blowing sand took an enormous toll on the exterior. Deck boards constantly required replacing, and nails seemed to work themselves up overnight to trip the unwary. They were excited about all that was under way: paint, new roof, new deck railing.

It was so wonderful to hear them happily making plans for the future that a few times I looked over at Todd and grinned before I could catch myself, a grin that faded abruptly when I realized where it was directed. The second time it happened, he looked puzzled and . . . hurt, maybe.

Still, their enjoyment carried dinner, that and the kids. Peter Phillip was wearing most of his by the end of the meal. Todd picked the food off his bib and wiped the worst of it from his face.

Carly rose and rested her hand on Uncle Jack's shoulder. "Why don't you two take the kids down to the beach for a little while?" she asked, looking from Todd to me.

My mouth fell open. What was going on here? I felt sabotaged. I dared a glance at Todd, but his face was expressionless. I decided in that moment that I wouldn't want to play poker with him.

"I—uh—it's getting kind of late," I stammered lamely. "Why don't I help you clean up and then head home?"

"Nonsense," Carly said briskly. "Jack can help me. He's making a special dessert and it will take a few minutes. Humor me," she added, when I made no move to get up from the table.

My mood of the morning came back tenfold. With belligerence that would have taught Darlene's twins a thing or two, I scraped back my chair. "All right," I muttered, lifting Peter Phillip off his encyclopedias and grabbing Suzy's hand.

I didn't exactly drag her down the deck stairs. Still, when she almost lost her footing it was Todd, who was a step behind me, who scooped her up in his arms. On the beach, I deposited Peter Phillip on the soft sand back from the water's edge. He happily toddled over and began looking for fiddler crab holes. It was a game we played on the dunes behind our houses. He would cover each hole with a shell, thinking he had the crab well and truly trapped. Too many Bugs Bunny cartoons, no doubt. I flopped down on the sand beside him.

Todd had put Suzy down and was kneeling, untying her shoes, which he placed side by side on the sand up from the water. He was wearing shorts and sandals with a t-shirt that read "Sebastian Inlet Beach Patrol." I wondered idly if he was really part of the volunteer organization that helped protect the endangered turtle population, or if it was one of those shirts they sold in tourist shops. In a way, it bothered me that I no longer knew him well enough to know. He removed his sandals and placed them next to Suzy's, which seemed to delight her for some reason. Then he took her hand and started walking down the beach away from Peter Phillip and me. For the first time, I realized he might be as uncomfortable with our forced togetherness as I was.

It was curious watching them walking down the beach side by side. Suzy was tall for her age. It could almost have been him and me so many years ago when he first walked into my life. Every few yards or so, they would squat down on the beach to examine some mysterious item deposited there by the outgoing tide, just as he used to do with me when I was fourteen. I could tell that they were talking, and I wondered what they found to talk about. What had he and I talked about during all those years of beach walking? Everything and nothing. Our fears. Hopes and plans.

A little of the early-evening brightness faded at that thought. I tore my gaze away from them, looking around me for Peter Phillip. He was still single-mindedly covering the crab holes with shells. What a lovely, self-contained child he was.

I looked up at the deck, but there was no sign of Carly or my uncle. What in the hell were they making, I wondered impatiently. The last time she'd made a special dessert was the night my uncle had told Darlene about the Parkinson's. What little goodie did they have in store for me tonight? Open-heart surgery?

I was shocked at my own thoughts. What in the world was the matter with me? Where was this mean streak coming from? I had always thought I was a better person that this. I remembered Stella's assertion that I needed to get laid. Maybe she was right. It had been a long time. I'd start looking around for a likely candidate first thing tomorrow. There was Paul at

Fischer's, of course, but he wanted love and I was looking for sex without complications. It wouldn't be fair. There were also a couple of decent-looking guys at the paper who probably wouldn't say no given the chance, but did I really want to get something started there? Something I had no intention of continuing?

"You look awfully grim," Todd said from beside me.

I jumped. I hadn't noticed them returning. He was standing not two feet away. My eyes traveled up the length of his body. I took in his bare, sand-covered feet, his muscular calves covered with blond, near-white hair that looked luminescent against his tanned skin. My eyes trailed higher. I swallowed hard, forcing my eyes up to his chest, his shoulders, made for lying one's head on. His arms in the short-sleeved Sebastian Inlet shirt. How well I remembered his arms.

Finally, after what seemed a year but was probably only a couple of seconds, I met his eyes. Swallowed again. "I was think-ing about—" I almost blurted out "getting laid," but at the last instant substituted "work."

"Not very pleasant thoughts."

We both looked around for Suzy. She had joined Peter Phillip in his game of "trap the crab." They both seemed to have forgot-ten we were there.

Todd joined me on the sand, turning so that he was facing the dunes and could watch the kids. I was facing the ocean, so it was like we were sitting on one of those old courting benches. I banished the thought the instant it appeared.

He wrapped his arms around his legs. "They're really cute kids," he remarked as if continuing an earlier conversation. "Whose are they?"

"My next-door neighbor's."

He looked surprised. "Stella has kids?"

I was stunned for a minute. Then I remembered Stella telling me she'd seen him around the inlet. I was tempted to ask just how well he knew Stella, but it was none of my business—just like so many things were none of my business. "Other side. Joyce and Leon Crenshaw."

"Oh. Suzy told me she's nine. How old is Peter Phillip?"

"Suzy is eight," I corrected. "Peter Phillip is two and a half."

Todd chuckled. "She's in a hurry to grow up. Like someone else I remember."

I thought of Freddie. Too much like someone else you remember. I said nothing aloud. He was right. I'd always been in such a flaming hurry to get older. That desire had died when I passed twenty. Now the years were beginning to speed by. It seemed like Christmas was last week.

"She's the one who has the crush on Freddie," he said, his voice reflecting his sudden realization. When I looked at him, he said, "Freddie told me."

"Did the two of you have a big chuckle over it?" I asked caustically.

He looked puzzled again. "No. Freddie told me he thinks she's cute."

I snorted. "Lucky Suzy."

He waited a minute before asking, "Are you upset about something?"

No, fool, I thought. I'm just thrilled to be sitting here on the beach with you where we spent almost four years building a relationship that I thought would last a lifetime and . . . "No." My voice sounded a little breathless from the intensity of anger that swept over me. It caught me totally off guard. I knew I'd harbored some residual resentment from his brutally abandoning me, but just then, at that moment, I felt as if it had all happened yesterday instead of eight years ago, and I was suddenly much too close to tears. My face must have looked gruesome, too, because he clearly didn't believe me.

"Hey, listen. I'm sorry if I said something that upset you," he began.

The dam burst. "Oh, will you stop with all that polite crap. God, I'm sick to death of it. Please. Thank you. Oh, excuse me," I mocked. "Real people don't talk that way, you know? Not real people who know each other. Strangers, maybe."

He was staring at me, shocked by my outburst. Suddenly his brow cleared. "Isn't that what you want us to be?" he asked quietly. "Polite strangers?"

I wanted to slap him for being so smug and so obtuse at the same time. I wanted to slap him for no reason at all. I wanted to run away as far and as fast as I could. I jumped to my feet, giving him one last withering look before I stalked away to collect Peter Phillip and Suzy. He stayed where he was on the beach, staring after us. I couldn't make out his facial expression, and I had the good sense to be glad I couldn't.

Up at the house, I had my mouth open to tell Carly I was leaving when she walked out of the kitchen carrying an enormous cake, frosted with whipped cream and decorated with strawberries. Across the top were candles that spelled out my name. My uncle was right behind her.

"Happy birthday, honey," Uncle Jack said, putting his arm around my shoulders. "I know it's four days early, but I was afraid you couldn't make it next weekend. Well, what do you think? I made it myself. It's still your favorite, isn't it?"

Carly was watching me anxiously, unsure from my face what my reaction was going to be. The kids saw nothing but the beautiful red and white cake she was holding.

I buried my face against my uncle's chest as a sob tore out of me. I knew that he wasn't afraid I couldn't make it next weekend; he was afraid his symptoms would be back. He was afraid he couldn't make it. "It's—it's beautiful, Uncle Jack," I stammered. All at once I was Suzy's age again and he was my universe. "It's still my favorite. It's beautiful," I said again.

Now the kids were watching me. Suzy's brow was furrowed, and Peter Phillip's lower lip began to quiver.

I let go of my uncle and knelt down in front of them. "It's all right," I assured them. "I'm just happy. See?" I pasted a big smile on my face. It was probably grotesque, but Peter Phillip seemed satisfied. He traced the smile with his finger. Suzy seemed less sure.

I reached out and hugged them both. "Now we're going to have my birthday party. Okay?"

Carly handed the cake to my uncle, then took Suzy and Peter Phillip's hands. "Will you help me bring in the presents?" she asked, leading them into the other room.

As soon as the cake was in my uncle's hands, the tremors began again. I started to ask him if I could help, but suddenly I knew he needed to do this by himself. I tried to stay close without hovering. His concentration was intense, which only seemed to make the tremors worse. Finally, he put the cake down on the table and turned to me with an embarrassed smile. He was trying to hide his obvious pride in having accomplished this feat that would have been meaningless to him a few years ago.

My heart felt like someone had reached into my chest and wrenched it in half. I walked over to him and put my arms around him, resting my head on his shoulder. "I love you, Uncle Jack," I whispered, letting the tears run down my cheeks unchecked.

Just then I caught sight of Todd standing just outside the sliding glass doors where he had obviously witnessed the whole thing. His face was a reflection of what I was feeling—intense sorrow, boundless love, and a slowly breaking heart.

The birthday party was a huge success. Carly had made me a copy of the dress I'd seen in the boutique window. I'd casually mentioned it to her, along with the fact that it had cost more than I made in a week, newspaper work not being known for its great salaries. The copy was perfect, and I loved it more than I ever could have the original. My uncle had bought me a leather-bound edition of Mark Twain's *Man Is the Only Animal That Blushes, or Needs To.* It seemed appropriate for that evening. Todd hadn't gotten me a present. I was grateful beyond words.

Peter Phillip curled up in my uncle's lap and was asleep by the time we finished our coffee. When I started making time-to-go motions, he looked over at Todd. "Will you carry him to the car?"

I protested that I could carry him, but Todd had already taken him in his arms. "You have Suzy and your presents to see to. I'll get the boy."

I hugged them goodnight at the top of the front stairs. The yard was dark and mostly soft sand, difficult for walking. "I love you both," I told them. "Thank you for my wonderful birthday surprise."

Peter Phillip didn't awaken when Todd strapped him into his car seat. He backed out of the Jeep and stood aside while Suzy strapped herself in.

As I started to get into the driver's seat, he touched my arm. "Happy birthday, dwarf," he said, leaning down quickly and brushing his lips over mine before turning and walking back toward the house.

I stood stunned, staring after him. The intensity of the moment had paralyzed me. How could a word so innocent, a kiss so gentle . . .

When he reached the front porch, he turned to look down at me. I felt gooseflesh spread down my arms and legs. With concerted effort, I climbed into the Jeep and found the ignition. After a minute, I was able to turn the key. Then I used all my powers of concentration to back the Jeep into the hard-packed turnaround.

I don't know how I made it home that night. I don't remember much of the drive, and not because of the wine I'd had earlier. That had worn off before the birthday celebration began. The drug affecting me was preoccupation, to a degree I'd never experienced before. Whatever thoughts were going through my head were traveling somewhere below the conscious level. It was as if a large part of my mind had clocked out and taken the rest of the night off.

It lasted until after I tucked Suzy into the guest room bed. Peter Phillip didn't awaken when I changed his sandy clothes for his pajamas. He snuggled up with his Pooh blanket and his teddy bear. It struck me that I wouldn't have minded having my old buddy Teddy in bed with me right then.

Even though Suzy was half asleep when I tucked her in, she hugged my neck and kissed me. "I like Todd," she told me groggily.

I groaned inwardly. "So do I," I told her miserably. So, God forbid, do I, I repeated silently.

I walked into the living room, knowing that sleep was a long way away. I couldn't leave the kids alone for my usual walk on the beach to the jetty. I considered having a glass of wine, then a cup of coffee, but I really wanted neither. I thought about reading or watching TV, but those activities didn't appeal to me. I wanted nothing. And everything.

I heard a soft tap at my front door and glanced at the clock. Eight-fifteen. Surely it couldn't be Joyce and Leon back so soon.

My front door was inset with frosted jalousies, the kind you could roll open to catch the breeze. I knew it wasn't designed for security, but Cape Canaveral wasn't exactly a high-crime area. I flipped on the front porch light and could see the outline of a man. A big man. I knew who it was before I opened the door. What I didn't know was what he was doing at my front door.

"What are you doing here?" I demanded, swinging the door open wide. It was more an accusation than a question.

Todd stood under the porch light looking pagan, all golden muscles and manhood. He held up the little overnight bag Joyce had packed with the kids' change of clothes. "I thought you might need this."

"Oh." I had totally forgotten the bag. "Well. Thank you."

He handed the bag to me. "Can I come in?"

I searched my mind for an excuse to refuse, then I immediately felt embarrassed by my ungraciousness. He had, after all, just driven twenty-eight miles to bring me what he thought I needed for the kids—the things I'd forgotten in my haste to get away from him. "For a minute. I was just getting ready to go to bed."

His eyes swept over my clothes and came to rest on the clock on the living room wall.

"To read," I added, making it worse. Impatient with my bungling, I held the door open and motioned him into the room. "Would you like some coffee?"

"Sure."

I started for the kitchen and he followed. The room, which had felt spacious just that morning, seemed crowded with him in it. I was painfully aware of him watching me measure coffee into the filter basket, then adding water to the coffee maker. This is your stepcousin, I reminded myself. That's all he is. A relative by marriage. An accidental family member. Who kissed you tonight, my other side countered. A brotherly birthday kiss, I argued. Then why did you turn to stone? I wished they'd both shut up.

"Are you heading back tonight?" I asked, more to drown out the voices in my head than because I wanted an answer.

He nodded. "Early shift tomorrow. But I'll be back."

I nodded absently.

"To stay."

My head came up. "To stay?"

"I'm moving back. I put in an application with Melbourne PD a little over six months ago. The job just came through."

I tore my gaze from his face. Automatically I poured two cups of coffee as I sorted through the implications. He would be around all the time, which would be awkward, but it also meant that Carly would have his support full time, which was good. For her. Probably for my uncle, too. "Where will you be living?"

He settled down in a kitchen chair, stretching his legs out in front of him. "With Mom and Jack for a while. I asked them if I could. Told them it would be cheaper for me to pay them rent than get some overpriced apartment."

I knew immediately what he wasn't saying, that his staying there would keep him close at hand for the increasingly frequent emergencies, and that he would be paying them money that they could really use right now. I was a little ashamed that I hadn't thought of it.

"I know it will make it a little more awkward for you to visit them," he added.

I gritted my teeth, waiting for the polite remark about staying out of my way.

"Tough," he finished.

It took a minute for the word to sink in. I blinked. "Tough?"

He nodded, taking a healthy sip of his coffee and, I hoped, burning his mouth. "You blew it tonight, Christie."

"I blew what?"

He looked at me over the rim of his cup. "You blew it."

"I don't know what you're talking about."

"Your anger." He took another, more cautious sip of coffee.

"You wouldn't still be angry if you didn't still care."

"I'm not angry."

"Right, and I suppose you're going to tell me that kiss meant nothing to you."

I felt the hated flush spreading up my neck. "That kiss back at the house?" His eyes dropped to my mouth, and my lips began to tingle. "That was a birthday kiss. Nothing more."

"It moved you, same as it moved me."

"Don't make something out of it that it wasn't."

"I'm not." His eyes drilled into me, making me see things in myself that I would rather pretend weren't there.

Furious with him, and myself, I jumped up from the table. "This is a ridiculous conversation. I'm tired and I want to go to bed, so I'll ask you to leave if you don't mind." Then my eyes came to rest on the kids' bag on the table. I pointed. "That was just an excuse, wasn't it?"

He shrugged. "Sure. I looked inside. No pajamas or anything."

"That was cheap and dishonest. Even for you."

"It was expedient," he countered.

The air in the room seemed to shimmer red. I gritted my teeth, determined not to show anger again. "I'd appreciate it if you'd leave now."

He got slowly to his feet and loomed over me. Suddenly I was afraid of what he might do. I took a half step backward, but he just picked up his cup from the table and carried it to the sink. Carly had trained him well. Then he came back until he was standing less than a foot from me, invading my space. "I'll go," he said, "but I'll be around. From now on. And you'll know it."

I looked up at him. As I did, his nickname for me floated into my mind. "Is that a threat?"

"Yes, ma'am," he said, tipping an imaginary hat. "That is indeed a threat."

I pointed at the door. "Please leave."

He smiled an infuriating smile. "Okay. For now. But I'll see you soon."

It took all my control not to kick him in the ass on the way out the door, but even I knew better than to assault a cop. Besides, I was afraid it would make him angry. I didn't want him angry. Angry was unpredictable.

Once he was out the door, I locked it and leaned against it, shaking. How dare he use that phony excuse to get into my house? Just to make me uncomfortable. That's the only reason he'd come, and to insinuate that I still cared about him. What monumental self-deception. His remark about the kiss had stung because it was true. So what? Hormones had no taste—and no feelings. Lust was lust. It was not love and it was not caring. It was wanting, base and primitive. That was entirely different. I hadn't cared about the man in over a decade. It was ludicrous to think that I'd suddenly start carrying a torch again. I wasn't eight years old like Suzy, and I wasn't eighteen, either. I was older and wiser now, entirely too smart to love a man who had already yanked the rug out from under my future once. What kind of fool did he take me for?

I stomped across the kitchen and, picking up his cup in two fingers, put it in the dishwasher. Then I turned off all the lights and went to bed.

When the alarm went off at six, I had been asleep for an hour and thirty-five minutes and felt like someone had dumped a pail of sand under each eyelid. At least during my brief sleep, I hadn't dreamed. Thank God for that.

I peeked into the guest room before I got into the shower. The kids were still sleeping. Something else to be grateful for. I didn't particularly want to deal with kids this morning, and certainly not before a shower and coffee.

I heard a knock on the door just as I stepped out of the shower and wrapped a towel around my hair. Joyce. It had to be.

I wrapped myself in a terrycloth robe and walked barefoot to the door. The outline through the jalousies was that of a man. A big man. I flung open the door sputtering with anger. I must have looked like a mad killer, because Leon stepped back and almost fell off the front porch.

"Oh." I clutched my robe around me. "Leon. Come in. The kids. Uh—come on in."

Mortified, I led the way into the guest room. Suzy was sitting up on the edge of the bed. Peter Phillip was still asleep.

Leon, once he got over his shock, looked haggard. He had dark circles under his eyes, and his skin had a loose, unhealthy look from his night of debauchery. I was pretty sure that, pill notwithstanding, May would bring a little brother or sister for the kids.

I was entirely too distracted to tease him about it, and he did nothing to encourage conversation. Within minutes, he had both kids up and dressed and out the door. I was grateful for the silence and grateful that I had a job to go to, one that would occupy my mind totally.

No one was in the newsroom when I arrived. I wasn't surprised. It seemed like little news occurred on Monday morning, unless there was a launch at the Cape or a particularly spectacular crash on one of the bridges. The excitement happened later in the week or on weekends, which was why so few reporters were in. Most of them had worked all weekend.

Mine was a small regional newspaper with a circulation of 55,000. Although the office was in Cocoa, we covered all of Brevard County, from Titusville to Sebastian Inlet, and most of us reported whatever came up at the time. There were no fine distinctions between crime reporters and those who covered social functions, although the guys in the newsroom repeatedly tried to foist the fluff pieces off on me or Masie Dixon, the only other female reporter on the staff. We fought it, but it was a losing battle. In retaliation, we always tried to stick them with local political pieces, the most boring of the boring.

We also did our own photography, scoped out our own leads, and, for the most part, edited our own pieces. At least we didn't have to actually print and deliver the damned things.

It was the way of small newspapers. When I'd interned at the *Miami Herald,* I had seen specialization in action. There was a reporter category for every news item. There also seemed to be editors for every category. I'm sure they printed the paper somewhere in the building, but I never found out where.

It was while I was interning that I fell in love with Edna Buchanan. She wasn't yet the *Miami Herald*'s shining star, but she was quickly making herself known. Not that I actually ever met or talked to her, but I did catch sight of her one day when she was tearing out of the building to cover some gory crime. She was the finest of the fine, fearless and unstoppable. Her stories didn't just report the surface facts; they searched for the truth under the news item and then spoke it aloud for all the world to hear. Back then, at twenty, I had wanted to be just like her. I still did, but it was kind of hard when most of the stories I was covering were about roadwork being completed and new hotels opening on the beach. Still, I was a reporter. Some day the perfect story would come along, and I would expose the truth to the entire world. I truly believed that was my mission in life.

The newsroom was pretty standard: a bunch of metal desks pushed too close together, each with a telephone and a typewriter. I scanned the notes on the bulletin board. A city council meeting Tuesday at two. Deadly. I put that one on Jake Elgin's desk. He had stuck me with a daycare center opening the week before. The fundraiser for the mayor of Cocoa, I gave to Alf Reed, a good-looking smoothie who had been making come-on sounds since the day he started at the paper. He definitely wouldn't be my choice for casual sex if I decided to take Stella's advice.

Neither would Gordon Bennett, who was forty and twice divorced and a former jock who tried to hog all the sports pieces. I hung onto the note about the Cocoa High football tryouts. It was petty, but I couldn't help it. I also took the ones about interviewing the new surgeon at Cape Canaveral Hospital, renovations at the Eau Gaulle Community Center, and a fire in the courthouse in Titusville. That should keep me running around for a while. I hung around for an hour, sipping coffee and hoping something more exciting than my chosen stories would surface.

Masie arrived at nine. Tall and blond, she looked like a cheerleader and talked like a marine. The guys hesitated to give her a hard time. She could, and did, out-cuss the best of them. Virgil breezed through, fresh-faced, with his shirtsleeves already rolled up and looking ready to tackle whatever came up. Marriage agreed with him, and he carried his self-satisfaction well. The others trickled in with less enthusiasm.

At ten o'clock, I finished my coffee, grabbed my camera, and got ready to head up to Titusville.

Virgil caught me before I got out of the door. He came out of his office holding a note in his hand. "Hey, Christie. Melbourne just hired a new officer. Want to do a profile on him?"

At first I thought it was a bad joke, then I realized Virgil probably wouldn't remember Todd from that brief meeting years ago. Too, he had no reason to link the name "Harrington" with "O'Kelly." I smiled sweetly, waving my stack of notes. "I've got my hands full. Why don't you give that one to Masie?"

Masie looked surprised, then pleased. "Okay," she said. "Sure. I'll do it." Lord, we were desperate for news.

The day passed almost pleasantly; the rest of the week was relatively uneventful. I began to think that Todd's threat was just that, a threat. I saw and heard nothing of him. I didn't ask Masie how her interview went, deciding I'd read it in the paper with the rest of the county.

Uncle Jack fell once climbing down the deck stairs to the beach, Carly told me when I called her on Thursday, but he wasn't badly hurt. He was having trouble buttoning his shirts, too. I could hear the desperation she tried to keep out of her voice and began to think again that Todd's coming might be a good thing.

Friday night I treated myself to dinner at Fischer's. I ate at the bar, staring at Paul and wishing to God I could love him. A nicer and more faithful guy would be impossible to find. I almost invited him over for a Saturday cookout and quickie, but I chickened out at the last minute. The only thing that could come out of it was his hurt feelings and my self-recriminations. Instead, I overtipped him outrageously.

I caught sight of Stella in Bernard's dining room as I was getting ready to leave, but I couldn't see whom she was with. Only our friendship made me quash my reporter's curiosity in favor of her privacy.

I ran into Alf on the way out; he had apparently been to a number of other bars on his way there. He heavy-handedly tried to get me to have a nightcap with him.

"Can't. I'm on my way out the door," I said blithely.

"Oh, come on, Christie. Just one."

"Sorry. Some other time."

"What'll it cost you? Not even the price of a drink." He took my arm and tried to turn me back toward the bar.

I heard Paul's voice behind me. "You heard Christie, Alf. She's headed home." It was a small town. Pretty much everybody knew everybody.

Alf turned and looked at Paul, then back at me. I could see his thoughts, or what passed for thoughts in his currently pickled mind, parade across his face. "Oh. It's like that is it?" When Paul stared at him stone-faced, Alf raised his hands in front of him, looking at me. "Okay. Never mind. Why didn't you tell me before?"

I smiled and patted his shoulder. Shooting a grateful glance at Paul, I escaped out the door, wishing again I could love the man as much as I liked him.

I had planned to see Uncle Jack and Carly on Saturday, but when I called, Carly casually mentioned that she expected Todd to be home that afternoon. I told her I was sorry that I wouldn't be able to make it down, that something had come up at the paper. There was no way I was going to invite another confrontation.

I was at loose ends. I spent the morning tidying my already clean house and the afternoon trying to work on my budding novel, but the words just wouldn't come. My hero seemed calculating all of a sudden, and I began to suspect he had lured the heroine into a relationship he knew wasn't going to last. I couldn't write a single love scene. Thomas—or rather, the hero—was suddenly unclear to me. I couldn't make out his face in my mind. Or, more accurately, that wasn't the face that appeared in my mind when I was writing. Maybe I wasn't a writer after all. Not a real writer, at least. Sure, I could write copy, but a book?

Discouraged, I stuffed the thirty-five pages into a drawer and started to write about Uncle Jack and Carly. Not a book or anything like that, just my recollections of their wedding and my snotty sisters. That was more like it. The words did come, and I even liked some of them, although I had to admit I came off looking like a smart-mouthed brat in print.

About eight-thirty, just as I was really getting into the swing of it, Joyce knocked on my door. As I opened it, I realized I hadn't seen her all week, not even to ask her how her date with her husband had gone. I thought she looked a little pale, but then, everyone looked bad to me these days.

"I'm sorry to bother you. I need to get the kids' clothes."

"Come on in." I swung the door wide. "I feel like I haven't seen you in ages."

She stayed on the front porch. "I've been pretty busy." She glanced over her shoulder. "In fact, I have to run right now. I just thought I'd get the kids' things."

I could tell something was wrong, but Joyce obviously didn't want to talk about it. "Sure. Just a second."

I went into the guest room and grabbed the bag Todd had brought to me. When I returned, Joyce was clearly edgy. "Thanks," she said, "for everything. Thanks." And she was gone.

I watched her hurry to her own house, noting that Leon's car wasn't there. Maybe that was it. He was due home soon. Or she'd left Peter Phillip asleep.

Puzzled, I settled back down to my story, into which Todd had crept unerringly, but my concentration was gone. Besides, I was hungry.

I fixed myself some scrambled eggs and ate them out of the skillet standing at the counter and looking out the window. Living alone did not make for good eating habits. I brewed some coffee and took it out on the patio. The night was beautiful. The ocean whispered softly on the sand, luring me down to the beach. After a few minutes, I gave in and, taking my coffee, headed north toward the jetty.

I walked along, leisurely kicking the sand and thinking about what I'd written. Putting my description of Carly on her wedding day on paper had made me realize just how much she'd changed. She had seemed so strong back then, to the fourteen-year-old child I had been, but I could see now that my uncle and his love for her were a lot of what had made her strong. From what Todd had told me about her earlier years, I could understand that she was a woman who needed a man. When her husband had died, she had married a brute and stayed with him longer than she should have.

Carly needed a man in her life to lean on, to look up to, and to admire. I had known other women like that. They weren't the happiest individuals I had ever known when the man they chose was the wrong one or when he did something to disillusion them. My uncle wasn't the wrong man, and the only thing he'd done to disillusion her was to get sick, which was hardly his fault. Still, I could see how his illness had changed her even as it had changed him. I wondered how she would handle her need for outside strength as Uncle Jack weakened. I didn't think she would have an affair. She loved my uncle too much for that, which was why his illness was killing her.

My steps slowed as the thought formed in my mind. Surely that was too dramatic. Depressing her, certainly. Upsetting her daily and probably nightly. I wondered if they still had a sex life. I could never even have thought about such a thing a few years ago, but now I could speculate about it almost clinically. I was pretty certain they'd had a dynamite sex life up until my uncle got sick. Carly was a sensual kind of woman, not the slut that Mother had accused her of being, but neither was she the prim, repressed tightass my mother had always been. Which made me wonder if my mother and Lamar had a sex life? Which made me wonder why I had sex on the brain?

I reached the jetty. Putting my cup down on the sand, I climbed onto the rocks. There was still talk about making the jetty a park and constructing some kind of boardwalk out over the rocks so people wouldn't scamper over them and fall. I hated the thought. They were taking all the fun out of life.

Grateful it was still granite under my bare feet, I picked my way out to the end and settled myself on a boulder, staring out over the water. There was magic out tonight. I could feel it in the salt breeze against my skin and hear it in the gentle slosh of the water against the rocks. The moon had risen and was spilling its liquid gold across the water, a trail that looked as if it would lead—or point the way—to heaven. I felt the hair on my arms prickle and knew I was being watched, and I knew by whom.

I turned and looked behind me. At first I didn't see him. He was dressed in dark clothes and sitting absolutely still a couple of rocks away. My preoccupation had been so complete that I hadn't heard him approach. That, or he moved with the stealth of a cat burglar. I could see him by turning my head slightly. His eyes held mine for a long moment.

"I don't appreciate being stalked," I said finally.

"I'm not stalking you."

"Why don't you go away?"

"Because I love you."

I felt like the night had sucked the air out of my lungs.

"I do, you know. I always have."

That gave me back my powers of speech. "No, I don't know, and I don't care."

"Liar."

Silence.

"I ended up married because of you."

"What?"

"It's true."

I turned and studied his unmoving form. "This ought to be really good. Tell me how you ended up married because of me."

"It was simple. I was horny as hell for you day and night and

I took it out on some other poor girl."

"Great," I spat out. "That crap about man's needs. So that was my fault."

"Not your fault, but it was because of you."

I suddenly realized I had suspected it all along. "Judging by the suddenness of your marriage, I guess she got pregnant. How noble of you."

"I married her when she told me she was pregnant with my child."

"So why were you divorced six months later?"

"Five. She lied. She told me she miscarried, but I talked to her doctor. She was never pregnant."

I felt sick, but he'd never know it. "Poor baby. Did it hurt you badly?"

"Yes."

"Good."

"Mainly because it hurt you badly."

"I survived the loss."

"So did I, but that doesn't mean I don't regret it every day."

"Too bad. Too late," I shot back.

"It's not, you know."

"Yes . . . it is," I said, the heat melting out of me. "I don't trust you, and I could never have a relationship with someone I didn't trust."

"You could learn to trust again."

I thought about that. "I don't think I could. I had a child's faith in you, and that child and her faith are gone."

"Then put a woman's faith in my love. It's been there since the first day I saw you standing there in your yellow dress. It's never faltered. Not even for one minute."

He remembered my dress. I shoved away the thought. "Those are just words. They're meaningless."

"I love you. That's not meaningless."

"Maybe not to you." I got to my feet. "Go away, Todd," I said, starting back toward the beach. "Let it go. It's over. Dead. Finished."

I passed within six inches of where he was sitting, but he made no move to stop me. I was almost to the sand when I heard him say, "No, it's not. Not by a long shot."

I decided to let him have the last word.

I let myself into the house and locked the door behind me. I took a bath and tried to soak out some of the knots in my emotions. Then I crawled into bed, falling asleep the minute my head touched the pillow.

The next morning, I awoke with a question in my head, a question I had asked many years ago. "Why is one of us always running away from the other?" I brutally quashed the answer before it could fully form in my mind.

I found my sandy coffee cup sitting on my front porch with a note stuffed in it. It read, "You love me, too, and that's not meaningless to either of us."

Sunday, I spent in Cocoa, looking into a story about a shooting on the infamous Highway 520. It was the two-lane road that was the main route between Orlando and the coast until the Bee Line Expressway was built.

The county was laid out like a ladder, with US 1 and A1A forming the outside supports. Causeways crossing the rivers formed the rungs. US 1 took you north to south to the cities of Titusville, Cocoa, Rockledge, Eau Gaulle, and Melbourne. If you crossed the causeways, they led to Cape Canaveral, Cocoa Beach, Satellite Beach, and Indialantic, which dumped you onto Melbourne Beach. You covered a lot of territory trying to cover Brevard County.

The shooting on 520 was pretty straightforward. A trucker passing on the two-lane highway had run a motorist off the road. When the trucker had stopped to make sure the driver was okay, the livid and somewhat inebriated man had pulled out a .38 and shot him. Fortunately, it was dark and the driver couldn't shoot in daylight when he was sober. He had only clipped the driver's shoulder. Then he had fainted from sheer excitement. The truck driver had taken away the gun, covered the motorist with a blanket from the cab of his truck, and had calmly radioed for the police. He was refusing to press charges.

The motorist was being released when I arrived at the Rockledge jail. He wept and shook the truck driver's good hand, vowing never again to handle a gun. I was disgusted. Even attempted slayings in Brevard County were half-hearted.

I was able to write a decent story, though. I bought the truck driver, his arm in a sling, a cup of coffee at the Dixie Diner while he waited for his relief driver to show up from Fort Lauderdale, and he regaled me with tales of the road that I used to write several human-interest pieces. *Wounded Man Forgives Assailant. Anger Stalks Our Highways. Truckers Are a Motorist's Best Friend.* I could keep it going for a week. Virgil was pleased, although I think he would have liked it better if one of them had bled more.

Sunday night, feeling more balanced than I had for a long time, I made a decision. I would maturely and gently set Todd right about this fantasy he had of us getting back together. Locking horns with him wouldn't work. It would only make him more determined to change my mind. Instead, I would let his easily spoken and meaningless protestations of undying love flow over and off me until, eventually, even he would see the futility of it.

By one o'clock on Tuesday, that resolve was history.

Chapter 16

It started at eleven, when Masie came bouncing into the newsroom to tell me she'd made lunch plans for us with "that new cop from Melbourne."

"Why didn't you tell me he was your cousin? I didn't even know you had a fucking cousin. Shit, he's a dreamboat. He thought I was cute. I could tell. God, what a fucking dreamboat. And those eyes! Wouldn't it be fun if we were sisters-in-law? He's not married, is he? I didn't even ask him. Jesus, I must be slipping."

As always, when that string of profanity-laced cheerleader jargon came out of Masie's pert, bow-shaped mouth, it took me a moment to adjust. "Uh—he's my stepcousin—sort of—and no and no. And no to lunch, too."

She was glancing through the notes on her desk. She spun around. "What do you mean, no? You can't mean no. I already told him yes. It's too late for no."

I turned back to my typewriter. "No means no. Go by yourself."

"What's wrong with him?" she asked, suspicious now.

"Nothing. We just don't get along."

Masie came and stood in front of my desk. "What do you mean, you don't fucking get along? He told me you two are really close."

"He lied."

My desk faced the newsroom door, and I looked around

Masie as Todd and Virgil walked into the room. Todd was saying, "Thanks for cutting Christie loose, Mr. Townsend. We don't get to see much of each other anymore."

"Call me Virgil, and don't think a thing of it. I understand family. She has to eat, doesn't she? You ought to try that new sub place on US 1. They make a dynamite sandwich." He beamed at me as they reached my desk. "You kids go and have a good time."

I was furious at Todd for this latest invasion of my world, and since Virgil was within a month of my own age, I found his entire manner condescending. Also, I could feel the eyes of the entire newsroom on me. Alf, in particular, was smirking at me. "I have too much to do," I mumbled, barely giving either of them a glance.

"Nonsense." Virgil came around my desk and nearly hauled me to my feet. "Nothing that can't wait. Go have lunch with your cousin and Masie." His voice held an edge.

I didn't want to make a scene, but his heavy-handedness irritated me. "Virgil, can I talk for you for a minute?"

"When you get back."

"Now."

I thought he was going to refuse. He looked at me from under his eyebrows. Then he tilted his head toward the door.

Once around the corner, he stopped. "What? What's wrong? What's this crap about not going to lunch?"

"I don't want to go to lunch with them."

"Why not?"

I felt trapped. I certainly wasn't going to tell him the truth. "I have too much to do."

"Bull. This is PR. We need all the PR we can get with the police."

"It won't be good PR. We don't get along."

"According to him, you do."

"But—"

"Don't make a big deal of it, Christie. You don't like your cousin, that's fine. He likes you. He specifically asked if you could go to lunch with them."

"Stepcousin, and—"

"Cousin. Stepcousin. What's the difference? Look, Christie," he said, putting an arm around my shoulder, a gesture I found as condescending as his words had been, "I'm not asking you to love him. I'm not even asking you to have lunch with him alone. Masie will be along. So eat a sandwich. Let them get to know each other. Smile. Pretend to be pleasant. God knows we need all the good relations we can get with the police."

While he was talking, he was edging me back toward the newsroom. "So," he said as he pulled me around the corner, "you have a good time."

They were all looking at me. Todd and Masie, Alf, Gordon. Even the mail guy had stopped and was waiting to see what happened. "You're right," I told Virgil. "That sounds like fun. I'll need your credit card."

I could see the color spread up around his collar, but he was smooth. He reached into his back pocket and pulled out his wallet, extracting the little green rectangle of plastic. "Sure." He handed me the card. "Have fun. Bring me the receipt," he muttered in my ear as he turned away.

I looked at Masie, who was frowning darkly at me, then Todd, whose face reflected a kind of amused admiration. I reached down beside my desk and picked up my purse. "Shall we?"

I insisted on driving. Todd climbed into the front seat and Masie, reluctantly, got in the back. Over the back seat, she managed to keep up a running conversation with Todd during the ten-minute ride. Out of pure spite, I chose the Land's End, the priciest restaurant in Cocoa. Masie raised her eyebrows at me in the rearview mirror when I pulled into the lot. "Good food,"

I said, the first words I'd spoken since we left the newsroom.

Todd made no attempt to come around and open my door. Good thing. A door handle makes a very effective weapon. Instead, he set about charming the socks off Masie. At first, I thought he was trying to make me jealous, but I had underestimated him.

He spent the salad and entree courses interviewing Masie, asking her trite and meaningless questions about the paper, while Masie basked in the glow of his attention. How did she get her stories? Which were her favorite kind? Had she always been a reporter? Then he turned to me. "How about you, Christie? Did you always want to be a reporter?"

Since he had been the one to set me on the road to a career in journalism twelve years before, I knew it was bait. "Yes." I nodded. "Since birth."

He grinned. "And what do you see as the mission of a reporter."

"To sell papers." When he looked blank, I added, "Stories equals sales equals money which, of course, equals job security. Simple."

"And that's it?"

"Close enough."

"What about all those things you used to believe in? Truth, for instance."

"I used to believe in a lot of things. Santa Claus. Truth. Justice. Loyalty." You. "I wised up."

"Sounds more bitter than wise."

"Not bitter. Realistic."

"Truth isn't realistic? Justice?"

"It's realistic to go after it. It's not realistic to expect to get it."

"Loyalty, then. Trust."

"Loyalty is in the eyes of the beholder, and trust has to be earned—and deserved."

"How can it be earned if you don't give the person a chance—"

"I believe in giving a person a chance. *One* chance. If they blow it, too bad."

"That's pretty cold."

"It's realistic. What would you suggest, allowing someone to let you down over and over? That would show a monumental lack of self-esteem."

"Would it? Or would trying again show courage?"

"It takes courage to know when to pull the plug."

Masie was so lost in our verbal tennis match that she forgot her company manners. "What the fuck are you two talking about?"

I almost burst out laughing at the look on Todd's face, but he recovered quickly. "Old family debate," he said smoothly, turning to her. "Christie and I get into it every time we get together."

"Because you won't let it go."

"And I never will," he said, giving me a look that burned through me. "Now, why don't we all order dessert since it's on your boss?"

Back at the newsroom, Todd gave me a chaste kiss on the cheek and did the same to Masie. She glowed and I glowered.

When he was gone, she rounded on me. "So what was that all about at the restaurant?"

I checked my desk to see which stories the guys had stuck me with while we were at lunch. "You mean our debate?"

"I mean all that bullshit about truth and justice."

"Amen, sister. Bullshit it is." When I looked up, she was still standing there, her arms crossed. "I warned you that we didn't get along," I said mildly.

"That wasn't 'not getting along.' That was a pitched battle. What's going on, Christie?"

"Nothing is going on. My stepcousin has some strange ideas about honor and commitment, that's all."

"I thought you were talking about truth and justice."

I waved dismissively. "Same thing."

"Hardly. I—" She broke off as my phone rang.

I snatched it up gratefully. "Newsroom. O'Kelly."

"What time are you getting home?"

It took me a minute to recognize the voice. "Stella?" She had never called me at work before.

"Yes. What time?"

"Why? What's the matter? Is it Uncle Jack?"

"It has nothing to do with your uncle."

"The house—"

"Is still standing. This is about Joyce."

"Joyce? What's wrong? Did something happen to one of the kids?"

"Not the kids. God, you ask a lot of questions!"

I had to smile at that. "I am a reporter," I reminded her. "What's wrong with Joyce?"

"I'll tell you all about it when you get home. I just want to know what time that will be."

I looked at my desk. I had to finish my trucker human-interest piece and three others for the morning edition. "Probably about seven."

"Good. That's perfect. Do you have any wine at your house?"

The question caught me off guard. "Uh—just the bottle you brought over Saturday."

"That won't do it." Pause. "Okay. I'll run up to the liquor store. See you at seven."

She hung up before I could ask what she wanted with wine. I sat for a moment, my hand resting on the receiver, trying to imagine what could have motivated Stella to call me at work.

Trying to imagine her calling about Joyce. They didn't even like each other.

When the phone rang again, it startled me. "Newsroom. O'Kelly."

"There's a fire at the Catholic Church in Rockledge," said a voice I'd recognize anywhere.

"Confirmed?"

"Yes."

I slammed down the phone and grabbed my purse and camera. "Fire in Rockledge," I yelled to no one in particular as I headed out the door.

Five hours later, I dropped my purse on my living room sofa, and then I collapsed beside it. I was filthy, sweat-covered and sooty. The fire had completely gutted the sanctuary. A priest had been injured trying to put out the flames with an altar cloth, and one fireman had been injured trying to stop him. I had raced back to the paper and pounded out the story, then had completed the other three. The human-interest piece could wait.

My eyes burned, and I was pretty sure my hair had been singed when a roof support collapsed, sending sparks shooting out ten feet. I was trying to decide if I had the energy to get back up when Stella walked in the front door. I groaned. I'd forgotten all about her.

"God, it smells in here," she said, juggling three bottles of wine and kicking the door shut behind her. "Did you burn something?"

I shook my head. "My hair. Church fire in Rockledge," I mumbled.

"Well, go get cleaned up. We have work to do."

"Too tired. I already worked."

"What kind of an attitude is that?" She sat the wine bottles down on the coffee table. "Your friend needs you."

"You don't need me."

She put her hands on her hips. "Not me. Joyce."

I pried off one shoe. "Joyce will have to wait until another day."

"Leon left her."

I came straight up off the sofa. "What?"

"Walked out on her," she said, satisfied that she had my attention. "And after you get your shower, I'll tell you all about it."

"Tell me now."

"Absolutely not. You stink. Go shower."

I hesitated, but I knew she was right. I couldn't bear to smell me, either.

The thoughts raced through my mind as I shampooed my hair. Leon and Joyce. It was impossible. I'd never seen a happier couple. Leon had always seemed satisfied, sitting on the living room couch clicking the remote. The questions formed in my mind faster than I could grasp them. When did it happen? Why? What about the kids?

That one stopped me. I closed my eyes and let the water hit me full in the face. What about the kids? What about Suzy? She adored her father. God, the poor kid. It would be easier on Peter Phillip, but the idea of that little guy growing up without his father broke my heart.

Then I caught myself. Here I was nearly weeping about their lot in life and I didn't even know if it was true. Joyce had said nothing to me. Stella's information might be wrong.

I rinsed the shampoo out of my hair and turned off the water, impatient now to get the facts. I quickly jumped into a pair of jeans and a t-shirt, not bothering with underwear.

Stella shoved a glass of wine in my hand as I walked into the kitchen. "Sit down. I fixed you a sandwich."

I had no appetite, but I ate anyway while she told me about

her friend who worked with Leon at the Cape.

"Harvey said that Leon told him he's on his own now, that he was ready for a change. He told Harvey he's got an apartment in Cocoa Beach. A bachelor pad, he called it." She made a gagging noise. "Apparently he's excited about living the single life again."

"That bastard!" I gulped my wine and reached for the bottle.

Stella pulled it away. "You have to keep a clear head. It's Joyce who needs to get drunk."

"Joyce doesn't drink."

"She will tonight," Stella said confidently. "We're going over to see her."

"Uh—" I looked at Stella, who was dressed in her usual shorts and halter-top. Although this one covered more of her than usual, it still didn't cover much. I was quite certain Joyce wouldn't want to say anything while Stella was around, and I wasn't sure how to tell her without hurting her feelings. "I'm not sure that's a good idea."

"Because she hates my guts? No problem. I'm going to soften her up." She reached behind her and grabbed a vase of flowers off the counter. Beside it was a yellow Whitman's Sampler box. The big one. She must have gone home to get them while I was in the shower. "You carry the wine. She has wine glasses, doesn't she? Oh, never mind. We can drink it out of tumblers if we have to."

"I don't think—" I stopped. She was right. "Oh, what the hell. Let's go."

Stella lit a cigarette the minute we were out of my house and puffed on it madly until we reached Joyce's front porch, where she flicked it into the bushes.

Joyce opened the door immediately at my soft knock, almost as if she were expecting someone. Her face said it wasn't us. She looked from one to the other, taking in Stella's attire, the wine, the flowers and candy. "What . . . ?"

"He's a bastard and we hate his rotten guts," Stella said, thrusting the flowers at her.

Joyce looked at her in amazement, then at me. Then her face crumbled and she collapsed in my arms.

"Oh, Joyce. I'm so sorry," I said, leading her back into the house and to the couch. "I had no idea. If Stella hadn't told me . . ." I sat close beside her, feeling awkward in the face of her tears.

"He—he j-just walked out," she sobbed, hiding her face in her hands. "He—he said it wasn't me," she looked up at me, her eyes swimming. "But if it wasn't me, why did he go? I mean, why would he go and leave the kids—" That brought on fresh sobs. I feared she was going to make herself sick if she didn't calm down.

Just then, the ever-practical Stella came back into the room carrying a box of Kleenex and a water glass full of wine. "Here, honey," she said, handing a tissue to Joyce, "blow your nose and drink this."

She vanished again as Joyce mindlessly did as she was told, making a face when she took the first sip of wine. She took another.

Stella reappeared, carrying two more glasses and an open bottle. She sat on the carpet on Joyce's other side. She half-filled each of the glasses and handed one to me. "He's right. It isn't you," she told Joyce. "It's that goddamn male menopause thing everyone writes about these days. These guys decide they're in a married rut and that they can do better. Then they get out there and realize no one else wants them. It makes me sick."

I wasn't at all sure Stella's diatribe was doing Joyce any good. I took her hand. "What did he say?"

"He said—" Her eyes cut to Stella. She gulped the rest of the wine in her glass, making a face. Stella refilled it. "He said he was in a rut, that he needed to find out who he was and what was im—important to him." Her lower lip trembled. "I thought *we* were important to him." The tears flowed unchecked down her face. "I had no idea he was unhappy. He never said—I mean, I thought—" She shook her head hard, as if denying what she was feeling.

She looked back at me. "He told me that night he took me out to dinner. I thought—" She choked on a sob. After a minute, she said, "I thought it was a special occasion, like he'd gotten a raise or something. Then he told me he was leaving. I didn't believe him. I mean, just like that. It's over and I'm leaving. I knew it wasn't a joke. He was too serious for that, but I kept thinking he'd change his mind." She took a deep, shuddering breath. "He drove me home. I think I was in shock or something. He wouldn't let me drive. The next morning, he took me back to my car. He must have packed while I was at work that day. He left that night as soon as I got home. He already had an apartment and everything." She studied the wine in her hand as if it might contain answers. "He had it all planned out, and I didn't know anything about it."

She looked so much like a bewildered child that it was all I could do not to wrap my arms around her, but that would have broken both of us down. "What are you going to do?" I asked gently.

"I—don't know. Nothing, I guess. I've put the kids in daycare, but it doesn't open until seven-thirty. The hospital's being wonderful about it. Oh, they don't know what happened. Just that I'm having to use daycare. They agreed to adjust my hours."

"What did you tell the kids?"

Her eyes filled again "I haven't told them anything. They think Daddy's on a trip somewhere. I—I couldn't . . ."

Stella handed her another tissue. "Is he paying for it? The daycare?"

"Oh, yes," Joyce said bitterly. "He told me he'd take care of his obligations. Obligations! They aren't obligations, they're our children. Even if he doesn't love me anymore, how can he turn his back on them? Why didn't he have a damned affair or something?"

I was shocked. "You don't mean that. You wouldn't have put up with that."

"As opposed to this?" she demanded. Then she sighed. "I don't know what I mean anymore. I don't know what I would have put up with. I just want my husband back. I want my life back."

"After this?" I asked, incredulous. "You'd take him back after this?"

Joyce looked up, her face gray with pain. "Yes. I'd take him back after this. I love him, Christie, and I want him back. Does that shock you?"

"Yes," I said softly. "I'm sorry, but yes." I bit my lip, but the question demanded to be asked. "What about your pride?"

If possible, Joyce looked sadder. "I don't give a damn about my pride. Don't you understand? I love my husband, and I want him back. I want my children's father and I want my marriage. I'd forgive an awful lot to have those things back."

Stella offered her more wine, but Joyce shook her head. "The kids might wake up and need me," she explained.

"Are you going to file for legal separation?" Stella asked.

"He is."

"No. You do it," Stella ordered. When Joyce looked surprised, she added, "Let him think you're taking control of the situation. It'll intimidate the hell out of him."

"I don't want to intimidate him. Besides, I don't know that he'll go through with it. He might change his mind."

"And he might not," Stella said with barely concealed exasperation. "Listen, you want him back?" When Joyce nodded, she said, "Then show him the woman he married isn't the wimp he thought she was. Shake him up a little. Whatever he thinks you'd do, don't do it. Throw him a few curves. That'll get his attention."

I heard Peter Phillip whimper in the other room. Joyce looked in that direction. "He's having nightmares. I haven't told either of them anything, but they both know something's wrong."

"Kids aren't dummies," Stella said. "They sense things we don't. Get your fight back, gal. Then those kids will tune into your strength. That's what they need right now, a mommy who's tough and determined."

I could see that Joyce was taking her seriously. I knew it was good advice, but I didn't see how Joyce could be strong enough to pull it off. I did see, though, that she wanted us gone. Stella must have seen it too, because she got to her feet.

"Go take care of him now," she said, leaning down and hugging Joyce. Both of them seemed surprised at the gesture. "Go in there with fire in your eyes and anger in your heart. The man's a bastard and a weakling. You're too good for him. When he comes back, remember that and make him pay."

She looked down at me. "You coming?" she asked.

I reached over and hugged Joyce. "Call me if you need anything. I mean that. Anything."

"I will."

"You promise?"

Joyce gave me a watery smile, but her posture had straightened. "I promise." She looked up at Stella. "Thank you, both of you, for coming over."

Stella smiled at her. "I'll be around if you need me, and you probably will. Just come on over."

Joyce nodded.

Stella looked at the bottle of wine on the coffee table. "You going to drink that?"

"I don't drink," Joyce said with a watery laugh.

"Good." Stella disappeared into the kitchen, returning with two unopened bottles. "No sense in letting this go to waste."

We crossed the lawn to my house. I expected Stella to come in, but she just handed me one of the unopened bottles.

I was still reeling from what Joyce had told us. "I don't know what she'll do," I said as we reached my front porch.

"She'll make it. She's a tough broad."

"I don't know—"

"Neither does she, but she is. You wait and see. She'll need some coaching, but she'll be okay."

"How can you be so sure?"

"Been there," she said offhandedly. "Goodnight, kid."

I watched her disappear out of the glow of the porch light. Been there? Stella?

I opened my door and went inside, automatically going to the kitchen and putting the bottle of wine on the kitchen counter. I stood for a long time, staring out the kitchen window into the blackness, thinking about Leon and what he'd done, about Joyce's words, "I thought we were important." I thought about his bachelor pad he'd already had ready and about him wanting to find himself. As Joyce's words played through my mind, a rage that was as indistinct as it was violent began to build inside me. Goddamn selfish pig! Tears filled my eyes, blurring the picture in my mind of Suzy and Peter Phillip crawling into Leon's lap, trusting him, believing in him.

I shook my head, but I couldn't shake out the memory of Leon picking up the kids the morning after his "date" with Joyce, knowing that he was going home to pack and walk out of their lives. They were obligations now. He had looked rough; I had thought he was tired from a night of lovemaking. How pitiful.

I opened the bottle of wine and poured a glass, chugging it before I walked out onto the patio. And Joyce, poor misguided Joyce, wanted him back. Despite his not wanting her, despite his wanting to try out the single life and, obviously, single women, she wanted him back. What was wrong with her? Where was her pride, her dignity? How could he be so important to her that she'd undergo any humiliation to have him? Was she like Carly, a woman who needed a man in her life?

No, I answered my own question. Joyce didn't want a man in her life; she wanted Leon in her life. She adored him. I had seen it a thousand times in the little things she did for him, in the way she looked at him. I couldn't imagine why. He was a nice enough guy, but he'd never seemed particularly bright or special to me. He was to Joyce, though. No one but Leon would do, and now he was gone.

The situation made me furious. I slammed my wine glass down on a patio table and headed for the jetty. I wanted to rail at something, and the sea was tough enough to take it. At the edge of the rocks, I jumped up and ran with angry abandon to the end, daring the rocks to trip me, daring the sea to make them slick. I wanted to fight. Something. Someone.

Luckily, he didn't disappoint me. As I reached the end, I heard quick steps behind me. I spun around, holding out my arms to balance myself, realizing suddenly that I had drunk more wine than I realized. "Great!" I yelled over the waves. "Just what I need. My own personal watchdog."

"What's the matter, Christie?" he asked, stopping two feet away from me.

"Matter? Nothing's the matter. What the hell could be the matter? And what are you doing here?"

"The fire. I wanted to know how it went."

"It went just lovely. Nice tip, thank you very much."

He was watching me closely. "Did something happen there?"

"Not much. Two injured. That's what sells papers, right?"

"What are you so angry about?"

"Angry? Me? Ha!"

"Tell me, honey. What's the matter?"

It was all the opening I needed. Visions of Joyce's ragged face floated in front of my eyes. I thought of Todd wiping the food off Peter Phillip's face and carrying his sleeping form to my Jeep. I saw Todd walking along the beach with Suzy, their heads together as he explained things to her. It all interwove in my mind.

The tide was coming in, and I felt a wave slosh over the rock I was standing on. I felt my footing give and held out my arms for balance. I glared at him, hating him more in that moment than I'd ever hated another human being. "Don't you dare 'honey' me, you bastard! You're just like the rest of them. Just turn your back on commitments, right? Who the hell cares if you made a promise? Who cares if someone else is counting on you? Just walk away, right? What'll it cost you? No big deal. You're sure she'll take you back anyway, so what does it matter? Just go out there and screw anything in skirts. When you get done, you can come back home figuring we'll just drop everything and take you back. Isn't that what you all want?"

He took a step toward me, watching me like I was a ticking, brown-wrapped package. "What are you talking about? Who are you talking about?"

"You! Leon! All of you! What difference does it make? You're all just alike. Goddamn selfish pigs! I hate all of you!"

I felt my footing start to give again. I'm not certain what happened next. I think Todd reached out to steady me. I don't know what I thought he was doing. He was standing balanced between two rocks that were water-slick, too, and his footing was none too sure as he reached for me. I lashed out with my hand and arm to ward him off and caught him off guard. I felt a solid connection with flesh and muscle, then nothing. I fell hard on both knees on the rock. I half saw him fall, and heard the crack of something striking rock. It registered that it might have been his head.

In that instant, I believed I'd killed him. I jumped to my feet, almost falling again. Blood was pouring down both legs from my skinned knees. I didn't feel them. I looked down into the water and thought I saw what might have been his shirt.

"Dear God," I cried, jumping off the rocks into the water. I got a handful of fabric and lugged it up to the surface. I tried to get what I thought was the neck of his shirt, but in another minute, I felt him swimming, pulling us both toward the rocks. Still in the water, he pushed me up on a rock and then hauled himself out of the water, choking and gasping.

"Oh my God, are you all right?" I knelt on the rocks beside him, completely unaware of the pain in my legs. My hands traveled over his shoulders, his head, and came away bloody. "Oh, Todd, you're hurt. Oh, God, I'm so sorry. Oh, Todd, I didn't mean—oh God, oh God, tell me you're all right."

He did. His lips came down on mine hard, as if he were punishing me for what I'd done. I returned the kiss in kind, making atonement for almost killing him. His arms came around me and mine went around him. We held each other as if our lives depended on it. Then we were frantic. Hungry. My hands examined him again as my lips devoured him. His back, his shoulders, his arms that were finally holding me. They crushed me to him, and I wanted nothing more in life than that, to be in his arms forever.

After a long time, his kiss became more gentle. He nibbled my lips, trailed kisses along my jawline and down my neck. I was having nothing to do with it. I felt frantic with needing him. I dug my fingers into the muscles in his arms. I could feel him shaking. Or was it me? I felt the wonder of it, the power.

"My God, I love you," he murmured into my mouth. "I love you more than life."

I knew he did, because I loved him the same way. The years vanished in an instant, and I was sixteen and standing on the beach, wanting him with every atom of my being. But this time it was different. This time I'd have him. Nothing was going to stop me.

"Come on," I said, getting to my feet and trying to pull him to a standing position. When he was upright, I reached up and touched his forehead. It was still seeping blood. "Can you make it to my house?"

He looked down at me, reaching out and grasping my other hand. "I could carry you to your house if I had to."

"Come on," I said again, leading him.

When we jumped from the rocks to the sand, he pulled me against him. I reached up to kiss him, but he drew back. "Tell me you love me."

I could feel the heat of his body against mine. I needed more. Now. "Come on," I said, trying to pull away.

"No. Tell me."

"I love you," I said, turning as I said the words.

He pulled me back against him, his eyes boring into mine. "Tell me again, Christie. Look at me and tell me you love me."

I looked up at him, at his beautiful face, all planes and angles, and at the cut on his temple that was still seeping blood, at his white-blond hair that glowed in the moonlight. I ran my hands up his arms and across his shoulders, biting deep into his flesh. I felt as if the words were being pulled out of my soul. "I love you, you goddamn bastard, and I want you." I pressed my body hard against his. "I want you inside me. I want to watch you wanting me. I want to climb on top of you and watch your face as you come inside me."

"Jesus." He grabbed my hand and started pulling me toward the house.

A few feet farther, he stopped, turning and taking me in his arms again. "I've dreamed for twelve years of having you. When you were a goddamn fourteen-year-old kid, I wanted you more than anything. I used to feel like a pervert, horny for a flat-chested kid. I'd dream of being between your legs and sliding into you. I used to watch you sleep and imagine crawling into bed with you and touching you until you woke up. I could feel my hands on you." He ran his hands down my arms, up my sides, then trailed them across my breasts. "I wanted to see your nipples get hard. I wanted to take you into my mouth."

I felt a surge of heat that made what had come before seem a weak preview. I laced my fingers in his hair and dragged his head down to mine. I took quick bites of his lips. I sucked his bottom lip into my mouth and chewed on it. Then his tongue.

He broke away, breathing hard. As one, we started slowly again for the house. After a minute, he stopped. "Then you went from being this cute-as-shit kid into a gorgeous almost woman, but it made no difference. I couldn't touch you, because if I had, I couldn't have stopped."

"You did, though."

He shook his head. "I did, but I shouldn't have. I should have thrown you down on the sand and taken you. I thought it would be a mistake, but it wouldn't have been. Everything that happened because I didn't was a mistake. You and me were never a mistake."

He kissed me again and, in his trembling control, I could feel the boy he had been then. I kissed him back just to feel the power I had over him. My hands slipped up under his shirt, and I caressed his bare back. I felt the violent shudders go through him as my hands traced his ribs to the front and caressed his stomach. I reveled in it. It was no different than the power he exercised over me as he ran his hands up under my shirt, caressing me, teasing me until I was ready to scream.

I made some kind of inarticulate sound and turned, pulling him by the hand. We made it as far as the dining room. As we stumbled in through the sliding glass doors, he spun me around, wrapping his arms around me. We somehow ended up on the floor with clothes flying. I think we both wanted it to last. I had a sense that we did, but we'd waited too long. The instant he entered me, I cried out. Seconds later, I felt him thrust, then collapse.

Then it was over. I'd been waiting for twelve years for this moment, and a moment was all it was; but it was a moment well worth the wait. I was still reeling with disbelief. Was this a dream? A wild fantasy? Could this really be Todd, my Todd, lying atop me, crushing the breath out of me? He was the first male I had ever wanted, the only male I'd ever really wanted. Could it finally have happened after so many years of waiting?

We lay there as if dead. Finally, he said, "I always thought our first time would be on the beach."

"It almost was," I answered breathlessly.

Our second time was on the living room sofa. We made it that far. Now that I look back on it, I'm amazed we left the dining room at all that night. Our clothes didn't. Eventually we found the bed, where Todd showed me again how much he wanted me.

As we lay, limp and drenched with sweat, I turned my head so I could see him. I couldn't seem to stop looking at him. We were spread across the bed, the covers somewhere on the floor. My ceiling fan rotated above us, cooling our flushed skin. His forehead had quit bleeding, but I think I'd forgotten he was injured. I had completely forgotten about my knees. I raised myself on one elbow and touched his face in the dim light, tracing its outline. I felt as if my heart would burst. At the same time, I felt like weeping.

He reached up and captured my hand. "Tell me again," he said, his voice husky with exhaustion. "Tell me you love me."

I closed my eyes. "I don't want to love you," I whispered.

"But you do."

"Yes. I do."

He let go of my hand and touched my drying hair, pushing it back out of my face. "Please give us a chance, Christie. I meant what I said. I love you. You're everything to me. You have been since the first day I saw you."

"You remembered the yellow dress."

He nodded. "I remember everything, probably every word of every conversation we had. I've played them over and over again in my mind the last twelve years. They were all I had. Except for a picture I stole out of mom's album."

He saw a tear leak out of the corner of my eye, and started to sit up. "Let me—"

I pushed him back down. "No. Let me." I walked to the bedroom closet and rummaged around, finally finding what I wanted. I pulled Teddy out of his place of honor, bringing him back to the bed. "I have a handkerchief," I said, untying it from around his neck and holding it out for Todd to see. "I remember a few things, too."

I could see the exact minute that comprehension dawned. He reached out and pulled me down on top of him, wrapping me in his arms while his jaw worked furiously. "Oh, dwarf."

I rested my forehead against his chest, my mind spinning backward to those days. "That's what you meant about not protecting everyone's morals. Just mine. You were already sleeping with her."

"Do we have to—"

"Yes!" Then, more softly, "Yes, we have to. It's like a festering splinter. I have to know. All of it."

He closed his eyes. I thought he was going to refuse to talk about it. I was ready to issue an ultimatum—talk or go—when he began speaking. "That last summer and Thanksgiving, I thought I was going to die. I couldn't get you out of my head. You wouldn't believe the fantasies that went through my mind. I'd be sitting in the living room watching you do something, just something dumb and ordinary like reading or something, and suddenly I'd have this erection. You were so innocent, or I thought you were until that night on the beach. Jesus, that was the kicker. 'Can't we pretend we're like them,' you asked me. Remember that?"

I nodded.

"I wanted to tear your clothes off and throw you down on the sand. Jesus, it was close. You were so beautiful looking up at me with those big, trusting eyes. That's what did it. That trust. You always trusted me to do what was right. What a bitch. I couldn't betray your trust. Can't you see that? Jack and Mom trusted me, too. They told me that they always knew you were safe when you were with me. How could I do it to them? To any of you?"

He took a deep breath and opened his eyes, staring at the ceiling. "When I went back after Thanksgiving, there was this girl at school. I had seen her around campus, but that was all. Then I busted her and her boyfriend one night when they were parked. I told you I had to do a lot of that. She kind of came on to me after that. She wasn't especially pretty or anything like that, but she let me know—you know—that she was—willing. I told her up front that I wasn't in the market for a long-term thing. I don't know. Maybe she didn't believe me." I saw him swallow hard. "I felt like a shit afterward. The whole time I was thinking about you, pretending she was you. God, that sounds sick."

He rolled his head until he was looking at me. "When I came home at Christmas, I felt like some kind of lousy hypocrite, pretending everything was the same. It was. I mean, my feelings for you were the same, but Melony was there."

"Melony."

He nodded. "I thought she was a nice girl, and that made it even worse." He swallowed audibly. "We kept seeing each other when I got back after Christmas. Then in March, she told me she was pregnant." His voice turned bitter. "I bought it. I'd used a condom, but, well, you know, they don't always work. I believed her. She cried and said her family would never forgive her and she wanted to die and she'd only done it because she loved me so much." His words slowed. "I felt like God was paying me back for what I'd done. I had used her and I had put this child in her. I knew what I'd been doing was wrong. I knew how wrong it was when I was doing it, but I did it anyway. I felt like I deserved to lose everything. And I did."

His eyes closed again. After a minute, he resumed speaking. "We were married by a justice of the peace in Tallahassee. Then she called her parents. They didn't seem very surprised. Later I found out she had already told them we were engaged. Anyway, I think she really did try to get pregnant then, but it didn't work. She didn't tell me anything until I realized she was having periods. Then she said she'd had a miscarriage and that she didn't tell me because she was afraid I'd leave her. When I asked her when, she said it had happened a couple of months before. I don't know why I didn't believe her. I just had this feeling. I called her doctor and tricked her into talking to me." He gave a bitter laugh. "She told me there was no reason Melony couldn't have children if we kept trying like we were. When I said something about a miscarriage, she said that she didn't know anything about that, but this woman had been her doctor for two years.

"So anyway, I confronted Melony. I acted like I knew all about it from her doctor." He reached up and covered his eyes with his hand. "It was awful. She said she had thought maybe she was pregnant and when she realized she wasn't, she was afraid I'd think she tricked me. She had. She knew it and I knew it. I left the next day."

I waited for him to go on. When he didn't, I asked, "What happened then?"

He blew out a breath. "I wrote to Mom and told her about the divorce. I told her why I'd gotten married. I quit school. I couldn't see your uncle shelling out bucks for someone like me to get an education. I worked at MacDonald's for a couple of months. Then I joined the army. Got in the military police. I waited until I was in boot camp to tell Mom and Jack. They took it pretty well. They wrote me a lot, always news about home and about you, what you were doing. I lived for those letters. They were the only things that kept me going."

I remembered his letters to Carly, how I had merely existed between them and only come alive as I slit open the envelope, and I understood.

"Your uncle always added a note to the bottom, some little something. Encouragement. Something upbeat. He's the best. You know that?"

I nodded.

"He should have hated me. He should have despised me for my weakness. I know Mom told him about Melony, about what happened. The first time I had to face him after that, I couldn't look him in the eye, you know? But he put his arm around my shoulders and told me that everyone makes mistakes, that that's how we learned in this life. I felt like bawling. Here I'd blown everything, I'd hurt you and Mom and him and tossed away all that money he'd spent on my college, and he was making excuses for me. Christ, I felt like a heel."

"Why didn't you come back after you got out of the service?"

His head turned toward me. "To what? I'd blown it. I couldn't show my face to you after what I'd done. I was sure Mom had told you all about it."

"She didn't tell me a thing."

"I didn't know that, and besides, I knew I didn't deserve you after what I'd done. There was no way I'd throw myself on your mercy. I knew that if it had been me, I'd have said forget it."

I might very well have said the same, I reflected. I'd been angry and bitter enough. I came up on my elbow. "Why now?"

"Why am I here?" I nodded. "Because once I saw you again, I couldn't get you out of my head. It was like no time had passed, like we'd just had a little fight or something and I had to make it up to you. It's hard to explain. Once I saw you, I knew you were it for me. Forever. I knew I'd never get over you. There's never been anyone else for me but you, and I knew then there never will be."

I laced my fingers through his and lay back on the bed as my mind raced back through the years. "Was that you? At graduation?"

"Yeah. Stupid, wasn't it? I figured you'd spit on me if you saw me, so I hid in the back of the auditorium. Pitiful. I couldn't stay away. I had dreamed so many times of what that night would be like, how Mom and Jack and I would take you out to dinner afterward and I'd give you your present."

"What present?"

He looked embarrassed. "Oh, nothing. It was stupid."

"What was stupid? What present?"

His eyes cut over to mine, then back to the ceiling. "It was just a typewriter. You know, for your newspaper writing."

"What's stupid about a typewriter?"

He chewed his lip, a habit I remembered from long ago. "I typed this note on it. Something about our lives being devoted to truth and justice and each other."

I saw a tear slip out of the corner of his eye. "Do you still have it? My note?"

"Yeah. Somewhere."

"I think I'd like to read it sometime."

He looked over at me then, a long, searching look that spoke of pain and hope, and he pulled me into his arms, burying his face in my hair. "I don't deserve you," he said, his voice tight. "I know I don't deserve you, but, Christ, I want you. I love you so much. You shouldn't do it, but please forgive me. Until I saw you again, I figured I knew what life would be like. I knew it would be empty but that was okay because I deserved it. Then when your uncle got sick, I was afraid you'd need someone. I knew Mom wasn't very strong, and I knew your mom wouldn't be much help to you. I figured I was your best bet, lousy as it was. So I came to see you. I was just going to be friendly, you know? Offer to help if you needed me."

His face cleared and he chuckled. "Jesus, you were all fire. The minute you opened that door, I was lost. When you marched out into the front yard with your little ass swinging in those jeans, it took all my self-control not to strip them off and take you on the sidewalk." He held me away from him. "That probably sounds pretty sick."

I remembered thinking he looked like a pagan god standing on my doorstep, but I said nothing.

He leaned on one elbow, looking down at me. "Then you laid down the law. No friendship. No concern. You were a big girl and I had no place in your life. I knew you were right, so I backed off."

"Until my birthday."

I could see the white flash of teeth as he grinned. "Yeah, well. Suzy kind of mentioned you weren't dating anyone."

I came up off the bed. "You were pumping Suzy for information?"

"Not pumping, exactly."

I lay back. "I'm surprised you didn't ask Freddie." I heard what sounded like a suppressed chuckle. "You were pumping Freddie, too?" I asked, incredulous.

"I didn't have to pump Freddie. He's my bud, remember? He told me you'd been seeing this writer guy, but he went back to Ireland. How serious was that, anyway?"

"None of your damn business," I shot out, but with little heat.

He gave me a lopsided smile. "Yeah, well, I'm satisfied with how it worked out. And I do mean satisfied." He reached over and trailed his hand along my face, my neck. "I started to think I might have a chance when you got pissed at me on the beach. There wasn't a reason in the world for you to be mad because I was being polite, unless that wasn't really what you wanted. Man, that tickled me. I watched you all evening with those cute kids and pretended they were ours. You know, like wishing they were. I was still pretending when I put them in the car. Then I kissed you. It rocked me, I can tell you that. That little kiss was like a punch in the gut. It got to you, too. I could feel it. That's when I decided I couldn't play by your rules anymore."

The moon topped the house and shone in the bedroom window, bathing his face in its white glow. I was struck again by how beautiful he was. Some men are masculine looking and some have almost pretty features. Some are outwardly strong and some openly vulnerable. He was all of that, and more. I watched as the smile faded from his face.

When he looked at me again, the vulnerability was there, and fear. "Don't send me away again, Christie. I don't care how dramatic it sounds. I can't live without you. There's no damned reason in the world to go on living without you. Not work or

Mom or Jack. None of it matters without you. I know you don't trust me anymore, but you will. I promise you that. It'll take time, but I'll prove it to you. I'll spend every day—"

I put my fingers against his lips. "Stop. Don't say anymore. We'll . . . take it a day at a time. Slowly. We'll see where it leads."

"I want to marry you."

I felt a smile try to fight its way past my determined expression. "That's not what I call slow."

"Okay. We'll wait until Friday."

I rolled over on top of him, straddling his body. "What makes you think we'll be out of bed by Friday?"

Later, when I thought he'd fallen asleep, I heard him ask sleepily, "What was that all about tonight? That part about all of us being bastards."

Was that only tonight? "My friend Joyce. Suzy and Peter Phillip's mom. Her husband left her. Walked out saying something about wanting to figure out who he was and what he cared about."

"Ahhhh."

He only said the one word, but there was a wealth of understanding behind it. He pulled me into his arms and nestled my head in the crook of his shoulder, kissing me lightly on the forehead. "I'm so sorry, honey."

"About us or Joyce?"

"Yes."

CHAPTER 17

He expected me to be a pushover. He showed up Friday night with a ring. It was beautiful, a blue-white diamond set in a wide gold band.

"Not yet," I told him, not without some disappointment.

"When, then?"

"When it's right."

"When will that be?"

"We'll know. We'll both know."

I held fast. It was six months before I let him slip it on my finger. Not that I wasn't sure about us until then. I was sure that first night, as sure as I'd ever been of anything, but I also remembered Stella's words. Make him work for it. Well, she'd said make him pay for it and she had been talking about Leon, but it was the same idea. Joyce also took her advice, although I was too much in alt to know it for a while.

I reveled in every minute Todd and I spent with each other. Imagine being force-fed tuna casserole at each meal for six months and dreaming every day about eating steak. Imagine that at the end of that six months, someone puts a thick juicy sirloin dripping with juice in front of you and hands you a knife and fork. That's how I felt. I couldn't get enough.

For the first month, each time we came together we were violent with need. He was working nights then. He would show up at my house at dawn, and we would make frenzied love until my alarm jarred us back to reality. We talked some, but mostly we touched and explored and learned one another. I discovered that he loved to feel my fingers in his hair and that he had never before had his feet massaged. He learned that he could reduce me to a purring feline with a back massage and that I was moved almost to tears by a kiss on the forehead. It was strange to know someone deeply on so many levels and yet be totally ignorant in others, but it was never strange to be in his arms. I belonged there. I'd always known it.

He had changed some. He was tougher in a lot of ways than he'd been at eighteen and twenty. He was still the idealist I remembered, but now his ideals were—not tarnished—but tempered with reality. Nor was he the fatalist he'd been at eighteen, maybe because he'd taken a hand at shaping his life after his divorce. He didn't always expect the worst now, but he seemed tough enough to deal with it if it came.

He handled his job as a cop philosophically, focusing on the good he could accomplish instead of the problems he couldn't solve. He kept giving me tips, nothing that could compromise a police effort, but solid leads that got me to the stories before anyone else. When Virgil and the others got suspicious about where I was getting my information, instead of telling them, I spread the wealth around, passing tips along to the others. It was enough to satisfy them.

I never told anyone where the leads came from. Todd was my secret. No one knew we were seeing each other. Well, I think Uncle Jack and Carly began to suspect, but they were too wrapped up in my uncle's rapidly deteriorating health to pay much attention to anything else.

Carly was back to working normal hours, thanks, I'm certain, to Todd's financial contribution to the household. Todd spent his days with Uncle Jack when my uncle couldn't work, which was more and more often as the months passed, walking on the beach or putting together model cars at his direction. I think he grabbed a nap after Carly got home. He couldn't have been sleeping more than three or four hours a day, but that seemed enough for him. I think he must have been existing on happiness. I know I was, although our happiness was always tempered with worry about my uncle and Carly.

Carly was changing quickly and dramatically. She was no longer the strong, levelheaded woman she had been during my teenage years. She was like a child, constantly asking for verification. When I mentioned it to Todd during one of our mornings together, he said, "It's like my dad all over again."

I was surprised. He'd never talked about his father except to tell me he died before Todd was five. "What do you mean?"

"He died of cancer. Mom didn't talk about it much. I could tell it upset her when she did. I know it was fast. They found pancreatic cancer. They started treatments right away, but five months later he was dead. I don't think it was pretty."

"This is different. Uncle Jack isn't *dying* of Parkinson's."

He was quiet for a moment. I could tell he'd thought about it a lot. "No, but he isn't going to get better either. He's not the man he was when she married him, honey," he said gently. "She's losing someone she loves, and she's losing him fast. She's terrified."

As terrified as she was, she was more angry. It came out in little ways. Todd was right. Uncle Jack was declining every day. It wasn't the Parkinson's by itself that was doing it. It was everything combined. Even the medicines for each of his health problems were at war, and his body was the battleground. Carly was angry at the illnesses, at the medication he was taking, at the doctors, and yes, at my uncle for being ill. I think she felt cheated. She began making little remarks in his hearing. "We can't go out to dinner anymore," she said one day. "Jack's afraid he won't be able to feed himself." And another time, "Jack was never much of a dancer, but at least we used to be able to get out on the dance floor together."

I don't think she meant to be cruel. I tried to believe that. My uncle pretended not to hear, but I often saw him wince at her remarks. So that I wouldn't begin to hate her outright, I tried to put myself in her place, to imagine what it felt like to lose two men you loved to illness. I would stare at Todd and try to imagine what it would be like if he were suffering from a degenerative disease. Of course, I was certain I'd never do or say anything that might hurt him. Youth is nothing if not self-righteous.

Still, I kept trying to understand. I tried to imagine what it was like to awaken every day and know that, however bad yesterday had been, today would be worse. I wasn't very successful, but I did try. I tried especially hard because she was Todd's mother and, in a very real sense, she was my mother, too. Carly had shown me affection when my own mother couldn't spare the time or effort. She had taught me how to cook and sew and, until now, how to forgive. I knew she loved my uncle, and I knew she was in pain, just as he was. I wished that intellectual knowledge could help more.

Todd was a buffer zone, much as I had once been between Joyce and Stella. Those two didn't need me anymore—they were getting thick as thieves—but I needed Todd's interference. He gave her the attention she seemed to crave in ever-increasing amounts when I would have railed at her. He calmed her down when she was angry and talked her back into spirits when she was weepy with self-pity, which was often. I was less patient with her. I, too, was losing someone I loved to illness. It didn't occur to me until much later that Todd was as well.

My uncle's life wasn't yet threatened, but its quality was diminishing daily. His good days were fewer; the bad days were very bad. Without work, time hung heavy on his hands. No longer able to drive, he was pretty effectively housebound.

Besides, it embarrassed him to go out in public. People stared. When he was home, the involuntary head and arm movements made it difficult for him to hold a book or read. He despised television, and yet it was the one activity he could engage in by himself. He became irritable and snappish. The doctors said that was partly the result of the medicine, although I thought he had plenty to be snappish about without it.

Because of my anger at Carly, I spent less time with him than I should have. At least, that's what I told myself, and yet I was furious with Darlene when she said she wouldn't allow the twins to go visit him anymore. He gave them nightmares, she said. I said things to her—well, something along the line that if she hadn't raised them to be such prima donnas, they wouldn't wither the first time they were faced with physical infirmity. If I had been perfectly honest, I'd have had to admit that it made me feel a bit wilted to see such a strong and independent man weaken to the point of near helplessness. I still took Freddie to see him occasionally, but while he never let it show around Uncle Jack, the visits clearly upset Freddie, too.

Into this morass of depression and despair strolled Stella, leading Joyce by the hand—a clearly transformed Joyce.

"Tell her she looks gorgeous," Stella ordered, pushing Joyce in my front door.

Joyce had lost fifteen pounds and was wearing makeup and nail polish and a little black dress that slithered over her new curves like water over smooth rocks. Her legs were encased in sheer black stockings, and her polished toes peeked out of three-inch sandal heels. She did look gorgeous. She also looked embarrassed.

"You look stunning," I said honestly.

"She has a date," Stella informed me.

"A date?" I echoed.

Stella nodded. "With that new surgeon at the hospital."

"Dr. McAuliffe?" I had interviewed him for the paper. He was a transplant from New Jersey, a bit of a dandy, I had thought, but successful enough to be semi-retired in Florida at the age of forty-five. "He seems—nice."

"He's filthy rich," Stella said, matter-of-factly. "Show her your walk," she said, making hand motions at Joyce.

Joyce strutted across the room—a Stella-choreographed walk if ever I saw one. At the kitchen door, she executed a tidy turn and headed back toward us.

I found my voice. "Very nice. Uh—what about . . ."

"Leon?" Joyce asked, speaking for the first time. Even her voice was different—not choppy and anxious as it had been, but slower, maybe even deeper. "Leon is currently cohabiting with a twenty-two-year-old waitress from the Ocean View Diner. That's what Suzy told me after her last visit. And I do mean last." She looked at Stella. "You don't think the shoes are too much?"

"The shoes are perfect." Stella turned to me. "We're double dating tonight."

"Double dating?" My voice squeaked on the last word. "Didn't that go out of style with sweater sets and poodle skirts?"

Joyce looked at Stella for reassurance, but Stella was busy raising her eyebrows at me. "Double dating is the prefect way to get to know someone," she said as if lecturing a dull schoolchild. "It's safe, and the entire burden of conversation isn't on either member of the new couple." She grinned. "I read that in *Cosmo*. Works for me. Okay," she said, taking Joyce's arm, "we just wanted you to see the new woman. We have to go. The boys will be here shortly."

"Boys."

"Goodnight, Christie. Tell Todd I said hello," she added as she pushed Joyce out the door.

"Tell . . ." So much for my secrecy.

I stared at the door for a while after they were gone. It made me sad that Joyce seemed to have relegated Leon to a past life, and yet I was proud of her for picking up her scattered pieces and carrying on. With a little help from her friend—which I had not been. My preoccupation with Todd had been complete. Joyce had undergone this amazing transformation and found her courage without any help from me. I realized I was a little jealous of her friendship with Stella.

I spent the rest of the evening writing. I was still working on my story about Uncle Jack and Carly. Writing about those early, happy years always made me acutely aware of how much Carly had changed. Before my uncle became ill, she had looked to him for confirmation of her attractiveness. She had depended on his strength. She saw her value reflected in his eyes. Now she looked away more often than not.

I did my writing on the typewriter Todd had bought me for graduation. Although he hadn't said so, I knew it tickled him when I refused to trade it in on a newer, fancier model. It tickled him even more that I had framed the note he'd typed me so long ago and hung it over the little desk in my spare bedroom.

I was writing about their wonderful first anniversary celebration when I felt strong hands encircle my throat. I'd been so preoccupied I hadn't heard him come in. He began massaging my tight neck muscles.

"Long day?" he asked.

"Mmmm. Endless." I moaned with pleasure as he worked on my shoulders. "If you keep that up, I may have to keep you around."

His hands froze. "Keep me around?"

"Um-hum."

"You mean permanently?"

I leaned my head back and looked up at him as he stood silhouetted against my ceiling light. "I think—yes."

His voice was tight. "You really mean that?"

I smiled. "I think I do. Yes."

His face was as serious as I'd ever seen it. His hands dropped to his sides. After a minute, he turned and left the room. I heard the front door open and close.

I looked after him in confusion. I hadn't planned my words, but I had meant them. I hadn't expected them to run him out of my house. Before I could react, I heard the door open again. He walked into the room carrying a small square box. When he was standing in front of me, he opened it and took the ring out of its bed of black velvet. Then he reached down for my left hand.

Tears filled my eyes as he slipped the ring on my finger. His eyes searched my face.

He dropped to his knees and buried his face in my lap. I stroked his hair. Neither of us said anything.

After a while, he lifted his head and looked at me. His eyes were wet. "I never thought it would happen. I was sure something would blow it." Then, "You're sure? Really sure?"

I laughed as the tears spilled down my face. "I'm really, really sure."

He got to his feet and pulled me into his arms. "Nothing will ever come between us again. I swear to God. I won't let it."

I buried my face in his chest. "I believe you."

After a long time, he tipped my chin up with his finger. "When?"

"Soon."

"Saturday?"

"Not that soon," I said, laughing. "I want a little time to enjoy this."

"But not long."

I took his finger from my chin and kissed it. "Not long at all."

I hadn't anticipated my mother's reaction.

"We don't want a big wedding, Mother," I told her for the third time.

We were sitting in her living room, Todd, Mother, and me. Lamar had gone to the kitchen to get champagne and glasses. I guess he kept a bottle chilled at all times for emergencies like this one. He was that kind of man.

We had told Uncle Jack and Carly first, of course. Their joy had spilled over in words and toasts and tears, theirs and ours. I had only called my mother as an afterthought, thinking it polite to mention to her that I was getting married. We were back on somewhat friendly terms and stayed that way by never allowing my uncle to come up in our conversations. When I made my announcement, she insisted that Todd and I join Lamar and her for dinner. They had never met Todd, although Todd had heard plenty about my mother.

"Nonsense," she said, bringing me back to the moment. "You can't deny me that. I had begun to think I'd never see the day. You agree with me, don't you, Todd? Besides," she went on without waiting for an answer, "it would mean so much to your sisters. They could be bridesmaids. Darlene's twins could be junior bridesmaids."

I couldn't imagine my sisters giving a flip if I ever married, but I kept my opinion to myself.

Mother rose gracefully and crossed to the roll-top desk in the corner of the living room, retrieving a writing tablet and a pencil. Mother and Lamar's house was elegant rather than homey. The outside was off-white stucco under a red tiled roof, with a wrought iron gate leading into an enclosed front garden. Very Spanish. Yucca plants lined the walkway to the house, their sharp, pointed leaves keeping incoming guests on the straight and narrow. Literally. The grass was almost unnaturally green and clipped to perfection. The interior had high ceilings with lots of white furniture tastefully arranged on pale green carpet. It was lovely. I couldn't live in it for ten minutes.

"Suzy could be a flower girl," Todd piped up.

I gave him a dirty look. I knew he was kidding, but Mother didn't.

"Who's Suzy?" she asked. "Never mind." She sat back down and crossed her stockinged legs. "Let's see. From our side of the family, we would want your aunt Jean and your cousins."

"They live in Seattle. Besides, I haven't seen Aunt Jean or my cousins in ten years, and I didn't like them then."

"Please, Christiana. Jean is my sister. Then there are the Carltons. They were always fond of you."

"Mother, I don't—"

"There you are," she interrupted, turning as Lamar came back into the room carrying an ice bucket with champagne and four glasses. "I was just beginning to compile the guest list for the wedding. We'll want to keep it small, but it's a wonderful opportunity for making contacts." She turned back to me. "Your uncle could pay for—"

"No." My voice was flat and brooked no argument.

"But—"

"No, Mother. Uncle Jack can't afford it. He can't afford anything. All his money goes for doctors and medicine."

"But isn't his wife working?"

"Hers, too. All their money goes for medical expenses. No." I got to my feet. "Forget it. We don't want a wedding anyway, just a quiet ceremony with family."

Lamar cleared his throat. He didn't speak often, so when he did, people tended to listen. "I might make a suggestion, dear," he said to my mother. He put the champagne and glasses on the table. Then he turned to me. "I never had any children, Christiana, and I'd consider it an honor if you'd let me finance your wedding."

"But dear—" Mother began.

"No, Lamar," I broke in. "Thank you very much. That's really a lovely gesture, but it wouldn't be fair—"

"I truly would consider it an honor. It's not a gesture at all. I've been able to help Darlene and Fred a great deal, and I was even able to assist Doug and Joanna at one time, but I've never been able to do anything for you." All that was news to me. Taking my speculative look as a sign of weakening, he added, "It would mean a lot to me."

There was no doubting his sincerity. I was trying to think of a kind way to refuse when Todd said, "I think that would be very kind of you, Lamar, as long as we kept it modest."

"That's decided then."

I groaned. Todd's idea of modest and my mother's were pots of violets versus the Biltmore Gardens, but I decided to give in for now. I'd fight each battle as we came to it. The first one surfaced even before I'd finished reaching that resolve.

"We were thinking about February," Todd said, which was news to me.

Mother clutched her throat. "February! We couldn't even have the invitations engraved by then. No, perhaps November. December wouldn't do because people are already booked up for holiday parties. Yes. Mid-November, before the Thanksgiving rush. Winter weddings are so *magnifique*. I can see trails of blue orchids against white satin. The bridesmaids could wear pale green. The garden in winter look."

Todd didn't clutch his throat, but he looked like he wanted to. "November is almost a year away. We wanted it soon."

Mother tapped her front teeth with her pencil. "Well, perhaps we could do it in October. Give it an autumn look, although I can't imagine what the bridesmaids could wear. Darlene looks dreadful in brown. Perhaps cream. Or peach."

"June," I said flatly. They all looked at me. "No later than June."

"But Christiana, everyone gets married in June. That's so common."

"June or not at all."

"You're so inflexible, Christiana."

"But that's six months away!" from Todd.

"June. Take it or leave it."

No one said anything for several minutes. Then Lamar pulled the champagne out of the ice and poured four glasses, handing them around. "Well!" He beamed. "let's drink to the first of many happy planning sessions."

The poor man. I really think he was serious.

Stella was smug, as if she'd known all along what was coming. "It took you long enough," she said when I told her. "Thank God you finally saw the light. Maybe you'll both be more pleasant to be around now."

"Just exactly when is it that you're around Todd?" I asked, wondering again what it was she did in her spare time. As usual, I got no answer.

I think Joyce truly was happy for me, but she couldn't keep the sorrow out of her face when she wished me congratulations. I understood completely, remembering how I had felt watching my uncle and Carly together after Todd abandoned me. It was in the presence of their love that I had felt my loss most acutely.

Reactions in the newsroom were mixed. Masie sulked. "You could have told me you two had a thing going."

"We didn't. Our thing ended eight years ago."

"Apparently it didn't," she countered with a sniff, but her pout didn't last out the day.

Virgil was alarmed. "You won't be quitting work, will you?" he asked, his eyes focusing on my abdomen.

"Not for a while," I answered sweetly, sticking my belly out as far as it would go.

Gordon's face fell at that. He made it no secret that he'd like my stories as well as his own.

Alf was predictably obnoxious. "I thought you and Paul were getting it on."

"We weren't, though."

That only slowed him down. "This Todd guy. Isn't he like your first cousin or something like that?" he asked with a leer.

"Something like that," I answered blithely. Let him figure it out.

Over the next few weeks, Todd and I settled in to a happy routine. He was still working nights by his own request so that he could have his days with my uncle. I rarely told him how grateful I was, but words weren't always necessary between us.

I saw him every day. He would get off work at six o'clock and come straight to my house. We would make love and then take our coffee and go for a walk on the beach. Then I'd shower and head into the newsroom, and Todd would head for home. I was going into work later and staying later. Virgil didn't care as long as I continued to pull my weight. With the tips I was getting from my own special source, that wasn't hard.

Things were so smooth, in fact, that I knew it couldn't last. It didn't.

The two ulcers that were eating my uncle's stomach hemorrhaged a month after Todd slipped the ring on my finger. Carly walked into the bathroom one evening and found him on the floor in a pool of blood. Two weeks later, he suffered a minor stroke. That time she came into the living room and found him sitting on the floor looking confused. He was unable to speak coherently for several hours, but there was, according to Doctors Johnson and Seegar, no permanent damage. I begged to differ. My uncle was living in complete terror of what his runaway body would do next.

Then there was the overdose.

There had been a horrendous accident on A1A at six-forty-five a.m. Four cars and an eighteen-wheeler had somehow managed to crash into each other, and two cars had ended up through the plate-glass window of a Laundromat in a strip mall. Two people were dead and twelve injured. Todd was normally off duty at seven, but all police and most of the fire rescue people in the area were called to the scene. Todd called me, so I was also at the scene. The sorting out and cleaning up took hours. It was afternoon before Todd and I were free, me to race off to the paper to write my story and Todd to go home to my uncle. Thinking Todd would be along any minute, Carly had left at nine.

When Todd arrived at the house, he checked on my uncle, who seemed to be taking a nap in his chair. Todd showered and fixed himself some breakfast. After about an hour, he went to wake my uncle to see if he wanted to go down to the beach.

By the time I was called, my uncle's stomach had been pumped and the doctors had determined he would live. He insisted that he must have taken the handful of pills they found in him by mistake, but I wasn't sure.

Carly was sitting in the waiting room, her hands fisted in her hair while she sobbed that she couldn't take any more. I felt sorry for her; really I did, but I couldn't see how hysterics could help the situation, even though I was feeling a little hysterical myself. Shortly after my arrival, Dr. Johnson came into the waiting room and gave her a pill. After a while she grew silent, with her head bobbing on her neck as if she were too weak to hold it up. Todd sat and held her hand while I went in to see my uncle.

I was used to him looking just a little worse—a little thinner or a little paler—each time I saw him, but once in a while his appearance deteriorated so dramatically that it shocked me. This was one of those times. His eyes looked too dark in his white face, and his skin seemed to sag loosely, as if all the connective tissue had given up and let go. I could see the bones close to the skin in his arms and hands. He looked pitifully frail and vulnerable.

"Really, Christie," he said, his voice raspy from the tube that had been down his throat, "it was an accident. I must have forgotten I took them earlier. They're giving me four pills three times a day. It's hard to keep up. Not that I haven't thought of it," he added after a minute in a whisper so soft I wasn't sure I had heard him right.

"Of what?" I didn't really want an answer, but I thought I'd better know if he were planning something so I could alert Todd and the doctors.

"Giving up," he said. I could feel the pain radiating off him as he said the words. "But . . . I don't know how."

I took his hand gently between my own, afraid I would hurt him if I squeezed too hard. I rested my forehead on our joined hands as if I were praying. "I love you, Uncle Jack." It was all I could think of to say.

Then followed what I thought of as two good months. Mother barreled ahead with the wedding plans even though I could muster no enthusiasm. I kept wondering how my uncle could give me away. He was so fiercely independent. Would he agree to use a wheelchair for just one day?

I quit taking Freddie to see him after the incident with the guitar.

My uncle had played guitar in a band when he was a young man, and he had kept it up all the years of his adult life. He was remarkably good. Before his illness struck, he was giving Freddie unofficial lessons on an old, patched-together instrument he had found in the back of a closet and had told us all that Freddie had real talent. Fred and Darlene had tolerated but never encouraged Freddie's love affair with music. Still, because he had kept it up year after year and, probably, because Freddie had nagged them unmercifully, they bought him a brand-new electric guitar. Freddie begged me to take him over to see Uncle Jack so he could show it off.

My uncle was having one of his bad days. He took one look at the beautiful shining instrument and turned away.

"Don't you want to try it?" Freddie asked—pleaded, really.

"No," he growled. A minute later, he got awkwardly to his feet and made his way to the bedroom with not a word of explanation, not a glance at Freddie or his pride and joy. He could be like that when the medicine wasn't working properly.

I tried to explain to Freddie that he had reacted that way because it hurt so much that he could no longer play the guitar, and Freddie pretended to understand. Still, a part of me was so angry with my uncle that I wanted to follow him into the bedroom and give him a piece of my mind. Another part wanted to hold him like a baby and weep with him. He had lost so much. But not as much, I discovered, as he would lose if my aunt had her way.

CHAPTER 18

It was a week or so after the incident with the guitar. I was curled up on my living room sofa one night, reading what I'd written the night before, when I heard a soft knock on the front door. I looked at the clock. Nine-thirty. Late for Joyce or Stella. I put my story aside and got to my feet. At the front door, I flipped on the porch light. The shadow on the other side of the frosted jalousies was obviously female. I opened the door.

"Hi, Christie," Carly said. She was alone and visibly upset.

I knew Todd was working an extra half-shift to fill in for a sick buddy. "Carly? Where's Uncle Jack?"

"That's—what I came to talk to you about. Oh, I asked a neighbor to stay with him," she added quickly, seeing the alarm on my face. "Nancy from next door. I do her hair. Can I come in?"

"Of course."

I felt a terrible sense of unease creep into me as I followed her into the living room. I could think of no good reason why Carly would drive twenty-eight miles alone at this time of night to see me. I could think of no reason at all, good or bad. She and Uncle Jack had rarely visited me here even when he'd been well. I had been at their house on Sunday and it was Tuesday. What could have come up in two days that couldn't wait?

She didn't keep me in suspense for long. She refused my offer of coffee, but accepted a glass of wine. The hand that was holding it shook as she took a sip. She looked at the stack of papers on the coffee table. "Were you writing?"

I reached out and flipped the pages face down. It was her story, but I didn't want her to see it. "Just rereading."

"Oh." She took another tiny sip of wine, then put the glass on the coffee table. "I wanted to talk to you. About your uncle."

I waited.

"He's—uh—I don't know how to put this." She looked miserably at me, then down at the hands clutched so tightly in her lap that the knuckles showed white. "I think your uncle needs more care than I can give him."

I relaxed slightly. I'm not sure what I'd been expecting, but this wasn't it. "You mean home nursing?"

Carly bit her lip. "I mean a home. A nursing home where he—"

"What?"

The word hung in the air, along with the accusation it contained.

She started talking fast then. "I just think it would be better for him, Christie. Surely you can see that. He's getting worse and worse. He can't be left alone for a minute. I'm scared to death if he even gets up out of a chair when I'm out of the room. He's fallen. He falls a lot. I haven't told you because I didn't want to worry you, but it's getting worse. He's going to injure himself. And his medicine. They increased the dosage again. He has to take it six times a day now, but he can't remember if he's taken it or not and I have to hide it or he'll try to take it himself. You saw what happened with that. And he's not sleeping. He just lies there and makes little noises. I can't sleep because I'm afraid of what will happen if I do. The doctors say this is just going to go on and on, and when you get married and Todd leaves, what's going to happen then?" She wrung her hands frantically.

"And Todd," she went on, barely pausing for breath. "Think of Todd. He's exhausted. He gets no sleep and he goes to work exhausted and he's going to get shot or something if it keeps up. And Jack has a gun. Did you know that? It used to be in the closet but he's hidden it and I can't find it. I'm afraid he'll—he'll do something, shoot himself or shoot me. He threatened me with it once at the beginning when the medicine was making him crazy. I didn't tell you. I couldn't tell you. But can't you see? It would be better for all of us if Jack were in some kind of home."

I felt a calm descend on me as her words assaulted me, a calm born of icy fury. "Have you already made arrangements?"

"Oh, God, no! Of course not. I haven't even said anything to Todd or your uncle. I wanted to talk to you first. I was sure you'd understand. I know you want the best for your uncle, but you don't live with him. You don't know what it's like. It's—it's horrible." She covered her face with shaking hands.

I sat and watched her, a pitiful sight, but I couldn't feel even a grain of sympathy for her. In fact, I felt something like hatred. My face must have reflected it, because when she looked up at me, she actually tried to move back physically.

"Do you think that's what he would do to you if the situation were reversed? Do you think he'd stick you in a nursing home if you were sick?" My words came out icy, and I aimed each one at her like a weapon.

"No," she said, crying harder, "but that's different. He is—he was strong. He could handle anything. But I'm not strong, Christie. I'm not strong and I don't know what to do."

"If you don't want him to live with you, I'll bring him here to live with me."

She looked around wildly. "But don't you see that wouldn't solve anything? It would be the same thing. You have to work, too, and he'd be alone and I don't know what would happen to him."

"Todd could live here. We'd work it out."

"But then I'd be alone," she wailed, covering her face with her hands.

I probably should have felt even greater anger at her incredible selfishness, or disgust, but what I felt was a tremendous surge of pity. The realization struck me with the force of a blow. This wasn't some evil stranger who was arbitrarily trying to harm my uncle. This was Carly. This was the woman who had taken a drab little fourteen-year-old smart-mouth under her wing and helped guide her to adulthood. It was the same woman who had lived with my uncle for the last twelve years and made his life wonderful. This is what the years of my uncle's illness had done to her—it had reduced her to a weak, rapidly aging woman who feared nothing as much as she feared being alone. This weeping woman in front of me was the result of the toll those years had taken. She deserved my support, not my condemnation.

I moved closer to her. She flinched when I touched her. "Carly, it will be all right," I told her. "Everything's going to be all right. We'll work something out. We'll talk to Todd about it. You've kept all this inside and it has eaten you alive. You should have talked to us about it. Come on, Carly. It'll be all right. You'll see."

My words went on and on, saying the same things, saying nothing. After a long while, her sobs subsided. She reached into her purse and pulled out a handkerchief that had obviously been used on the way to my house. I hurt for her. I wanted to help her.

In a few minutes, she pulled away, wiping her eyes. "How you must hate me."

"I don't hate you, Carly," I said, taking her hand. "I love you.

I haven't shown it much lately, but I do. We'll get through this somehow. All of us. Together."

She shook her head and looked down at her lap.

"We will," I insisted. "I'll call tomorrow and get some information on some kind of home health care. We'll see about getting a nurse to stay with him. You need a break. You've been through too much. We'll get you some help. I'll talk to Todd, too. He probably knows some people who can help."

Her eyes registered alarm. "You won't tell him—"

"No," I assured her quickly. I remembered another time when it had been me begging her to keep her silence. I owed her at least that much. "I won't tell either of them about the nursing home. We'll just forget about that. Okay?"

She nodded. Tentatively. She looked around the room as if trying to think of something else to say, but in the end, she just picked up her purse and stood up. "I have to get back. Nancy . . ."

I got to my feet. "Are you all right to drive?"

"I'm all right," she said quietly. She started out the door, but she stopped without turning. Her head was bowed. "I'm— sorry," she whispered.

After she was gone, I sat back down on the couch, staring at some point in front of me and seeing nothing, feeling everything. I was exhausted. I was bone tired from living an hour with the kind of emotion that she lived with twenty-four hours a day, seven days a week. I vowed then to do everything I could think of to help her get through this terrible time, no matter how long it took, not knowing as I did just how short a time I would have to make good on my vow.

When Todd arrived the next morning, I found it harder than I'd expected to keep my silence. He walked into the bedroom, where I was sitting propped up in bed. I had slept a little, if you could call it that, those hours of tossing and sweating and getting tangled in bed sheets and dreaming hideous things. I was more tired now than when I'd dragged myself to bed at two.

"What's wrong?" he asked, stopping in the doorway.

"Nothing. Bad dream."

He came over to the bed and pulled me into his arms. "Because I wasn't with you."

"Mmmm." I let him stroke my back for a few minutes.

"What's really wrong?" he asked after a few minutes, pulling back from me and searching my face.

"Nothing. Really." I could see he didn't believe me. "I spent the whole night thinking about Uncle Jack and Carly." That was true, and he could see the truth in my face.

"You poor thing." He stroked my face.

"Not me. Them. Your poor mother. I can't stand what she's going through. We have to get her some help."

I could see skepticism cross his face, then suspicion. I couldn't blame him. I had been openly critical of Carly for a long time. "What kind of help?"

"Nursing help. I was thinking about it last night. Uncle Jack is having a hard time taking care of himself, and you and Carly can't be there every minute. You need a break. She desperately needs a break."

He got up and walked over to the dresser, emptying his pockets. "What brought this on?" he asked, not looking at me.

"Nothing in particular. I've been thinking about it for a while. I decided last night that I'd do some checking into home nursing care. Joyce should know something. I could start with her."

He glanced over his shoulder. "So for no reason at all, you just started thinking about this?"

"Not for no reason," I said impatiently. "Because it's something that needs doing. Don't you think she needs help?"

He came back and sat on the edge of the bed. "Yes. I do. But it's the first time you've said anything about it."

I couldn't meet his eyes for a number of reasons; primary among them was guilt that I hadn't even considered that Carly—or he—needed help until her visit. It was one more of those times when my own selfishness astounded me.

I traced the veins in the back of his hand with a finger. "I've been a real ass, Todd," I said, not looking up at him. "I've criticized your mother when I should have been trying to help her. I—I guess I wouldn't let myself think about what she was going through. I've let the two of you do it all because I'm too far away and my job is—" I broke off, impatient with my own self-deception. I looked up and met his eyes. "That's not true. Not entirely. I've let it fall to the two of you because it was easier to pretend that everything is okay, that he wasn't really that sick. Then last night when I knew you were working, I started thinking how one of you had to be with him all the time and—and it's just too much to ask. Of either of you. I know Carly can't be sleeping after everything that's happened lately. She needs to get away from it once in a while, and you can't be there all the time. So I decided to do some investigating."

He nodded his head slowly. "You're right. It's getting pretty hard to stay on top of it. Mom doesn't say much—not that much," he added quickly as if expecting me to argue. "I mean, she tries to be tough, but she's right at her breaking point. She does need help."

"And you need some sleep," I said, unbuttoning his shirt and pulling it free of his trousers.

"It may be what I need," he said, his first smile of the morning teasing his lips as he pulled my nightshirt over my head, "but it isn't what I want."

What I wanted, I decided a week later, was to elope. Mother

was up to her knees in lists: caterers, florists, dressmakers. She kept asking me what I thought and then choosing what she'd wanted in the first place. After a while, I learned to nod and smile. It seemed enough for her.

My big surprise that week was Joanna, who descended on me without warning. I looked up from my typewriter in the newsroom, and there she was. I almost didn't recognize her. I hadn't seen her in over three years, and during that time she had gained more weight than Joyce had lost, all of it in her chest. With her long skirt and stern expression, she looked—God forbid—matronly.

She was in town for her fitting. No one had thought to mention it to me, or if they had, it hadn't registered in my cluttered consciousness. I bought her lunch.

"You could have knocked me over when Mother told me you were getting married. And to Todd Harrington. Isn't that a hoot? After all these years. I remember way back when you were a little thing, you had this big crush on him. Remember that?"

I nodded, smiling. This was a different, effusive Joanna. Her southern accent, a recent addition, wrapped around her words and dragged them out endlessly.

She had finished her pasta and was eyeing my plate. I pushed it over toward her. "Oh, no thanks," she said. "I'm stuffed." But she started poking around, finding buried pieces of sausage and nibbling on them as she talked. "He was good looking. I sure remember that. Wouldn't give any of us the time of day. Oh, well, water under the bridge now. I remember his mother." She speared another piece of sausage. "Anyhow, Mama dragged me down here for this fitting. I told her I could just send her my measurements and take my chances or get my woman in Birmingham to whip me up something, but no. I had to hightail it down here to be poked and prodded Florida style. She told me you picked out your dress. Tell me all about it."

It was a minute before I realized she had quit talking. "I—uh—"

"Does it have a cathedral train? I really love a cathedral train."

"I'm . . . not sure. It's white."

She whooped at that. People at the tables around us turned to stare, but this new Joanna was oblivious. "Well, I sure hope it's white. Even if you aren't one, you don't want to announce it at your wedding, now, do you? What's the neckline like?"

"It's—" I drew a blank. "I don't know," I said, embarrassed. "Mother had all these pictures for me to look at and I guess I picked one, but I don't remember which."

Joanna looked incredulous. "You don't know what your own wedding gown looks like? You haven't changed so much after all. Well, no matter," she said, picking up the dessert menu. "We'll know this afternoon at the fitting. That's at four. What do you want to do until then?"

"I really should get back to work—"

"On my one and only day in town? I should think you wouldn't. We could go shopping, even if there aren't any decent stores around here. Not like in Atlanta."

"I thought you and Darlene—"

"Darlene." Her voice was scornful. "She's doing some stupid something with the PTA. You won't see me doing PTA on my day off. I do enough of that kind of stuff at home. No ma'am. I am not doing PTA today."

"We could go see Uncle Jack."

She looked surprised. "Isn't he working?"

"No, he's home."

"Well, it must be nice."

"It's not nice," I said more sharply than I meant to. "He can't work anymore."

"Why ever not?"

Now I was mystified. "Didn't he tell you about the Parkinson's."

"Oh. That. Years ago. I figured he must be doing pretty well. I haven't heard anything else."

I swallowed hard. "He's not doing well at all. He's had a lot of other problems. Arteriosclerosis. Arthritis. He has some stomach and heart problems. He had a minor stroke not too long ago."

Joanna was staring at me, her eyes wide. "Darlene never said a word."

How could I tell her that Darlene's only acknowledgment of our uncle's illness was her refusal to let her children visit him? "She—doesn't see him a lot. She doesn't like me to tell her how he is."

"Is he in the hospital?"

"No. He's at home."

"Will that wife of his be there?"

Time had stopped for Joanna when Uncle Jack had married Carly. For her, Carly was still "that woman."

"No, Carly will be at work."

With a nod, Joanna pushed the pasta plate away. "Okay. If you think we have time, but let's get some dessert first. It's gonna be a long time till dinner."

I have seldom felt worse for anyone than I did for Joanna that day. I had almost daily witnessed the changes in our uncle, and yet it still upset me to see the difficulty he had doing simple things. Eating. Drinking a glass of water. Joanna was completely unprepared. When Todd ushered us into the living room where Uncle Jack sat in his recliner, Joanna shrank back from what confronted her. Seeing him through her eyes, even I winced. The last time she'd seen our uncle, he had been six feet two and a hundred and ninety-five pounds, proud and strong and independent and, on rare occasion, even fierce. Now his weight struggled to reach a hundred and twenty, and arthritis had rounded his shoulders. He reached for her hands, but his own shook so violently that it took several attempts before he could capture them. His joy contorted his face until I thought he might burst into tears.

It was minutes before she could speak. Joanna was finally able to steel herself enough to kiss him on the cheek. After that, she sat on the couch and let Todd and the nurse carry the conversation. I could see her eyes dart quickly to Uncle Jack every few minutes. Her expression was painful to watch. I could almost see the denial trying to form layers around her as it had Darlene, but Joanna must have lost that particular family skill.

We spent half an hour there. When we were back in my car, she sat staring at the fists clenched in her lap. "He's real sick, isn't he?" she whispered as if afraid her words would carry back into the house.

"Yes."

I saw the fists tighten. Suddenly she blurted out, "God, it's so awful! He's so sick. Why didn't Darlene tell me? Not that I could have done anything, but still, I didn't even know!"

"I think it's too hard for her to face. I probably should have told you myself, but I thought Darlene had told you and that you were too busy . . ."

Joanna sat back, biting her knuckle. Her eyes were dry, but her face was alarmingly red. "I probably deserve that. No," she said when I started to protest, "I probably do. I never made a secret of how mad I was at him for deserting mama and I sure didn't spare much time for him when I lived here, but—"

"Deserting mama?" I echoed. "What are you talking about?"

Joanna's eyes rounded and she covered her mouth.

"*Joanna.*"

She took a deep breath and sat back against the seat. I could hear the occasional car passing on A1A. After a minute, she looked over at me. "Well, why don't I just blurt out the family secrets?"

"*What* family secrets?"

I could see the war going through her. Finally, surprisingly, honesty won. "Mama had a real thing for Uncle Jack way back when. Before she married Daddy." She hesitated, then blurted out the rest. "I guess he didn't have a thing about her, though. Then after Daddy died, I think she thought she and Uncle Jack—well—you know. Not that they did," she added quickly. "Have an affair or anything." She glanced at me out of the corner of her eyes. "Then there was the inheritance."

"Inheritance," I repeated, still trying to make sense of what she had said before.

"Uncle Jack got half of Daddy's insurance money. She told me that herself. She said it wasn't because he loved Uncle Jack so much, but because he hated her. I think she was sure then that Uncle Jack would do the right thing since he got half our money. She was really pissed when he got married again and it wasn't her."

I could barely believe what I was hearing. "When did you find all this out?"

She looked mystified. "I'm not sure. She dropped little hints sometimes. It kind of all came together after Uncle Jack got married again. I'm not making it up," she added defensively.

No, I didn't think she was. I could clearly see our mother concocting this scenario in her mind, letting imagined betrayals infuriate her. It amazed me that it had all been going on around me in my home, and I'd never had a clue. I started the car.

We were ten minutes late for the fitting, and Mother made an issue of it. "It's unbearably rude to keep Marcelene waiting," she said to the air between Joanna and me. "After all, it wasn't your uncle who paid your airfare down here, you know. If I had known you'd spend your day visiting with him . . ." She let the threat hang.

I studied my mother, trying to see her differently in light of what Joanna had told me about Uncle Jack, but it was impossible. Maybe I had known her too long.

"I didn't spend a day, mama," Joanna said. I could see how upset she was, even if our mother couldn't. "I spent exactly half an hour, and it may be the last time I ever see him. He's really sick—"

"Oh, nonsense," Mother said, waving Joanna's words away. "People don't die of Parkinson's."

"It isn't nonsense," Joanna erupted. "The man's half dead already."

My mother's gaze flew to mine, and in hers was something close to panic. In mine, I'm certain, confirmation of Joanna's words.

Mother seemed to be making an effort to collect herself. After a minute, she said, "Well, let's get these fittings taken care of. Lamar is having dinner brought in at six."

CHAPTER 19

I begged off the minute the fittings were done. I still had no idea what my dress looked like. Not, I hoped, like that muslin thing Marcelene had pinned on me. At the moment, I truly didn't care.

I needed a Todd fix, but Todd was, I hoped, sleeping. I went back to the newsroom to finish my day's work. The place was nearly deserted, and eerie. I wrote my copy as quickly as I could and dropped it in Virgil's box. Then I went home, dreading the empty house.

When I arrived, light was blazing from my front windows. As I cautiously approached the front door, I heard music coming from inside. If there was a burglar in there, he or she was a country rock fan. I turned the key and pushed open the door in time to see Stella being dipped nearly to the carpet. By Leon.

"Am I in the wrong house?" I asked, looking back at the numbers on the front door.

"Christie, honey!" Stella bellowed, alerting me immediately that she'd had too much wine, which, for Stella, meant a hell of a lot. "I thought you'd never come home."

"So you decided to do it for me?"

She burst out laughing, almost losing her balance. Leon pulled her back up to a standing position, a sheepish grin on his face. "Hi, Christie."

I nodded at him without smiling. I still hadn't forgiven him for walking out on Joyce. Finding him in my living room dancing with his wife's friend wasn't going to hasten the process.

Just then Joyce's voice called out from my kitchen, "Is that Christie? Is she finally home?" I had a sudden uneasy feeling that Joyce, the Joyce who didn't drink, had also had too much wine.

As visions of kinky threesomes leapt into my mind, Jackson, of the bait shack, walked into the room, carrying a bottle of beer. He grinned at me shyly. "Hey, gal."

I blinked. I was beginning to feel a little like Alice through the looking glass. Would the Mad Hatter arrive next? "Uh—"

"It's a long story," Stella said, pulling down her shirt from where the dip had hiked it. "Jackson, honey, would you get Christie a glass of wine? You sit right here," she said to me, dropping down on the couch and patting the seat beside her.

Jackson, honey? I fell more than sat. Joyce walked into the room. She was barefoot and had her shirt—one of Leon's, actually—tied up under her breasts, leaving her flat and tanned stomach bare. Her shorts should have been outlawed. She must have been spending more time with Stella than I'd realized.

Leon grinned at her stupidly, leading me to believe they were all drunk. In my living room. At nine o'clock in the evening.

"The long story?" I prompted, looking at Stella.

Jackson, in his usual cutoffs and tank top, entered the room just then and handed me a glass of wine. Then he perched on the couch arm beside Stella. She looked up at him and winked. Then she rubbed her shoulder against his bare leg.

Jackson? And Stella? As if he read my thoughts, he rested his hand possessively on her shoulder.

"Well, I guess my little secret about my honey here's out of the bag," she said, patting his leg. "And you must have guessed about Joyce and Leon."

Leon looked at Joyce and Joyce looked at the carpet.

"Our boy saw the error of his ways and asked Joyce to take

him back. So to celebrate, we went deep-sea fishing with this guy Jackson knows from our fishing camp."

"Your fishing camp."

"Oh, that's right. You don't know. Jackson and I are partners in a fishing camp—among other things," she said with a stout laugh. "We built it on some land we bought down by Sebastian. Right on the river. You'll have to come down and see it. Todd thinks it's the greatest."

"Todd."

Stella's eyebrows knit together. "Yes. Todd. Harrington. Honey, are you all right?"

"I don't know," I answered honestly. "I feel like I was just dropped in the middle of a grade B mystery. I'm not sure who's who here."

"Well, you've been busy lately, and a lot's been happening." Stella sighed happily. "Let's just say everything worked out for the best. We came over because we wanted you to go out and celebrate with us."

"You broke into my house to wait for me?"

"We didn't break in," Joyce said, looking hurt. "I used that key you always hide under the flower pot." She pulled the key out of her shorts pocket. "See?"

Was nothing secret—or sacred—in my house?

"Are you mad?"

I looked at the four faces watching me. Stella, world-wise and at the same time as innocent as Bambi; Jackson, somewhat detached and amused; Leon, who still wore the stupid grin; and Joyce who, although she still seemed embarrassed, looked happier than I'd seen her in months. I melted a little. "No. I'm not mad. But I think I'll take a rain check on the celebrating if that's okay."

"But honey—"

"My sister Joanna is in town, and I took her over to see Uncle

Jack for the first time in years. She was pretty upset."

"Oh, Christie," Joyce said, coming over and leaning down, giving me a hug. "That must have been awful."

"It was."

"She's lucky she has you as a sibling," Jackson said. "A lot of sisters would have resented her neglect of her uncle all these years. Especially if they were bearing the burden of that neglect."

I blinked. I had never heard Jackson say that many words at one time before. Maybe he really had been a professor. Stella was grinning at my expression.

"Of course we'll give you a rain check," Joyce said to all those around her. It was an order. She had slipped back into her nurse persona.

"You want us to stay here with you and cheer you up?" Stella asked. She had definitely had too much wine.

I couldn't help but smile. "Not tonight," I told her, getting to my feet. "Tonight you guys go out and celebrate. I'll talk to you tomorrow. Oh, and you might want to put on some clothes. It's chilly out there."

They all looked at each other. "Yes, Mother," Stella said with another laugh.

After they were gone, I tried to get my thoughts about them in order. Stella was right. A lot had happened. Apparently Leon and Joyce were back together. I wanted to be happy for them, but I was terrified for Joyce instead. Could this be for real? Could it last, or would Leon control the remote for another few years until his identity crisis flared again? I knew there were no guarantees, but I suddenly and desperately wished that there were. For Suzy and Peter Phillip's sake.

Stella and Jackson were even harder to reconcile in my mind. All this time I'd been picturing Stella down on the beach lounging around with some millionaire, and all this time she'd been— where? At Jackson's bait shack? In Jackson's trailer? It was true,

Jackson was a nice-looking man and probably very intelligent, although I'd never seen any obvious signs of it before tonight, but Stella and Jackson as partners in a fish camp? Built on property they had bought? Where would Jackson get money to buy riverfront property? He sure as hell hadn't made it at the bait shack selling cups full of bait shrimp and Cokes for fifty cents, or by changing less than a dollar for a beer. My suspicions gained momentum. For that matter, what did I really know about Jackson? He had showed up one day claiming to be from Minnesota and having the fish-belly white skin and accent to prove it. Could Jackson be taking advantage of Stella?

It all gave me a headache, or was aggravating the headache I already had. So instead, I thought about Joanna. My snotty big sister. I had been writing about her just days ago, about the eighteen-year-old Joanna whose nose was perpetually out of joint and in the air. Today's Joanna had shown real sensitivity, something I had not witnessed once in eighteen years of living with her. Her pain about Uncle Jack's illness was genuine. She had even stood up to Mother about it. Could her years away from here have made that much of a difference in her? What was her life like in Alabama? I had always begged off when Mother and Darlene went to visit her. Now I had to wonder. Was she happy? Had her miserable husband improved any? Or her equally miserable son?

It hit me suddenly how out of touch I really was with my family, except for Uncle Jack and Carly, of course. And Todd. Todd. Why wasn't he here? I needed him.

I was ashamed the minute the thought formed in my mind. Too many of us needed him. Too many of us leaned on him. Who could he lean on?

I pulled on a sweater and, taking my glass of wine, headed inevitably for the jetty. This time when I reached it, I didn't bound from rock to rock but made my way carefully to the end.

The tide was out, and the sea a gentlewoman, brushing up against the rocks and swirling gracefully between them. I settled myself down on a flat boulder, crossing my legs and pulling my sweater closer around me.

The breeze was soft, a feather against my skin. My eyes misted as I looked up into the dark night sky at the million stars you can only see at the seashore or, I had been told, in the desert. The slosh of the water as the waves broke on the rocks and the sucking as the sea pulled them backward toward their origin was as soothing as it was friendly.

The night wasn't really that chilly. The chill I felt came from inside, from a certain knowledge that something somewhere was wrong. My uneasiness was unspecified, and I attributed it to feeling too much empathy for Joanna's pain. On top of Uncle Jack's and Carly's and Todd's and my own, it was very nearly unbearable. I almost envied Darlene her wonderful coping tool, denial. It did work for some. For a while. That seemed good enough for me. I put my mind in neutral and let the night and the damp salt air wash over me.

I jumped when I heard a sound down on the beach, but when I looked, my heart filled with love and gratitude. Todd was making his way toward me. He was dressed in his uniform and looked official and threatening and goddamned gorgeous. I got to my feet and met him halfway, walking into his arms. I hugged him tightly.

"I got worried," he said into my hair. "I called and you didn't answer. I know how tough today was on you."

I had called and talked to him briefly after I left Joanna. I thought I'd put a good face on it. Not good enough, apparently. "Oh, God, how I love you," I said, burrowing into his chest. "Do you have any idea how much I love you?"

I felt the chuckle in his chest. "I have all night if you want to show me."

I pulled away. "All night? What about work?"

"Mitch is going to take my shift. He owes me one after the other night. I thought you might want me with you."

I rested my head against him again. "Always," I said, "please."

Joanna left the next morning, but she stopped by the newsroom to see me on her way to the Orlando airport. "Todd seems nicer than I remembered him."

I was still basking in the afterglow of the night before. "He's wonderful."

"Well, take advantage of it," she cautioned. "They change after the wedding."

I wondered if she realized how much she was telling me about her own marriage. As she waited for the elevator, she said, "You'll keep me posted, won't you? About Uncle Jack? Darlene's useless. All she can think of is her dopey kids and her dopier husband, and she won't talk about Uncle Jack at all."

"I promise."

We hugged. It was still awkward for Joanna, but she got through it just fine. Then she was gone. I stared at the closed elevator doors, sorry for the first time to see the back of one of my sisters.

For two weeks after Joanna's visit, nothing untoward happened. I suffered through the visits with Mother while she talked about flowers and food. I made all my fitting appointments on time and tried mightily to feign interest in the proceedings. Lamar smiled and wrote checks. Todd teased me about being the bride of the decade. Darlene pretty much stayed out of the way.

I was able to talk to Stella and Joyce, separately for once. Stella told me she'd been seeing Jackson for over three years. He was her Mister Right, she told me, although in Stella-like terminology. I couldn't bring myself to voice my uglier suspicions to her directly, but I did ask her why Jackson?

She smiled, a smile I'd never seen before. "Because he's everything I've ever wanted in a man."

"You feel comfortable going into business with him?"

Again the smile. "I feel comfortable going into anything with him."

Jackson? Of the bait shack?

When I asked Todd about it, he confirmed that Jackson and Stella were partners in a fishing camp. I broached the subject of Jackson possibly using Stella, but gently, as I suspected Todd and Jackson had become close over the years.

"Using her?" He burst out laughing.

"I didn't mean physically or emotionally," I said, not entirely pleased at his reaction. "I was thinking more financially."

"Honey," he said, taking my hand as I started to turn away, "Jackson is a Bergstein."

"What's a Bergstein?" I asked, turning back.

"One of the richest families in Minnesota, that's what. Jackson is rolling in money."

I was astounded. "But—but the bait shack. His clothes—And I thought he was a professor or something."

"He was and he loved it, but he couldn't get away from being a Bergstein in Minneapolis. That's why he came down here. No one knows him."

"He could have taught here. Why . . ."

Todd shrugged. "He said he wanted something completely different."

I wasn't sure I believed him. The next day, grateful for the newspaper's resources, I did some investigating. Jackson was indeed a Bergstein. Not the heir apparent, but a second son who could be allowed to stray. I saw pictures of their mansion, the family yacht, and I thought of Jackson's bait shack. It appeared that Jackson had succeeded. He had definitely got something completely different.

My talk with Joyce came a few days later. She arrived on my front step and asked to come inside. I led her into the kitchen and poured her the cup of coffee she asked for when I offered wine. In some ways, at least, she was back to the old Joyce. But not quite.

"You probably think I'm weak, taking Leon back," she said with little preamble, managing to sound both embarrassed and defensive.

I sat down at the table across from her. I remembered my reaction to her a few months before when she'd said she wanted her husband back. "What about your pride?" I'd asked her. What an arrogant ass I had been. "No. I don't think you're weak. I think you're courageous."

"You mean to take back someone who'll probably walk out on me again."

I cringed. "No. That's not what I mean. I mean you're courageous because you have the guts to fight for what you want and get it." When she looked surprised, I went on. "I don't know if Stella told you about Todd and me."

"About you being engaged?"

"About our history."

She looked blank. Bless Stella's discreet little heart. "Todd and I go a long way back," I said, suddenly feeling the need to tell her. "He's my stepcousin, you know."

She nodded.

"Well, I fell madly in love with Todd when I was fourteen years old. Four years later, he got married."

"He's divorced?"

"Yes," I said, determined not to be distracted. "We had made plans for the future. He dumped me without any warning. I was devastated for years." I bit my lip. "For a lot more years than even I realized. He was only married for six months. It was a disaster. When he finally showed up again, I was hell-bent on protecting my pride. I wouldn't have anything to do with him. I thought only someone who was wishy-washy would give a guy like that a second chance. If I hadn't—" Suddenly the backs of my eyes burned. I took a deep breath and let it out slowly. "If I hadn't been so self-protective, we'd probably be married right now, and—and my uncle could have walked me down the aisle."

"Oh, Christie," Joyce said, reaching across the table and taking my hand.

I had to bite my trembling bottom lip hard to keep from crying. "So now, because I was so busy protecting my pride . . ." I couldn't finish, but I didn't need to. Joyce squeezed my hand. "Anyway," I said, shaking off the emotion that had blindsided me, "I think it shows a lot of courage to take the kind of risk you're taking."

"You just weren't ready yet to forgive him." It was a statement. A true one.

I released her hand and picked up my coffee cup. My hand was shaking. "Sometimes I feel so young and so dumb," I told her. "Carly worked so hard to teach me forgiveness when I was younger. I remember her telling me that I'd be a lot happier if I learned to forgive. I thought I had. When I forgave my sisters and mother for being jerks, I thought I was the most forgiving person who ever lived. But, you know, I never thought of forgiveness when it came to Todd. I didn't think that had anything to do with what happened between us, but the truth is that I was angry and hurt and unwilling to forgive. I've been just as bad with Carly lately. She came to tell me she wanted to put my uncle in a nursing home, and I felt like I hated her." I shook my head slowly. "I just don't seem to be able to get a handle on this forgiveness thing."

"Is your uncle that bad?"

I brushed the hair out of my face. "No. Yes. He probably is. I called that nursing service you told me about and got someone who could stay with him during the days. It will give Carly a little break. It won't help during the nights, though."

Joyce nodded. "It's really hard on the family. On everyone."

"Do you think he should be in a nursing home?"

She looked at me sympathetically. "I can't answer that, Christie. Oh, it would be easy for me to sit here and say yes or no, but that would be a clinical evaluation. You're not in a clinical situation. You're in a tough personal situation with your uncle and aunt. You all have to make that decision."

We sipped our cooling coffee for a few minutes. Then Joyce got back to the subject we had been discussing. "I'm not a fool. I know it might not work with Leon. He's told me he made a mistake and it'll never happen again." She laughed ruefully. "I wish I had a dime for every time I've had women tell me their husbands said that. It'll be hard to forgive him and trust him again, but—" She shrugged.

"Well, in my newfound wisdom, I can tell you that you have to try. If you love him and there's a chance to make it work, you have to try."

When she left, I felt closer to her than ever before. She was, I realized, a very brave woman.

The feeling of dread that had been with me day and night for weeks increased as the days passed. It was as if I was waiting for something to happen, which made no sense. My uncle was doing—not well, but not too badly. He was walking a little better and even keeping some food down. Todd spent all day Saturday with me since Carly was home. He left at ten-thirty that night to go to work. Sunday we both spent with Uncle Jack and Carly. We cooked chicken out on the grill, and Carly and I made Uncle Jack's favorite potato salad. He ate a little of it. He was sick afterward, but he told us it was worth it. He seemed pitifully frail. You could tell he had to work at being cheerful, but he did make the effort.

Todd was on duty that night, and I headed home about ten, content that I could give Joanna a decent report.

The next morning, Todd didn't show up. I figured he had gotten tied up with work. It happened occasionally. I dressed and headed in to work.

It was quiet in the newsroom, a typical Monday morning. I was sitting at my desk trying to decide which of the fascinating stories I would pursue for the day when I looked up and saw Todd standing in the doorway. He was still in uniform.

"Todd?" It was then I noticed his eyes were red. I stood up. "What is it?"

CHAPTER 20

He crossed the newsroom in four strides and took me into his arms. "It's your Uncle Jack, Christie. He's gone."

I pulled back. "What do you mean he's gone?"

"He died last night in his sleep."

"No." I tried to fight my way free of his arms. "No!"

I don't really remember what happened after that. There are gray recollections of being bundled into Todd's car. I think Virgil was there. Todd strapped me in. The seatbelt felt like a straightjacket. My arms and legs didn't seem to be working properly. I stared out the window of the car as tears ran down my face. I remember the morning sun glinted on the water as we crossed the causeway, and pelicans swooped and plunged beak first into the river in search of their breakfast. I have no memory of arriving at my house. Suddenly it seemed full of people. Stella was there. And Joyce. Why wasn't she working? Where were the kids?

Stella forced brandy on me, then led me to the bathroom and held my head while I was sick. Joyce stuffed a pill in my mouth and held a water glass to my lips. I had no resistance inside me. I swallowed.

It was early afternoon before my mind swam back into focus. I was stretched out on the living room sofa. Todd was sitting on the floor at my feet, watching me. He had changed into clothes he kept at my house. His face looked gray, his eyes dragged down by exhaustion and sorrow.

As I looked at him, pain and sorrow filled me as I remembered. Tears filled my eyes. Without a word, he pulled me down into his lap, wrapping his arms around me, and I huddled against him, crying quietly.

"He wasn't that sick," I whimpered.

"He was, honey."

"He seemed better."

He stroked my hair. "Christie, he wasn't better. You know he wasn't really better."

After a minute, I whispered, "What happened?"

"His heart gave out. That's all. Dr. Johnson said his heart quit beating. Carly said it happened sometime during the night. When she woke up, she realized he wasn't breathing."

I felt the sobs well up in me, and I let them overwhelm me. Then suddenly I pushed myself away. "Carly!"

"She's all right. Dr. Johnson gave her something. I left the nurse with her."

"Oh, God," I moaned. "Poor Carly." The guilt she must be feeling after trying to send him to a nursing home not a month ago. Todd knew nothing about that. He saw my concern as more pure than it was.

"She'll be all right, honey. Don't worry about Mom. Let's just take care of you."

It struck me then that taking care of me was all Todd had been able to do. I had been lying around in a stupor for half a day while my uncle was who knew where and Todd was taking care of me and Carly and everything. I looked at him then, really looked. His face was haggard. His eyes were red, partly from lack of sleep since he'd been on the go for more than twenty-four hours, but partly because he'd lost the stepfather he'd loved for as long as I had loved Todd. It seemed a lifetime to me.

"Are you all right?" I asked, reaching up and touching his face.

"I'm fine." Then he gave me a half-smile. "Well, maybe not fine, but okay."

"Where is he?"

"Dr. Johnson arranged for him to be taken to Smathers' Funeral Home." After a second, he asked, "Do you want me to take you there?"

I knew he'd collapse if he tried to take me anywhere. "No. Not now. I have to call Darlene and Joanna—"

"Stella already did. I didn't think you'd mind."

"No, I don't. How did she know where to call?"

He gestured toward my purse by the front door. "Your address book."

"Oh." I nodded, still studying his exhausted face. "What I'd like to do right now is to drive you to—to your mom's house. You haven't slept at all. You can take a nap while I spend some time with Carly. Okay?"

"You don't have to do that. I can drive."

"You can nap while I drive," I insisted gently. "How about that?"

I could see his desperate need for rest warring with his concern for me. "Are you sure?" he asked.

"Positive," I said, getting to my feet. "Let me grab a change of clothes. We won't drive all the way back here tonight."

He was asleep before we hit A1A, two miles down the road. As I headed south, I felt a hollow ache well up inside of me and threaten to choke me. I fought it back. Todd needed me now, and so did Carly. I'd had my time to react, and I'd have more time later to grieve. Right now I had to function.

Todd awoke when I turned off A1A. The nurse was at the door before we were out of the car, middle-aged and gray and looking fierce. I raced toward the house, afraid something else had happened. "What—"

"Shhh." She held her finger to her lips. "I just wanted to tell you to come in quietly. I gave her another pill a little while ago and she's sleeping. The poor thing," she said, her face softening as she led us toward the kitchen, "Sleep's the only thing that'll help her now."

She didn't need to silence me; the atmosphere in the house would have kept my voice at a whisper. I wasn't usually fanciful, but I could feel the turmoil and grief in the air around me. It was eerie and terrible, as was being in my uncle's house and knowing that he wasn't there, would never be there again.

At my urging, Todd went on into his bedroom to get a little more sleep. I sat in the kitchen with the nurse for a while, not really listening as she chattered on about who knew what. She didn't seem to mind my inattention. At least, it didn't stop her talking. Her fierceness had abated. She was all motherly now. She fixed me tea with enough sugar in it to satisfy even Stella's sweet's craving. I hate hot tea, but I drank it anyway, hardly noticing what was in the cup. When I finished it, I got to my feet and headed in the direction of Carly's room. I needed to see her, even if she was asleep.

"She's in the other room." She pointed toward my room. "She couldn't bear to stay in there."

I don't think I could have, either. I headed in the other direction.

I opened the door and peeked into my room. Carly was stretched out on her back on the bed, covered with a light cotton blanket. She was sleeping but moving restlessly. Her face showed the ravages of the day. Even in sleep, her expression moved constantly from sorrow to pain and back to sorrow. Tears had left tracks on her face.

I sat down gently on the bed, just wanting to be close to her. As I did, she reached automatically beside her to where, I'm certain, my uncle had slept in their own bed. When her hand found empty space, her eyes fluttered open. As they focused on me, an expression of horror crossed her face. She bit her fist and curled protectively on her side. I knew she must be remembering what had happened, as I had when I'd awakened earlier to find Todd watching me.

"Carly, it's okay. I'm here now. Todd and I are both here. You aren't alone."

I could feel her sobs shaking the bed, although she made no sound. I thought then about what it must have been like for her to wake and realize my uncle wasn't breathing, to think that she had slept on after his heart had quit beating. It was almost too terrible to grasp.

I gently rubbed her back for a while. It was all I could do. After a long time, her sobs subsided. A little while later, her breathing evened. I thought maybe she'd fallen asleep.

As I rose from the bed, I heard her voice, little more than a hoarse whisper, say, "Christie. I'm so sorry. I . . ." Her voice trailed off.

"I know," I said. "Don't think about it now. Just rest."

Back in the living room, the nurse was sitting on the couch, an unopened magazine on her lap. She was unruffled in her white uniform and shoes. I guess this was routine for her. "Would it be possible—I mean, I'll have to go to the funeral home. Make arrangements. Could you stay for a while?"

"Long as you need me, Miss O'Kelly. I already called my daughter. She's bringing me an overnight bag in case I need it. I'll just stay here with your aunt as long as you want me to. Poor thing doesn't need to be dealing with all that right now. Couldn't anyway, if you ask me. Dr. Johnson left me enough pills to get her through the next few days."

Relieved, I headed into Todd's bedroom.

It was the first time I had been in it since he left to go back to college that winter so long ago, and it had changed little. That was comforting. He was face down on the bed, still dressed in his clothes. I decided to leave him where he was and go alone, even though I dreaded the thought. As I tiptoed toward the door, I heard him stir, then his voice, "Christie? Is Mom okay?"

I turned back, coming to sit beside him and curling my hand in his, still sleep-warm. "She's asleep again. I thought I'd go over to the funeral home to see what they'll need."

He sat up, running his fingers through his hair. "Give me five minutes to get a shower and I'll go with you."

"You don't have to do that."

He looked at me levelly. "Yes. I do. Wait for me. Okay?"

"Okay," I said, swallowing hard with relief.

Going to the funeral home was a nightmare. It was a long, low-slung building, all dignity and soft music. Someone had made a feeble attempt to dress up the interior with silk trees and flowers, as colorless and without life as most of the residents, including the funeral director who met us at the door. He spoke in a low monotone. My uncle, he informed me, had not wanted a funeral. He had requested cremation. I remembered then that long before his illnesses had rendered him incapable of humor, he had joked about wishing he could be an organ donor but fearing he would have no organs worth salvaging by the time he died. I hadn't laughed then and I didn't laugh now. I told them I wanted a memorial service. What I really wanted was my uncle back.

When we arrived back at the house, the nurse told me my sister Joanna had called. I felt sick as I dialed the number. Joanna answered on the first ring. Her voice was husky, and she broke down as soon as she realized it was me. "I can't believe it. I just saw him. I can't stand it that he's gone. What if I hadn't come to Cocoa Beach for my fitting? I would never have seen him again. Oh, God! Why did I ever move to this godforsaken place? I should have been there. I could have seen him all the time. Now it's too late."

I listened for what seemed like hours. Joanna needed to talk. Her guilt was tearing at her. I told her I felt the same way even though I'd lived here the whole time. That it must be some strange phenomenon that occurred when you lost someone you loved. We both felt we had given him too little of our time, although, as Joanna pointed out, she had good reason to feel that way. I told her what little I knew, that he had died in his sleep, that his heart had just stopped beating. She didn't ask about Carly. We hung up with her promise to be at the memorial service. Then I called Darlene. She was sad but calm. "Thank God he's finally out of pain," she said, but I felt she was talking more about herself.

I hung up the phone and sat staring at it, unsure about what I was about to do. Why should I? Would she even care? After a few minutes, I picked up the receiver and dialed my mother's number.

"I wanted to tell you," I said when she answered, "that Uncle Jack died last night."

I heard her sharp intake of breath, then silence. I started to apologize for bothering her, but she said softly, sadly, "Thank you, Christiana. Thank you for letting me know."

Then I laid my head down on my folded arms and wept, for love and loss and for people who didn't know how to show they cared.

There was no casket at the memorial service; the cremation had taken place almost immediately. Instead, a picture of my uncle taken years ago rested on a pedestal table, surrounded by flowers. Attendance was larger than I had expected. A lot of people were there from where my uncle had worked, and a number of Uncle Jack and Carly's neighbors.

Paul from Fischer's came. He shook Todd's hand. Then he hugged me and kissed my cheek. I saw his eyes come to rest on my left hand, on the beautiful diamond in the wide gold band. "I'm so sorry, Christie," he said. I knew his words were sincere, but I thought maybe he wasn't talking about just my uncle.

Joanna was there, along with Doug and Edwin, her son. Neither Doug nor Edwin seemed much improved by age. Doug had put on a lot of weight and clearly didn't want to be there. He avoided me, not that I made it hard for him. Edwin kept checking his watch as if the service were keeping him from some important appointment. Joanna was in too much pain to be embarrassed by their behavior, and I loved my new, caring sister enough to overlook them altogether.

Darlene and Fred, along with the twins and Freddie, came. Darlene remained dry-eyed, but Fred Senior seemed deeply touched. I fear I had always underestimated the man. The twins were quiet and respectful. Freddie tried to be brave, but halfway through the service, he broke down and turned his face into his mother's shoulder. To her credit, she put her arm around him and held him. Darlene sincerely loved her children.

Carly went through the days before and after the service in a drug-induced daze. She cried silently all the way to the funeral home and accepted condolences from well-meaning friends without hearing any of them. Todd and I supported her between us during the service itself. No one seeing her that day could have doubted how deeply she loved the man to whom we had come to say goodbye. Her tears continued all the way back to the house, where she collapsed as she got out of the car. Todd carried her inside while I wondered what people who didn't have a Todd did at times like this.

The nurse, Ethyl—I had finally remembered her name—stayed with her when Todd and I went back to the funeral home to collect my uncle's ashes and carry out his last wishes, wishes that Carly wanted no part of. I felt strangely peaceful as we drove back to the beach that day. Jackson took us offshore in his fishing boat, where we sprinkled my uncle's ashes into the Atlantic, knowing they would wash back up on the shore to mingle with the sand. Now, I felt, he would forever be a part of this place that had been his happiest home. I guess that was where I really said goodbye to him.

Todd put his arm across my shoulders. We were silent all the way back.

For the next three weeks, I pretty much moved into the house on Melbourne Beach. We kept the nurse on, although we really couldn't afford to. Dr. Johnson insisted it was necessary so that the insurance company would pay some of it. Todd switched his hours to days so that we could both be with Carly at night, when her demons seemed to be the worst. I made the twenty-four-mile commute each way every day. I reduced my hours. Virgil was patient with me, and the rest of the newsroom, although sympathetic for my loss, was glad to get my stories.

Carly continued to sleep in my room. I slept in Todd's bed one night while he slept on the couch. The next night I brought him to bed with me in his room. A month before, such behavior would have been unthinkable, but Carly was too drugged now to notice or care.

According to Ethyl, she spent her days staring at the television. Todd and I knew she also spent her nights that way. Whatever time we awoke, we could hear the television in the next room. It was as if she couldn't bear the silence. Or the dark. When she did sleep because we forced a sleeping pill on her, she had to have both the television and a light on in the room. If we tried to slip in and turn them off, she awoke immediately.

And cried. It seemed impossible that one human being could

shed so many tears. After the second week, I became seriously concerned about her health. She ate no more than a few bites at each meal. Her skin was hanging on her frame. Her eyes never met ours, and no matter what they say, it didn't work to tell her, "Uncle Jack would want you to go on," or "Uncle Jack would want you to take care of yourself." I tried both, and we had to put her to bed with medication each time when she became hysterical.

Finally, in desperation, I called Dr. Johnson. It was late on Thursday afternoon. I had come home early since Ethyl had to baby-sit her grandchildren. Todd was on duty, so just Carly and I were in the house.

Dr. Johnson was in with a patient, but he called me back minutes later. "Christie? What's the matter?"

"It's Carly, Dr. Johnson."

"What about her?" His voice sounded tense. He must have been expecting my call.

"I'm worried about her. She's barely eating or sleeping." I glanced toward the bedroom, where Carly was taking a nap—or pretending to. "I don't know what's going to happen to her if this keeps up. I wondered if you had any ideas about what we should do?"

"There's nothing you can do, Christie," he told me in that perfectly reasonable voice that set my teeth on edge. "Just give her time."

"But it's been weeks already."

"Each person reacts to grief differently. She just needs time."

I wasn't satisfied. Time didn't seem to be doing Carly a bit of good.

I peeked into her bedroom a little later. She was lying on her side on the bed, staring at the wall. In a moment of inspiration, or maybe it was exasperation, I swung the door wide open. "I need your help out here, Carly," I said matter-of-factly. "I can't keep doing all this alone." Then I turned and walked away.

I went into the kitchen and pretended to start preparing dinner. I listened for a sound in the hallway. I was about to give it up as another failure when I heard uneven footsteps coming toward me. After a minute, she came into the kitchen. She had quit dressing in street clothes. Instead she wore a bathrobe over her pajamas. That was fine with me. At least she was out of bed.

I feigned nonchalance. "Why don't you sit down there," I said, motioning toward a kitchen chair. "You can peel these potatoes for me."

She functioned like an automaton, wordlessly following my orders. I had her setting the table when Todd got home.

He was astounded to see her up and out of bed. "Mom," he said, going to her and putting his arms around her, "you're up."

She collapsed against him as if she couldn't hold herself up any longer. His eyes met mine over her head, questioning. I shook my head slightly at him. "You need to put out the napkins, Carly," I said in the same businesslike voice I had been using all along.

With what seemed like an enormous effort of will, she pulled herself up and went to the sideboard drawer where she kept the napkins.

Todd looked troubled, but he followed my lead all through dinner. I instructed Carly to pass things and to try her potatoes and vegetables—meat seemed beyond her—and she obeyed like a child. It was awful, but it was a start.

After dinner, I told her to go take a bath. When she was gone, Todd turned to me. "What's going on, Christie?"

I motioned for him to help me clear the table. "I think we're guilty of loving Carly too much," I said. I told him about my unsatisfactory conversation with the doctor. "I know he said we have to give Carly time, but time doesn't seem to be helping. I think our patience has enabled her to give up." I felt out of my element, but determined all the same. "I think we're going to have to kick-start her motor. Give her simple things to do until she starts functioning on her own again."

Todd seemed unconvinced, but he agreed to go along with it.

Before I left the next morning, I gave Ethyl instructions that she was to get Carly involved in her day. "I want the TV off. I want her to help you fix lunch. She used to love to cook. I want her to help with dishes. I want her to bathe herself and fix her hair and get dressed. She has to get busy. She never could stand to be idle."

"I think it's too soon," Ethyl said with a huff.

"Maybe, but let's try it anyway."

Our gazes met, clashed. Then she looked away. "I'll try—if you insist. But I wouldn't count on much success. You can't rush things like this."

"Thank you, Ethyl," I said, gracious now that I'd won the battle. "I'll call you this afternoon to see how thing are going."

As it turned out, a minor boating accident took me to Sebastian Inlet that afternoon, so I stopped by instead of calling.

The television was off. Carly's hair was brushed and she was out of the bathrobe I had come to hate. The next day, she was in the kitchen helping Ethyl fix dinner when I arrived. She seemed a little better, Ethyl admitted grudgingly when Carly was out of earshot.

After a couple of days, she could participate in a conversation. She wouldn't initiate it, but she'd answer questions if they were put to her. I considered it a milestone.

I called her neighbor, Nancy, the next week. I explained what we had been through with Carly and what we were trying to accomplish. Nancy was more than happy to help. She dropped by at least once a day and engaged Carly in conversation. After two weeks, Carly agreed to go with her to the grocery store. Another milestone.

Although she said nothing, I could tell that Carly was uncomfortable around me. I wasn't surprised, since I was the one ordering her around. She seemed a little better with Todd, and even more so with Ethyl. That was fine. I could bear her resentment as long as she came back to life.

I called Dr. Johnson to report on Carly's progress and thought he seemed relieved. It occurred to me that maybe he had been concerned after all.

Before another week had passed, Carly was functioning somewhat normally. Not happily, but adequately. According to Ethyl, she got out of bed in the mornings without being told and showered and dressed. She fixed her meals, although she took little pleasure in the process. She cleaned the house. Nancy was still dropping by every day or so, and Carly now agreed to go wherever Nancy suggested. She cut Nancy's hair. A couple of days later, she announced that she was going back to work.

I felt such relief I could have wept. Todd hugged me and told me I was a genius. I packed the clothes that had accumulated during the weeks and prepared to go home. When I announced my plans to Carly, she seemed relieved. I thought she was tired of me standing over her shoulder and passed off her stiffness when I hugged her to the same thing.

I headed back to Cape Canaveral in blissful ignorance, thinking that the worst was behind us now. It wasn't until later that I began to realize that Carly wanted me to leave because of the guilt she felt every time she looked at me.

CHAPTER 21

Realization comes in a rush sometimes; at others, it creeps in like the fog over the river. That's how it was with me.

I postponed my wedding, of course. I even suggested we forget the wedding altogether. Todd and I could have a civil ceremony later in the year, I told Mother. She took the postponement better than I expected, but she asked me as a personal favor to go through with the wedding. She acted like it was important to her. I couldn't tell her no. She had seemed subdued since my phone call the night after my uncle died. I think, like all of us, she had thought that Jack O'Kelly and endurance were synonymous. Beyond that, I don't know what she thought.

Carly showed no interest in our wedding plans. She ignored any reference to them, except when I mentioned gently that Lamar had asked if he could give me away. Then she froze. Not looking at me, she said, "He couldn't have walked you down the aisle anyway." It was a strange remark, but she made a lot of strange remarks during that time.

She seemed to be functioning on autopilot, going through the motions. She went to work, came home, fixed an unimaginative dinner, and sat in front of the television until bedtime. From Todd's reports I knew that she still slept in my room and kept the light and television on throughout the night. I saw little of Todd unless I went to Melbourne Beach, because he still didn't want to leave Carly alone at night. She clung to him as she had never clung to my uncle. I told myself I understood, but I was beginning to want my life—our life—back.

My birthday came and went. I received a card from Joanna, the first I could remember ever receiving from her. I was touched, but more than anything, I was sad. It had been just a year ago that my uncle had made me the strawberry shortcake. I remembered the pride that had filled his face when he carried it to the table without dropping it, and I shed more than a few tears.

Shortly after that I suggested we pack my uncle's things away. It was a painful process, but long overdue. Todd agreed. While the room remained untouched and unlived in, it would serve as a constant reminder of what we had lost. Carly, not surprisingly, refused to help, although I caught sight of her more than once hovering just outside the door.

We started with the closets, carefully folding and packing my uncle's clothes into cardboard boxes. Then the drawers. In the back of one of them, I discovered a journal, a small, leather-bound book with lined pages. On the first page were the words, "I was born in Mississippi on the banks of the river, but I never truly felt at home until my father moved us lock, stock, and barrel to Florida."

The writer in me felt a rush as I realized my uncle had at least begun to write his autobiography. I flipped forward. There was writing on almost every page.

"Todd, look at this," I said as he walked back into the bedroom. "I think it's a journal. I didn't even know he kept one."

"Let me see," Todd said, reaching for the book.

At that moment, Carly hurried into the room. She took the book out of my hands. Then she looked startled at what she'd done. "It's—mine," she said, letting the hand holding the journal fall to her side. Glancing quickly at each of us, she turned and left the room.

Todd and I looked at each other. Even for Carly, it was odd behavior. "Maybe she felt it was personal," he said. "She might have wanted to read it first." It wasn't so much an explanation as an apology.

Carly came back after a few minutes. "I'll help," she announced without meeting either Todd's or my eyes.

The next weekend, Todd and I painted the room a different color and changed the bedspread and drapes. We rearranged the furniture. We were a little desperate, I think.

A few days later, Carly moved back into the room although, according to Todd, the lights and television remained on at night.

I continued to journey down to Melbourne Beach several times a week. I would have dinner with Todd and Carly. Then he and I would walk on the beach for a while before I headed home. It was less than satisfactory as a courtship, and I was sure the strain was coloring my take on things. Still, it began to frustrate me that Carly seemed so uncomfortable when I was around. I knew I resembled my uncle, in coloring at least, but there was little I could do about that.

"Give her time," Todd said. It seemed to be the advice of the year. What choice did I have?

I gave her time. She withdrew, either physically or mentally, whenever I came into the room. She flinched when I touched her. She made other odd remarks. One night, without preamble, she said, "He wasn't getting better. He was getting worse every day."

It took me a minute to realize what she was talking about. "I know."

"He really was," she insisted. "Dr. Johnson said he was deteriorating fast."

Another time, she said, "He wanted to give up. Did he tell you that?"

"Yes."

She examined my face. Her eyes looked a little wild, or maybe it was just the light. "He told me he wished he knew how to give up."

"I remember," I said carefully. It didn't take much to set her off.

Appearing satisfied, she went back to watching television.

Little alarm bells began to sound in my head.

Then came the night I asked Todd to attend a banquet with me. It was one of those deadly boring political affairs I would normally refuse to attend, but I was hoping I could choreograph another little affair to follow, this one at my house.

"It shouldn't run late," I told Todd and Carly. "These things seldom last later than ten or eleven o'clock." It would be over at eight and I knew it, but I had plans for Todd afterward, plans that his mother had no business knowing about.

Todd must have picked up on my excitement. He looked from me to Carly.

She gave each of us what passed these days for a smile, forced and wobbly. "You kids go on to the dinner. I'll be fine." Saying that, she slowly pushed herself out of her chair and headed into her newly decorated bedroom, closing the door behind her.

I felt my cheeks go hot. "Who is that woman that's inhabiting your mother's body?" I demanded of Todd.

He looked from the closed door to me. "Honey, I know it's a little exasperating—"

"A little exasperating!" At his signal, I automatically lowered my voice. "It isn't a little exasperating. It's mind numbing, Todd. Good God, you'd think she'd allow you a night out now and then. Even lowly servants get a day off."

"Christie—"

"I'm sorry, Todd," I said, not feeling a bit sorry. "I just don't know how much more of this poor-victim routine I can take. I know she lost her husband, and I'm terribly sorry. But, you know, I lost my uncle at the same time. Life has to go on. You remember life. That thing we used to have?"

"Honey, you're being unreasonable."

"I am not being unreasonable. I'm being honest with you, and I'm being normal and maybe lonely and horny."

"Shhh . . ." He held his finger to his lips.

It was the final straw. I slammed my hand down on the table. "What do you mean, 'Shhh?' Are we going to pretend now that our relationship is platonic? After we spent weeks sleeping in your bedroom while we took care of her?" I jumped to my feet and stomped across the room. Then I came back and stood in front of him, all but seething. "I'm sorry, Todd. I've had it with this. I know you love your mother. I love her too, but we've lived our lives around her sorrow for months. I never even had a chance to grieve my uncle's death because it might bother Carly. It's too much. We're never together anymore. We can't be together here because she's here. We can't go out because you don't want to leave her alone. You might be all right with that, but I'm not."

"Is the banquet really that important to you?"

I thought the top of my head was going to blow off. "This is not about a damned banquet. To hell with the banquet. Don't you see? It's everything. I'm not going to spend the rest of my life tiptoeing around Carly's sensibilities. I want to live life. I want to live it with you, but one way or another I'm going to live it."

He looked at me. Then he looked toward the room where Carly was holed up. He hesitated too long. I spun on my heel, saying over my shoulder, "Give me a call when you get your priorities straight. You probably still remember the number."

I took a water tumbler of wine to the jetty that night. It seemed impossible that I was back here alone. After all that Todd and I had been through over the years, was it to end here because of this? I didn't think I was being unreasonable but, even if I was, I had meant what I said. I had loved my uncle deeply, but I didn't intend to spend the rest of my life grieving his loss or being controlled by someone else's grief.

As a martyr, Carly was beginning to make my mother look like an amateur. I simply could not understand it. I knew she was grieving—we were all grieving—but why was she blatantly vying for pity like this? The Carly I had long known and loved wouldn't have done this, wouldn't have tried to manipulate her son's life by playing on his sympathy. Yes, she had suffered a loss, but lots of people suffered losses and went on with their lives. She acted like it was all her fault.

The thought stopped me, glass halfway to my lips. I breathed in. Breathed out. That was exactly what she was acting like. Was she playing on our sympathy because of guilt? Did she think we couldn't pity her and blame her at the same time?

I got to my feet and headed back toward the house as a vague sense of unease settled on me and ugly thoughts flitted through my mind, thoughts that refused to be pinned down. As I jumped to the sand, I saw Todd coming down the beach toward me. I stopped and waited for him.

"You came," I said when he reached me.

"I love you, Christie."

I wasn't that easy. "What about Carly? Did you get someone to stay with her?"

He shook his head. "She's the one who told me to come. She overheard our conversation. She said you were right, that we had to get on with our lives. She said for me to tell you she's sorry she has been such a problem."

I gritted my teeth against words I knew I'd regret later. He was here now, and I loved and needed him. It had to be enough. For now.

Our lives improved just slightly after that. The unfocused thoughts that had threatened to come forward that night at the jetty remained unfocused. Todd and I had some evenings together. Alone. I spent some evenings with him and Carly. She was pleasant and more like normal than she'd been for a long time, but I still wasn't comfortable. She . . . watched me, as if she were waiting for something. I quit trying to put her at ease. My efforts weren't working anyway, I reasoned, so why bother. It was a foot-stomping, immature reaction, but I wasn't feeling particularly mature at that point in my life. I was feeling frustrated, and something more I couldn't quite put my finger on.

Todd was a bird on a wire, trying to balance his loyalties. I felt for him, but I wasn't about to go back to the way things had been. I informed him of my plans. If he wanted to take part, I included him. If not, I went on without him. It was about to kill me.

I told Mother to hold off a little longer on the wedding plans. It looked like she'd get her winter wedding after all. Or maybe it would be spring. Or maybe there wouldn't be a wedding at all. I wasn't sure anymore, but I was sure that I wouldn't marry a man who only came to me because his mother told him to. Todd had to make some hard choices, and I wasn't at all certain what his ultimate choice would be. My love life was pretty shaky.

Life was better in other areas. I got a call from Joanna late one afternoon when I was feeling particularly down. "I'm back," she announced in a singsong voice.

I felt warm just hearing her voice. "That's great. For how long?"

"Forever."

I was stunned. "Forever? What about Doug? And Edwin?"

Her laugh barked out over the phone. "What about them? I left them in Alabama."

"But—"

"I'll tell you all about it, but not over the phone. Come out with me tonight. Let's get drunk."

Joanna drank? "Uh—sure. Where and what time?"

"It's your town. It is now, anyway. You tell me where. What time is right this minute as far as I'm concerned."

I looked at my cluttered desk, at the half-finished story in my typewriter. "Now is perfect. I'll meet you at Fischer's in . . . what? Half an hour?"

"Fischer's?"

"Bernard's Surf. The bar."

"I'll be there."

My head spun with questions as I drove across the causeway. What in the world had prompted Joanna to leave Doug? Well, knowing Doug, I could imagine what prompted it, but why now? Where was she going to live? What kind of job could she get? As far as I knew, Joanna had never worked a day in her life.

I arrived at Fischer's in just over forty minutes. The room was so dark after the sun's glare that it took a minute for my eyes to adjust. I heard Joanna before I saw her.

"There she is. I told you she'd be early," she told Paul.

I walked up to her and hugged her before she could react. "I'm so glad you're here," I told her with sincerity that surprised even me.

"Me, too," she said, laughing.

I turned to Paul. It was the first time I'd seen him since the memorial service. "Hi, Paul."

His grin was almost back to its usual wattage. "Hi yourself, stranger. Coke or beer?"

"Beer. Thanks."

"I beat you here," Joanna said, pushing her glass away. "Of course, I didn't have far to come."

I dropped my purse on the floor beside my stool. "When did you get back, and where are you staying?"

"Last night, and at Mother and Lamar's, although that won't last long. Lamar's a soft touch. He'd give you the shirt off his back and the money to buy a matching coat, but Mother's a different story. I'll play on Lamar's sympathy until I decide what I want to do."

I grinned. If this new Joanna was still a manipulator, at least she was a candid one.

Paul came back with my beer. As he put it down on the napkin in front of me, I saw his eyes once again come to rest on the ring on my hand. "I didn't get to congratulate you on your engagement, Christie. Todd. He's your uncle's stepson, isn't he?"

I nodded.

"Well, I wish you happiness. You deserve it."

His words touched me because I knew he meant them. "Thanks, Paul."

"If it couldn't be me, I'm glad it's him," he added before moving off down the bar.

Joanna was looking at me through narrowed eyes. "Do you have every guy in this town in love with you?"

I blinked, sitting back. "Don't be silly. Paul was kidding."

"Was he? Who else are you stringing along?"

"No one," I protested.

As the words came out of my mouth, the outer door to Fischer's swung open. I groaned as Alf Reed and Gordon Bennett strolled into the room.

"Christie!" Alf bellowed when he spotted me. "So this is where you ran off to." He advanced on us, Gordon a step behind.

They both eyed Joanna with open curiosity. There was no getting out of it. "Joanna, this is Alf and Gordon. They work with me at the paper. Guys, this is my sister, Joanna Dawson."

"O'Kelly," she corrected me, offering her hand to Alf and then Gordon. "I intend to take my maiden name back after the divorce is final."

"Divorce?" Gordon echoed. It was a subject with which he had a lot of experience.

They started to settle at the bar on either side of us. I felt the beginnings of panic. "Guys," I said, "Joanna and I have a lot to catch up on. If you don't mind."

Alf looked sulky, but Gordon winked at Joanna. "Sure, Christie," he said, getting back to his feet. "We're just going to grab a quick one and head down the beach." He nudged Alf on down the bar. "Maybe we'll run into you two again later," he said over his shoulder. "Sounds like your sister and I have a lot in common."

I breathed a sigh of relief as they left. Joanna looked amused. "So Alf is number three."

"Alf is—" I began, then lowered my voice. "Alf is after anything in skirts. What he really wants is a piece of—" I broke off, scandalized at myself

"You can say ass in front of me, Christie," Joanna chuckled. "I've seen a few. Known a few, too." She shook her head, regarding me. "I just can't believe it. My baby sister, the late bloomer, turns out to be the vamp of Cocoa Beach."

"I'm not the vamp of anywhere," I argued. "I'm engaged—"

"With a string of broken hearts behind you." She looked down the bar to where Paul was listening to Gordon and Alf with half an ear as he watched Joanna and me. "Like our boy Paul there."

Thank God her voice was low enough that Paul couldn't hear her. "I never even dated Paul," I hissed.

"I'll bet that wasn't his fault."

Just then he smiled down at us. "He really is a great guy," I said, meaning it.

Joanna was looking down the bar with her head tilted to one side. "And adorable," she agreed. Then she turned back to me. "But Todd's greater?"

"Todd is—" I faltered, not sure what to say.

Joanna raised her eyebrows. "Uh-oh. That doesn't sound good. Trouble?"

I wasn't ready to talk to Joanna about Todd. As strange as it sounded, I didn't feel like I knew her well enough for that. "No you don't," I said, reverting to my light tone. "We're here to talk about you."

Joanna picked up her beer and took a sip. "Me? Wow, what can I say?"

"Start at the beginning. We have all evening."

An hour later, I felt like weeping. Joanna was home because she had walked in on Doug and his fifty-five-year-old secretary while they had been engaged in kinky sex in her marital bed.

"I never knew he went in for that kind of stuff. No wonder he never wanted me," she said without excessive self-pity. "I thought I was too old or ugly and here he wanted me to grow gray hair and spank him." She shuddered. "God, it was hideous. They acted like it was my fault for getting home early. Doug actually told me I should have called." She laughed, then her eyes filled with tears. She blinked them back, biting her lip. "I felt like I was the one who'd been screwed. He refused to give me a divorce until I threatened to tell his mommy."

"Oh, Joanna, I'm so sorry."

"Don't be," she said, sitting back and crossing her legs. "He finally agreed to a divorce and a hefty settlement in return for my silence. He's really a bigwig in old hell-hole, Alabama. President and CEO of his daddy's company, and that company is the only thing that keeps the town alive. He has a lot to lose if he doesn't keep his end of the bargain."

"What about Edwin?" I asked gently.

"That little spawn of Satan?" she said, but her face was bleak. "I don't mean that, but God, he's his father all over again. Oh, not the sex part. At least, not as far as I know. He informed me in no uncertain terms that even if I was going to abandon his father, he wasn't. I couldn't tell him the truth. That's part of the deal." Her eyes pleaded with me to understand.

"What do you mean?"

She finished her beer and motioned to Paul for another. "I mean that I leave town quietly, Edwin remains with his father and his loving Alabama relatives, and Doug files for divorce on the grounds of irreconcilable differences and he sends me a check for a million."

I gasped. Exactly how rich was Joanna's husband? "Still—"

"Oh, it's all right," she said, knowing where I was going, "I got myself into it by acting like a slut in my mother's bedroom."

I groaned. "You remember that."

She grinned at me. "I certainly do. You were a mouthy little shit back then."

"I still am."

She laughed as Paul placed another beer in front of her and moved away to give us privacy. Her smile wavered a little. "You were more than that. You were the one who made my wedding dress fit me. I'll never forget that. After the way Darlene and I treated you all those years, you should have cut it up in ribbons and thrown it back at me."

"I was paying back a debt," I said, my mind traveling back-ward.

"What do you mean?"

Now it was my turn to grin. "Remember that bathing suit I stole from you?"

It was after midnight when I got home. The lights were on in my living room and Todd's car was parked in the driveway. I frantically searched my mind. I was certain we hadn't made plans. In fact, I hadn't seen or talked to him for a week, and I wasn't particularly happy about it.

The front door was unlocked. Todd was standing at the window.

"Todd?" I said as I went in. "Is everything all right? Is Carly okay?"

"Carly's fine." He continued to stare out the window. "Did you have a good time?"

Something in his voice sounded a little off. "Yes," I offered tentatively.

"Was that Paul who was with you?"

I groaned inwardly. Paul had insisted on following me home to make sure I made it all right. We had both followed Joanna to my mother's house for the same reason. "He wasn't with me. He followed me home. Joanna and I were at Fischer's all evening. We had a lot to drink."

"I didn't know Joanna was in town." His voice was still calm. Entirely too calm.

"I didn't either until this afternoon. She called me at the office and asked me to meet her."

He glanced over his shoulder. "It would have been nice if you had let me know. Maybe I could have come with you."

I bristled. "We were catching up. She's left Doug. She wanted to talk about it."

"I guess you wouldn't have wanted me there. Still, it would have been nice to spend an evening with you."

I felt the temper boil close to the surface. "I feel the same way. It would be nice to spend an evening with you, but you haven't been available."

"I was tonight."

"And exactly how was I supposed to know that? You didn't call to tell me about it. Joanna didn't call until four, and I hadn't heard a word about your free evening by then. Maybe I should have checked with you before I made plans with my sister."

He turned to face me. "It would have been nice."

I actually stomped my foot. "What the hell is it with you, Todd?" I demanded. "Here we've spent months barely seeing each other because we're too busy coddling your mother and that's just fine. I don't see you or hear from you for a week but that's fine too. Then I spend one damned evening with my sister and you're jealous."

"I'm not—"

"The hell you aren't," I said angrily, pacing the floor in front of him. "Well, join the club. Don't you think I'm sick and tired of you choosing your mother over me? Don't you think I'd like a little bit of your time that she doesn't bestow upon us like a gift? I know all about jealousy. I've been sick with it ever since you started acting like she was more important to you than me—than us. So don't talk to me about jealousy!"

He flinched at my words, and his face went pale. "She needs me."

"She needs a shrink!" I spat out angrily.

He rubbed his hand over his face. "I know," he said.

That brought me up short. "You know?"

"I'm not blind, Christie."

"You sure have acted like it."

He winced.

"I'm sorry," I said, meaning it. "That was a low blow." All the anger left me as quickly as it had come. I took his hand and led him to the sofa, sitting down beside him. "Come on. Talk to me. Why haven't you at least called? What's going on?"

He sat on the edge of the cushion, staring at the floor, his hands clutched between his open knees. "I don't know exactly. Something's not right. She's—" He glanced over at me. "It's strange, Christie. One minute she's acting like everything's all right. The next—" He threw his hands up in the air. "I don't know. Somehow it's all connected with you. If I say I'm going to call you or come over, she gets weird. I don't know what the hell is going on. She loves you. I know she loves you, but . . ."

I nodded. Thank God he'd finally seen it. Thank God I hadn't imagined it. "I think it's guilt."

"Guilt? For what?"

"I'm not sure." I bit my lip as I realized that wasn't entirely true. "Well, I know part of it, at least." Now it was my turn to stare at the floor. "I shouldn't even be telling you this." I took a deep breath and let it out slowly. "She came here alone about a month before Uncle Jack died. She told me she wanted to put him in a nursing home. She tried to get me to agree to it."

"What? What are you talking about?"

"Carly came over one night and told me that living with Uncle Jack was horrible. She said she couldn't take it anymore, that she wanted to put him in a nursing home. I told her to forget it."

"You never said a word about it."

"I told her I wouldn't. She acted ashamed afterward. She was afraid I'd tell you and Uncle Jack. I promised her . . ." I looked over at him. "I guess my promise didn't mean much, but if that's what is making her act like this, maybe it would be better to get it out into the open. Maybe we can be a family again."

He opened his arms to me, and I went into them. "I don't know what's happening to us anymore," I said against his shoulder. "Is this mess what's going to finally do us in?"

He buried his face in my hair. "Nothing's going to do us in.

Remember? I promised you."

"I hope you're better at your promises than I am."

"Christie." He kissed me lightly, then drew back. "You never would have told me if you didn't think it would help Mom. I know that."

I held him tightly. There was so very, very much I loved about this man.

After a long time, he said, "What about Joanna? How come she left Doug?"

I had forgotten all about my sister. "I don't want to talk about Joanna," I said, slipping my hand inside his shirt.

He made a sound deep in his throat. "What do you want to talk about, then?"

I began undoing his shirt buttons one at a time. "What makes you think I want to talk?"

Later, I lay propped up on one elbow staring down at him. The moonlight shone through the window, providing just enough light for me to see the beautiful sharp planes of his face. I loved every bit of it: the square chin, his lips, full and soft, the tiny lines at the corners of his eyes. I traced his cheekbone, then his jaw. "What were you doing here anyway?"

He stretched out his legs, trapping my ankle between them. "I told Mom I was going to call you. She went all weird again, and I got pissed. So I left."

I smiled. "Were you really jealous of Paul?"

He looked up at me, his face serious. "I wanted to go out there and beat the hell out of him."

"Paul's just a friend."

"Yeah. Right," he muttered. "I've seen the way he looks at you."

"Paul," I repeated, tracing his lips with the tip of my finger, "is just a friend. You are the man I love."

He pulled me down on top of him, holding me tightly, his vulnerability back in an instant. "Don't change your mind. Hang in there with me, Christie. We'll work this out. I swear to God, somehow we'll work this out."

The next evening we confronted Carly.

I went over for dinner. Todd cooked out on the grill. I felt my uncle's presence on the deck. Carly was still watching me carefully. This time she had a good reason.

I hadn't betrayed her trust lightly. I was frightened for her, terrified of the changes I was seeing in her. She was unstable and becoming more so. I saw Carly in two distinct ways: as the mother who had guided my adolescence with a gentle and sensible hand, and as the widow of my uncle who had become unhinged by his death. Somehow I couldn't bring the two images together into one person.

After dinner, we sat in the living room. When Carly started to turn on the television, Todd stopped her. "We want to talk to you, Mom."

She looked alarmed. I could see her struggling for control as she sat down on the couch. "About what?"

"About Uncle Jack," I said gently.

She flushed and started to rise. Todd stopped her. "Wait, Mom. We need to talk about this."

She sat back down, her hands clenched into fists in her lap looking at neither of us.

"Carly," I began, unsure what to say now that I was actually talking to her, "I told Todd about you wanting to put Uncle Jack into a nursing home."

She flushed a bright red, but I didn't know if it was from anger or embarrassment. I went on before she could say anything. "I know you're feeling guilty about it, and it's making you—it's tearing you up. I understand how you felt when you said it was horrible living with him. I—"

"That's a lie," she blurted out, glaring at me. "You're a liar. I never said that. I never said anything about wanting to put him in a nursing home. You made that up. You're trying to poison my son's mind against me."

My mouth fell open. Of all the reactions I had envisioned to this conversation, this hadn't been one of them.

"No I'm not, Carly. I'm trying to tell you—"

"You're a liar!" she cried out, jumping to her feet. "I never would have said that about Jack. I loved Jack."

"I know you did," I began.

"You don't know anything. Oh, you think you do. You think you know everything, don't you? Well, you're wrong. I loved my husband and I never would have done anything to harm him." At that, she burst into tears and ran from the room, slamming and locking the door behind her.

"Jesus," Todd said, rubbing his forehead.

I sat frozen in my chair. I had just been called a liar. I had no proof. It was my word against hers. I was waiting to see which one of us he believed.

He looked up at me. "What are we going to do, honey?" he asked, his face deeply creased with worry. "She's going off the goddamn deep end."

I got up from my chair and came to him. He stood, and I wrapped my arms around him. "I don't know, Todd. I wish to God I did."

It was her denial that caused my suspicions to begin to crystallize. If Carly had called me a liar, there was a reason. Her words haunted me. *I loved my husband and I never would have done anything to harm him.* It hadn't occurred to me that she had. Or had it? *He wanted to give up. He told you that, didn't he? That he didn't know how?*

It had not been my imagination that he'd been better right before he died. He had been sick, but sick enough to just quit breathing? For his heart to just stop beating? And if it hadn't?

The alternative was too horrible to contemplate, and yet I couldn't let it go. It was with me every minute I was awake; it haunted my dreams.

Had Carly murdered my uncle? The idea was too outrageous to contemplate, and yet I did. I envisioned hideous scenarios. Carly holding a pillow over his head until he was dead. Could she have done that? He had been a strong man at one time, but when he died, he had weighed just over a hundred pounds. Still, could she have done something that cold? Could she have felt him struggle and held the pillow over his head knowing that she was killing him? She had been stressed to death taking care of him, watching him deteriorate, but she had genuinely loved him. I knew she had loved him. Surely she couldn't have . . .

If not the pillow, what then? My thoughts went round and round until they settled on the obvious. His sleeping pills. Dr. Johnson had prescribed them because Uncle Jack wasn't sleeping at all. It was as if he was afraid each day would be his last, and he wasn't able to let go of each one as it came to a close. He had told me that himself. Finally, knowing exhaustion was weakening him even more, he had agreed to take the pills. He hated it that the pills took his last lingering control from him, that they knocked him unconscious whether he was ready for it or not. He had only taken two before he decided he would rather lie awake all night. Could Carly have slipped enough pills into something so that they killed him? I could see that scenario more easily than I could see the pillow thing. It was . . . more impersonal. He would just go to sleep and not wake up, which was exactly what had happened. But had it happened that way?

As the days passed, I became frantic to know the truth. The truth, that thing I had always valued more than anything else.

How in God's name would I ever know? They couldn't do an autopsy. My uncle's ashes were mixed forever into the ocean he had loved so dearly and the sand at its shore. There was nothing to autopsy.

It wasn't lost on me that this was the story I had always said would show up, the career maker, the story every reporter wants to stumble across. Only now I didn't want a story. And yet . . . and yet I couldn't let it go. I wanted the truth, and I was determined to have it at whatever cost.

I had no outlet for my suspicions. I couldn't talk to Todd. Even if he had believed me, which I doubted, I just—couldn't. I couldn't talk to Joanna. She had no love for Carly. Darlene was out of the question. So were Stella and Joyce, because—well, because.

In the end, I wrote my suspicions down. The beautiful story I had been writing about my uncle and Carly's love affair took a vicious turn. I wrote about the sleeping pills, because the other notion, the pillow, was too terrible to contemplate, even as fiction. As I wrote it, it became more plausible to me. It took on a reality that terrified me.

Somehow I managed to work while all this was coming together in my mind and on paper. I talked to people, but I don't know how I did it. I put one foot in front of the other and must have seemed pretty normal, because no one regarded me strangely.

I spent time with Joanna. She hinted that she would love to be my roommate. After all, she reminded me, I had an extra room. I suddenly realized that I vehemently didn't want Joanna as my roommate. I loved my sister better now than I ever had, but I didn't want to live with her. I wanted to live with Todd. I wanted to be married to him and have his children, but the possibility of that ever coming to pass seemed more remote with each day that passed.

Joanna took my decision well. I think she was used to rejection by then. She looked around and finally found an apartment a couple of miles from my house. We spent a lot of time together.

She confessed to me one night that she had been jealous of me while we were growing up.

"Of me? What for? You were the sister that had it all. Looks, popularity."

"Yeah. Big deal," Joanna said offhandedly. "You had the brains and—and Uncle Jack." She looked at me, not casual at all now. "You always had Uncle Jack."

"We all had Uncle Jack," I corrected, astounded by her words.

"No we didn't," Joanna said, but without accusation. "He tried to pretend he loved us all equally, but you were the apple of his eye. Hey," she added, "it wasn't your fault you were just like him."

That stopped me for a minute. Just like him? What an incredibly lovely compliment. Nor could I argue with her, remembering Carly's words so many years ago about him having to try a little harder to love Joanna and Darlene.

"If I had him," I conceded, "you had Mother. You and Darlene, but especially you. She never loved me like she did you."

Joanna didn't argue. "I know. I think part of it was because you were so much like him," she said, "and part of it was because you tried so hard to be unlovable."

"I did not!"

Joanna grinned. "Well, maybe not, but you were always so damned superior to us all. You had the brains and all the answers, and you didn't hesitate to let us know it. Face it, sis, you weren't always the easiest person to love."

My bristles went down before they were fully up as the truth of her words sunk in. I had always felt smarter than them. I tolerated them, mocked them, albeit silently most of the time, looked down on them as lesser than I. I thought they were too dumb to realize it. I remembered when Carly was giving me my first real lesson in forgiveness, her saying that my mother and Joanna and Darlene were trying to get through life the best way they knew how. I had pretended to accept her words. Now, suddenly, they made sense, and I could clearly see that I must have been a very difficult person for them to love.

I looked over at Joanna with new and even stronger affection. "Well, I was jealous of your boobs."

She looked at my chest. "You still should be."

When I gaped at her, she laughed. "Don't sweat it, little sis. Less to droop later on."

Joanna was becoming a true friend. It was miraculous to me. I even introduced her to Stella and Joyce. A part of me could envision a future in which we were all friends. Another, more perverse, part refused to envision any future at all.

While it was growing easier to talk to Joanna, it was becoming impossible to talk to Todd. Not until I had something definitive to say. He was a cop, but this wasn't some stranger or casual acquaintance I suspected. It was his mother. I couldn't share my suspicions with him if there was a single doubt in my mind.

I became frantic to know the truth, whatever it was. If I was wrong and Carly was blameless, maybe we could begin to rebuild some kind of relationship. If my suspicions were right . . . I couldn't go there. I couldn't think of that. I had to focus on finding the truth. It had always carried me through. I could only hope that it would this time, too.

I began to plan. I remembered that when we had boxed up my uncle's things, they had only included clothes and shoes. No toiletries. The sleeping pills might still be in the bathroom medicine cabinet. If they were, I could see how many were missing from the bottle. I didn't think Carly had taken any of them. She'd been afraid to sleep at all while my uncle was alive, and Dr. Johnson had prescribed sleeping pills for her after my uncle's death with enough refills to carry her into old age.

How to get into the medicine cabinet was tricky. Carly wouldn't welcome me into the house after my last visit. I had a key, but I would have to make sure Carly was at work when I went. And Todd. I didn't want to have to try to explain why I was sneaking into their house in the middle of the day.

I chose the next Monday. I knew the beauty shop was always swamped on Mondays. I left the newsroom under the guise of covering a gas main break in Melbourne. That took just over an hour. Then I headed across the causeway toward Melbourne Beach.

I had never broken into a house before. Maybe, technically, I wasn't breaking into this one. I was using my own key to let myself into my uncle's house, my fiancé's house. Who was I kidding? I was going to raid a medicine cabinet because I suspected Carly of murder. I was paranoid as hell.

I saw Nancy watching from her deck as I approached the front door, but she was so used to my comings and goings that I decided she wouldn't think it was strange. To make sure, I waved and smiled at her as I opened the front door and went inside. The fear that shortened my breathing told me that I was indeed breaking and entering.

Quickly, I crossed the living room and went through Carly's bedroom and into the bathroom. I swung open the medicine cabinet and saw the pill bottle immediately. I had meant to glance at the date and quickly count the pills, leaving the bottle where I found it. I had even entertained the thought of searching her bedroom for the journal, but I couldn't bear to be in the house a minute longer than necessary. Instead, I dropped the bottle into my pocket and headed out of the house.

Nancy was no longer on her deck when I hurried down the front steps to my car. I pulled out onto A1A with my heart pounding. After a few miles, I began to relax. Then I saw Carly's car coming toward me. I felt lightheaded. As we passed going in opposite directions, I tried to scrunch down in my seat, holding my breath as if that would hide me. Carly didn't appear to notice me. She was staring straight ahead out the windshield, apparently lost in her own thoughts.

As soon as she disappeared from my rearview mirror, I pulled the Jeep to the side of the road. I was shaking so badly I could barely get the car into park. I dropped my head on the steering wheel. What was I doing, for godssake, sneaking around trying to gather evidence? Was I out of my mind? I wasn't a cop, and if this little fiasco was any indication, I wasn't cut out to be an investigative reporter, either. What in the hell was I trying to prove? Nothing, was the answer. I was trying to find out, not prove. Proof was impossible, but I needed the truth. Desperately.

When I had calmed down enough, I put the car in gear and headed for the office, where I could at least pretend to be sane.

Bennett was sitting at his desk, doodling on a piece of scrap paper. "Hey," he said as I came in. "How did it go?"

"What?" I asked, alarmed.

"The gas main break."

"Oh." I felt foolish. "Fine."

"Fine?" His pencil was poised over the paper. He chuckled. "I never heard of a gas main break that went fine before."

His attempt at humor irritated me. "You know what I mean." I sat down at my desk, turning my back to him.

"That's some hot sister you got."

I glanced at him over my shoulder. "I like her."

"Got her number? I thought maybe I'd give her a call."

"She's in a new place," I said, turning back to my desk. "No phone yet."

"Well, when she gets one, I'd like the number."

"I'll tell her," I lied.

★ ★ ★ ★ ★

That evening, I went over to Joyce's. Leon was working and the kids were glued to the TV. Disney. A rerun of *Fantasia*. Even the newly mature Suzy was mesmerized. She gave me a vague "Hi, Christie," never taking her eyes off the screen.

Joyce led me into the kitchen and fixed me a glass of iced tea. Joyce was back to being the happy homemaker, but she still looked gorgeous. I had a feeling she'd hang on to that part of what Stella had taught her.

She sat down across the table from me.

"Can I ask you a professional question?" I began without preamble.

"You're pregnant!" she said, smiling. At the look on my face, the smile faded.

"No. It's about my uncle."

I could see her change gears. "Of course you can."

I took a deep breath. I hadn't realized this would be so hard. "I know—at least I've read—that Parkinson's isn't fatal. So how—what—what do people with it die of? I mean, is there—" I floundered, unsure how to ask what I needed to know.

"You mean, is there a common complication?"

I nodded.

She tilted her head to one side, thinking. "Not really. But some are more common than others. Often a Parkinson's patient's resistance gets so low that infection gets out of hand. If they're bedridden, pneumonia is always a risk. As the Parkinson's progresses, their system is weakened. Diseases that are normally responsive to meds become a lot more dangerous for them."

"Could it weaken them so much that they quit breathing? That their heart just quit beating?"

"It's . . . possible," Joyce said, in that slow, cautious tone of voice that all medical professionals adopt when they don't want to commit themselves.

"But not common?"

"I'd have to read up on it, but I don't think so."

I let out a shaky breath and pulled the pill bottle out of my pocket. "How many of these would it take to kill someone?"

Her eyes widened. She took the bottle from me and read the label. "Your uncle's."

I nodded.

I could see the wheels spinning. I knew she couldn't misunderstand my question. I half-expected her to tell me I was crazy. In fact, I think the words were on the tip of her tongue. Then she seemed to make a decision. "What's going on, Christie?"

"I don't *know*," I blurted out. "Maybe nothing. I just don't know."

She put the pill bottle on the table between us and leaned forward, folding her hands together. "Tell me."

The floodgates opened. I told her all of it, about Carly wanting to put my uncle in a nursing home, about his brief improvement before he died, about Carly's strange behavior since his death, her odd, out-of-sync remarks. "And the journal. She all but snatched it out of my hands that day. I don't know what she thought was in it. I'll probably never know. I didn't have the guts to look for it today, and it's a good thing I didn't. She would have caught me searching her bedroom." I shuddered at the thought. "I might have been able to explain being at the house, but not in her room."

Joyce had remained impassive throughout my tirade. Now she picked up the pill bottle and opened it, looking in. "In your uncle's weakened condition, probably four or five pills. Maybe fewer, but I don't think it would take more. Barbiturates are respiratory depressants, and these are whoppers. They could stop his breathing and his heart."

"Then you think—"

She held up her hand. "I don't think anything. I'm just answering your question."

"Okay." After a minute, "You don't think I'm crazy?"

She smiled sadly at me. "No. I don't think you're crazy. I think you're heartbroken over your uncle's death. I know that it's normal to look for something or someone to blame when we lose someone, but I also know that you've dealt very well with his death. I can also tell you that what you've told me would make me wonder, too." She closed the bottle. "How many are missing."

I gritted my teeth. "Six more than should be missing."

"Maybe Carly couldn't sleep and took them."

"She had her own sleeping pills."

Joyce closed her eyes.

She got up and brought the pitcher of iced tea to the table, refilling our glasses. "Have you talked to Todd about it?"

"No."

"You're going to have to, Christie."

I said nothing.

She handed me the pill bottle and I put it in my pocket. "What are you going to do?"

I had thought long and hard about it. "I'm going to talk to his doctor."

CHAPTER 22

Dr. Johnson seemed surprised and not particularly pleased to see me. Or maybe it was my imagination.

I had made an appointment for a consultation. I hadn't wanted to fake an illness to see him, but I needed to talk to him in person. His nurse led me into his cluttered office and left me there, announcing that he would be with me directly. I took a seat in one of the two available chairs. The other furniture consisted of an ordinary-looking desk stacked high with patient charts and two ancient steel file cabinets. The room smelled of old books and dust. For a lunatic moment, I considered looking in his files for my uncle's chart. It was a good thing I didn't, because directly turned out to be less than three minutes.

He hesitated when he walked in and saw who his next patient was, but then he came in and shook my hand. He wore a white lab coat over suit trousers; a stethoscope hung loosely around his neck. Even with that, he looked to me more like a weasel in medical garb than some kindly old family doctor.

"So what brings you here to see me, Christie? I hope you're not sick."

I thought his smile looked insincere. "No, Dr. Johnson. I'm fine. I wanted to talk to you."

He went behind his desk and sat down. "Of course. About what?"

"My uncle."

His smile wavered, then faded altogether.

"I have a few questions about his death," I went on when he said nothing.

He sat back in his chair and crossed his legs, raising his eyebrows. "Yes?"

"Todd told me that the cause of death was his heart stopping."

"That's right, in a general sense."

"What was it in a specific sense?"

He seemed taken aback, but he recovered quickly. "Congestive heart failure."

"And what caused that?"

He waved his hand impatiently, as if to shoo away a pesky insect. "His weakened condition caused that. It wasn't too surprising, you know. I'm not sure why you're asking these questions now."

"I'm just trying to understand why my uncle died. He seemed better right before—"

"It wasn't genuine improvement," he interrupted, frowning. "You know how his condition waffled. He was deteriorating rapidly. The arthritis kept him in constant pain. The ulcer had begun bleeding again. The arteriosclerosis put a constant strain on his heart. Surely even you realized he wasn't getting better."

His sarcasm wasn't wasted on me. Neither were my years as a reporter. I asked without hesitation, "You told Todd he stopped breathing. Do you think his sleeping pills may have shut down his respiratory system?"

His eyebrows came together in an angry V. "Those pills were perfectly safe taken as directed—"

"What if he somehow ingested too many?"

"What are you implying?"

"Nothing. I'm asking. Could that have caused his congestive heart failure?"

"No," he said angrily, starting to get to his feet, "and I don't appreciate you coming here and suggesting that I—"

"I'm not suggesting anything about you, Dr. Johnson," I said. "I'm just trying to find out what happened to my uncle."

"Your uncle did not kill himself."

It was my turn to be shocked. "I know that." After a moment of tense silence, I asked, "Did you know that Carly wanted to put him in a nursing home?"

He seemed to take a mental step back. "She—discussed it with me. I wasn't surprised. In fact, I thought it might be the best thing. Parkinson's is very difficult on the primary caregivers."

"So you advised her to put him in a home?"

His face reddened. Now he stood. "I advised her to do what she felt was best, which is what I always recommend in situations such as hers. Your aunt spent years taking care of your uncle. She did the very best she could."

He crossed the room to the door, stopping with his hand resting on the knob. Consultation over. I got to my feet reluctantly, but in truth, there was nothing else to ask.

As I neared the door, he opened it and stepped back, as if my closeness would contaminate him. "Your uncle was ill, Christie," he said. "Terribly ill, and getting no better. He was in a tremendous amount of pain twenty-four hours a day. You didn't live with him, so you don't understand how bad it was. He was also terribly unhappy. I don't know what you're hoping to accomplish here, but I would advise you to let it go. Just—let it go."

I felt him watching me as I made my way down the hallway toward the red exit sign. I wondered if he'd bill me for his time.

I had been fishing when I went to see Dr. Johnson, but his final words solidified my suspicions. I reported the conversation to Joyce who, understandably, took up for the medical profession. "I'm sure that if the doctor had suspected unnatural death, he would have reported it."

"Even if he thought it was the best thing? Even if he thought it was what my uncle wanted?"

"He is a doctor. His job is savings lives, not covering up murder."

I was less convinced.

I met with Dr. Seegar, the neurologist, and learned nothing. He explained sympathetically that Dr. Johnson had been responsible for my uncle's general care. He agreed with Joyce that infection of some kind due to the patient's weakened condition was frequently the cause of death in Parkinson's cases, but he said that congestive heart failure certainly wasn't unheard of. He wasn't defensive in the least. More importantly, he failed to pick up on my suspicions. He patted me on the back as he walked me out of his office, telling me to feel free to call him if I had any more questions.

Joanna was beginning to realize that something was troubling me deeply. She hinted around several times that she would be happy to listen and seemed hurt when I failed to take her up on her offer, but I simply couldn't talk to her.

Nor could I talk to Todd. He called me the next evening at the newspaper as I was trying to finish up a story. "Hi, honey. Working late?"

I hadn't seen Todd in days, much to my relief. "Not much later. Why, are you free?"

I could hear the sigh in his voice. "No. Not tonight. Mom said you might have come by the house day before yesterday."

I felt like a cornered animal. "I did," I said breezily. "I was looking for my red t-shirt. I thought I might have left it over there." A lying cornered animal.

"I told her it must be something like that." There was relief in his voice, then he lowered it, "But you know what she's like these days."

"Not any better?"

"Worse. She's been searching the house like a madwoman. She won't tell me what she's looking for. I think she thought you took something."

I thought of the pill bottle now in my own medicine cabinet and avoided the truth. "Have you talked to her about counseling?"

"I've tried," he said, his voice still low. "She's not having any of it."

"Why don't you suggest she call Dr. Johnson? Maybe he can recommend someone." A sneaky, lying cornered animal.

"I might do that. Oh," he covered the phone with his hand, but I could hear him say, "She was looking for a shirt she left here." Then, to me, "I gotta go, honey. Mom tells me dinner's ready."

"When will I see—" But he had already hung up.

It was better, I reminded myself as I climbed wearily into my Jeep. I didn't know how I could talk to him without telling him my suspicions, and I wasn't ready to do that. I didn't know if I'd ever be ready to do that.

The trip across the causeway seemed inordinately long. The glare of oncoming headlights aggravated the headache that had been nibbling at the edges of my consciousness all afternoon. I began to almost look forward to a quiet night. I stopped at the Winn Dixie where the 520 causeway ran into A1A and picked up a roasted chicken at the deli. It would feed me for a week. I added a pint of coleslaw and one of potato salad to my cart. Might as well make it a picnic. As an afterthought, I grabbed a bottle of chardonnay. An elegant picnic.

I headed north on A1A with visions of the evening ahead soothing my aching head: a bite of dinner, a soak in a tub, the usual mental wrestling match with myself. That scenario faded as I drove into my driveway. My living room was lit up, but no car was in the driveway. That meant Stella. Or Joyce. Or both. Or maybe another damned celebration. I really was going to have to change my locks.

Joyce and Stella were comfortably settled on my sofa, apparently sharing a bottle of wine. It occurred to me that Stella might be a bad influence on Joyce. I looked around but saw no sign of other visitors.

"Come on in," Stella said as I stepped inside, juggling my grocery bags.

"Thank you for your hospitality," I said, kicking the door shut behind me.

"She's tired," Stella told Joyce. Then to me, "Come sit down, honey, and have a glass of wine."

"I don't want a glass of wine," I told her petulantly. "I want some time alone."

Stella and Joyce exchanged glances. Joyce took a deep breath and let it out. "Uh—Christie, I told Stella about it, about what we talked about the other day."

"You did *what?* Jesus, Joyce, why didn't you just take out an ad. I told you that in confidence—"

"Thanks a lot," Stella said, hurt. "I used to think we were friends."

"This is different—"

"I told her because I'm worried about you," Joyce broke in.

"Because you think I'm crazy," I said bitterly.

"Because I think you need your friends—all your friends—around you right now. This is a rough time for you."

I felt ashamed of myself. Joyce was right. I did need my friends right now. More than I wanted to admit. "I'm sorry," I said, dropping my purse on the floor and coming over to them. I dumped the bags on the table. "Dinner."

Stella brightened. "I'll get us some plates," she said, heading for the kitchen.

I sat on the floor. There was a glass waiting for me on the coffee table. I made use of it. "This thing is about to make me as crazy as I deny being."

"No wonder," Stella said sympathetically as she came back into the room. "Thinking your aunt would do something like that and then with Todd spending all his time down in Melbourne Beach—" She broke off, looking away.

"Is there anything you don't know about my life?" I asked, my voice laced with sarcasm. "Oh, never mind." I pulled the chicken and salads out of the bag. "It's a small town. I don't need to take it out on you."

"He told Jackson how much he missed being with you," Stella said defensively. "That's the only reason I know. Look." She got to her feet. "If you'd rather I left—"

"No." I grabbed her hand and pulled her back down on the couch. "I'm sorry. I'm just . . ."

"You're stressed out," Joyce said, standing up. "You forgot the silverware, Stella," she said, heading toward the kitchen.

I looked up at Stella when she was gone. "Really, Stella. I'm sorry. I would have talked to you about it, but I was sure you'd think I was nuts. I only told Joyce because I needed to pick her medical brain. I know all this sounds preposterous—"

"No, it doesn't," Stella said, her face serious. "With what Joyce told me, it sounds about right. That's why Joyce is so worried."

Joyce returned then with the silverware. I sipped wine as she and Stella carved the chicken and spooned food onto the plates. I had thought I was hungry, but the smell of cooked meat nauseated me. I had always been one of those people who ate when they were upset. This was different, and I didn't like it. I ignored the plate they pushed in front of me and stared at nothing. The past paraded through my mind as it had for weeks now, hazy images in no particular order. Todd as he'd been at the church the first night I'd seen him. Carly playing with my hair, laughing at my reactions.

"What are you going to do if you're right?" Stella asked.

I looked up. "I haven't thought that far ahead." In fact, I tried to think no further than the end of each day.

"You need to, you know," Joyce said around a mouthful of coleslaw.

I glanced at her and pushed my plate toward her. "I don't know how I'll ever know I'm right," I said miserably. "I mean, it's not like they can do an autopsy or anything. Dr. Johnson will never admit anything—if he knows anything," I added, seeing Joyce's look, "and Dr. Seegar doesn't know anything. There's no smoking gun, so to speak."

They ate in silence for a few minutes. I was glad to have them there after all. Their belief in me mattered. It was more than I had in myself.

"That morning after your uncle died. What happened?" Joyce asked.

I thought for a minute. There seemed to be a hole in my memory. "I know Todd showed up at my office," I said slowly.

"I mean with Carly. What happened there?"

I looked at her blankly. "I'm—not sure. I got the impression that he walked in and Carly collapsed immediately."

Joyce took a last bite of potato salad. "What did she say about it?"

"I don't think I ever asked. Todd told me he quit breathing. That's what Dr. Johnson told him. He said Carly woke up and realized he wasn't breathing."

"Did she call an ambulance?"

"I don't know. With all the confusion after his death and Carly being so drugged afterward, I never thought to ask about it. Do you think it's important?"

"What would you have done under the circumstances?"

I tried to imagine waking in the middle of the night and realizing the man I loved had quit breathing. "You mean after I woke the neighborhood screaming? God, who knows?"

"It might help you if you knew what happened. Could you ask Todd?"

"At this late date? I think he'd suspect something."

"He's going to suspect something anyway," Stella interjected. "You'll have to talk to him eventually. You can't keep something like this to yourself."

I didn't want to hear her words, even though I knew they were true. "I don't think I can talk to him."

"And your aunt," she went on as if I hadn't spoken. "You'll have to confront her."

I almost dropped my wine. "Are you crazy?" Confronting Carly was one thought that had never entered my mind.

Joyce nodded. "Stella's right, Christie. You're going to have to." At the look on my face, she added, "Maybe she can explain if it's not true."

"You're both crazy. What do you expect me to do, go over and say, 'Excuse me, but I think you might have killed my uncle. Would you like to confess?' "

I started to laugh, but it turned into a sob. They were both beside me on the floor in an instant. "Don't you understand?" I said, looking from one of them to the other as tears streamed down my cheeks. "This woman was a mother to me. She loved me, and she loved my uncle. I know she did. If I do that—" I stopped, shaking my head. It was too huge to grasp. If the words were ever spoken, if my suspicions ever came to light, it would destroy any chance there might be of having a relationship with her again, even if she weren't guilty. And I knew with a certainty born of all that had transpired in the past months that I would lose her son as well.

I closed into myself as the magnitude of it all overwhelmed

me. I hugged my knees to my chest. As it had so often in the last weeks, my mind went back to a happier time. "Did I ever tell you what Carly did the time I stole my sister's bathing suit?"

I talked long into the night, telling them tales of my years with Carly, of all she had taught me, of all she had done for me. They listened and refilled my wine glass. They laughed and even wept with me. They were, in short, the perfect friends.

Before they left, Joyce hugged me. "I know you love your aunt, Christie, and I know you love Todd, but this whole thing—this wondering night and day—is going to make you sick, honey. I think you have to at least try to find out the truth."

"She's right, sweetie," Stella said. "You've got to try and get to the bottom of it or forget it, and I don't think you can do that."

I looked from one to the other. "For the first time in my life, I'm not sure if I really want to know the truth," I said honestly, "and that scares the hell out of me."

I hugged Stella, wishing they'd both stay the night. I didn't want to be alone.

I went to bed no wiser, no more decided than I had been when I arrived home in a snit, only now I felt loved and valued. Trusted and believed. It was a gift only true friends can give you. I slept soundly for the first time in a week.

The next night, there was a car in my driveway when I got home from work. Todd's. I suddenly didn't want to see him. How perverse of me. Last night I wanted a slumber party; now I wanted solitude.

I heard the shower as I walked into the bedroom. I stood in the middle of the room trying to decide what to do. The shower cut off, and he walked into the bedroom, a towel wrapped around his waist.

"I thought I heard you," he said, putting his arms around me. He lowered his head and his lips brushed mine.

I was mentally accusing his mother of murder as I accepted his kiss.

He took a step back. "Bad day?"

"Several," I said, kicking off my shoes. I walked to the dresser and pulled out a pair of shorts and a shirt. Anything to avoid looking at him. I searched my mind for some way to ask him what he was doing here without sounding accusing, but nothing came to mind.

As I pulled off my blouse, he came up behind me, slipping his arms around me. "Anything I can do to help you forget?"

I froze. I couldn't do this. I could not make love with Carly's son. I could not lie in his arms and pretend everything was all right. I wasn't that big a hypocrite or that good an actress.

He must have felt my reaction. He dropped his arms. "What's wrong, Christie?" he asked, turning me around.

I dropped my head in my hand and rubbed my forehead. "Headache. I don't feel well."

"Let me get you some aspirin," he said, turning toward the bathroom.

The bottle of pills sitting in plain view on the glass shelf flashed into my mind. "No!" When he turned and stared, I said, "No. I took some before I left the paper. I think I'll take a shower."

He watched me, clearly uncertain what was going on.

I grabbed my change of clothes and headed toward the bathroom.

"Would you rather I left?" he asked my back.

"No." Then, "Yes." I finally looked at him. My eyes prickled with tears that demanded to be shed. "I'm sorry. I really don't feel well."

"What's wrong?" His face held a confused mixture of disbelief and concern.

"Nothing. Really. I just don't feel well. I want to go to bed."

He was still watching me. "Okay," he said after a minute. He pulled on a pair of jeans and a shirt he had lying on the bed. Then he scooped up the uniform he had draped over a chair. "Will you call me if you need me?" he asked, coming to stand in front of me.

"Yes," I said, looking up into his beloved face. My eyes filled and overflowed.

"Honey—"

"No. Really," I said, brushing the tears off my face. "I just need to lie down. Some quiet. That's all. Please."

The desperation in my voice must have convinced him. "Okay. Sure. But call, okay? If you need me?"

I nodded, not trusting myself to speak.

I watched as he turned and walked out of the bedroom, his shoulders rounded with defeat. I wanted to call him back. I wanted to throw myself into his arms and have him make everything all right like he always did, only this time, Todd couldn't make it right. No one could.

The air grew chill as he left the room. Suddenly I wanted my mother. Not my mother, I realized suddenly. I wanted Carly. I desperately wanted Carly. The thought was like a knife in my heart. Knowing what I thought I did, suspecting all that I suspected, I still wanted Carly, the old Carly I could love and count on. Almost as much as I wanted her son. The magnitude of the loss that faced me overwhelmed me. I heard but didn't see the front door open and close. My eyes were closed, my head flung back as I realized the truth. It was over for us. There was no way around it. I had to bite my clenched fist to keep from screaming.

Late, late that night, I remembered to take the bottle of pills out of the medicine cabinet. I looked around for a place to hide them, somewhere I was certain Todd wouldn't find them if he showed up unexpectedly again, but I couldn't make even that simple a decision. I knew I should flush them down the toilet and throw away the bottle, but I couldn't do that either. They seemed to be the only link I had with the truth about my uncle's death.

Finally, I dropped them in my purse. Tomorrow. I would decide tomorrow what to do about them.

I crossed to my closet, reaching into the far back corner. My hand closed around comfort, or the closest thing to it I was likely to find. I pulled Teddy out and brushed him off, straightening Todd's handkerchief around his neck. Then I lay down on my bed and hugged him tightly to me, feeling not one bit embarrassed.

CHAPTER 23

When Todd called the next day to invite me to lunch, I made an excuse. His words accepted it; his voice called me a liar. He asked what I was doing later, and I told him I'd be working late. I knew I couldn't hide forever, but I was willing to try. When I let myself out of the building, I half expected him to be lying in wait for me in the parking lot, but his car was nowhere to be seen. When I reached the intersection of A1A, I turned the car south instead of north. I didn't want to go home.

Fischer's wasn't crowded. It was the lull between the lunch crowd and the dinner bunch. Paul's face lit up as I walked into the door, the first ray of sunshine I'd seen in my otherwise black day. "Long time no see," he said, walking down to my end of the bar. "The usual?"

"Please." I dropped my purse on the floor beside my stool and my keys on the bar.

He studied my face for a minute as he put my Coke in front of me. "Everything okay?"

I nodded.

"How's your sister?"

"Joanna's doing great. She found an apartment in Cape Canaveral. She's working part time at the boutique with my mother."

"She tell you she was in here the other night?"

"No." I wasn't surprised. I hadn't given her much of a chance to tell me anything.

Paul nodded. "With that guy you work with. Not the rodent. The big guy."

I laughed. It had been so long that the sound felt alien. "Bennett." I sighed. "Well, she's a big girl. He sure wouldn't be my first choice."

"Speaking of your first choice," Paul said, nodding toward the door.

Todd walked in and looked around. When he saw me, he ambled slowly in my direction.

I felt a little sick, as guilty as if he had caught me in bed with another man. I tried to manage a smile, but it was a weak effort. "Hi."

"Hi," he answered, his face serious.

"Can I get you something, Todd?" Paul asked with an easy friendliness that only I knew cost him.

Todd nodded at the Coke in front of me. "One of those, maybe."

When Paul was gone, we sat in silence. I stared at the bar and Todd stared at me. The clink of glasses and low conversation barely registered in my mind. I heard someone laugh and felt jealous.

After Paul put the Coke in front of him and moved away, Todd said, "You going to tell me what's going on?" His voice sounded tight and a little frightening.

"Nothing's going on."

He gave his Coke a little push with one finger. "I see. Just a night out with the girls?"

When I ignored the question, he said, "Where are they, anyway?"

"Who?"

"The girls."

I turned to him, ready to tell him it was a night out with

myself, when he looked over my shoulder. The surprise on his face caused me to look around.

Joanna walked into the bar. She grinned when she saw me. "My long lost sister!" she called out from across the room and headed in our direction.

Todd rose from his stool. He reached into his wallet and pulled out a five-dollar bill, dropping it on the bar. He stared at me for a long minute. "See you," he said. Nodding at Joanna, he turned and walked out.

Joanna perched on the stool beside me. "Whew," she said, looking after him. "That wasn't very friendly. They're not supposed to act like that until after the wedding. What did you do to him?"

I shook off the dread I felt building inside me. "Nothing. What are you doing here?"

"Meeting someone."

"Bennett?"

"You told!" she said, grinning at Paul as he sat a napkin in front of her.

"Guilty," he answered. "What'll you have, Joanna?"

"Dewars and soda." She turned back to me and frowned. "Are you all right, Christie? You've seemed kind of . . . oh . . . distracted, I guess."

"I know, Joanna. I'm sorry. I've just had a lot on my mind."

"Anything your big sister can help with?"

For just an instant, I considered telling her. After all, where was the harm? It certainly couldn't make her hate Carly any more than she already did. But I couldn't. "No. It's nothing like that."

Her face reflected her hurt before she could cover it up.

I couldn't stand it. "It's not you, Joanna," I said, touching her arm. "This is just something I have to think out before I talk about it. Have you ever felt like that? Like you have to sort it out before you talk to anyone else?"

"Yes," she said, her face clearing. "Actually I have. Lots of times." She took a sip of her drink and made a face. "It sounded so sophisticated. Dewars and soda. God, it tastes awful." She pushed the glass away from her. "If you decide you want to talk, you can call, you know. Or come over." She gave a little laugh as Bennett walked up beside us. "But call first, okay?"

I forced myself to smile. "Hi, Bennett."

Bennett had the grace to look embarrassed. "Hi." He turned to Joanna. "Our secret's out, huh?"

"Not completely." She looked up as Paul walked over. "I don't think it would be a good idea before my divorce is final. Paul here won't tell another soul, will you, Paul?"

"My lips are sealed, but if you want to keep it a secret, I don't think I'd meet here."

She nodded thoughtfully. "You're probably right. I've run into half of Mother's neighbors in the last few days here. Let's go somewhere else." She turned to me. "Want to join us?"

"No," I said, gathering up my purse and keys, "but I'll walk out with you." I smiled. "Maybe people will think Bennett's with me." I blushed as I realized how that sounded. "You know, a work thing." That only made it worse.

Shaking my head at my own ineptness, I fished in my purse for my wallet. Paul shook his head. "Coke's been paid for," he said, nodding at the five-dollar bill still lying on the bar beside Todd's untouched glass. "Hey," he said as we started out. He looked at me, his face clouded. "Take care. Okay?"

His concern touched me. "Okay," I said, giving him a genuine smile.

Then his eyes went to Joanna, narrowed when they got to Bennett. "You, too, Joanna," he said, not looking at her.

Joanna blinked in surprise, then she smiled. "Yes, sir," she said with a snappy salute.

I expected Todd's car to be in my driveway. It wasn't. I expected him to show up at the jetty when I walked down later that night. Tempting fate? Torturing myself?

The next day when I walked out to go to lunch, I saw him as I was unlocking my car. He was in uniform but he was in his own car, which he had parked next to mine. "Lunch time?" he asked through the open window.

"I—was going to grab something to take back."

I could tell he saw through it, but he was polite enough not to call me a liar. "Got a minute?"

There was no way I could say no. I stuffed my car keys in my pocket. "Sure," I sighed, climbing into the passenger seat of his car.

"You ready to talk about what's going on?" he asked.

"Nothing—"

"Something is. I saw you leave with Joanna and some guy. I saw them get in his car and leave, so you weren't meeting her."

"Were you—"

"No. I wasn't spying on you. I was sitting in the parking lot wishing I didn't have to go home." He turned in the seat so that he was facing me. "So are you worried about something, or is there another guy?"

"There isn't another guy," I said, surprised that he could even think it.

He didn't bother to hide his relief. "So you're worried about something."

"Not worried," I lied. "Preoccupied."

"With?"

I thought about putting him off again, but suddenly I wanted to know. I dropped my purse on the floor of his car and sat back, crossing my legs. "That night Uncle Jack died. What happened?"

He blinked. "What do you mean?"

"I mean what happened?" I gestured impatiently. "Where were you? Did Carly call you?"

He regarded me steadily for several minutes. "Why is that bothering you now?"

"I just want to know."

"You never did before."

"I do now."

"Why?"

"I just do."

When he looked like he was going to refuse, I got him started. "You said she woke up and he wasn't breathing."

He watched my face for another moment before he came to a decision. "All right," he said slowly. "That morning when I got home from work, I thought I heard something in their room. Mom was always up by the time I got home from work. She usually had breakfast made. You know how she is. Was," he corrected.

I nodded, studying his face intently.

"That morning the house was quiet. Too quiet. I don't know what made me look in their room. I thought I heard something. Like someone—oh, crying or calling or something."

He looked at me and I nodded again. He rubbed the back of his neck. "She was on the floor by the closet, curled up on the carpet like she was scared or something. She didn't look at me when I came in. She was staring at the bed. Just staring. I knew then, but I decided to make sure. Then I—"

"How long?"

"How long what?"

"How long had he been . . . dead?"

"Jesus, Christie. I don't know. What difference—"

"How long do you think?"

He closed his eyes, shaking his head. "Hours, anyway. Dr.

Johnson said at least four hours."

So for four hours she had huddled on the floor waiting—for what? To see if the pills worked? To see if he would come back to life and point his finger at her? My stomach churned. "Did she say why?"

"Why what?"

"Why she didn't call the doctor or an ambulance or the police."

"No," he said angrily. "She didn't say anything. She—" He stopped abruptly, then continued. "She collapsed. When she saw me walk over to the bed, she started crying and kind of collapsed on the floor. She didn't say anything."

He was watching me now, closely. I didn't know what my face looked like. It felt frozen. "Why are you asking all these questions now?" he asked, his voice level.

I met his eyes. "It didn't seem strange to you that she didn't call an ambulance? Or her own son?" I asked, my voice as impersonal as I could make it.

He answered in kind. "No. She was obviously in shock."

"What made you think so? Was she cold? Shaking?"

"I've seen people in shock before."

"Dilated pupils?"

"What is this, Christie?"

"It's questions, Todd. Questions I should have asked when my uncle died."

"Why?"

"So I could get at the truth."

His voice grew harsh. "What *truth?*"

"The whole truth."

I saw a muscle twitch in his jaw. "What the hell are you trying to say? Just spit it out."

"I—" Couldn't. I could not say the words. I looked at his beautiful strong face, angry now, and knew that I could never say the words to him. I could never look at his face and accuse his mother of murder.

I grabbed my car keys out of my pocket and jumped out of his car.

He made no move to come after me. I realized as I drove out of the parking lot that I hadn't expected him to. He was no more anxious for me to give my suspicions a name than I was to name them.

CHAPTER 24

Because he knew. I realized it as I turned onto the causeway, and the realization forced me off the road. I pulled off onto the wide, grassy shoulder that sloped down to the river, shaking as if palsied. Todd knew. He might not believe my suspicions, but he knew what they were.

When I could, I pulled back out on the road and headed home. It was the middle of the day. I would have to call the paper and tell them where I was. As I put my key into my front door, Todd drove up in my driveway.

He walked toward me, my purse in his hand. When he reached me, he handed it to me. "You left this in my car."

I swallowed hard, praying the fear didn't show on my face. "Thank you." I turned and went inside.

His voice stopped me just inside the door. "How many are missing?"

I turned slowly, hoping I'd misunderstood his question. He reached into his shirt pocket and pulled out the pill bottle, holding it up in front of him.

"Please, Todd—"

"How many?"

I closed my eyes, but whether in prayer or to avoid seeing his face when I answered, I wasn't sure. "Six."

"Six—"

"Eight, with the two he took."

His hand closed around the bottle, and I heard the plastic crack.

Eons passed. I heard a car and hoped it was a tourist, lost. It pulled up into the driveway and Joanna jumped out.

"Hi, guys!" she said as she advanced on us. "I'm glad I caught you. I wanted to invite you to . . ." Her voice trailed off as she looked from one of us to the other. "Am I here at a bad time?"

Todd took a step backward, his eyes never leaving mine.

"I can come back," Joanna said, edging away.

"No. I was just leaving." He held my eyes for another minute before he turned and walked away.

When he was gone, Joanna shook her head. "God, I hope no man ever looks at me like that while he's wearing a gun. What's going on with you two? Are you still fighting?"

I rubbed my forehead. "No. Yes, I guess." I searched my mind for a lie that would satisfy her. Suddenly it seemed like too much trouble. I slipped my purse strap on my shoulder. "I was just about to head back to work," I said, ushering her out of the door and locking it behind us. "What did you say about inviting us somewhere?"

"Oh. Mother. She and Lamar want to have a dinner party. She wants all her girls to come."

I almost laughed at the absurdity of sitting down to a pleasant family dinner with all that was going on around me. "When?"

"Friday."

"Okay. Probably. I'll call her. Okay?"

"Sure. I'll tell her." She looked like she wanted to say something else, but she changed her mind. She turned and headed down the walk. When she reached her car, she glanced back at me. "Hey, kid. Call me if you need me, okay?"

I nodded, blinking back tears as she climbed in and started the engine.

As soon as she drove away, I let myself back into the house. I called the office and told Virgil I had cramps. I had found that men never questioned that. I changed into shorts and a shirt and, putting on my tennis shoes, headed to the jetty.

I had only been there a couple of minutes when I felt Todd beside me. I turned. He was glaring at me, his face distorted with anger. Hostility radiated off him, and yet I felt calm. The damage was done now.

I looked back down into the water. The tide was almost in. The rocks were slick with it. We were alone. No one was fishing in the middle of a workday. His size and strength were a separate presence there with us. I thought how easy it would be for him to destroy the suspicions against his mother. No one would witness it. I actually saw myself floating face down in the water, my hair spreading out around me, yet I felt not a single grain of fear.

"So you've decided she killed him," he said without preamble.

I looked up at him. "Pretty much."

I could see the muscle in his jaw clenching and unclenching. "Did it ever occur to you to talk to her? To give her a chance to defend herself?"

Had it? "No."

"I think it's the least you can do. Everyone deserves a hearing."

I looked at him then. His face had aged years in the space of an hour. "Don't you think you owe her that much?" he asked when I didn't speak.

I knew I owed her that much and more, infinitely more. But I didn't have it to give. Still, "All right."

We walked back toward my house, careful not to touch. I remembered the night he had come to me and broken through the wall of resistance I had erected around myself. I remembered our frantic lovemaking, our breathless exploration of one another's bodies, and I wanted to go backward in time, back to when our lives were coming together as surely as they were now being torn apart.

I saw Joyce and Stella staring out of Joyce's kitchen window as we passed, their faces identical studies in worry. I couldn't bring myself to so much as nod in their direction. I reflected idly that Joyce must be back on the night shift. I wondered how it was working with Leon. We hadn't talked about that in a long time. We had only talked about what was going on in my life. Self-involvement, my nemesis. I hoped the marriage was going well, for all their sakes. They deserved happiness, didn't they? Didn't everyone deserve at least a chance at happiness? If Leon cheated, I hoped Joyce never found out, never suspected, because suspicion was evil.

Stella and Jackson, improbable as they were together, deserved happiness, too. I wished it for them with all my heart. I think I prayed then that everyone would find happiness. Or if not happiness, at least peace.

"I want to change clothes," I said when we reached my sliding glass doors.

He nodded curtly. He stood in the middle of the living room with his hands in his uniform pockets as I headed for the bedroom.

I pulled off my damp shorts and put on jeans. Exchanged my soaked sneakers for loafers. My shirt was dry. I stalled as long as I could. When I walked out of the bedroom, Todd was hanging up the phone.

I raised my eyebrows.

"She was at work. I told her we were coming down to talk to her. She'll be at the house."

"Did you tell her why?"

"I told her you found the pill bottle and wanted to talk to her about it."

"Do you think that was wise?"

"Why?" he asked bitterly. "Do you think she's going to destroy the evidence?"

"No." I thought she already had.

He turned and left the house. I followed. It was a labor to put one foot in front of the other. I ached with the effort.

We were silent on the way down. It was another beautiful day. Puffy clouds floated gently across a sky of brilliant blue. People say they can see things in clouds: animals, faces. They all looked like pills to me.

Todd pulled up in front of the house. Neither of us made a move to get out of the car. After a long time, I turned to him. "I want to be wrong, you know. More than anything, I want to be wrong."

His face contorted before he pulled back on his professional mask. As he opened his car door, a shot rang out.

We were both out of the car in an instant. Todd bounded up the stairs two at a time. I was right behind him. He raced into the house, but I stopped at the front door. I could see him kneeling over his mother. Carly was crumbled on the floor like a broken doll. I could see blood splattered on the wall near her head.

I doubled over, gagging. It was a strictly physical reaction. It was minutes later before I grasped the full meaning of what I was seeing. When I did, I froze where I stood.

He checked her pulse. Then his hand dropped at his side. He knelt beside her, not moving.

Finally, he reached down beside her and picked up a piece of paper. He read it, then folded it and put it in his shirt pocket, the same pocket where he had earlier kept the bottle with the six missing pills.

I backed away until I felt the railing against my back, then turned and stumbled down the stairs. I somehow made my way over to his car and leaned against it, dropping my head to my chest. I hugged myself as the chill of it all penetrated me.

Then I heard a noise on the porch above me.

I looked up as Todd came slowly, unsteadily out of the house. I made no move toward him, but watched as he walked down the wooden steps and across the sand to where I stood waiting beside his car, trying desperately to deny what I had just witnessed.

"She's dead," he said unnecessarily.

The words stunned me, even though I had already known.

I saw him tremble with the effort to hold himself together. His face flushed, then paled. Sweat that had formed at his hairline trickled down the sides of his face like the tears he couldn't shed. His fists clenched and unclenched, the muscles in his arms cording and stretching his skin like separate, living things trying to force their way out.

I don't know how long we stood there. After a while, he reached out as if to take my hand. Instead, he moved off across the white sand dunes and toward the water's edge. I followed him, just as I always had.

Everything seemed unreal to me, all of it except Todd. He was real, a forceful presence that kept me from flying apart as we moved down the deserted beach. Finally, he stopped and lowered himself to the sand.

I dropped down beside him and studied him as he stared out to sea. After a while, I licked my dry lips, tasting salt. "I'm sorry," I said.

He looked at me then, his eyes hazed with pain. "Isn't that my line?"

"We'll have to call the police," I said finally.

The muscles in his jaw worked. He looked down at his uniform. "I am the police." He shook his head. "There's no rush. It's not like a crime's been committed." His eyes searched mine.

The cries of the gulls dimmed to silence. The waves no longer whooshed up on the sand. The sun no longer shone. There were Todd's eyes, and there were mine. Nothing else.

"I love you," I whispered.

The air between us clouded, and then cleared. He reached over and brushed my hair back from my face. He traced the outline of my face with his cupped hand. Then he looked back out to sea.

After a long time, Todd got to his feet, pulling me up beside him. The sun reflected off his hair, light within light. His arms went around me, and I clung to him as the gulls cried overhead. He pushed me away slightly and reached into his shirt pocket. He drew out the folded paper. He held it out to me.

With a shaking hand, I reached out and took it. For an endless space of time, I looked into his eyes.

For maybe the first time in my life, there were no questions in my mind. I had valued truth all my life and I valued it still, but not above everything. I suddenly understood what Carly had tried so hard to teach me without even knowing how desperately I would one day need the lesson. She had been my greatest teacher.

There was no decision to make. My eyes still on Todd's, I tore the paper across without looking at it, then tore it again and again until all that existed still were tiny bits of white, not as small as ashes, but near enough. I walked to the water's edge and released them into the sea, where they would wash up on the sand and mingle with all that comprised it.

I turned back to Todd. He met me halfway. His hands shook as he took my face between them and kissed me gently on the lips. Then, with his arm across my shoulders and mine around his waist, we walked back to the house.

CHAPTER 25

August 1977

It had taken us fourteen years to get here, and despite hating all the stage management that accompanied a large wedding, I intended to enjoy it. We had discussed waiting a while longer, but Todd finally said we had already waited too long. When I thought about it, I knew he was right.

I stood dressed in ivory satin and outrageously expensive lace in the choir dressing room. At least I finally knew what my dress looked like. It looked—good.

I tore my gaze from the full-length mirror and peeked out the door at the multitudes spilling into the wooden pews of the church. It seemed appropriate that we were being married here, where we had first met so many years ago. The minister—a different one—was even on time.

I had been certain that I would feel their presence here today, my uncle and aunt, but if their spirits were around, they were keeping a low profile. I was glad. Not that I wouldn't have welcomed them both here in any form for the day they had both so looked forward to, but it seemed to me that if they weren't around, they had probably made their necessary peace and were done with us here on earth.

My eyes scanned the crowd, looking for familiar faces. Mother had invited so many of Lamar's banking friends (*Christie, think of the gifts, dear!*) that I hadn't expected to recognize a soul, but I was wrong. Todd's side of the church was crowded with blue and brown. At least half the members of the Orlando and Melbourne police departments had shown up. While I might not know them all by sight, I couldn't help but recognize the uniforms. I prayed no one was in the mood to rob a bank. The mayor also sat on Todd's side. A pretty impressive showing for a man with no living relatives.

My side was equally full. Lamar's cronies made up the largest group, of course. I also spotted Alf and Jake sitting toward the front, with Masie wedged between them. I half expected Masie to whip out a pad and start taking notes. "And the bride wore . . ."

Virgil and Becky Townsend sat beside her. Gordon Bennett had sent a gift instead. As many times as he'd been unhappily married, that didn't surprise me. Still, the newspaper was well represented.

Stella and Jackson sat side by side, although I knew Jackson would soon excuse himself to go stand with Todd. Jackson, bait shack and fish camp owner, looked every inch the history professor he used to be, dressed in his three-piece worsted wool suit. He must have sent to Minnesota for it. If it had hung in the closet of his trailer for a decade, it would have been gray with mildew. I only hoped he wouldn't expire from the heat before the ceremony was over. Stella was equally stunning and looked a great deal cooler, dressed in frothy pale pink chiffon that showed quite a bit of well-tanned cleavage. Her hair was shorter now, gentle red curls that softened her face. Carly would have approved.

Darlene had her brood lined up like soldiers in the front pew. Fred looked complacent, the twins adorable and identical. Freddie's face was a kaleidoscope of emotion. I knew he was torn between the loss of Todd and me as separate individuals and the joy of always getting to see his two favorite people at one time, but I was certain joy would win out in the end.

There was movement at the rear of the church. I could see Joyce back there, important as the mother of the flower girl and ring bearer. She fussed with Suzie's frilly dress in a way that was strongly reminiscent of Darlene on a bad day. Leon stood off to the side, not quite a part of his family group. That saddened me a little. Would it ever be completely right between them again?

Near the door, I could see the back of Paul's head as he stood talking to someone. Then he moved a few inches to allow an elderly couple to move past him. That's when I saw Joanna looking lovely in all her matron of honor regalia. When she looked up at Paul and his eyes met hers, I saw a whole lot more. I took a step back. Paul and Joanna? Had I been this out of touch? What had happened to Bennett? Was that why he had sent a gift instead of attending? Had I missed something? For just an instant, the thought of losing Paul's undying devotion saddened me. Then I felt a jolt of exhilaration. Paul—and the new and improved Joanna? Could anything be more perfect?

Suddenly my mother filled the doorway. "Christie, we have to hurry. Everyone's seated." She fussed around me, straightening my dress and checking my veil, and I let her. It was her day as much as mine, even if she had complained about how hopelessly impossible an August wedding would be. "The guests will be fainting in the aisles, dear. Don't you think December . . . ?" She had finally given way with good grace. Out of my newly discovered feelings for her, I had stood through endless fittings as my gown was taken in to compensate for the weight I'd lost in the last eight months.

She had never again mentioned my uncle's death, or Carly's. I told her about it, just the basic facts, knowing she would read about it in the newspaper anyway. Officially, Carly had died of grief, a suicide. Mother's only remark—and it had rung with sincerity—was, "What a terrible tragedy. I am so sorry for both of them." Those words earned her back a lot of the points she had lost over the years.

Now she grabbed my hand and pulled me down the hallway to the back of the church, where a nervous and happy Lamar stood waiting, very dashing in his tuxedo.

Joanna turned to me with a wet smile. "You look even prettier than I did," she said, giving me a hug before she moved to just outside the doorway. Paul gave me a sad little smile and kissed my cheek before slipping into the doors that led to the sanctuary.

I turned to face my mother and Lamar, and was surprised to see a suspicious shine in my mother's eyes. She reached out and took both my hands, pulling me closer. "You look just like him," she whispered into my ear, "and you wear it very well."

Before I had time to react, I heard the opening strains of the wedding march. I took Lamar's arm automatically, and we began to make our way down the aisle.

Most of the ceremony was a blur. We had decided on traditional vows, as we intended to have a long and traditional marriage. Watching Todd's beautiful face, I mouthed the well-rehearsed words by rote until the minister said, "in sickness and in health." As I opened my mouth to repeat the words, my breath hitched and tears filled my eyes.

Todd leaned closer to me. "We'll make it, dwarf. Trust me. We'll make it now."

Suddenly I knew he was right. I swallowed back the feelings of loss that had filled me for just an instant and, looking into his clear, blue eyes, I repeated in a voice that rang with conviction, "In sickness and in health . . ."

ABOUT THE AUTHOR

A native Floridian, **Lynda Fitzgerald** has lived in Georgia for the last thirty years with her lifelong friend and current crop of rescue dogs—but that hasn't stopped her from heading back to Melbourne Beach and Sebastian Inlet most years for a week or so of self-imposed down-time. The area, which remains somewhat wild and natural despite the public's best efforts to tame it, has always held a particular fascination for her. She always knew she'd write at least one book about it. Maybe more.

Lynda has been writing all her life. She studied creative writing at Emory University and Georgia Perimeter College, where she won a creative writing scholarship with a pair of powerful short stories. She spends her non-vacation time in tiny Snellville, Georgia, a suburb of Atlanta.